ELIXIR

By Christopher Buecheler

Elixir
By Christopher Buecheler

http://elixirnovel.com
http://cwbuecheler.com/writing

Elixir is a work of fiction. Names, places, and incidents are a product of the author's imagination or are used fictitiously.

First Edition: December 2018

Cover Design by Christopher Buecheler

Cover Imagery via 123RF.com
- Oleg Gavrilov
- Konstantin Kalishko
- isoga

For Kirsten

CHAPTER 1

Brooklyn Beat

The kid on the rooftop was holding a shard of glass to the girl's throat, fingers clenched, pumped so full of Elixir that he didn't realize it had cut the living shit out of his hand. He just stared out with his dinner-plate eyes, shouting obscenities, threatening to let what was inside of her out all over the tar paper. The girl was probably high, too; she wasn't crying, didn't even look scared. She was just standing there, mute and confused, waiting for whatever end was coming.

Clay Foster clenched his teeth, kept his weapon extended, and chose his next words with care. "Buddy, you need to let her go or I'm going to shoot you in the face."

"Bull-*shit*!" The kid drew the first half of the word out and emphasized the second with bared teeth. "Fuck you and your fat friend. I know how this works! You put your fucking guns down or I will do this bitch right here."

Clay's partner, Kellen, heaved a huge sigh. "Oh, ain't I had just about enough of this?"

"If we lower our guns, you'll let her go?" Clay said. He got what he was expecting.

"Let her go right off the fucking side, man! She stole my shit!"

They'd taken a few turns on this merry-go-round already; the kid wasn't going to stand down. He'd been licking for too long, and if he'd ever had a brain rattling around in that skull of his, it was beyond fried. You could see it just by looking at him. Crazy eyes. Hair like he'd carved the hide from a mangy golden retriever and glued it to his head. Pants that looked like they'd been pissed more than once. Clay could smell him from twelve feet away.

"How you want to go about resolving this?" Kellen said.

"You ready for some paperwork?"

"Suppose I am."

"The fuck you talking about paperwork?" the kid shouted, and Clay pulled the trigger. The bullet hit just below the kid's left eye and punched that half of his skull in, sending his brains out over the side of the building and down into the street below. The kid's hand jerked, squeezing the shard of glass so tightly that it cut his pinkie finger most of the way off. Clay thought he would drop it, but his seizing fingers held on, and as he began to fall backward the glass slid along the girl's face, charting a jagged course that left a flap of skin dangling from her jaw.

Could be worse, Clay had time to think, and then realized it was—the kid's momentum was going to take him and the girl both tumbling over and down to the sidewalk below. Eight-story drop.

"Shit, grab her!" Clay leaped forward, knowing even as he said it that there was no possible way his partner could keep up. The kid was already over, and the girl was going, her eyes just beginning to register that something, somewhere, was happening. *Christ, she must have dropped a whole ampule.*

The girl made a tiny sound—"oh"—as she flipped backward, and her little black foot with its ridiculous pink-plastic fuck-me heel kicked tar-paper sand in his face as it swung upward. Clay reached out for it, half blind from the sand, hoping for the best. He felt his hand close around something and grabbed tight, falling to his knees, throwing himself backward for leverage. The band dug deep into his fingers, but it held. He heard the girl make a startled "guh!" as her back collided with the bricks.

"Shit, man, I can't believe you made that catch," Kellen said from somewhere behind him.

"Shut up and help me, you fat asshole!" God knew how long the shoe was going to hold.

"Oh my gawd," the girl said from the other side of the brick parapet. There was no fear in her voice, only something like surprise, or maybe amazement. Like she was enjoying some incredible new experience. As if to confirm this assessment, she began to laugh.

Kellen finally arrived, wheezing, and Clay heard slapping sounds as his partner wrapped his giant meaty hands around the girl's ankles and planted his feet. "Got her, bro."

"Great, can you ... Christ, just hold her." Clay stood up and tried to rub the grit out of his eyes.

"What the fuck is even happening?" The girl's voice was plaintive, a note of deep confusion running through it.

"That's a good question, right there," Kellen said, and Clay grunted out a laugh. He turned back to help, leaning over the low wall. The girl's skirt had flopped up around her belly, revealing bruised thighs and an unkempt bush of jet-black pubic hair. Clay reached down, wrapped his fist into the cotton fabric of her T-shirt, and hauled upward.

When they had her back over the ledge, they let her go. The girl dropped immediately to her ass, making a grunting noise as she landed, and sat with her back against the wall. The blood from her jaw, which had run up her face and into her kinky hair, now began to soak her T-shirt.

"It's fucking ... is it cold in here? I feel cold." Her eyes rolled up, and she went to wherever it was that people went when they poured an entire ampule of Elixir down their throat. Sometimes that trip ended up at the morgue.

Kellen brushed his hands on his pants. "Well, this lady's gonna have a story to tell."

"If she remembers it." Clay picked up the gun he'd dropped in order to catch the girl's fall and holstered it.

His partner leaned down and inspected her face. "How old, you think?"

Clay glanced over at him. "Nineteen?"

"No way. I got sixteen. Bet you lunch."

"Yeah? Tell you what—I'll bet you the actual lunch. You lose, you go hungry."

Kellen laughed. "Not a fucking chance."

"Didn't think so. Should we try to stop that bleeding?"

"Nah ... ain't that bad. We should call us some EMTs and let them deal with it. You just filled the rest of *our* night with paperwork."

"You said you were okay with that."

Kellen nodded. "I am. There's no way that asshole wasn't gonna get himself shot ... You saved her life and saved us some extra paperwork."

Clay nodded. That echoed his thoughts exactly. He glanced over the wall at the junkie lying splattered below. "You suppose he was somebody?"

His partner shrugged. "If he was, he took a long walk down Nobody Road way before he ever met you."

* * *

"When the hell you going for lieutenant?" Kellen asked. They were doing the cop thing: sitting in a diner, drinking bad coffee, eating shitty food, filling out reports. They'd flirted with Maggie-the-waitress, thrown waves to Joe-the-cook, nodded to Steve-the-regular. It was like a bad television series, some cop show from a hundred years ago, back when "just the facts, ma'am" had meant something.

Kellen took a forkful of pancakes, dunked them in syrup, speared half a breakfast sausage, and shoved the entire mess into his mouth. The man ate like someone had dared him to. Forty-six, about five-eight, barrel-chested and strong-armed, Kellen was the product of a Puerto Rican father from Sunset Park and a redhead WASP from Massachusetts. He had close-cropped brown hair speckled with more than a little gray, green eyes, and skin that was both tanned and freckled.

Kellen was looking at him expectantly. Right, the question. Lieutenant.

"Been thinking about it." Clay didn't know how to explain to Kellen that he wasn't sure they'd ever pass him and was afraid to find out.

His partner laughed. "Yeah? Best hurry up. How the fuck am I ever going to stop drawing these shit assignments without friends in high places?"

"Maybe someday." Clay tabbed over to the next page full of form fields. He doodled concentric circles with his stylus while looking it over, hit "undo," and began answering questions. "Guy was licking, right?"

"You do not have to worry even a little about anyone claiming that motherfucker wasn't lit up," Kellen said between bites.

Clay sighed. He had a long history of shooting people, and adding this prick to the list wasn't a concern. What was happening to his city, though—that ate at him. Elixir was tearing Brooklyn apart like a tsunami, a relentless wave of destruction eating everything in its path.

"If we hadn't-a got that call when we did, that girl would be dead right now," Kellen said. Someone had seen the two kids up on the roof, fighting, and had actually given enough of a shit to call it in.

Clay nodded. "She's lucky to be alive, but I don't think they have any nanotreatments to help with the scar back where she comes from."

The girl had turned up empty on the scanner—no prints, no DNA match, nothing. That meant she hadn't been born in any hospital that shared data with what was left of the United States. That ruled out most of the hospitals in the industrialized world except China, and China wasn't known for breeding tall black hookers and shipping them off to Brooklyn. No, the girl had probably been born and raised in The Hook, which was like being born and raised in hell, only wetter.

Kellen slugged down some coffee. "Still can't believe you made that catch."

Clay shrugged. He was younger than Kellen. Faster. Not nearly so fat. During his days in the shit, in North Carolina, he had been incredibly quick and agile. Most of that was still with him, and it had been enough to save the girl's life.

Clay's tablet chirped and he brought up the text, a note from his wife.

"Woman saying goodnight?" Kellen said, and Clay grunted an affirmative. He had three late shifts a week and Terry always texted him before she went to bed.

Clay sent her a quick response. *All's fine. Sleep well. Love you.* He wasn't going to tell her about the junkie and the girl. The less Terry knew about the things he had to do in the line of duty, the better. They both had blood on their hands, but hers had come only from the soldiers she'd spent years tending to, and she hated the ugliness of Clay's world. She wouldn't want to know he'd added one more name to the list.

Kellen put his tablet to sleep. "You about finished with that shit?"

"Yeah."

"All right. Let's settle and then make a run up Kingston. I want to see if Escobar's already back to his old tricks."

They'd put Escobar away for what was supposed to be a long time, but he'd been sprung a week ago. Overcrowding was the official explanation, but Chief Baker hadn't been able to look them in the eyes when he gave it to them.

Escobar. Piece of shit handed out Elixir to kids. Once they were hooked he'd use them as runners, and every few weeks one of them would turn up dead, a little boy playing at being a gangster, killed for the drugs he carried. It had taken ages to piece together enough evidence to link the dead kids back to Escobar, and the son of a bitch had only spent six months at Rikers. Hadn't even made it to trial. Brooklyn justice.

Outside, the wave of stink hit him like a solid wall, and Clay made an involuntary noise of disgust. A hundred and six at midnight and the whole city steaming, sweating out the poisons trapped in its bays and marshes. Brooklyn nights in July were like having your face jammed into the crotch of a wet, filthy dog.

"Jesus, Lord, I swear it's still getting worse," Kellen said, but Clay barely heard him, wasn't entirely there anymore. This stench ... He tried not think about struggling through the brackish swamp that had once been Greenville, North Carolina, dogs on his trail and men with guns intent on murdering him not far behind. It had smelled like this, there, on the night when he had shot that little girl.

"Unlock the fuckin' car, man," Kellen cried. "I'm dying, here!"

Clay pulled his thoughts away from Greenville and forced himself back to the present. Their car, a Mercury Z-Cell with an amped-up engine that could still burn gas if it needed to, bulletproof glass, and a reinforced frame, was set to respond to the proximity of the biometric fobs that he and Kellen carried. Only problem was that Kellen forgot his about 90 percent of the time. Clay took two steps forward and heard the doors unlatch.

"You should try to remember your—" he began, and Kellen overrode him.

"*You* should try getting the hell into the car and turning on the AC, brother. Save the lectures for someone who gives a shit."

Fair enough. Clay opened his door and sat down. He pressed the ignition button, listened to the faint hum as the electronics came on, eased the car out onto the road. Flatbush was falling apart—you could see it in the details. More junked cars, more junked lives. A girl on the corner raised two middle fingers at them as they drove by. Kellen waved to her, gave her a cheerful grin, called her a *puta* through his clenched teeth.

Flatbush was bad. Crown Heights was worse. Clay signaled a right turn and pointed them toward it.

*　*　*

The sign that they'd crossed into Escobar's territory was half a cinder block bouncing off their windshield, tossed from a roof or window high above. Other chunks of debris followed, and Clay could hear the occasional shouted obscenity, muted by the thick glass. The Brooklyn PD had lost its hold in Crown Heights, and the place had gone feral.

"Why the hell did we come here?" Kellen muttered.

Clay glanced over at him. "It was your idea."

"Doesn't answer my question."

"Guess not."

The rain of rocks and garbage eventually ended as people got bored and went back to whatever it was they did in this place. There was a woman headed down the street—well-dressed for the area, with a tailored blouse and a skirt that almost looked like real leather—and Kellen motioned toward her with one hand. Clay slowed down as Kellen rolled down the window.

"Oh, not *this* wetback motherfucker," the woman said to no one in particular as they pulled up, but she stopped walking and turned to face them.

"You would know your wetbacks," Kellen told her. "Escobar still putting it to you, or did you find some new daddy to buy you that fake Gucci trash while he was locked up?"

"Why don't you go fuck yourself?"

"How about you tell me where to find Arón and I won't bust your ass for soliciting?"

The girl sneered. "I ain't never solicited shit in my whole life and you know it. You best get up out of here before you get your ass shot."

"Where's he at, Janelle?"

"I don't even know *who* you're talking about."

"Sure you do. Short, scarred up, crazy eye ... bangs about fifteen other girls behind your back."

"Oh, you fucking fat shit—"

"You got fifteen seconds! After that, we haul your stupid ass downtown. I say she's soliciting, so that means she's soliciting, right, partner?"

"For fucking sure." Clay didn't even bother to look over at Janelle. This was Kellen's play, and it was fine by him. Better than wasting time hunting for Escobar, and at least if they had to bring her in, it would mean going back to the station.

"God*damn*! He's at the fucking Loco, all right? That's where they all moved to. Can I go buy my smokes now, you wetback spic pig?"

"Hope you don't think Escobar keeps you around for your personality." Kellen rolled up the window, cutting off her retort. She kicked the car as Clay began driving again.

"Shoulda known," Clay said, and Kellen murmured assent. The Loco—a bar that had been called Locomotive 18 in some distant past when its neon still worked—had been Escobar and his crew's preferred hangout even before the man had been sent away and lost his previous headquarters to a rival gang. Clay and Kellen had been in the place more than once, after the bust, looking for Escobar's underlings. If the drug lord had taken it over, getting in was no longer going to be a matter of walking up to the front door and showing their badges. Clay didn't know if Kellen intended to try, but if he did, they would need backup first. Clay would have thought about calling the National Guard before storming that fortress from the front if the Guard still existed.

As if reading his mind, Kellen heaved a weary sigh. "Ain't going in there ... but I want him to know we're watching. If we have to put that piece of shit away six months at a time, that's how it'll be."

Clay nodded. He wasn't sure it mattered—even if they put Arón Escobar away for life, the vacuum would end up filled by some other thug or petty mafioso. The only thing that was consistent with crime was the crime; the names and faces changed with a rapidity that was mind-boggling. Escobar had lasted long enough for them to have learned who he was. That was a testament to the man's survival instincts, but it didn't mean he was irreplaceable. Still, Clay had to admit it had felt good when they'd finally rolled up on the man at a traffic light, dragged him out of his car, and put the cuffs on.

The Loco was set farther back from the street than the buildings that surrounded it, and its windows had been blackened, barred, and partially blocked with debris scavenged from the crumbling remains of the burned-out buildings that littered the neighborhood. Multiple concrete barriers were strewn about in front of it, and a dozen or so thugs, openly carrying heat, were standing around or leaning against the barriers. Talking, smoking, looking tough. They watched as the police cruiser rolled forward, and one of them turned to the others to make some sneering joke. They were still laughing when Kellen rolled his window down again.

"Seen Escobar?" he asked the nearest gangbanger, and the man gave him a cool glance. He was tall and white, with the kind of skim milk-blue skin that can only be cultivated by long nights and little time under the sun. Built like a dumpster, thick and solid and square, he had a long brown ponytail, squinting eyes, and obvious Elixir blooms at the corners of his mouth. His clothes were mostly loose synthetics, popular among gangsters, but like all of Escobar's men, he wore a black cotton bandanna tied around his left calf. Clay knew from experience that if you shone a black light on the bandanna, a hidden pattern of fleurs-de-lis would show up.

He spat on the pavement. "Ain't seen shit except some stupid pig thinks he can roll into Crown Heights and ask me dumb questions."

"My mother always did say I was hurting for brains."

"Gonna be hurting for blood in a few more minutes, you don't roll out."

Clay could see several of the other thugs looking toward the cruiser, their anger and desire for violence visible on their brows like gathering thunderheads.

"You and your buddies aren't dumb enough try and jump two armed police officers, are you?" Kellen said.

The man ran his gaze along their cruiser, unimpressed, and turned back to Kellen. "You got nothing that scares us. We heard all about you two from the boss. Couple-a pussies is all. Had to sneak up on him just to take him in. He said he's got something for you if you ever get in his way again. Said he'll make you regret ever hearing his name."

"Motherfucker, I regret that every day already," Kellen said.

The guy sneered but didn't respond.

"Tell your boss we said hello. Tell him we're watching."

"Head on in and tell him yourself."

"Maybe someday I will."

The thug ran a hand along the butt of the revolver slung at his hip, a too-big piece of garbage that probably wasn't accurate beyond twenty feet. Clay wondered how fast the man could draw something that size and thought it likely he could shoot the thug dead three times over in that span of time. In the old days he would've tried it—just the attitude this piece of shit was throwing would've been enough. Clay's training had beaten some of that out of him, and Terry had helped, too, but the instinct was still there. Swing or shoot first, worry about the consequences after. It had served him well on occasion, kept him alive, but now wasn't the time.

He made a show of yawning and kept his voice pitched low. "Let's fuck off before the rest of his boys decide to come over here."

Kellen made a noise of assent. They weren't scared of these assholes, but a shootout in the streets of Crown Heights would piss off the brass.

"We're rolling on," Kellen told the thug. "You tell Escobar what I said."

"Go fuck yourself," the man replied. Clay put the car into gear and drove forward. The group of men stood staring until they had turned the corner.

"Think that guy will actually convey the message?" Clay said, and Kellen nodded.

"Come on ... Escobar owns these guys. They'da told him even if I hadn't given them anything to tell. Nothing happens in Crown Heights without him hearing about it. Hell, he probably saw it from upstairs."

"Right. So now he knows we're watching. Suppose he's scared?"

Kellen laughed, sighed, shook his head. "I doubt that drug-pushing pimp is scared of anything in the entire world. If he thought we were a threat, those boys would've just opened fire."

"What's the plan now?"

Kellen glanced at the time. "Clock out, go home, see if I can get an hour or two of sleep in before the kids wake up. Put on the disco show and let's get the fuck out of here."

Clay pushed the pedal down and took the car up to sixty. He turned on the flashers and burned through streetlights, heading for downtown.

* * *

Terry murmured as he slid into bed next to her. She was on her side, facing away from him, the bedspread and sheets pushed down, only covering the lower half of her naked body. Even with the AC cranked, it was still warm on the third floor. Clay didn't mind, but Terry had grown up in houses with real insulation that could hold their cool air, far from the heat and stink of the city, let alone the Carolina swamps. She talked about moving back upstate someday, getting away from Brooklyn and all its bullshit, but Clay thought it was just idle daydreaming. They'd been here ten years now. The city was a part of them.

Clay rolled onto his side and moved up against her, putting one arm under his head and slinging the other over her, pressing his face to her hair and inhaling. Her shampoo was made with orange blossoms, a scent they both loved; the candles at their wedding had given off the same smell.

"Wh'time issit?" Terry said.

"Almost five. Sorry I woke you up."

"S'okay. I was dreaming."

"About what?"

Terry took his hand in hers. She led it down along her belly, past the little patch of reddish-brown curls, and pressed between her legs. She was a furnace down there, slick and wet, her clit poking out and begging for his fingers.

"Oh." Clay could feel himself growing hard. He began to rub gentle circles around that stiff little nub, and Terry made a sound that was half sigh, half moan. She reached back with her hand, found his erection, stroked him.

"I dreamed you were fucking me in the living room," she murmured. "You were sitting on the couch and I was kneeling on top of you, naked. All the windows were open and I knew people could look right in from the street, but I didn't care."

Clay made a noise of approval, pressed hard against her clit and made her gasp, went back to circling. He snaked his other hand under her and teased a nipple with his fingers, pinching and rolling it.

"You were grabbing my tits and saying the most dirty, awful things, and I was so hot, and I was just ... just *riding you*. You woke me up right as I was about to ... about ... oh, God."

Terry had stopped stroking him now, lost in what he was doing with his hands, and he felt her begin to tense, pressing forward hard with her hips. He pushed back with his fingers, circling rapidly, and he heard Terry make a sort of choked cooing noise—the sound she always made when she came. In another moment she pulled away from his fingers, unable to take any more. They lay for a time not speaking, Terry panting and Clay running his hand along the freckled skin of her thigh and ass and back.

"That was fast," he said at last.

Terry laughed. "Told you ... I was close when you woke me up."

"Glad I was here for it."

"Me, too." She rolled over to face him, her deep brown eyes half-lidded, and reached down again to take him in her hands. She kissed him, and Clay put his hands in her curly red hair, kissing back, letting her do what she was doing. It didn't take her long.

"That was pretty fast too, mister," she said when he was done and smirked at him as he reached for tissues.

"Someone got me all riled up," Clay said.

Terry snorted laughter and clapped her hands over her mouth in embarrassment. "I can't believe I just snorted," she said through her fingers.

"You do that all the time."

Terry took her hands from her face and made a noise of mock outrage. "Well ... I couldn't believe it any of those times, either!"

"When's your alarm?"

She reached over to her nightstand, tapped her tablet, glanced at the clock. "Eight thirty."

"You should get some more sleep."

"Okay. Can I lie on you?"

"Sure."

"Even though it's hot?"

Clay nodded, lay back, took her in his arms. She closed her eyes and rested her head on his chest.

"I love you, baby," Terry said. "You should go for lieutenant. I hate these night shifts, and I don't think being on the street is helping any with ... everything else you have to deal with. It's too close to what you did before."

Clay smiled. "I'm okay. Maybe this winter."

"All right." Terry's voice was drifting off. "I've got brunch with Cynthia tomorrow, so I won't be around before you have to work. Let's have a date night at Pascale's ... maybe Sunday night? I'm craving puttanesca."

Clay thought about mentioning that he had dragged a screaming line chef out of Pascale's two weeks ago and booked him for distributing Elixir on the premises, but he decided it didn't matter. "Sure, baby. Whatever you want."

Terry gave a contented sigh and kissed his chest. In five minutes she was asleep, and in ten more she pulled away, returning to her side like always. Clay lay there on his back, trying to relax. The sex had helped, but for him sleep was always a long time coming. He was glad for Terry; before her, nights had been all but impossible, sleep arriving in little ten-minute bursts between what felt like hours of tossing and turning. She'd told him it was PTSD. He'd thought of it as penance.

Clay leaned forward and kissed the back of Terry's head. He flipped over onto his belly, closed his eyes, and tried to empty his mind. Eventually sleep came. When he woke up six hours later, Terry was at brunch. Five hours after that, his life had changed forever.

CHAPTER 2

The Fall

Clay would forever remember the few seconds after it happened, when there was nothing but silence and the strange chill that wrapped around him like the arms of a malevolent ghost. It was almost interesting, in its own terrible way, this moment in which his body emptied so completely of feeling.

The news was squawked out at him over a dispatch radio in a room full of yammering cops. Brooklyn precincts had been crowded even before consolidation had moved most operations downtown. Now this central location was stuffed to the gills. The room held fifteen desks, with barely enough space between them to maneuver, and all were occupied. It was hot, under-lit, stinking of pastrami and old, sour coffee. Kellen's desk, next to Clay's, was heaped high with papers, binders, and discarded sandwich wrappings. The cleaning crew had given up trying to tend to it.

Sergeant McCarran—a textbook example of the fat, corrupt Irish cop, though he was at least five generations removed from the Emerald Isle—was in the middle of an unapologetic and brutally racist joke that Clay thought might get him socked in the eye when the dispatcher's words cut through and caught Clay's attention.

"Ten fifty-four at 145 Willow Street. Officers dispatched. Paramedics dispatched."

I can't have heard that right.

He had, and a part of him knew it, and when he shouted at the other cops in the room to shut the fuck up, something of that knowledge must have come through in his voice. The whole place went graveyard silent, every eye turned on him. Clay sat and waited for the confirmation, and when the dispatcher said it again there could be no doubt.

One forty-five Willow Street. Ten fifty-four. Possible dead body.

That was when the cold feeling descended, and for a few moments it seemed as if everything were moving at a fraction of its normal speed. No one in the room was speaking, and the radio had fallen silent. Everyone was just staring, and Clay had time to wonder what his face must look like to cause such expressions of shocked concern. He heard his heart beat once, twice, and realized that the strange tightness he was feeling stemmed from the fact that he hadn't taken a breath in what seemed like months. He tried to take one now, couldn't, and for a moment was glad for it. Maybe it would just end here, and he would be spared the agony of learning the details.

It might not be her. With that everything snapped back into full speed. Kellen was opening his mouth to speak, but Clay cut him off, sucking in a deep, ragged breath. "That's my fucking house!"

And then he was moving, heading for the cruiser. Kellen was making a valiant effort to follow, but Clay rapidly outdistanced him. He heard Kellen giving up the chase and shouting to someone else for a ride. Clay never stopped moving, racing through the halls and shoving his way out the door through a group of officers standing outside.

"What the shit, Foster?!" someone shouted, but Clay just kept moving.

His cruiser was parked in a ready position, rear half up over the curb, nose facing out toward the street. Clay reached it at such speed that the car barely had time to detect him and unlock before he was hurling the door open. He dropped into the seat, pushed the ignition button, and slammed the car into gear. It lurched forward, tires shrieking on the hot asphalt, and he almost lost control of it. Clay cranked the wheel hard to the left, just missed the front bumper of another parked cruiser, and then straightened out, accelerating, flipping on the lights and the noise.

By the time he reached the end of the street he was doing eighty miles an hour, and he barely tapped the brakes as he swung a hard right. His house, and Terry, were less than a mile from the Eighty-fourth Precinct. The trip would take him four minutes at the most. To Clay, this seemed an eternity, an unacceptable ocean of time to be sailed on a foundering ship. Watching cars ahead of him pull over and people scatter from the streets, he kept the pedal pressed to the floor and tried not to think about his wife's still, silent form stretched out on some cold metal table somewhere deep in the bowels of the precinct.

* * *

They hadn't even started taping up a line yet when Clay screeched to a halt amid a cluster of four other squad cars.

Down the block, he could see the lights of an approaching ambulance, and he leaped from the car cursing their lack of haste.

Clay's neighborhood was still the ritziest in Brooklyn, even as the city decayed around it. The quiet, tree-lined streets and stately brownstones had seen their share of lickers, but the money here allowed many of his neighbors to pursue their Elixir habit without resorting to violence and petty crime or losing their homes. Still, Clay had more than once found himself hauling stoned and sleeping people from his steps, and it was not always possible to tell whether they were transients or merely locals who'd been on a multi-day binge without showering or changing clothes.

He wasn't supposed to live here; cops didn't earn enough to rent a single-floor apartment in a Brooklyn Heights brownstone, let alone own the entire building, but Clay wasn't like other cops. Uncle Sam, what was left of him, had set Clay up for life after the things Clay had done for that bony, bearded, finger-pointing bastard. Clay was a cop not for the pay or the benefits or even the action but because Terry had thought it might help him ease back into civilian life, and because she hoped he might be able to do some good for the city. This latter ideal amused Kellen to no end, and Clay didn't blame him, but he'd found himself hoping Terry was right. He might have done more measurable work as a soldier, but he liked being a cop better.

There were four officers standing around his front steps, and when Clay pushed past them, one of the patrolmen grabbed at his shoulders. "Foster, don't."

"Get off me!" Clay pulled away from the man's grip, thrusting forward up the stairs and toward the door. Behind him, he heard another car pull up, heard Kellen call his name.

Clay kept moving. In through the front hallway, past the staircase, toward the rear of the building. He could see into the kitchen at the back and, past that, another group of officers standing on the iron stairs that led down to the concrete patio and postage-stamp backyard. One of them saw Clay coming and her eyes widened. She took three quick strides through the kitchen and stood blocking the doorway.

"You don't want to come out here," she said, and the words hit Clay like a volley of knives. He knew in an instant, from the tone and from her expression, that the paramedics would be worthless. They were required to call it in as a 10-54, but what was really outside was a 10-55. A coroner case. His wife was dead, and she wasn't going to be revived.

Clay felt anger well up within him, anger like he had never before experienced, and another emotion that was foreign to him despite everything he had done in the past. For the first time in his life, Clay wanted to murder something. He could taste the desire for it rising within him, bitter, like bile at the back of his throat. He bared his teeth at the woman.

"Get out of my way, Mendez."

"Foster, if you ever take one piece of advice in your entire fucking life, make it this one: Do not go out that door."

She was short and stout, half his weight and no real threat if he decided to go through her. A crimson wave of rage surged within him, and for a moment he grappled with the desire to pick the woman up and hurl her across the kitchen. Then something seemed to snap inside him and the rage left him all at once. In its place was a kind of vacuum, a feeling of emptiness so profound it seemed as if his entire body would collapse into it, like stars dragged into a supermassive black hole. Before meeting Terry, he had never been able to imagine the kind of life he had built with her. Now the prospect of a life without her seemed impossible. What was he going to do?

"I have to see her," Clay said, his voice jagged and broken, barely more than a whisper. Mendez shook her head.

"Not like that. No, you don't." She looked over Clay's shoulder. "Ruiz, get your goddamn partner *out* of here."

Clay felt Kellen's meaty hand on his shoulder. "Come on, brother. Let's let the medics help her."

"Christ, Kel ..."

"I know, man. Come on."

Clay allowed himself to be led back toward the front of the building. As they walked, Kellen glanced over his shoulder. "He knows that he owes you one, Mendez."

Clay, who felt at that moment as if he knew nothing at all, kept his mouth shut.

* * *

Clay had first met Terry ten years earlier, in 2048. He'd been sitting in graying bed sheets at a shitty VA hospital in Virginia, three pieces of metal still embedded deep in his hip, awaiting a surgeon. Unlike the injuries to most of the civil war veterans in that place, so near the front lines, his was not life-threatening, and so he had been left to sit in his bed and watch the lying bullshit that the government called news, sucking down pain medication every few hours. The inability to sleep had only added to his convivial mood, and when Terry had first shown up in his room with the latest batch of pills, Clay had been bent over in agony, and his first words to her had been "It's about time, you cunt."

Terry, two and a half years into dealing with men who'd suffered indescribable trauma, had taken it in stride. She'd given him his meds, told him she hoped they would help, and moved on. The next time Clay had seen her, a few days later, he'd apologized. Terry had hit him with that broad smile of hers, and that was it: the end of everything that had come before. In the days and weeks that followed, as she waited with him for the surgery, nursed him back to health when it was over, and agreed to leave Virginia and come back to New York with him, Clay must have apologized fifty more times for what he'd called her. Every time, Terry had laughed and told him that, of all the people who had ever called her a cunt, he was by far her favorite.

They married three years later, a small civil ceremony in front of a few close friends and her parents, who'd made the trip from Rochester. Terry in a white gown, Clay in a rented tux. He'd just finished that morning with the legal wrangling that had made him rich and had waited to be alone with her so he could break the news. Terry had cried when he'd told her, when he'd promised that her parents would never have to worry about money again, and she'd thrown her arms around him and kissed him. They'd made love while streaks of eyeliner were drying on her cheeks, her white dress hiked up around her hips, breasts peeking out from above its strapless top.

Christ, she was beautiful, and Clay could still summon up that night in near-perfect detail, had done so a hundred thousand times since. When what was happening to Brooklyn seemed ready to overwhelm him, swallow him up, cast him into inescapable despair, Clay needed only bring that image up to remind himself that there were still things that were good in the world.

His beautiful girl was lying in front of him now on a cold steel table under bare blue-white bulbs, her pale little feet poking out from under the sheet that was draped over the rest of her. She'd painted her toenails purple. In a minute, the coroner was going to pull down that sheet and he was going to have to look at her cold, dead face and say yes. Yes, that is my wife.

Others had volunteered to make the ID—Kellen had practically begged Clay to let him do it—but Clay wouldn't have it. He wanted to see her, wanted the reality and the finality of it, no matter how awful it was. It seemed to him the least he could do for Terry, after all she had done for him, to look at her like this, at the end.

She'd fallen from the third-floor balcony, the place where she kept her marigolds and tiger lilies and that goddamned unkillable spider plant she'd had since she was thirteen and hated but couldn't bring herself to abandon. She'd stepped onto a stool to water it, lost her balance, and toppled over the railing. The concrete below had done the rest. A neighbor, out on their own balcony, had seen Terry lying there, her body and limbs piled up in a pool of blood, and called the police.

The medics had briefed him. She went quick, they'd said. Probably didn't even have time to realize what was happening, they'd said. It didn't hurt, they'd said. At least he could feel good about that. As if it were possible for Clay to feel anything right now, let alone anything good.

No one had tried to tell him she was in a better place, and that was probably for the best. Clay thought he would hit a man who told him that, send him to the oral surgeon, but he would've been acting on principle, really, rather than out of rage. It seemed his ability to feel anything except a kind of helpless emptiness had abandoned him.

Truth was, no one had said much of anything to him, except that they were sorry. He'd heard that one a hundred times, a thousand, since the news had come in from the paramedics that there was nothing they could do. It was impossible to describe how little the words *I'm sorry* meant to him right now, and so he hadn't tried. Clay wasn't sure he'd spoken at all in the last four hours.

The coroner came into the room, and he was not what Clay had expected. Men like this were supposed to be balding, bespectacled, hunched and pale and sickly. This man was tall, blond, and good-looking. Young. Tan. He looked like the type who might spend the weekends golfing at a country club in Smithtown or Brentwood. His face was set in an expression of sympathy that Clay was certain the man had practiced in front of a mirror.

The coroner glanced at his tablet, then back up, and took in a slow, deep breath. Clay felt adrenaline flood his body. Here it was, and he wasn't ready. He could have spent a thousand hours sitting here in this cold room that smelled of antiseptics and preservatives and it wouldn't have made a difference. He would never be ready. Clay clenched his teeth, steeled himself, met the man's gaze.

"Are you sure you want to do this?" the coroner said.

"No. Get on with it."

The man nodded and stepped forward. He grasped the sheet and moved it quickly but without flourish, not pausing for suspense or theatrics. Clay was, for a moment, impressed with his professionalism, before the sight of his wife blew all other thoughts from his mind.

He had expected damage to her neck, and there was indeed some bruising visible, but it looked remarkably intact. What caught him off guard were the eyes—huge and puffy, standing out purple-black against skin that was otherwise waxen and pallid—and the large abrasion where the concrete had stripped a chunk of skin from her forehead. They had cleaned off the blood, and Clay supposed he should be thankful for that, but he had never in his life imagined that he might one day know what the bone that made up his wife's skull looked like.

He understood in an instant the terrible mistake he had made, understood why Kellen had fought so hard against it. He would never be able to wipe this image from his mind, and now whenever he thought of Terry's smile, her laugh, the way she had looked perched atop him on their wedding night, that beauty and joy would be followed in his mind by this atrocity.

"Oh, fucking hell." Clay's voice broke, and the coroner said nothing, eyes on the floor, giving Clay the time he needed to digest the blasphemous site before him.

"Put it ... Cover her up, please."

The man did so, glancing up now. "I'm sorry."

Clay couldn't seem to find a response to that, so he ignored it. After a moment, the coroner nodded. The man was a pro; he'd seen all of this before, knew not to take anything personally, probably even had a script to follow if things got aggressive.

"Will you make the ID?" he said.

"That's my wife. That's ... She's Terry Foster. Or Brooks. She used to be Brooks. Terry Elizabeth Brooks. Christ, I have to call her parents. Jesus Christ."

What was he going to tell them? Tim and Emily, people he had come to love more than he'd ever loved his own parents, would be devastated. What was he possibly going to tell them that could take away the pain of knowing what had become of their daughter, a beautiful and caring woman who had given all of herself to injured soldiers for more than three years? They had sent her off to Brooklyn with some useless man who had failed to protect her, who had let her go tumbling to a stupid, shitty death on a concrete patio. What could he possibly say, what could he possibly do, that would ever absolve him of this sin?

The coroner was looking at him, nodding in sympathy, an expression on his face that seemed to say, *It's OK if you need to cry. I've seen it before.*

"I have to get out of here," Clay said.

The coroner made a noise of assent. "We'll do everything we can for her."

"There's nothing left you can do," Clay said as he left.

* * *

The sun had set by the time Clay stepped out of the precinct, showered and changed into a pair of jeans and a T-shirt. Brooklyn was glowing; even with the city going to shit, and even with its much prettier sister shining across the East River, the place still had the capacity for beauty. Clay could usually see it, but at the moment it seemed the whole world was gray and ugly, coated in ash and decay. He felt exhausted. Defeated. Sucked dry. The thought of going home to his dark, empty building to make dinner and trying to fall asleep seemed as remote and impossible as growing wings and flying away.

"Chief says you're on a mandatory two-week vacation," Kellen said, stepping up beside him. "After that, you go talk to him. He'll decide if you're even ready for a psych eval or if you need another two weeks."

"Terrific," Clay said, not looking over at his partner.

"Listen, I got two offers. Your pick."

Clay looked up the road, toward the cars flashing by on Tillary Street. "Let's hear the first."

"I can drive you home, spare you the walk, if you want to get started on ... you know, preparations."

Clay grunted. Shook his head. "No fucking way. What's the other one?"

"Shot of whiskey and a beer at Breaker's. Then maybe another shot of whiskey and another beer. Then we evaluate our situation and determine if another shot of whiskey and another beer are required."

"Angela going to let you get away with that?" Kellen's wife didn't typically enjoy it when her man came stumbling home drunk in the middle of the night.

"Angela spent the afternoon crying and told me I wasn't allowed to come home until I was sure you were all right."

Clay glanced over at him. "That the plan?"

Kellen gave him a sad, sorry grin and shook his head. "When you think you're going to be 'all right,' bro?"

"Might be a while."

"A long fucking while. I got your drinks, and your dinner if you can eat, and I will get you into a cab when you need it. That's offer number two, but it's all I got. I can't ... If I could do anything more ..."

Clay pressed his thumbs to his temples. Closed his eyes. "It's fine, Kel."

Breaker's was two blocks away, a pool hall whose tables might have been new at the start of the war back in thirty-five. Located so close to the precinct, it was popular with their fellow cops, and Clay considered requesting a different location where there wouldn't be so many people around prone to staring or, worse, expressions of sympathy.

Kellen seemed to catch his hesitancy. "Ain't no one going to bother you in there, brother. Everyone in the precinct knows to leave you be."

"If you say so. First person to ask if I'm okay gets his nose broken."

"Fair deal." The two walked in silence for a bit.

Clay ran a hand through his hair. "I called her parents."

Kellen winced, muttering some Spanish profanity under his breath. "How'd that go?"

"They'll be in tonight, but late. I'll see them tomorrow."

"Yeah, but how'd they—"

"I had to tell them their baby girl fell off a balcony and broke her neck, man ... How do you think that went?"

Kellen nodded, gave a disgusted sigh, scratched his head. "I'm thinking not well."

"You're thinking right. You ever hear a sixty year-old man cry like a little kid?"

"I have not."

"Try to keep it that way."

They had arrived at the bar. Clay could hear music and the clack of pool balls, muted by the door, and even from outside he could smell the sour scent of stale beer. Through the few small windows, he could see televisions playing sports networks. He paused again and Kellen noticed.

"Your call, man," he said.

Clay shrugged. Where else was he going to go? "Fuck it, let's get drunk."

CHAPTER 3

Dead Ends

Clay woke up in a cold, empty bed at four in the morning, head throbbing and guts roiling. He stumbled to the bathroom, hauled the toilet seat back, and vomited until all the muscles in his abdomen hurt. Afterward, he lay on his side on the cool tile of the bathroom floor, still half drunk, exhausted and sick and miserable. The unpleasant taste of bile, bourbon, and beer had coated his tongue. Somewhere outside in the dark, a dog barked once.

He wished then that he was still the man he had been before Terry. Wouldn't it be easier not to care? To go back to those days when he could zero in on a six-year-old's head through the scope of a rifle, consider for a final time not the moral implications of what he was about to do but instead the reliability of his planned escape route, and then pull the trigger? It would be easier, yes, but he was no longer that man.

He thrust himself up and got first to his knees and then to his feet. Standing at the sink, he tried to avoid looking at his reflection as he filled the glass they kept on the counter with cold water and drank the entire thing down. Clay filled the glass again and brought it back with him to the bedroom, where he set it on the end table and went to stand at the window, looking out into the yard in which Terry had died.

There wasn't much to it. The stairs, the patio, an eight-by-twelve plot of trimmed grass, vibrant green even in late July thanks to the frequent thunderstorms that had accompanied the rising ocean. There was a solar-powered pole lamp in the yard that bathed the area in a gentle glow. Clay could see moths batting against it. He watched them for a long time.

He almost missed it when he turned around, just as he had when he'd stumbled into the room, full of bourbon, to pass out in his clothes. He'd missed it again when he'd awakened in those same clothes and ran to the bathroom to throw up. He was less drunk now, and not moving with such urgency. It was a small thing—a minuscule thing, really—but it stopped him in his tracks. Their wedding picture was turned to face toward the bed.

That wasn't right. Terry had a thing, a hang-up Clay had never understood, about that picture always facing the window. She bitched every single time the people from the cleaning service moved it while dusting, and the last such time had been less than four days ago. The cleaners hadn't been back since, and Clay had seen her move the thing with his own eyes, turning it to face the window. Why was it facing the bed?

He stepped over to look at it. Staring, he tried to will his addled brain to think. Was he sure? Was he goddamned positive about this? And if he wasn't, why that creeping feeling at the back of his spine? Why that certainty—which he hadn't felt since his days in Carolina, in those moments before a mission went suddenly bad and the shooting began—that something was not right?

Clay reached out to turn the picture back toward the window and stopped dead, arm outstretched, fingers trembling just a little. At the back, stuck to the wall only by the very tip and near to falling entirely behind the dresser, less than an inch of it exposed, there was a hair. Just a single hair, but it glowed silver in the moonlight streaming in from the bedroom window. At any other time, he might not even have noticed it, because it wasn't one of Terry's long red-brown curls and barely stood out against the white wall. If he even breathed the wrong way it was going to fall behind the dresser and be lost forever.

Carefully, very carefully, Clay reached forward and pinned the hair between two fingers. He drew it forth, holding it up in front of his eyes, confirming what he already knew: this was not his wife's hair. Eight or ten inches long, blond and straight, this was not the hair of anyone he knew, and certainly not anyone who had recently been in his bedroom.

At least, not that he was aware of.

Another man? He shook his head. *Impossible.*

No, not impossible ... but improbable. His relationship with Terry had been strong. They'd been happy, made love often, rarely fought, enjoyed spending time together. He didn't live at the office, hadn't treated her like shit, hadn't taken her for granted. There were none of the hallmarks of a relationship in distress. Besides, he was a cop and a soldier, a man trained to notice things out of place. If Terry had been fucking some longhaired stranger in their bed, man or woman, he would have known something was amiss.

Had she had a friend over at some point? Why would they have been in the bedroom, and why would that person have moved a picture? That possibility made no sense. What else was there?

While you're asking questions, how likely do you really think it is that she fell over that railing?

His eyes narrowed and it seemed that the last of the alcohol fuzz slipped from his mind. The analytical, observant part of his brain, the part that had been trained for nearly two decades to notice every detail, was taking over. For the first time since he had heard the 10-54 come across the radio, Clay began to question the circumstances of Terry's death. The more questions he asked, the more came to mind, and there weren't enough answers to make him happy.

Still holding the hair between the thumb and index finger of his right hand, Clay turned on his heel and went to call the Forensics Unit.

* * *

"Couldn't find a damn thing, man."

The tech's name was Mike, and he'd been working on crime scene investigation for at least thirty years. He'd done just about every job there was to do in that area, but his specialty was DNA analysis, and Clay'd asked him to personally investigate the blond strand of hair. This was the conclusion, which meant that whole angle was a goddamned dead end. If Mike couldn't find anything, then no one could.

"Is it synthetic?" Clay asked, running a hand over his scruffy face. He wasn't even supposed to be here at the precinct, but no one ever came down to this dim, windowless set of offices full of chemicals and computers. At least no one who was going to give a shit if Clay was hanging around.

"Define *synthetic*," Mike said with a shrug, glancing back at one of half a dozen holo monitors sitting on a desk behind him. "It's real hair, not plastic, if that's what you mean ... but it could be vat-grown. That's how they make mid-price wigs."

"Even if it's vat-grown, it has to have DNA."

"Sure, I mean, we've got matches, mostly ancient stuff from the USS public database, but nothing anywhere near a hundred percent. If that hair came off a real person and not out of a vat, about the best we could do is point you toward relatives ... but distant ones. Her closest match is from almost fifty years ago."

"You know she's female?"

Mike shook his head. "Guessing. The hair was ten inches long, dude."

"There are plenty of guys with—" Clay stopped himself. Mike's graying hair was pulled back in a ponytail and reached halfway down his back.

The other man favored him with a grin and turned back to his monitors, pointing to one. "If you look at the data, you can see that she's haplogroup I-one. So if it's not a wig, she comes from generic European stock, maybe Scandinavian, given how light the hair is."

"It's not bleached?"

"Nah, it's legit."

"Is that ... what the fuck did you call it? Haplogroup? Is it uncommon?"

Mike shook his head. "About 20 percent of white people around here. So you're looking at a couple million in easy driving distance alone."

"Why aren't there any recent matches?"

Mike shrugged. He was a big guy—not fat but broad through the shoulders and ribs. When he hunched over his screens he seemed too big for his desk and chair. Now, though, he was leaning back, hands folded over his fiftysomething belly, chewing on his lower lip. "It's weird. It's like someone scrubbed the DNA group from the records past a certain point."

"Why would someone do that?"

"The better question is 'how?'"

"Okay, so—"

"I don't know. That's why it's a better question. The 'why' seems obvious, man. If your DNA isn't on the list, you can do ... stuff."

"Like throw a woman off a balcony?" There was no point beating around the bush. By calling the investigation unit in for a full sweep of the house, Clay had all but announced that he suspected foul play in Terry's death.

"Maybe?" Mike seemed unconvinced. "Or maybe about a zillion other reasons."

"So what you're telling me is you've got nothing for me." Clay slumped back in his chair and closed his eyes. He'd already heard this from everyone else. It didn't matter that the picture was out of place, or that the drawers in the bedroom had clearly been tossed. No one gave a shit about all the little things wrong with Terry's office, the way all the random crap she'd collected and displayed on her shelves was just a bit off, the way her books were out of order.

"Well, not nothing," Mike said, and he frowned. He turned to yet another holo monitor and tapped at his lightkeys, bringing up a gigantic image of what looked like a black swatch of cloth.

Clay raised an eyebrow. "How incredibly helpful."

"Hang on. Filters." Mike tapped at his keys and then swiped a hand in front of the hologram. It went blue, and suddenly there was an image, faint but visible, printed on the cloth. When he saw it, Clay fought to keep his cool, to not show the bright red streak of rage that ran through him. To most people, the design would have meant next to nothing, but to Clay it held a deep significance. He knew it very well.

"Where the fuck did you find that?"

"I didn't find shit," Mike said. "That was all Rogers. He found it in the kitchen, caught on a nail or something. Brought it down here for me to work my magic."

"Why didn't he tell me?"

"That he found a random piece of black cloth in your million-year-old house that might not even have anything on it? Come on. He just filed it with everything else. Wasn't worth a call."

"Have you shown it to anyone else? O'Connor needs to see this."

Mike gave him a cool glance. "You want to give me any other tips? I showed it to the detective. Showed it to the rest of the team down here, too. We tried to get prints or DNA off the cloth, but no dice."

"I need to talk to O'Connor," Clay said, standing.

Mike stayed seated, looking up at him. "You recognize it, don't you?"

"Maybe. Listen, thanks for the hair thing. If you stumble on any more info ..."

"I'll let you know. No worries. Buy me a beer sometime."

Clay said he would and headed for the door. As he reached it, he glanced back over his shoulder. Mike had returned to his work but had left the image up on one of the screens. The image sat there, seeming almost to mock Clay. Just a little icon, no bigger than a thumbprint, but Clay knew it would be repeated across the entire cloth to which the swatch had once been attached. It was a fleur-de-lis, Arón Escobar's symbol, worn by every single one of his thugs.

* * *

Detective Shereece O'Connor was an imposing presence, nearly six feet tall and built like a grizzly bear. She'd made the junior Olympic team as a weight lifter before coming to the force. Now in her mid-twenties, she still had plenty of muscle; it stretched the cloth of her uniform at her biceps and thighs. She had brown skin and curly hair that she dyed a deep auburn and kept pulled back in a tight bun. Her sunken eyes sat above a long nose that seemed too thin for her face. She was peering down it at him with an expression of skepticism.

"Aren't you supposed to be on leave, Officer Foster?"

Clay shrugged. "Let's say I'm here informally."

"Bet you'd prefer I not say you were here at all."

"I'd appreciate it."

"All right, but this better not be some sit-down where you tell me I'm not working on your case hard enough."

O'Connor could be intimidating when she needed to be, but her greatest talent was an impeccable eye for detail combined with a dogged work ethic. Her rise to detective had been meteoric by Brooklyn standards, and Clay doubted it would be long before she moved up the chain. "No way I'd ever accuse you of that, Detective."

"Good. So why the visit?"

"You've seen the cloth that Mike found?"

"No, I saw the cloth that Rogers found and Mike stuck under a black light to show off a little picture of a Saints logo."

Clay rolled his eyes. "Don't play dumb. You know about those bandannas. They were in our reports on Escobar's men. I'm sure you've read them."

"More than once," O'Connor said. She wrapped a massive hand around a mug Clay would've had a hard time gripping and took a long slug of coffee. "Listen, it's an interesting little piece, but—"

"Interesting? Is that all it is?"

"If you're looking for 'conclusive,' you should keep looking."

"Jesus Christ, Shereece, one of Escobar's men was *in my house.*"

"Were they? Foster, that design's been around forever. It's older than you and me combined, and that particular ink goes back at least thirty years. I know for a fact you've only owned that palace of yours for eight years. Hell, it could have come in stuck to your shoe. It's not like you haven't spent plenty of time in Crown Heights."

"So you think that we left a piece of cloth lying around our kitchen for eight solid years and it just coincidentally happens to point a guy who hates me and recently threatened me?"

O'Connor raised an eyebrow. "Does that seem any less likely than that Arón Escobar, less than three months out of jail, decided to send one of his goons to your house to kill your wife? And that for some reason this guy didn't notice that his gang marker got caught on your kitchen door? And that he failed to notice it even though he managed to rearrange all of your stuff while leaving exactly zero fingerprints or DNA evidence?"

"There was the hair."

"Vat-grown wig, probably a previous tenant. Foster ... Clay ... I can't pretend to understand what you're going through, but—"

"But you're ready to tell me I'm crazy anyway."

The detective folded her hands and rested her chin against them, regarding him for a moment. "What do you want from me?"

"I want you to get a fucking warrant, search the Loco from top to bottom, and haul Escobar in for questioning."

"And you want me to do this based on a swatch of cloth that might be thirty years old and a hair that belongs to no one. You think I'm going to get a warrant out of that ... how? Let's not even consider how connected Escobar is. Even if he were small-time, that is some thin fucking evidence."

Clay was silent for a moment, considering. "How far up the line did you take this before it got shot down?"

O'Connor regarded him for a time, lips pressed tight together, as if considering whether she wanted to answer the question. "Not that far," she finally said.

"So it didn't get to Baker?" The police chief was no fan of Clay's, but securing a warrant wouldn't require his permission.

"Not even close."

"Even if we can't get the search, we have enough to at least bring Escobar in for questioning. The threat, the fleur-de-lis, the rearranged shit in my house—"

"Maybe you think we do, and maybe so do I, but the higher-ups don't seem to agree."

"Who was it?" Clay leaned forward in his chair, looking her in the eyes. "At least let me know which one of our bosses is bought."

"What if they're not bought?" O'Connor said, taking another sip of coffee. "What if they just think that there's a simple, sad explanation and that you're grasping at straws because you don't want to accept that something so terrible could happen for no reason?"

"Does that sound like me?"

She shrugged. "Not really."

"So help me out here."

"I'm doing what I can, Clay. Forensics has spent more time on this than they would've on most other cases. I've been talking to Escobar insiders, seeing if they've heard anything. I've got friends undercover who are digging. If anything comes up, we'll reevaluate, but I'll tell you ... if this was Escobar's hit, he does *not* want anyone to know about it."

"Of course not. He killed a cop's wife."

"If you can prove that, I'll bring him in. Hell, if you can make the brass a little more suspicious, I'll bring him in. You want to talk to them, I'd start with a captain. That's a step higher on the chain than I got before getting shut down."

"By the time I'm allowed to talk to anyone on the record, it'll be over. Escobar probably already knows we're looking, and he'll pay off whoever he needs to pay off to make sure it doesn't go any further."

O'Connor spread her hands. "That's out of my control."

"Christ." Clay grabbed the back of his neck with his hand, squeezing, trying to relieve the tension.

"If it's worth anything, I'm sorry. I'd like to at least haul the son of a bitch in. I don't know if he killed your wife or not, but there's enough that's weird about this to make me want to find out for sure."

"I'll take it up with Captain Peters," Clay said. "I'll see if we can at least get him in for questioning, even if we can't search that dump he calls a headquarters. Goddamn Escobar."

"Baker won't be happy that you're chatting up half the department when you're supposed to be on leave."

"Chief Baker knows he's got a standing invitation to kiss my ass." Clay stood up.

O'Connor laughed a little. "Everyone knows that. Good luck, Foster."

"Thanks, Detective. Keep an ear open."

"You know it."

Clay turned and left the office. Peters wouldn't be in right now, but it didn't matter. He had no intention of talking to the man; the Brooklyn PD wasn't going to be interested in Escobar unless Clay could come up with conclusive evidence that the thug had ordered Terry's murder. Even then, the system would drag it out for ages and the eventual outcome would probably be another six-month stint at Rikers before Escobar got himself back on the streets.

There was only one real path left for him. If he wanted Arón Escobar to be held accountable for what he'd done, Clay was going to have to handle this himself.

CHAPTER 4

Crown Heights

"Clay, man, this is not a healthy line of conversation."

Kellen picked up his cheeseburger, bacon poking out from the sides, and took a hearty bite. They were sitting in a Brooklyn Heights deli, where Kellen had agreed to meet Clay for a late-afternoon lunch. Kellen glanced up, chewing, waiting for a reaction.

"Bullshit," Clay said. "Listen, Kel, it wasn't an accident. I'm sure of it."

Kellen took another bite, chewing slowly, looking contemplative. At last he set the burger on the plate, took a giant swig of Pepsi, and shrugged. "That's not even what I'm talking about."

"They're not going to pursue this. What choice do I have?"

"There's always choices," Kellen muttered. He snagged a french fry, held it up, and jabbed it at Clay. "Anyway, you're supposed to be on leave, not doing cop shit."

"I'm doing cop shit because none of the cops are," Clay said.

"You really think O'Connor and the forensics boys half-assed the inspection on a cop's wife? No signs of struggle, no bruising anywhere that doesn't make sense, nothing. No one heard any screaming, no one saw anybody go in or out of your place. It wasn't even dark out. You got a hair, a piece of cloth, and some knickknacks that Terry herself mighta moved."

"Someone tossed that bedroom and the rest of the place, too. Whoever did it was good. This wasn't some B&E asshole. It was someone wearing gloves and working with a delicate touch, but they were in a hurry and they missed a few things. Someone was looking for something in my house, and someone threw my wife off the balcony. Goddamn it, Kel—"

Kellen held his hands up. "I'm not saying you're wrong, or crazy, or anything like that, all right? I'm saying it's hard to believe, is all. How's it go? The simplest explanation's probably the right one?"

"Not this time."

"How you been sleeping?"

"Fuck you. I'm not crazy."

"Calm down. I never said you were crazy. You went home drunk as a motherfucker the other night, probably slept like shit, called Forensics ... Now you've had a couple days sitting alone in your apartment overthinking this shit, right?"

"Not even close. I spent five hours today with Tim and Emily, organizing the funeral."

"How are they?"

"Don't change the subject."

Kellen rolled his eyes. "Christ, man, I promise, we are not done talking about this shit. Not by a long fucking ways. You want to tell me how her parents are doing, or you want to keep acting like I'm not on your side?"

"Are you?"

"You fucking bet. I just need to know that when I get hauled in front of Chief Baker after you do something stupid while you're supposed to be on goddamn leave, I can nod emphatically at that pompous shit and say, 'Yessir, I did everything I could to convince that loco son of a bitch that he was out his damned mind,' and be telling the truth. Covering my ass, bro. You know I'll back whatever play you want to make, right after I tell you every single reason you shouldn't make it."

Clay leaned back in his seat, closed his eyes, rubbed his forehead with one hand. "Her parents are dealing. They don't blame me, which I don't understand, but I guess whatever."

"Did you tell them about all this?"

"Of course not. They think it was just a terrible accident, just like everyone else who hasn't heard all the details does. Tim told me he was trying to think of it like a lightning bolt, just a random thing that happens and no one can control. Emily kept talking about God's fucking will, as if that has anything to do with anything."

Kellen looked unimpressed. "Plenty of people out there who think it has something to do with *everything*, brother."

Clay didn't even want to get started on that merry-go-round. "Sure. Look, I think you should send Angela and the kids out of the city for a few days."

Kellen considered this for a time, eating his burger. Finally he gave a disgusted shake of his head. "Arón fucking Escobar. Goddamn it."

"He lost six months thanks to us, lost some turf, probably had to put down a few petty rebellions when he got back. Then, just as he thinks maybe we learned our lesson about Brooklyn justice, we roll up on his joint and start threatening him again. Hell, his boy fucking told us he had something planned for us. Remember?"

"That was bluster, man. Come on. I ain't heard nothing from the usual lines of communication regarding Arón Escobar putting a hit out on anyone, let alone a cop's wife."

"Doesn't mean it didn't happen. Escobar's good."

"Better'n average, anyway," Kellen said. It had taken them much longer than it should have to put together enough evidence to make it worth bringing Escobar up on charges. The man was smart. Slippery. Hard to pin down.

"Maybe he kept it quiet," Clay said. "Maybe he—"

"When that motherfucker has someone put down, he's not real subtle about it. You remember how his boys did Sal Lobello? Word that Escobar called in that hit came down before they even found the pieces, and they left those lying around in broad daylight."

"Chopping up a small-time thug who's cutting into your action isn't the same thing as assassinating an innocent civilian who's married to Brooklyn PD."

Kellen nodded. "That is true."

"I think we spooked him, and I think he called in the hit, and I think you need to be worrying about your family."

"I am, now ... and thanks real fucking much for that. Man, we still don't even know Terry was killed. I know you're convinced, but goddamn ..."

"It's the only thing that makes any sense."

"No. I'm sorry, man, but it also makes sense that she got up to water her plants and just ... fell."

Clay shook his head. "If I could get five minutes alone with him, I'd wring his neck until he gave up the truth."

"Good luck with that. You want to get near that fucker, you best bring half the cops in the city with you."

Clay scratched at his stubble, thinking. "We're not going to storm the Loco."

Kellen finished his meal, slid his plate away, and dropped some bills onto the table. "We ain't doing anything yet, all right? This isn't cop shit, brother. What you are engaged in right now is what we in the business call 'idle speculation,' and that's not good enough. You know the rules."

"The rules say I can't do anything except sit in my house and wait to bury my wife, Kel. That motherfucker killed her. I need to do *something*."

"I know. I told you, I got your back, but I am still on duty and the cop shit I gotta do is the cop shit I'm told to do by my superior officers. You got some time off ... so go use it. Hit the streets, shake some motherfuckers down, get some information. Lickers in Crown Heights won't know you're on leave, and they didn't take your badge, so flash it and get some news. Put together something convincing, man. You won't get anywhere trying to get them to move on Escobar with what you've got."

Clay nodded. He understood. Kellen wasn't dismissing him, but neither was he going to accept Clay's hypothesis without further proof, and there was nothing else to deliver right now. Nothing but—how had Kellen described it?— misplaced knickknacks.

What had he been searching for, this mystery man? Was he hoping to find evidence of corruption? That made no sense; there was no reason to kill Terry in that scenario, and anyone who knew him enough to care would also know that Clay was the cleanest cop between the Atlantic and the Pacific. All his dirty secrets were property of the United States Government; he had none of his own.

No, the only motive that made sense was revenge. Could it have been someone he'd harmed in the war? Clay had destroyed more than one family in North Carolina, and it wasn't impossible that someone might be doing the same to him. Still, he'd never been caught, never identified as an operative, at least not by anyone who'd lived. The more immediate solution made the most sense: he and Kellen had put Escobar away and the man wanted to hurt them for it.

Kellen's suggestion was busywork. Clay wasn't going to find what he needed by wandering the streets and asking junkies if they'd heard anything. If Escobar had meant for the truth to be known, it would be known by now, and no one as good as the guy who'd tossed Clay's house was going to blab. This was just a little payback, a little "fuck you" from Arón to Clay, kept quiet because the gangster knew that to openly kill a cop's wife was tantamount to signing a declaration of war with the entire force.

There were only two people in the city who knew what had happened to Terry: the man who'd killed her and the man who'd ordered the hit. He knew where that latter motherfucker was: holed up at the Loco in Crown Heights, surrounded by men with guns. Clay could feel prickling at the back of his neck as rage rose within him, thinking about that smug piece of shit kicking back in his chair, grinning, feeling untouchable. The killer was out of Clay's reach for now, so he was going to have to start with Escobar.

Clay thought back to his time in North Carolina, alone, vastly outnumbered, and tasked with matters of blood and politics. He was no longer the man he had been in those days—

Terry had reshaped him into something new—but the skills he had used weren't gone. They never really left you once you had them; that was the beauty of the training. He hadn't grown fat or lazy, hadn't lost his speed, his agility, or his steady hand. Escobar's men were not soldiers. They were thugs, nothing more, just a band of rough-and-ready lickers with too-big guns strapped to their hips. No training. No tactics.

Kellen held his hand out, forcing Clay out of his reverie, and Clay shook it.

"I'm off tomorrow," his partner said. "You want me to stop by, help with the planning?"

"Sure. Kel, I'm serious about Angela and the kids."

"I know. I'm thinking they could use a trip up to New Haven. She's got a brother near there with a beach house, always says he'd love to see us. I'll send her up tonight, catch them on the weekend. We'll spend a little time swimming, fucking around in the woods ... summer vacation shit."

"That sounds like a good idea."

"I'll see you tomorrow around noon. You can show me the data on that mystery hair. You know how I love looking at data ..."

Clay gave him a tired grin and nodded. Kellen stood, gave a quick semi-salute, and headed for the door. Clay sat and stared at his plate of food, rolling the idea around in his head. Escobar. He would need to go alone. Kellen couldn't be involved in this, couldn't even know about it. If what Clay was thinking of doing ever came back to haunt him, it couldn't drag Kellen and his family down with it.

I can do this. I have to.

Clay stood up, tossed his own bills onto the table, and left his food. He had plans to make.

51

* * *

Getting into Crown Heights was easy if you weren't trying to do it in uniform. Clay went in a pair of jeans and a beat-up linen shirt, a baseball cap pulled over his head, a canvas messenger bag at his side. He was not famous, even among the city's underworld; no one other than Escobar was going to recognize him. The movies said a seasoned criminal could spot a cop just by the way he talked. That was bullshit. It took time and effort to sniff out a rat, and Clay didn't intend on giving Escobar the opportunity.

To the people around him, he was just another guy looking for an ampule of Elixir or a piece of pussy. Clay was happy to let them keep that illusion, moving at a steady pace but not hurrying, not speaking, keeping his eyes down. There was nothing suspicious about heading toward the Loco; it sat on a strip of road that held at least half a dozen bars and whorehouses.

Clay was neither skilled nor suicidal enough to attempt a frontal assault on Escobar's stronghold, and casually walking up to the front door wasn't going to work. They'd take his bag and gun, and inside the place was a rat's warren of dimly lit rooms and thudding music, with access to Escobar's upstairs office tightly guarded.

What Clay wanted was a little one-on-one talk. Just him and Escobar, going over the fine details of what the man had done to his wife. Clay wasn't worried about getting Escobar to open up and expound on the subject; it was just a matter of getting the man alone and finding the right buttons to push. The little girl in Carolina had been a button; when Clay had pushed it, her senator father had folded and shifted his vote, ending the war.

The building on the Loco's southern side was a six-story housing project, not quite a tenement, one of many that had gone up in the twenties during the city's last real boom. Brooklyn had been flush with money from the construction of the walls that had separated Manhattan from the rising water. That the walls might also be used to keep out those who had built them hadn't seemed to cross anyone's mind, but over the ensuing decades the island had become next to impossible to enter. When it became apparent that few in Brooklyn would ever again be considered worthy of a pass, the borough had revolted, withdrawing from New York and petitioning to become a city of its own again.

It had taken five years, but Brooklyn had eventually gained its independence. Manhattan, supplied with low-wage workers from the Bronx and Queens, had said good riddance, cut the number of passes available to Brooklyn residents to an absolute minimum, and gone about its business of becoming the center of both wealth and political power in what was left of the country. Brooklyn had established its own local government, and within months that entity was thoroughly corrupted. The long, slow decline had begun. Now Elixir seemed more likely with each passing day to be the death blow to a once-proud city.

Clay climbed the tenement's exterior staircase, glancing from the corner of his eye at the toughs idling in front of the Loco. They were paying him no attention, which was perfect. When he tried the front door, it swung open easily, the lock having long ago been pried away. Inside, it was stifling and smelled even worse than it did outside. He could hear the sound of a television blaring from the nearest apartment, and somewhere deeper in the building a couple were either fighting or fucking with extreme zeal. Clay turned and pushed open the door to the stairwell.

There were shattered Elixir vials everywhere, crunching underfoot and glittering in the dim light cast by the few working bulbs. The walls were covered in spray-painted tags, and an acrid odor in the air made him think something chemical had burned here not long ago. The building wasn't a squat, so there had to be a landlord and maybe even a super, but neither seemed interested in cleaning the place up.

He had just passed the third floor when there was a crash as someone flung the door open behind him. Clay stopped climbing and glanced back. A man came stumbling into the stairwell, leaned over the edge, and vomited out a long stream of black fluid. Clay heard it spattering on the tile floor below.

"God … Christ …" the man moaned and vomited a second time. Clay began to climb again, but the man, who had finished throwing up for the time being, called out.

"You got an extra ampule, my man? I'm hurting bad and the niggers in number four won't open their door."

"I don't lick," Clay said, not stopping.

"Course you don't. Me neither. Never touched the stuff in my life, and anyway I'm giving it up next week. I promised the Father. Have you got an ampule, bud? Those *fucking* niggers, you know? Took our jobs and our women, now it's our fuckin' drugs … hey! Listen to me!"

Clay came to a halt again and looked over his shoulder. "I don't take that shit, and if you're smart, you'll shut the fuck up before I let the guys in number four know how you're talking about them."

The man gave him both fingers, told him to go fuck himself, and leaned over the railing again, dry heaving. Clay idly considered tossing him over it. That made him think of Terry and her own fall, which sent purpose running through him. He began to climb again, and the man gave him no further trouble.

The roof access, a hatch in the ceiling, had also had its lock torn out. Someone had chained it shut, securing it with a huge padlock. Clay rifled through his messenger bag, looking for his set of picks. He could not spring a modern mag-lock—not with a set of little brass tools anyway—so most of Brooklyn's front doors would present a challenge should he ever take up cat burglary, but something like this padlock was easy work. He had it open in three minutes.

The air on the roof was fresh, a welcome surprise. The building was tall enough to get some breeze and to sit above most of the stink from the street. The Loco sat next to him on the north, four stories tall—two shorter than its neighbor. Too far to jump from here. He was going to have to climb down to the fire escape and launch himself from its iron railing to the Loco's roof. He hoped the bolts would hold.

Clay opened his bag and went through his tools. There were the lock picks, a handgun—not his service pistol, of course—and a pair of handcuffs. There was also a bundle of parachute cord, a heavy bandanna, two razor blades, a lighter, a capped syringe, and three small glass bottles. While there was no such thing as a truth serum and probably never would be, the cocktail Clay could make from the vials' contents would leave the recipient both pliable to suggestion and in no small amount of discomfort. He hoped he wouldn't have to take the time; the gun was faster.

As soon as Clay was certain that Arón Escobar had ordered Terry's death, the drug lord was a dead man. Clay was not going to wait for Brooklyn's lazy-assed justice system to try the man, was not going to let a jury of imbeciles picked by conniving lawyers decide Escobar's guilt, was not going to see the man buy his freedom again six months down the line. The moment he was certain, Clay was going to put a bullet in Escobar's head, even if it meant being gunned down in the process.

Clay pulled the last item from his bag and turned it on. The tablet was top-of-the-line, using tech not available to the civilian workforce and featuring a high-speed data connection secured with four-gig encryption. Development on devices like this had stalled somewhat in the last thirty years, as efforts had been focused primarily on the war and halting the rise of the oceans, but it had not ceased entirely. The latest model, combined with the Brooklyn PD's classified databases, allowed him access to detailed satellite imagery, floor plans, and other information about the Loco. Everything he needed to know was here in his hands.

Clay didn't need floor plans to tell him where he'd find Escobar. The Brooklyn PD had plenty of informants, and within twenty-four hours of learning where the drug lord had holed up, those in charge of gathering information at the precinct had put together a pretty thorough dossier. Escobar's office was in the northwest corner of the building, on the second floor, as far from the street as possible. The man was known to spend hours there each night, venturing down to the club only in the morning, when the crowds had thinned and his business was done.

With dawn only a couple of hours away, Clay's time was running out. After packing his gear, he made his way to the fire escape and climbed quickly down the ladder onto the iron balcony that rested perhaps six feet above the Loco's roof. The metal groaned a bit when he stepped onto it, but it held.

Clay looked down at the roof. It seemed to be in decent shape, and he hoped that when he made his leap, he wouldn't plummet right through it and into the building below. Not wanting to delay and give Escobar the chance to leave his office, Clay clambered up onto the metal railing. There was no way to get a running start from this position; he was going to have to make the jump from a crouch, cover the space between the buildings, and land on the roof in a way that didn't break any bones.

This is crazy.

Yes, it was, but if he wanted the man who had ordered Terry killed to answer for that crime, there was little else to be done. Catching Escobar singlehandedly as he drove through the city with five bodyguards in an armored truck would be next to impossible, and breaking into the man's home was out of the question. He lived in a luxury condo somewhere in Williamsburg, with private security patrolling the grounds, cameras, a security system—the works. No, it had to be the Loco, and it had to be from above, which meant Clay was going to have to make this jump.

"Didn't come all the way up here for nothing," he muttered and sprang forward, aiming in the direction of the other building's fire escape so that, in case he missed the roof, he might at least find something to hold on to before beginning a four-story descent to the pavement below.

It didn't matter. The arc of his jump took him just past the parapet, and he hit the tar paper on the balls of his feet, his knees absorbing some of the impact, and rolled. One elbow scraped painfully along the leg of a derelict water tower, but he was otherwise unharmed. After a moment, he climbed to his feet, breathing deep, already focused on the next task. Arón Escobar, and the answers Clay craved, were sitting somewhere below him. All he had to do was go and get them.

CHAPTER 5

Escobar

The best thing Clay could say about the crumbling brick building that housed the Loco was that he was glad its windows hadn't been updated for more than fifty years. They were still made out of safety glass, popular in the early twenty-first century, rather than the polymer more common in post-war buildings. This made it easy to climb down a fire escape to the metal landing outside a darkened room, crack the glass with the butt of his gun, and kick it in.

Clay waited a moment, perched outside the newly broken window, but no one seemed to be coming. He climbed through into the room. The top floor of the building was largely deserted, given over to boxes of junk slowly collapsing in on themselves and shattered furniture that had seen too many fights in the bar below. The walls were grungy and cracking, vandalized, damaged by water, rats, and the slow progression of the years.

Clay set his tablet on a pile of boxes to use for illumination. He slid his gun into his waistband, at the back. He hated carrying like this; it was inconvenient and dangerous. A belt holster was optimal but too bulky for the messenger bag, and it was too hot out to wear something that would cover an underarm holster without arousing suspicion. He made the weapon as secure as it could be, picked up his tablet, and ventured into the interior of the building. The lights were off and there was no noise coming from anywhere on this floor. Clay doubted anyone came up here very often. There were no bedrooms, and no one to—

He rounded a corner and found himself inches from what he at first thought was a statue but quickly realized was a human being. The man was mountainous, tall and broad-shouldered, the kind of guy who seemed like he'd been born and raised at the gym. He was wearing what looked like crocodile-skin pants and silver-metallic cowboy boots. A machine pistol—an old Mac-10—was hanging from his side.

The man was leaned up against the wall, arms crossed, eyes closed. Clay quickly took three quiet steps back and around the corner again, killing the light on his tablet. *Shit.* He should've realized that someone would be guarding the staircase. He didn't want to start shooting now—there was no way he'd make it to Escobar before the man fled the building—but neither was he enthusiastic about trying to take this guy on hand-to-hand.

Do I kill him? He'd done it before—come up on soldiers unaware and broken their necks or crushed in their windpipes before they'd known Clay was there. This man was probably a licker, almost assuredly a piece of shit, and the world would perhaps be better off without him, but Clay was a cop now. He was no longer the man who killed first and worried about the details later. Being put on leave hadn't changed that.

This wasn't going to be any fun for the guy in the crocodile pants. The decision made, Clay didn't hesitate, setting his tablet down and spinning around the corner again. This time he wasn't so lucky—the guy had opened his eyes, and they went wide at Clay's sudden appearance.

"Hey, what the fu—" he began, and Clay dropped low and drove a hard uppercut directly into the man's crotch. It was a dirty move, and one he should perhaps have been ashamed of, but Clay didn't have time to wrestle with this hunk of meat.

The guy made a strangled noise of agony, grabbed his balls with both hands, and began to double over. Clay didn't give him the time. He pulled the gun from the back of his pants and, with an artful flip, took hold of the barrel, leaving the polished wooden grip exposed. It was a heavy thing, and if Clay miscalculated this next swing he was going to kill this man instead of leaving him snoring on the floor.

He didn't, cracking the man just above the left temple with the butt of the gun. The guy crumpled and flopped forward. Clay put the gun back in his pants, reached into his messenger bag, and pulled out the short length of parachute cord. Kneeling, he pulled the guy's hands back and tied them up. Then he shoved the bandanna into the man's mouth, forming a crude gag. It wasn't great—the guy could still get to his feet pretty easily if he woke up—but it was all Clay could do. Besides, by the time this guy was conscious again, Clay would have reached Escobar, and it wouldn't matter anymore.

He made his way quickly down the central staircase, wary of encountering any further danger. No one was stationed at the next two landings—perhaps Escobar had only been concerned about someone's gaining access via the roof. He left the staircase and headed for the drug lord's office. He stopped, reviewing his plan of attack before making the turn that would take him in sight of the man guarding that room.

Part of him—the part that couldn't stop picturing Terry lying on that steel table in the coroner's lab, her feet sticking out from under the sheet, the skin of her forehead missing— wanted simply to turn the corner, draw his weapon, and begin firing. He forced that part away and focused on assessing the situation.

There would be at least one man between him and Escobar. Clay had spared the life of the guard above because that man had been lucky enough to be dozing. Escobar's personal guards wouldn't dare to rest with their boss so close. Decisive action was required, but if Clay simply turned the corner and shot the man, it would give Escobar ample time to react. He needed to get closer to the door first.

Clay pulled his cap down tight over his head, hunched his shoulders, stepped forward, and turned the corner in a kind of lurching stumble. He reached out, steadied himself against the wall, breathed deep, and let the air out with a "whoooah" noise. He took two steps forward, heading toward the guard, and the man stiffened.

"Back the fuck up and head downstairs," he said.

"I got … Is the staircase over here?" Clay asked, taking another two steps forward. The guard drew his gun but held it at his side.

"Staircase is back the way you came. Turn around before I put a cap in you."

"I took too much," Clay said, coming to a halt. He let himself reel, looking off balance, as if about to fall backward, before lurching forward another step or two. He was less than eight feet from the man, close to grappling distance but not quite there. This was going to be tight.

Apparently tired of issuing warnings, the guard began to raise his weapon, and Clay leaped forward, transforming in an instant from Elixir-addled junkie to something much more dangerous. He came in low, from the side, doing his best to avoid the man's line of fire while simultaneously drawing his own weapon. The guard was big, almost as big as alligator-pants upstairs, but fast. Christ, there was no way to reach him in time, and it was too early to start shooting.

Clay grabbed the bill of his ball cap and flung it at the guard's face. It wasn't much, just enough to make the man flinch for a fraction of a second, but it was all the time Clay needed. He finished closing the distance and swung his pistol around, smashing its butt into the guard's jaw. Bone snapped, teeth shattered and went clattering against the wall, blood sprayed.

Clay gave the man no time for recovery, driving his knee into the guard's stomach and landing another blow with the gun, this time at the back of the man's skull. The guy went down; that kind of hit could be fatal, but Clay was beyond caring. He'd started his play, and now he had to see it through. He swung around again and kicked out with his heel, and the shitty pine door separating him from Escobar gave up readily. As it swung inward, Clay saw Escobar scurrying across the room toward a table on which sat another Mac-10. He brought his gun up. "I really wouldn't do that."

Escobar must have heard the deadly clarity in Clay's voice and understood that he was in real danger. He came to a halt and turned to face Clay, his face like stone. The man was fifty-three, short but thick and muscular, with heavy dark brows and close-cropped hair going gray and thinning in the front. His face was badly scarred. Some of those scars were the product of fights engaged in during the long journey up to his current position. The rest …

Like a celebrity obsessed with appearance, Escobar liked to tinker. Where those in Hollywood sought higher cheekbones or the perfect nose, Escobar was interested in more drastic changes. He was notorious for chasing the latest biomodification tech, but when you had to acquire that shit from the black market and could only find disgraced surgeons to install it, things sometimes went wrong. The ugly burst of blue-tinged scar tissue around the man's right eye spoke to that.

"It would seem I need a better man at the door," Escobar said. His voice had nothing of the streets in it, no grammatical flaws or gangster appropriations, no trace of an accent. The words came out strangely smooth, as if run through an auto-tuner. Clay remembered the sound of it from the gangster's trial.

"Guess so."

Escobar was sizing Clay up, head tilted, lips pursed. He was dressed simply: a pair of dark slacks and a stone-colored button-down shirt. A crimson tie hung loose at his neck. The Louis Vuitton logo embroidered on it was just obnoxious enough to be real. One of his hands was covered with a black leather glove.

"This seems a far cry from legit police procedure, Officer Foster."

"Must've left my book on procedure back with my badge and uniform. Take a seat." Clay used his foot to swing the door backward. The knob had torn away from the wood, but at least no one would see him from the hallway and shoot him in the back.

Escobar shrugged, spun, and headed for his desk. There was nothing on it but a holo screen, a set of lightkeys, and a crystal decanter filled with clear liquid that Clay assumed was liquor. Escobar walked with a limp, and Clay could hear the slight whir of a motor or servo whenever he moved his left leg. That was a new one; at the trial, his mods had been limited to the upper half of his body.

"Keep your hands on top of the desk," Clay said.

"This is your show." Escobar sat down and folded his hands in front of him. The gloved one hit the desk with a heavy thud. "So ... what do you want?"

"First? The name of the guy who killed her. After that we can talk about why you needed to toss my place."

Escobar raised his eyebrows and for a moment looked amused. It was a strange expression to see on the face of a man staring down the barrel of a gun. "Killed who?"

"This is not a good time to fuck with me, *Arón*."

Escobar seemed to consider this, tenting his fingers and touching them to his face. At last he spoke. "So ... who died? I hope it was someone you liked."

Clay felt his trigger finger tense. Escobar seemed to notice this; his expression became more serious, but he didn't move, not even to put his hands down. He simply sat and waited.

It was the right choice. Clay got control of himself. "I want a name, and I want an explanation."

"I haven't ordered any hits on anyone who matters to you, so I have no idea what you're talking about."

"I've got reason to think you do. Your man on the curb told us you had something for us, that you were going to make us regret ever hearing your name."

"Did he, now?" It was impossible to glean any insight into Escobar's emotions from his modified voice or the expression on his face. Guy should've been a poker player. "And you believed him?"

"Why wouldn't I?"

"Most of my guards are degenerate lickers with half-rotted brains. Whoever you spoke to made something up to frighten you."

"Sure, and that's why I found a piece of cloth with your boys' logo on it in my kitchen the night after my wife was killed."

Escobar's lip twitched, but he managed to suppress whatever expression wanted to come out at this news. "My condolences ..."

"Fuck you."

Escobar ignored this, cracking the knuckles on his left hand with the gloved fingers of his right. "You're not worth my time, and you're definitely not worth earning the enmity of the rest of your department. Even the men I own in your precinct—and I own a lot of them—wouldn't stand for a hit on an officer's wife."

Clay considered this. "Maybe. Or maybe you're trying to talk me out of putting a bullet through that robot eye and out the back of your head."

Escobar shrugged. "You could've solved all of this with one visit to the Chink."

"Right, or I could've asked Bigfoot. I'm not interested in myths."

"Pretty persistent myth."

The Brooklyn PD had been looking for a man operating under that name for years. No one had ever managed to find any concrete evidence that he existed, and yet the rumors continued to swirl that the man was real and that he lorded over The Hook like a god-king, his hand in everything that happened there. If Escobar was telling the truth, no one else in the city would be more likely to know who had ordered Terry's death.

"You've met him?"

"Maybe."

"Tell me how to reach him and maybe I won't shoot you in the face."

Escobar tapped one of the fingers of his gloved hand on the table. "Not a chance."

Clay took a step forward, baring his teeth. "Listen, motherfucker, right now I'm pretty sure you had my wife killed. If you think I won't blow your fucking brains right out just because I'm a cop, you're wrong. So start talking."

Escobar sighed. "I don't understand why you think you can come in here and threaten me."

"Because I'm the one who has the gun." Clay understood as he said it, even before the smirk appeared on Escobar's face, that he was wrong. He wasn't the one with the gun, or at least not the only one.

"Are you?" Escobar asked, and his smirk widened into a grin.

Shit. "Where is it? Let me guess … in your eye?"

"That would be fancy, wouldn't it? Tim, why don't you let Officer Foster know where the gun is?"

Clay hadn't heard the guard's approach, but he certainly heard the unmistakable sound of a shotgun being pumped from behind the door. Christ, that easy?

Escobar stood up. "I tripped the alarm as soon as I heard my man at the door telling you to back off. They've just been waiting for a code word to blow your guts out all over my floor."

"Why didn't you use it?"

"Didn't feel like I needed to. We can take care of you without getting blood everywhere. Drop the gun."

Clay did as he was told. Escobar ordered him to do the same with the bag and then to take two steps backward. Clay complied, and he heard the door open behind him, heard footsteps, felt the hard metal of the gun's long barrel press against his back. It was angled down so that a shot would hit the floor rather than Escobar.

"All right, boss?" the man behind him said. Clay saw a second man, tall and pencil-thin, dressed much like Escobar and apparently unarmed, walk by to his left. The man picked up Clay's bag and gun, set them on the desk, and moved off to the side.

"I'm fine," Escobar said. "Check him for anything else."

The thin man stepped forward and performed a quick, thorough search. "He's clean."

Escobar came out from around his desk and leaned against it, regarding Clay. "Here's what's going to happen. We're going to call up a few more guys and we're going to escort you somewhere a little more private. Eventually you're going to end up sunk down in Bushwick Swamp with all of the other corpses. The ones no one wants found."

"You're too smart to kill a cop's wife, but a cop's all right?" Clay said.

Escobar made a scoffing noise. "You killed yourself. You came in here with no badge, no warrant, and no proof. No one will ever find what's left of you. They'll know … but they'll know it was your fault."

Clay looked him in the eye. "Guess you'd better get on with it, then."

Now Escobar grinned, wide and wolfish. He took a few steps forward and stood in front of Clay. "You've got balls, *cabrón*, I'll give you that. I'll make sure they cut those off before you die."

Clay didn't have much to say about that, so he kept his peace.

Escobar gave him a grim smile. "You putting me in Rikers? That was easy time. That place is the Hilton compared to where I grew up. It was like a vacation, except the food … the food was *shit*, my friend. So here's a little bit of payback for six months of crap meatloaf and stale fucking bread."

He drew back his fist—the mechanical one—and rammed it forward, driving it full force into Clay's gut. The punch felt like a wrecking ball swinging into his intestines, but if Clay could've done anything beyond controlling his rising gorge, he would've thanked the man. Might have kissed the motherfucker. The punch had made him bend over, and the motion forced the guard with the shotgun to take a step back and pull the gun from Clay's spine, and that was all the room that Clay needed.

He opened his mouth, letting air out and directing it around the edge of his left cheek. The razor blade secreted in there dislodged and flew forward, landing neatly in his cupped hands. It was an old trick, keeping a blade lodged between your cheek and gum like that, a gangster trick from the days when the crack pipe had been Brooklyn's vice of choice. Clay had practiced it first with a filed-down blade, then with a real one, learning to speak without cutting his mouth to shit in the process. In all the many times he had been searched, whether he had the blade on him or not, no one had ever thought to stick their fingers in there.

Clay brought the razor up in a flashing arc and added another scar to Escobar's face, slicing a deep red line from jaw to cheek to forehead. The blade hit the man's right eye, and rather than the burst of blood and ooze Clay had expected, there was instead a shower of sparks. Escobar covered his face with his hands, profanities pushing their way out from between his fingers.

Clay spun on the guard behind him and ran the blade in a jagged line up the man's arm. The guy shouted and let go of the shotgun's pump. Clay flicked the blade aside, reached out, and broke the guard's right arm over his knee. Bone pierced the skin, and Clay felt blood spatter against his face as the guard's shout became a shriek.

The thin man was raising Clay's gun. Clay grabbed the shotgun from the guard's limp right hand, spun it around, and fired one barrel into the thin man's arm. Clay's gun went bouncing away, and the thin man voiced a reedy wail. He fell backward against the wall and slid to the ground, clutching at the wound.

Clay rounded on the guard whose arm he'd broken, shucking the shotgun. He pressed the muzzle up under the man's neck. When he pulled the trigger, most of the top half of the guard's head hit the ceiling. Clay turned, bringing the shotgun back to his shoulder.

Escobar had reached the table and had his fingers on his Mac-10. Sparks and a viscous green liquid were still belching forth from his robotic eye, but the good one was open wide.

Before Escobar could raise his gun, Clay aimed his own weapon down and gut-shot the gangster. Escobar's mouth dropped open and he lost his grip on the Mac-10, staggering backward and hitting the desk. He reached to steady himself and knocked the bottle of clear liquid to the floor with a crash, the scent of alcohol—probably vodka—drifting up from the remains. Leaning against the desk, Escobar clapped a hand over the new sopping wet hole in his shirt. Clay took two strides forward, swung the stock of the shotgun, and cracked it against Escobar's temple.

The man went down, landing a foot or two from the expanding pool of alcohol. Clay couldn't have asked for better than what happened next: the sparks from Escobar's eye set the vodka ablaze, the flames leaping up with a whoosh. The thin man, whose screams of pain had been reduced to whimpers, suddenly cried out again. Clay tossed the shotgun away, picked up his gun, and leveled it at the man. "Shut the fuck up. You can stay there, keep quiet, and not move, or I can shoot you in the head."

The thin man opted for the first choice, and Clay turned his attention back to Escobar, kneeling down by him. The drug lord was groaning.

"You feel that fire, Arón? In about two minutes, you're going to feel it real good unless you tell me what I need to know."

"Didn't … didn't kill your wife!" Escobar shouted.

"Yeah, I think we're clear on that point. The Chink, motherfucker. How do I find him?"

"Don't know. Don't remember." Escobar took a swing at Clay with his metal hand, but it was weak. Slow. Clay grabbed his wrist and shoved it back down. Escobar moaned.

The wooden floor below the flaming pool of vodka, dry and old, had caught fire now. The heat was becoming tough to take. Clay glanced up at the ancient sprinkler system overhead. *Yeah, no way that's working.*

"You tell me how to contact the Chink and you might live. You sit here lying to me and you're going to burn alive."

Escobar swallowed. The sparks from his eye had finally stopped, but it was still leaking fluid. Clay smacked him on the side of the face. "Fire's getting pretty fucking close, man, so if I were you—"

"Exo-Net four!" Escobar cried out and then stopped to cough. He moaned in agony but continued. "Exo-Net four. Twenty-two, forty-eight, six. Just say you're looking for information."

"Then what?"

"Then nothing. Once he knows you're ... you're looking, he'll know everything about you ten minutes later. Then he'll decide if you're worth his time."

Interesting. "If there's anything else I should know, now's a good time."

"That's all there is!" Escobar shouted. "Fuck!"

Half the room was on fire now, and the heat was becoming unbearable. Clay stood. He grabbed his bag, slung it over his shoulder, and picked up the Mac-10. He pointed his pistol at the thin man, who was still lying sprawled in the far corner of the room. Clay didn't think the wound was that bad. The shot hadn't spread much, but it also had hit the meaty part of the man's bicep, causing mostly surface damage.

"Get up."

"I can't!"

"That right? Think you'll still feel that way in a few minutes? This place is about to burn to the fucking ground."

"Brady, get up, you pathetic, weak shit!" Escobar called from behind him.

Clay glanced over his shoulder and saw that the man had flipped onto his leaking stomach, dug his nails into the wooden floor, and was dragging himself away from the flames.

Clay pointed the gun at the thin man. "Stand the fuck up."

Brady sucked in air through his teeth and held his breath. He pulled his legs up underneath him and then, good arm steadying himself against the wall, shoved upward. His legs nearly buckled when his bad arm swung away from his body, but he managed to hold himself up, taking in little gasps of air through his teeth. He grabbed his elbow with his good hand and held the bad arm to his body.

"Now you have a choice," Clay said, and he gestured at Escobar with the gun. The drug lord had dragged himself a short distance from the flames and was lying on his stomach, panting, in a pool of blood. "You can help your boss or you can piss off. I truly don't give a shit."

Brady looked at Escobar. The flames were licking at the drug lord's shoes. Then the thin man looked back at Clay and his face hardened. "Fuck him."

"You coward fucking—" Escobar said, but the thin man was already moving out the door at a run, headed for parts unknown.

Clay, who was not about to give Brady time to rally the troops, followed. Behind him, Escobar roared something incoherent, and the roar turned into a shriek. That would be the flames, finally catching up to him, giving the man the same sort of torturous death he'd no doubt handed out to dozens of others.

The building might have been old and decrepit, but its fire alarms still had some life in them; they went off just as Clay turned into the hallway that led to the stairs. The sound startled a man standing at the end of the hallway and his first shot was wild, thudding into the drywall to the right of Clay's head. Clay dropped to one knee, raising his pistol and firing. His shot was true—it caught the guard in the shoulder and spun him around. The guy bounced off the wall and fell to the ground, clutching his arm, shouting for help.

Clay sprinted forward. He didn't want to deal with any reinforcements. If they got the drop on him here, in this little hallway, with a steadily increasing blaze at his back, he was a dead man. There wasn't time to pick them off one by one, and even the Mac-10 didn't have enough bullets for him to just blindly spray them around.

At the end of the hall he turned the corner and saw three more men running from the central area by the staircase. He fired off some rounds from the Mac-10, hoping the gun would prove reasonably accurate in close quarters. Two of the men went down; the third had a gun in his hand—Clay thought it was a Beretta—and came to a halt, steadying himself for better aim. Smart guy.

Clay was able to shoot on the move and did so, putting a bullet into the man's kneecap. The guy threw his hands into the air, firing his shot into the ceiling, and collapsed. Clay made a beeline for the stairs. It sounded like there were more guards coming, and he wanted nothing to do with them, especially with the Mac-10 nearly out of ammo.

He took the stairs at a run, two at a time, ignoring the burning in his calves. Behind him he could hear the men shouting for more help, but there were no thuds of boots on the stairs. Perhaps chasing Clay had lost its appeal when they'd seen the size of the blaze; he could smell the smoke even three stories up and knew that by now the fire had spread too far to contain. The whole building was going to come down.

At the top of the stairs, the man he had bound and gagged was just coming to. Clay kicked him in the side as he passed. "Fire! Get the fuck out!"

Then he was at the window. He shoved his pistol back into his pants and threw the Mac-10 out over the edge. Then he hauled himself through the frame, out onto the fire escape, and scrambled up the ladder to the roof. Across the alley was another metal fire escape, this one attached to the building from which he'd originally come.

This wasn't the same as jumping down onto the Loco's roof. He was going to have to leap straight across and grab the metal. Clay wasn't sure the bolts in the bricks would hold when his full weight came down on the fire escape. He wasn't sure his arms or ribs would hold when he hit it, either, but he was going to have to try.

"Jesus, this was such a stupid idea," Clay said to himself, and then he sprinted forward, planted his foot firmly on the parapet, and leaped.

CHAPTER 6

Contact

"Word on the street is the Loco burned to the bricks last night."

Clay glanced up at Kellen, affecting mild surprise. "That so?"

"That is so. You won't believe this, but their fire suppression system hadn't been checked in a while and it didn't work so good. Word is also that Escobar was in the building when it happened and never made it out."

"Shit, seriously? That's good news." Clay tried to pitch his tone right, a sort of muted pleasure—you never wanted to seem too happy about someone's death, not even a drug-dealing pimp like Escobar—mixed with surprise. He thought he'd nailed it, but Kellen raised an eyebrow for a minute before going back to his lunch.

"What?" Clay said.

Kellen glanced up from his shitty takeout enchiladas. "Well ... nothing, I guess."

It would have been easier to just let the thing drop, but Clay knew it would hang between them. He wasn't going to tell Kellen that he'd bruised up his ribs pretty good jumping across an alley to grab hold of a rickety fire escape that had pulled halfway out of the bricks and almost sent him tumbling to his death. Neither was he going to tell his partner that he'd hiked his way back home from his adventure in Crown Heights, cursing himself the entire way for letting his emotions get the best of him. The more he'd thought about it, the more he'd realized how absurd it all was; there wasn't any conspiracy. There wasn't any murder. There wasn't any Chink. There was only the fact that he'd gone on an insane rampage based on a scrap of cloth and a hair that belonged to no one, ending up with more blood on his hands and nothing of value to show for it.

He wasn't going to tell Kellen all of that, but he didn't want the man to bottle up whatever it was he had to say. "Come on, Kel."

"We should get back to these funeral plans, brother. That's what I came here for, not to learn shit I don't want to know."

"I have no clue what the fuck you're talking about."

"Well, that's sure a relief, man, because I heard from Jackie Skins that someone shot Escobar in the gut before burning up his place."

"Rival gang, I'd think," Clay said. Kellen looked at him for a long time, long enough that Clay – no stranger to such inspections – began to grow uncomfortable.

Finally, Kellen stabbed a bite of enchilada, forked it into his mouth, chewed, and swallowed. "I hope so, because what we do *not* need is someone who thinks he's Batman running all over the damn place."

"When did you decide you and Arón Escobar were tight?"

"Don't even start that shit. I put in every hour that you did sending Escobar away, and I wasn't any happier when he came back, but I am a fuckin' police officer, all right? That has to mean something or what's the goddamn point?"

Clay sighed. "Relax, Kel."

Kellen's expression softened. "Now, I suppose it's possible that it was just gangers being gangers. Anyway, that motherfucker deserved what he got, and maybe we should just let it go."

Clay agreed with this line of thought. He knew he was supposed to believe that Escobar was entitled to a fair trial, but Escobar had bought his way out of Rikers before ever getting one of those. He knew he was supposed to feel that he'd acted wrongly, that going around the law in order to get at the gangster and having it result in the man's death should feel wrong to him, but it didn't. It was as Kellen had said: *the motherfucker deserved what he got*, and if Clay had any regrets, it was only that he'd wasted his time and nearly gotten himself killed going after an absurd delusion.

"Maybe that's exactly it. Gangers being gangers, right? Or some other underworld bullshit. Escobar had more enemies than God, and God's made a lot of fucking enemies."

Kellen considered this and nodded. He snagged another forkful of enchilada. "Lot of folks at the precinct hoping it's okay to come to the funeral. They maybe didn't know Terry so well, but they saw her around, you know? Bake sales and Christmas parties and that fucking cookout every year where Mick pretends he knows how to make Texas barbecue."

"It's a big church." Clay picked up his burger, thought about taking a bite, put it back down. "They'll fit."

He tried not to think of the idea of sitting in front of a hundred people or more, listening as a priest droned on, the body of his wife set in a wooden box in front of him. This was going to happen in two days? Christ.

"That's not even close to what I'm asking, bro." Kellen's voice was soft, tinged with equal parts sympathy and humor. It was a good tone, and it helped Clay break through his reverie. There would be time for that later, hours and hours of time to spend alone in his empty house. Right now, he had plans to make.

"They're welcome to come. Look, Kel, you know I've had my share of disagreements with people at the precinct—"

Kellen made a derisive snorting sound but said nothing.

Clay gave him a look. "But they're good people, most of the time, is what I'm trying to say. Sure, most of them are on the take and some of them do half the work you or I do, and that's when we're feeling lazy, but they're not bad people, and if they want to come and ... and say good-bye to Terry, they can do that. She would have liked that. She would have ..."

Clay rested his elbows on the table and put his head in his hands. "Jesus Christ," he croaked.

"Take a breath, bro. We're here to do what's right for her."

Clay nodded. "I know. Doesn't make it any better."

"Course it doesn't. If this shit was easy, God wouldn't make good people deal with it."

Clay glanced up at him, eyebrows pulled in tight, head tilted. "That ... doesn't make any fucking sense."

"Made more sense before I said it out loud."

Clay found himself laughing despite everything. He closed his eyes, shaking his head. "Let's finish this. I need a walk. Been cooped up in here too long."

"All night, ain't that right, brother?" Kellen said, and there was only the slightest edge to his voice.

Elixir

Clay gave him a grim nod. "All night."

* * *

When it was finally done, when he was through the doors and out on the street and he was alone for the first time in what felt like days, Clay decided that Terry's funeral had been the most harrowing experience of his life. Being chased by dogs and men of murderous intent through a Carolina swamp paled in comparison with the deluge of well-meaning but clumsy words of sympathy. Had he been given the chance during the funeral to switch places with that faraway him of ten years ago, Clay would have gladly taken it, even knowing the amoebic bowel infection that lay ahead of him.

The church service had been meaningless to Clay, but it had meant a great deal to Terry's parents, and to her younger brother, Michael, who had flown in from Ohio. Clay had sat next to Emily, Terry's mother, for the duration, and the woman had spent most of the service wracked with sobs. Terry's best friend—a woman named Tamara who'd known Terry since the two of them were four years old—had delivered an eloquent eulogy between breaks to compose herself. Terry was well-liked; perhaps a dozen old school friends had made the trip from upstate New York, and nearly forty of her co-workers had attended. With Escobar dead, Kellen's wife, Angela, had felt safe enough to return to the city with the kids, and the whole family was there, along with a few other Brooklyn friends. Clay's fellow police officers had also made an impressive showing.

Clay himself gave a short speech. He hadn't the words to tell these people what Terry had meant to him, how she had not only changed his life but fundamentally altered him as a person. He certainly wasn't about to tell them he'd killed people earlier that same week under the mistaken belief she'd been murdered. It wasn't the time. It probably never would be.

After the service, they took Terry away; Clay would be allowed to pick up her remains in a day. Terry didn't have a will—they'd been too young to have a will, goddamn it—but she'd specified very clearly to both Clay and her parents that she was to be cremated and her ashes scattered in autumn from the Walkway Over the Hudson, in Poughkeepsie. "I want to follow the river to the Atlantic while the trees are changing colors," she'd told Clay. When the fall came, he intended to carry out her wishes. Her parents had given their blessing, asking only that he give them notice so they could attend. Until then, her remains would stay with him in Brooklyn.

Spacious as it was, Clay's brownstone was ill-equipped to handle such a large group. Anticipating this, he'd rented a Cobble Hill restaurant and for the next four hours had been forced to mingle. All he'd really wanted to do was go home and get blackout drunk by himself. Finally, at eight, Clay had made his way through the now mostly drunk crowd of mourners. He thanked them for coming and let them know the space would stay available to them until midnight before making his exit. He'd never been so happy to step out into the heat and reek of a summer night in the city.

The walk home was long, but it did him good. Clay had been tightening up all day, from the moment he had given up on sleep sometime around four in the morning until he had said his very last good-bye and stepped outside. Alcohol might perhaps have helped with this, but he hadn't wanted to drink in public. It had seemed a bad idea; something inside him was near to breaking. As he walked he could feel the strain subsiding. It was over. All of it. Escobar hadn't killed his wife. Most likely, nobody had killed his wife. It was a pointless waste of time to try to hunt down the Chink. If the man even existed, he would just tell Clay what everyone else already knew: Terry had slipped and fallen, and that was all there was.

He ignored the call the first time it came through. Requests for an encrypted, scrambled connection from an unknown number usually meant some kind of scam. Clay let his tablet buzz and go silent, continuing to sit on the sofa, staring at the wall, drinking bourbon. When the tablet lit up again, he glanced over in aggravation. The temptation to throw the goddamned thing against the wall raced through him, and he held his hands up, fingers splayed out, until it passed. Then he grabbed the device, tapped the screen, held the tablet to his ear.

"What?!" It would be someone asking him to wire them funds in Nigeria or trying to sell him underwater land in Jersey. It always was.

The voice that spoke up was garbled, and not only from the enhanced security measures that had been requested as part of the connection. It was being run through some kind of pitch modulator that made it warble and shift unnaturally. Clay thought he could also hear a white-noise generator, a trick that made computer analysis of a call's content more difficult.

"Clay Foster?"

"Yes, that's me," he told the robot voice, suddenly much more interested than he'd been a moment before.

"I have some important information regarding your wife."

"That right?"

"It is, so I thought I'd call you. First, I need an answer. When she was fifteen, your wife went on a date that ended disastrously. What was the guy's name?"

What the fuck? The question caught Clay off guard, and for a moment he was lost. Then it clicked: verification. Even someone who had done their research on Terry would be unlikely to know the answer to that question. Clay remembered the story, which involved a bottle of blackberry vodka and his wife's first attempt at a hand job, during which the young man had vomited all over her head and passed out.

"His name was ... Christ, give me a minute ..." Clay searched for the memory, and after a moment it tore through him: Terry telling the story and laughing so hard that tears streamed down her face, every word a supreme effort just to get past her lips. Clay felt his whole body clench and found himself unsure if he was stifling a laugh or a scream. Then the name came to him.

"Trey. Trey Halstead, or Halton ... something like that."

"Close enough," the voice said. "This call will end in sixty seconds, so listen carefully. Your wife's death was not an accident. You'll need her SynchDrive, her data key, and her personal encryption key. Don't bother searching the house for the drive. If you don't know the keys, tell me now and don't waste my time."

"I know them," Clay said. He and Terry had agreed on the need for advanced security and had committed each other's keys to memory. Terry's secure encryption key was a twenty-seven-word passphrase. In combination with the data key, itself a sequence of thirty-two random characters, it guaranteed information security that was almost impossible even for the fastest computers to brute-force hack.

The voice continued. "I'll meet you at Martyr's Monument in Fort Greene Park at exactly eleven a.m. tomorrow. Stand on the topmost southern point. I'll approach wearing a Yankees cap. I'll say the words *Even hotter than usual, isn't it?* to identify myself. Respond with 'I've felt worse,' and we'll go from there."

"Are you serious with this cloak-and-dagger shit?" Clay said, but he was talking to a dead line. He held the phone there for a moment more and then set it down on his desk and glanced out the window. The neighbors across the street had left their curtains open and Clay could see the news holos running on their gigantic setup.

What was left of the United States was still arguing with the United Southern States over the disputed Tennessee territory. The Association of Free States, in the West, was having trouble with energy delivery, resulting in widespread brownouts in Colorado. Elixir was spreading outward, becoming entrenched in Boston and Philly and starting to turn up in locations as far away as Detroit, Lexington, and Charlotte.

Disgusted, Clay turned away from the window, stood up, and went to the kitchen. He got a glass of water and stood in the dark, thinking about the phone call. The man's words echoed in his head. *Your wife's death was not an accident.* So here, then, it was being stated as fact. Not an accident, which meant she'd been killed, just as he'd suspected. He'd assumed the hit had been put out by someone meaning to get at *him*. Now he wondered where her SynchDrive was, what was on it, and why the mystery voice on the phone knew more about it than he did?

"Baby, what the hell did you get yourself mixed up in?" Clay said out loud, but if Terry's ghost was somewhere in the room listening, she gave no response. The only sound was the click-hum of the refrigerator's compressor coming on. Terry was gone, and the only answers he was going to get would come tomorrow, in Fort Greene Park. Until then there was only the prospect of another long, lonely night.

Clay went to pour himself another glass of whiskey.

* * *

The man who had killed Terry was a professional. The man who had arranged to meet with Clay was not. Clay spotted him fifteen minutes beforehand and took the time to observe him from a distance before making his approach at eleven.

The man had left off his Yankees cap until the designated time, and that was something, but everything else about him screamed amateur. He was standing at the top of the monument's stairs, pacing in circles, periodically staring down passerby, and frequently glancing over his shoulder. About five-eight and built like a scarecrow, he had short curly black hair and a bit of a hunch. Pale skin, squinting eyes. Even though it was ninety-five in the shade, the guy was wearing black jeans and a button-down shirt with the sleeves rolled up. There were sweat rings half the size of the Atlantic under each arm. He might as well have printed *conspicuous* across his chest.

Clay was wearing a pair of khaki shorts and a faded Brooklyn Nets T-shirt. Sandals. Sunglasses. His messenger bag was slung over one shoulder and rested beside him, holding his pistol, his tablet, and a pair of cuffs in case things went poorly. He was sitting on a bench in the shade, pretending to talk into the tablet, watching his contact pace and twitch and generally make a spectacle of himself. Clay almost felt bad for the guy.

At one minute to eleven, Clay stood up and made his way to the monument, not looking at the guy in the black jeans while he went. He stood at the southern end, hands in his pockets, reading the inscription and waiting. Soon, the guy in the jeans had moved close to him.

"You forgot your hat," Clay said, and the guy turned to look at him.

"Excuse me?"

"Come on, just ask me if it's hotter than usual and let's get out of this fucking sun."

The guy looked at him like he'd grown three heads. "Is this … is this some sort of gay sex thing? Because thanks and all, but—"

Clay cut him off. "You're not here to meet someone?"

"No. I mean, well … I am, but not … not a dude."

Before Clay could respond, a woman's voice said, "I'm sorry to interrupt, but is one of you Gerald?"

"I, uh … well, excuse me," the man said to Clay, and he turned to face the speaker, a brown-haired woman who was eyeing his sweat stains with distaste. "That's me."

"She said you were taller," the brunette said.

"Well, I guess the people I was with when she met me were maybe kind of short," Gerald said, and he gave a snickering little laugh that made Clay want to punch him just to get him to stop. Gerald was staring at the woman's rack, and she glanced over at Clay with an expression of regret. Clay looked at his tablet, saw that his contact was now more than five minutes late, and suddenly felt very exposed.

"Well," he said, adopting a tone of nonchalance, "I'll let you guys get to know each other without me standing around. This guy doesn't even know me … Thought you were someone else, man. My bad!"

He wandered off, leaving Gerald and the woman looking perplexed. He was sure they would get over their confusion and move on with what would no doubt be a disastrous date. He kept his pace slow as he returned to his bench, not wanting to draw attention to himself, but inside he was furious. Amateur mistake, making assumptions and jumping into action. All those years of training and he was still doing it.

Now he'd gone out into the open, marked himself in the eyes of anyone watching, all because he'd let his anxious need to learn more about Terry's death make him sloppy. On top of all that, the motherfucker from the phone call hadn't even shown. There was no one in the park wearing a Yankees cap, and now that Gerald and his blind date had departed, there wasn't even anyone standing on the monument steps.

Clay gave it fifteen more minutes, but he knew his man wasn't coming. He thought it likely that this entire meeting had been an excuse to get him out of the house, and he wondered if he would find everything just a bit out of place again, when he got home.

Maybe they'll leave a fingerprint this time.

Clay began to walk. There was no point trying for a subway. It would take longer to walk to a station, wait for the train, make the ride, and walk to his house than it would to just hike the mile and a half back from the park. He could have hailed a cab if any were open in the middle of lunch rush on a

Wednesday, and with the traffic that would maybe have saved him ten minutes. What did it matter? Terry's SynchDrive wasn't in the house, and that was the only thing they were interested in.

Nothing seemed out of place at first glance when he got home, but Clay didn't have time to make a thorough inspection before there was a knock on the door. Reaching into his messenger bag and keeping a firm grip on his pistol, Clay went to answer. When he opened the door with his other hand, he found himself face-to-face with a tall woman, fit, in her late twenties or early thirties, dressed in a smart black business suite. She had high cheeks, blue eyes, and streaky brown hair cut at the shoulders. Her lips were tinted crimson, and she gave him a sympathetic smile as he opened the door.

"Mister Foster?"

"That's right."

"I'm Kendra Disanto. I worked at Shun Ten with Terry. Well, I mean ... not really *with* Terry. I'm in R&D and we didn't actually interact much, but we were friendly."

The woman's eyes flicked down to Clay's hand, still stuck in the messenger bag, and then back up. She tilted her head a little, clearly curious but too well-mannered to ask. Clay let go of the gun and pulled his hand out of the bag, offering it to the visitor.

"Sorry, you caught me right as I was digging around for my tablet."

Kendra shook his hand, smiled a little, and glanced down again as she let go. "I think you'll find it's in your pocket, Mr. Foster."

Clay gave her a thin smile. "Yeah. Whoops. You can call me Clay. What can I do for you, Kendra?"

"Well, first I wanted to say that I'm so very sorry about what happened, and I apologize that I couldn't make the funeral on Sunday. I had urgent business outside of the city."

"It's all right," Clay said. "Thank you for your condolences."

"Terry was a lovely woman. I can't even believe ... Oh, Lord, I'm sorry. I'm being terrible. You don't need any more of this."

Clay, who surely didn't, nonetheless smiled, shook his head, told her it wasn't a problem. "If there's something I can do for you, though ..."

"Yes, right. I thought I'd come over and ask in person instead of calling. Terry was working with Doctor Imran, as I'm sure you know, and one of the things they were doing was testing the C-spikes in our latest—well, it's technical. The thing is, Doctor Imran had a crash and lost the data, and we were hoping Terry made a backup. There's nothing on her terminal, but we were thinking maybe her SynchDrive ..."

Clay tried not to react and must have succeeded, because the woman's expression didn't change from the look of cautious hope she'd adopted as she began her explanation. Here was another person interested in Terry's SynchDrive. What a fine and interesting coincidence.

Get your shit together and stay calm. This woman probably just wants her C-spikes or whatever the fuck it is she's talking about. She probably has no idea that someone else was willing to kill for that SynchDrive.

Terry had worked for a company called Shun Ten Industries, headquartered in downtown Brooklyn. A chemical production enterprise, Shun Ten was responsible for the production of a wide variety of component parts that were used in things like household cleaners, acid etching supplies, and personal care goods. Terry had been a senior lab technician and had indeed worked closely with Doctor Imran, head of the test lab.

"I'm afraid I haven't found Terry's SynchDrive. I'm still ... still going through her things, but mostly stuff that's been stored for years. The drive's not anywhere obvious. I actually thought it might be at the office."

"They haven't forwarded you her effects yet?" Kendra asked, a tone of horror touching her voice.

"It's all right, I asked them not to. Had too much else to deal with. They said I could pick them up at my discretion. So maybe the SynchDrive is there?"

Kendra bit her lip. "I hope this won't offend you, but I asked Doctor Imran and she said she had looked through Terry's things and couldn't find it."

"Well, the data should be backed up, right? That's the point." SynchDrives were so named because each contained an always-on connection and synched its data with a distributed server system multiple times per minute.

"We hope so. Doctor Imran ... she's a bit scatterbrained. She'd stopped using her SynchDrive for a bit, and then the crash ... Terry's copy is really our only hope. Do you have access to the backup?"

"It's bio-printed, so I can't just bring it up. You have to have a thumb and retina match to get at the backups, but as her ... sorry, this is still hard to say ... as her next of kin, I should have legal rights to it. Might take some wrangling."

A brief flash of frustration crossed Kendra's face, but she forced it away and nodded. "I understand. Could I leave you my card? You can get in touch once you have her backups, and we'll see whether she has the data we're looking for. It would really mean a lot. It will take months to replicate, otherwise. But I guess we'd better get started on that too, just to be safe."

Clay took her card without hesitation. "I'll make it a priority."

"Thank you very much, Mr. Foster. It was ... I'm sorry we had to meet under such circumstances. Again, you have my sympathies and those of everyone at Shun Ten."

She offered her hand again and Clay took it. The handshake went on just a moment too long, and there was the briefest flash of something hungry in her eyes. Clay was no model, but he was tall and muscular, with chestnut hair not yet falling out or going gray, hazel eyes, and a strong jaw. He'd gotten this look from women before, and might even have appreciated it at some other time. Right now it only made him think achingly of the times when Terry would stand in the bedroom door with nothing on but one of his T-shirts, smirking, beckoning him to join her.

Then it was gone, and Kendra smiled, letting go of his hand, and he wondered if he had even seen it at all. She turned and moved down the steps, heading back in the direction of downtown Brooklyn. Clay watched her go for a moment before closing the door.

"What the fuck is going on?" he asked himself, leaning against the wall. He felt like a man doing a jigsaw puzzle made entirely of transparent pieces, half of which were missing. Almost nothing had fallen into place. Clay felt confused and desperate, and he missed his wife so badly it was almost a physical ache. He wished he could talk this through with her and found the absurdity of that idea painfully amusing.

It seemed there was only one man in the city who could give him a few more pieces to work with. Escobar had given

Clay the means to contact the Chink, and it was time to do it. He headed for his terminal and once there quickly found his way to the sub-net that Escobar had mentioned. He left a message, just as instructed. Then he went and made lunch, a roast beef sandwich that he devoured while staring at the kitchen wall, barely tasting it, thinking about Terry. He was still sitting there, the sandwich long gone, when his tablet chirped.

Clay fished it from his pocket and opened the encrypted message that had just come in. At first glance the subject meant nothing to him: "July 28th is Available." But when he opened it, he realized its significance.

Mr. Foster,

Your interest in speaking with my employer has been noted. We believe that we possess information that will be of value to you. You are welcome to join us at our place of business on July 28th, in order to conduct the meeting you have been seeking. Transportation to and from said location will be your responsibility. You may ask at the entrance to The Hook for further directions. Expect to wait until at least midnight, as my employer is a busy man.

If you wish to confirm this appointment, you will make payment to an anonymized account, the details of which will be sent, along with the amount, in a follow-up message. My employer's services are not inexpensive. We expect full payment up front and will not issue any refunds, whether the meeting provides any information you consider of value or not. This fee covers the meeting only. Additional information may be bartered for at that time.

We look forward to speaking with you.

-M

There it was. The disastrous visit to the Loco had proven valuable after all. *You could've solved all of this with one visit to the Chink.* So it seemed.

The Chink. The most powerful information broker in Brooklyn, and quite possibly in the Northeast. If Clay wanted the person in the city most likely to hold a few more of the puzzle pieces he was so desperately seeking, that was his man.

Visiting the Chink meant visiting The Hook, and The Hook made Crown Heights look like a fucking black-tie cocktail party. There was no law there. There was no *city* there, not anymore. There was nothing except survival of the fittest. You couldn't even roll a police cruiser into the place; it would fall right through the boards and into the quagmire below, and there wasn't a man, woman, or child there who would reach an arm down to save you from drowning. It was the Wild West, if the Wild West had been full of assault rifles and synthesized opioid-stimulant hybrids so powerful that a single use could hook a man for life.

July twenty-eighth. Visit The Hook. See the Chink.

Clay was beginning to warm to the idea.

CHAPTER 7

The Hook

The cracked and splintered boards that made up the bulk of The Hook's exterior walkways were black with years of accumulated grime. Thick and slippery but also able to suck a man's shoes from his feet, the filth made it difficult to walk. Visitors often found themselves taking on a peculiar gait the locals called the Virgin Shuffle. The boards spanned the gaps between the flooded buildings whose upper floors housed The Hook's residents. In a way, the layer of filth was a benefit; it was essentially waterproof and kept the wood from rotting away.

The walkways crisscrossed between the buildings, haphazard and rickety, with no obvious attention paid to planning or safety. Some were three or four stories above the water and offered little in the way of railings or handholds. Between them, ropes and cables spread out in a tangled web, clothes and flags and bare LED bulbs hanging from them. They had electricity here, most of it illegal, none of it reliable; what wasn't stolen from Manhattan Water and Power was provided by biodiesel generators, purloined or salvaged solar panels, the occasional wind turbine, and methane collected from the shit produced by humans and animals alike. The air was fouled with exhaust and the gut-wrenching, malodorous combination of excrement and hot, rancid vegetable oil.

Manhattan had built its walls, but here, over the years before science finally stopped the rising waters, the ocean had taken hold. The warming of the oceans, long fretted over by scientists and eco-minded citizens, had taken a sudden and dramatic leap. Ice caps had melted, and water level predictions that had once spanned centuries were revised to cover just a few decades. The world had worked together, even while continuing its petty squabbles and resource wars, to find a solution, and one had at last been reached, but for places like The Hook, without the means to build walls against the rising seas, it was too late. Seven meters of ocean, more than twenty-two feet of salt water, now existed where before it had not.

The Hook was not by the sea or even at its edge. Instead, it crouched, steaming and smoldering and stinking, three meters above the high tide mark, built on the skeleton of a flooded neighborhood. Its crumbling buildings poked from the oil-slicked and fetid black water like twisted, poisonous fungus. Men sometimes dived into those waters to make the structural repairs that kept the ocean from absorbing The Hook. Sometimes they came up bleeding and screaming, attacked by something in those dark, inscrutable depths. Sometimes they never came back up at all. Rumors swirled of giant fish with bulging, sightless eyes. Crocodiles and alligators and anacondas. Mutant babies with gills, ravenous, their needle teeth gnashing away at flesh and bone.

It had been two weeks since Clay had received the message from the Chink's emissary. During that time he had returned to active duty. It was proving difficult to be around Kellen, pretending that Escobar's death had cleansed him of his rage and hate, that he was not still spending every off hour looking for answers. Still, they had quickly settled back into the old routine, making drug busts and dealing with Brooklyn's ever-increasing homicide rate. They didn't talk much about Terry, which made it easier for him to hide his feelings. Sometimes Kellen looked at him askance, as if still suspicious, but Clay didn't want Kellen to have to bear the burden of knowledge. He went about his business, waiting for his chance to meet with the Chink.

He had tried to learn more about the man, but there wasn't much out there. Most of Clay's normal contacts in the underworld had proved useless. They knew of The Hook but gave it a wide berth, preferring the comparably safe streets of places like Crown Heights, Bensonhurst, and Bushwick—places held in thrall by crime lords but not yet completely lawless. Someone died in The Hook every night—often more than one someone—and rarely in a way that could be considered pretty or dignified. It was a poor, broken place, but the man who ran it was wealthy, like a king out of the feudal era, commanding absolute loyalty and taking as he saw fit.

It had cost Clay just to make the appointment and would cost him more to extract anything useful from the Chink, for whom information was currency. Clay had little of that type of payment—at least, little that he was willing to offer—but he had much of the traditional type, and the word was that the Chink would at least consider cash deals. The sum would probably have to be outsize; the Chink had little use for token payments. He owned a piece of every whore, every bar, every gambling table in The Hook. The town was not officially a town, was not officially even an acknowledged entity—on maps it was shown as part of the ocean—but it belonged to the Chink.

The nearest working subway station was at Carrol and Smith, the end of a line that had once hooked eastward and delved deep into Brooklyn. The flooding Gowanus Canal had filled the tunnels with filth and toxins sometime in the twenties, and the city had never bothered to excavate them. The Carrol Gardens stop itself was barely used; half of it had been closed down and subsequently taken over by a gang of violent addicts.

Clay was standing at the water's edge, eyeing the wooden ramps that led upward to the walkways. The edges of these walkways, those that might have been accessible by any means other than the ramp, were lined with great loops of razor wire, and behind them sharpened stakes stuck outward like the fortifications of a medieval fortress. Someone had erected a hastily built sign, little more than a couple of planks held together with baling wire, and splashed on it in chipped and cracking red paint were the words *The Hook*.

"Go on and state your business," said a voice, and Clay saw a man emerge from the shadows past the entrance.

"My business?" Clay raised an eyebrow.

"You know ... whatchyer here for. Whores? Booze and drugs? The tables? Or maybe you're just here to cause trouble."

The man had a drawn pistol in one hand and what looked like a gargantuan blunt in the other. Staring at Clay, he puffed at the latter, its light illuminating beady eyes and a scabbed, pock-marked face below a tangled mass of blond dreadlocks.

"What, you're the welcome wagon? City assign you that job?"

"Ain't a part of your city. Answer the fuckin' question."

"I'm here to see the Chink."

The man grunted, shifted, shrugged. "Never heard of nobody by that—"

"Right. I have an appointment."

"Well, it ain't got shit to do with me anyway. Here are the rules: you fuck with anyone, you get beat down, rolled and stomped by the locals. Be lucky to only get your head cracked and not end up food for the big daddy gulper fish down below."

"Yeah, I get it. Tough town."

The man appraised him, shrugged again, stepped back. "You're pretty, but you look like maybe you seen some shit. I'll let you in."

"What if I'd decided I was coming in anyway?" Clay said.

The man grinned. A few rotting teeth still poked from his gums. "Six rifles pointing at you right now, my friend. I bring this gun up and you go down."

Clay had thought it would be something like that. He nodded. "Six is enough to guard the door?"

"Oh, we got more. Six is fine for a lone motherfucker coming up the way. We don't get a lot of big groups all at once. Don't get that many people coming in and out at all. Folks who show up tend to stay a while."

"Planning on spending the night myself." Clay's meeting with the Chink was still two hours away. No trains would be running by the time he was done—the days of twenty-four-hour subways in Brooklyn were long gone—and a walk back would be lengthy and dangerous. Not worth it, especially as he didn't want it to get back to the precinct that he'd been wandering around The Hook and its surrounding neighborhoods in the middle of the night.

Clay stepped onto the wooden planks and made his way up the entrance. The gate man stepped a few feet back, hand still holding tightly to his gun, and made a sweeping gesture with his blunt before jamming it back between his lips.

"Welcome to The Hook," he said and dragged deep. He held for a time before letting the smoke out in a series of coughs.

"The Chink. Where is he?"

"A ghost can be anywhere." The guy gurgled nasty fake-sounding laughter and gave another rotting grin. "But you might try the old Westin. Tables and booze, rooms and girls, Elixir all over fuckin' everywhere. Nice place."

"Directions?"

"Walk straight. Five blocks. Can't miss it."

"Last question: what if I actually was here to make trouble?"

This time the man burst forth with genuine laughter. He brought the blunt to his mouth again, dragged, held, let go. Clay was enveloped in a stinking cloud of cannabis.

"If that be the case, brother, you going to fit right in."

* * *

By the time Clay reached the building that had once been an eight-story chain hotel, his shoes were covered in sticky black filth. The locals had observed him doing the Virgin Shuffle with glee but had otherwise left him alone, with the exception of four women who had propositioned him, three for sex and one holding out ampules of Elixir with cartoon characters on them.

The hotel resembled a rat's nest, with wooden platforms poking out at every level, twisting around and around the central frame. Wires and cords extended out to touch every nearby building. There was music coming from inside, and lights burned in nearly every window, some flickering or pulsing, others holding steady. Standing outside, Clay could hear people shouting and laughing from within. Above him, girls for sale leaned out of their windows, holding their bare breasts in their hands and encouraging passerby to come inside. Men and women lay comatose around the building's edge. Clay saw a group of six filthy children moving from one to the next, rifling through their pockets.

The man at the door asked him if he had weapons. Clay saw no advantage in lying to someone built like a silverback gorilla and said that he did.

"This is a no-carry zone. Whole building. Walk forward, turn to the left, and go check anything that's on you. We have a scanner that'll find anything shoved up your ass, metal or not, so don't bother. Move in any other direction or try to draw and you'll be dead before you get there. I'm fast as hell with this piece. You can get your shit back when you're done."

"I'm here to see the Chink," Clay said.

"I truly don't give a fuck," the man replied and turned his eyes away. Clay headed for the weapon check, blowing the razor blade from his cheek as he did so. At least in a no-carry zone anyone who jumped him, other than the Chink's men, would be doing so hand to hand.

The guy at the window looked like a bulldog that'd been stabbed in the face. One eye was milky and blind, the scar tissue rising around it pink and smooth, stretched by age and the man's slow descent from muscled hulk to potbellied, jowled fat ass. He had three days of graying stubble and was wearing a comically small bowler hat; Clay was reminded of an old cartoon character from the antique vids he'd used to watch as a child, but he couldn't bring more than the ghost of a memory to the front of his mind.

"Weapons go in the drawer," Bulldog said as Clay came up, turning away from a bank of old non-holo flat screens. "Close the door, slide them through, wait for clearance. Booze, too. Drugs you can keep, but no smoking, shooting, or licking at the tables. Go to the bar or rent a room."

"You don't sell here?"

"You can get anything you need inside, but we prefer to let the freelancers handle that shit. We get a piece either way and don't have to stock it. Hurry it up. As you can see, I'm a busy man."

Clay put his gun and his razor blades into the metal tray. All he had on him now were his tablet, his keys, his wallet, and a few hundred in cash. He rarely carried bills—they were being phased out entirely in many parts of the city—but it seemed likely that he would need them here. Like before, with Escobar, he'd left his badge and service pistol at home.

"If I have an appointment with the Chink, who do I see?"

Bulldog eyed him for a moment. "I'd mention that to the bartender."

Clay nodded, closed the drawer's lid, slid it through. Bulldog opened it on his end, glanced into it, and bent the corners of his mouth down, looking impressed.

"Nice. Pre-war? That's not one of those Korean pieces of shit."

The gun was a Smith and Wesson semiautomatic, one of the last the company had made before being absorbed by an overseas conglomerate. Clay nodded. "Practically an antique at this point."

"Must be worth a fortune."

"You can see how I'd be pretty upset if it didn't come back to me when I was done here."

The man laughed. "You'll get everything back. Even the razor blades, if you think you want to stick 'em back in your mouth."

Guess he saw that on the monitors. "Keep 'em."

"You're a prince." Bulldog turned back to his screens. Grinning a little, Clay made his way to the scanner. A guard directed him through it without speaking, indicating for Clay to hold his hands above his head as the machine spun around him. After a moment he was waved on. Clay passed through a small hallway and into the central area that had once been the mezzanine floor of the hotel.

The interior of the building had been stripped, most of the walls torn down to make one giant room. The carpeting was worn bare, ripped and torn at the edges, covered in muck. Sand had been scattered on the central pathways to keep them from growing too slick. The lighting was low and tinted red, the air full of incense smoke and the powerful reek of the waters below. There were a great number of tables set up; they were in notably better condition than anything else in the place. Clay could hear the clack of roulette wheels, the clatter of dice, the curses and cheers of the gamblers, the cooing encouragement of the prostitutes working the floor. He hadn't been in a place like this since the war.

The bar was at the back of the room, a gigantic thing made of massive wooden blocks tossed atop huge chunks of slowly disintegrating concrete. Behind it were shelves and shelves of liquor, more bottles than Clay had ever seen gathered in one place. Half of them hadn't been produced since before the war, and Clay wondered if their labels actually reflected their contents. A chalkboard had been hung from the ceiling and angled down at the drinkers. The prices listed on it were outright robbery, so much so that Clay wondered how any man who called The Hook home could afford to drink there, but the bar was packed.

He leaned against the wood, looking over the bottles and listening to the sounds of the casino. Someone near him was screaming profanities, just a constant litany of invective that ended with a sudden meaty sound that Clay recognized as a fist connecting with a man's face. There was a burst of laughter at this. Clay resisted the urge to turn and look, and after a moment a man behind the bar with long, black hair slicked back and a bushy handlebar mustache wandered over. He had skin like coarse sandpaper and a huge hooked nose riddled with at least half a dozen gold rings.

"Help ya?" The guy stood with his arms crossed, dressed in biker's leathers and a pair of jeans so grimy Clay wasn't sure what color they'd originally been.

"I was told you were the man to see if I had a meeting with the Chink."

"You were told correct. What's the name?"

"Foster."

"I'll let him know you're here. It'll probably be a while. He runs late."

"So I should have a drink," Clay said.

"That would be my strong recommendation." The bartender scratched at a rash on his neck. "Almost as strong as avoiding Mary over there, who is eyefucking the back of your head right now."

"Why's that?"

"She's a goddamned lying, stealing, sore-covered cunt is why," the man said, turning his head and spitting on the floor but never taking his eyes off the woman. Clay heard her voice protest at this but didn't bother to turn around.

"Not here for the girls."

"If you want the fellas, you need to go to the baths."

Clay shook his head. "That bottle of Maker's Black actually have Maker's Black in it?"

"It does."

"I'll know if you're bullshitting me."

The bartender gave him an amused look. "Tell you what, Foster ... you put the fucking hundred down on my bar first, then you can question the quality of my whiskey, all right?"

Clay laid a few bills on the bar and the man turned, grabbing the bottle, and set it down in front of Clay. "Everything here is legit. If you can afford it, we can get you just about anything that's left in the world. You see that bottle up there? Pre-phylloxera cognac. Hundred and ninety years old."

"You ever actually sell a glass?"

The bartender nodded. "Twice."

"Same guy?"

"Nuh-uh. First guy got eight inches of steel in his throat the same night. Waving his fucking money around. Rich motherfucker, slumming ... little like you."

"That's me." Clay nodded at the bottle. "I'll stick to the Black."

"Water back?"

"I've been advised not to drink the water in this town."

"It's bottled."

"The man who advised me also told me that your bottled water comes right out of the tap."

The bartender barked out a laugh, snagged a glass, uncorked the whiskey, poured out two fingers. "He sounds well-informed."

His work done, the man wandered off. Clay sipped his whiskey, listening to the ebb and flow of conversation around him and trying to avoid making eye contact with the prostitutes. He wasn't afraid or ashamed; before Terry, during the war, women of that type had been his principal means of release whenever he could secure leave. He didn't know many soldiers who'd been able to resist the allures of cheap, uncomplicated, and usually unprotected sex, particularly once nanotreatments had made HIV, syphilis, and other such diseases mostly nonfactors.

The treatments did nothing for pregnancy, though, and plenty of hookers and johns couldn't be bothered to reliably use the stuff that did. It was as it had ever been in that department: many a bastard there was who'd been fathered by a civil war soldier, and while Clay didn't know of any of his own, he supposed it was possible. He wondered sometimes if one day he would answer a knock at the door and find there a young man or woman whose face looked like his own.

Eventually Clay felt a tap on his shoulder. He glanced backward, jerked, and spun fully to face the person who had touched him. She was taller than him by at least three inches, her scalp shaved bald and gleaming under the red-orange lights, her skin so pallid it looked almost translucent. Her lips were stained a deep red, as if she'd spent the evening eating cherries. She was wearing a single-piece silver gown that hugged every inch of her; there was clearly nothing on underneath it. No weapons were visible on her person, but her bearing was that of someone who held no fear, had perhaps never known the emotion at all.

All of this was striking, but it was the eyes that got him. They were depthless black oceans, no white to be found, and lined further still with heavy black eyeliner. The effect was ghoulish. Clay had never seen eyes like these. Were they tattooed?

"Clay Foster," she said in a voice neither high nor deep, devoid of any emotion or even interest, its volume low, its diction precise.

After a moment more to digest the sight before him, Clay nodded. "Yeah. And you are?"

"That information is irrelevant. Follow me up the stairs, please, to my employer's office. Outside, I will frisk you."

Clay bristled. "I already went through the scanner."

"Do you want to see the man you came all this way to see, Clay Foster?"

She seemed almost bored by what was happening. Clay clenched his teeth, forced himself to take a breath, and nodded.

"Then outside of my employer's office, I will frisk you. Follow me."

She turned and began to walk, not looking back to see if he would follow. The material of the dress was stretchy, clingy, and her haunches moved beneath it like those of a wild animal. Clay thought the outfit an intentional distraction and had to admit it worked; for a moment all he could think of was peeling that dress off of those muscular legs. Then he thought of Terry and the desire waned. He stepped away from the bar and allowed himself to be led up the stairs. Somewhere above, the man he had come to see was waiting for him.

CHAPTER 8

The Chink

The first words Clay spoke upon meeting the most powerful information broker in the Northeast and one of the city's premier crime lords were "You're not Chinese."

The man behind the desk broke out in a grin. He leaned back in his chair and turned to look at the bald Amazon in the silver dress, who merely raised her eyebrows, returning the man's gaze without sharing his mirth. After a moment longer, still smiling, he turned back to Clay.

"Very good," the Chink said, and his voice was an odd, high-pitched croak, like a jungle frog's. He spoke slowly, deliberately, as if each word were an effort. "I believe you're the sixth person to make that observation. Mayors and mob bosses alike have failed to detect that detail."

Clay shrugged. The man's features were Asian—tan skin, straight jet-black hair, slightly slanted eyes, broad nose—and at gunpoint Clay would have guessed Filipino, but it was obvious that he was not ethnic Chinese. That no one else in Brooklyn could be bothered to make the distinction wasn't his concern.

"But you let everyone call you the Chink anyway ..."

The Chink's eyes shone. "Let's be honest with each other, Mr. Foster, and admit that for a man who deals in information, there may be great ... value ... in the spread of falsehoods."

Clay considered this, found it reasonable, moved on. "Where are you actually from?"

The Chink regarded him for a moment, and Clay realized he couldn't determine the man's age. He might have been in his late twenties or early fifties. He was dressed in a jade-colored, expertly tailored three-piece suit that had to have come from Manhattan and a cream-colored shirt. He wore no tie; instead, around his neck there was an odd choker-like collar.

"I'm 'from' Brooklyn, Mr. Foster, born and raised. As to my ethnicity ... well, such things are not parted with for free in this room. Would you care to make a bid?"

Clay didn't care and shook his head. "I think you know why I'm here."

The Chink nodded. "It seems the lovely Mrs. Foster has recently come to a terrible end."

"Someone wanted her SynchDrive. They're still looking for it."

"I can't tell you what is on her SynchDrive or where it can be found."

"That's not what I came here for ..."

The Chink nodded. "Of course not."

"... but I'm not stupid, either, and I know that 'can't tell' doesn't mean 'don't know.'"

This earned Clay a long slow smile, and the Chink glanced again at his bodyguard. She hadn't moved, hadn't said a word, was standing with her back to the window and staring straight ahead, seemingly uninterested in the exchange. It was a fine charade, and Clay imagined that many forgot her presence entirely, but he could almost feel the woman's readiness. If he moved in a way that displeased her, she would swing into action. He found himself wondering what action that might be, given her lack of weapons.

The Chink looked away from her again and back to Clay. "You're not stupid, Mr. Foster, and I have never thought of you as such, not once since I began my research into your particular ... situation. So, then, we proceed. You've come to me to find out who did bloody murder. The hows and whys and whats are of less importance to you than the who."

"Yes."

"And it doesn't interest you at all to learn what the data on her SynchDrive might be?"

"It interests me, but I doubt I could afford it even if you were selling. Isn't that right?"

"I would consider trading a general description of its contents for your precinct's encryption codes."

Clay shook his head. "Can't do that."

"No. Very well. And what do you have to offer, then, for the piece of information you seek? I can tell you much, but every bit has its price."

"I want to know who killed my wife. I understand that a man in your position values information more than money, but if I had information, I wouldn't be here. I don't have anything else to offer except cash."

"That's not entirely true." The Chink reached forward, gripped a crystal decanter at the desk's edge, and opened it. "You have abilities that may be useful to me if you are willing to barter them. Port, Mr. Foster? It's a lovely vintage."

"I'm good, thanks. My services aren't for sale."

The liquid inside was deep crimson, rusty-colored where the light shone through it, and gripped the sides of the glass. The Chink finished pouring, set the decanter down, held the glass under his lips, and inhaled deeply. He sipped, closed his eyes, smiled.

"Everything is for sale," he said, and looked again at Clay.

"It would have to be a compelling offer."

"That is the only type I'm known to make. Mr. Foster, you have a curious history. Born in Brooklyn, abandoned by your father, dirt poor. You were thirteen years old when the South seceded. You were outspokenly, some said virulently, pro-North in your youth."

"I was pro-USA. At the time, that still included the West."

"An unusual stance considering how unpopular the war was even at its start."

There had been protests from day one, and they'd only gained strength as the war had gone on and more men and women came home in boxes. "I thought the South was full of goat-fucking inbreds who wanted to bring slavery back, lock up gay people, and send their women back to the nineteenth century, all while spewing bullshit about Jesus's loving gaze."

"After you enlisted in the Army, how did you feel?"

Clay shrugged. "Turned out it wasn't like that at all."

"You'd bought into a great deal of propaganda, I suspect."

"I was young and dumb. Spoiling for a fight. So believing the shit on the news was easy. But the war wasn't about that stuff ... not really. It was about things like how badly we fucked up and how many thousands died after that hurricane hit Charleston, how we let Miami turn into a breeding ground for malaria and dengue fever. How clear it was that no one gave a shit about anything south of D.C."

"But none of this new knowledge kept you from doing your job." The Chink waited, but when Clay was not forthcoming, he smirked again, nodded, and continued. "You did a tour in Missouri."

"That's right. We lost the state in the end, but they must have seen something they liked from me."

"Your reports were exemplary. *Glowing* is not a term one normally uses with the American military, but there it is. It seems ... you've a flair for soldiering, Mr. Foster. Near the end, you saw men gassed and nearly met the same fate, correct?"

"Sarin gas, yeah."

The war had split the military right down the middle, with each side laying claim to countless vehicles and weapons, stockpiles of ammunition, bombs and missiles. Chemical agents. It was something of a miracle that no supergerms had been deployed during those thirteen years.

"The use of nerve gas is a violation of international law."

"I don't think a bunch of redneck skinhead militiamen hopped up on meth and white dog give much of a fuck about international law."

"I imagine not. After Missouri, you disappeared for three years. How interesting."

"Training," Clay said. "A whole lot of ... specialized training."

"Training for what?"

Clay laughed a little. "What'll you give me for that? Better be good."

The Chink considered for a moment. "After you reemerged, you were set loose alone behind enemy lines. You spent two years in southern Virginia, and once the U.S. had secured that entire state, they sent you into Raleigh for another year."

Clay was impressed. He had never told anyone, not even Terry, exactly where he had spent that time. "Now *that* is pretty good info."

"How many people did you kill, Mr. Foster?" He sipped his port.

"Who says I killed anyone?"

"You were sent to R-9 for three years. Even I have few details about the program, but what I do know is utterly fascinating. They ... rebuilt you, made you into an assassin. Governments don't expend such resources to create that kind of weapon and then not point it at anyone."

"Maybe you're right."

"This is an information exchange, Mr. Foster. By answering my questions now, you are gaining access to answers, when it becomes your time to ask, that money alone would not unlock."

Fine.

"Six people." Clay met the Chink's eyes, unapologetic, not embarrassed. "That's official targets. I lost track of how many I killed while fighting."

"Do you sleep well, Mr. Foster?"

Clay looked at the man across the desk for a long time. "If I don't, it's not because of those six."

"Not even the last one?" The Chink finished his port, set the glass on the table, and studied Clay.

"If you know the details, why ask me how many there were?"

"The only thing I know about your final mission is that it must have been very special."

"Why's that?"

"The rapidity with which you received your honorable discharge was quite something, but even more impressive was the sum ... the government handed over to you approximately two years later. Another such sum comes every year on that same date. You are not a poor man who needs to get by on a policeman's salary, *Officer* Foster."

"Let's stick with *Mister*. I'm not here officially."

"If your superiors find out you were here at all, it won't matter how official the visit was. They look rather unfavorably on my organization ... those who believe it exists."

"No shit."

"You were injured during your last weeks in North Carolina and met your wife at this hospital?"

Clay nodded. They had reached the part he didn't want to talk about, but when he glanced up at the Chink, he saw that the man was staring intently, a tiny smile on his face that said he understood Clay's discomfort and cared not at all.

Clay looked away, not wanting to match the Chink's gaze as he spoke. Outside, The Hook smoldered and fumed, wisps of vapor passing by the stringed bulbs that spanned the buildings.

"Terry was two years into her degree in Applied Chemistry when the stuff she was seeing on the news just got too bad for her. She couldn't keep working at UCONN while people were getting blown to shit every day. She took a leave of absence and headed for Virginia. She worked as a nurse's aide there for three years. After we moved to the city, she transferred her credits to Brooklyn College and finished her degree. That was right before Elixir hit."

"The scourge of our time, isn't it, Mr. Foster? Do you think they will ever find a way to combat it?" Something in the Chink's tone, audible even through his croaking voice, made it seem as if he were enjoying some colossal joke.

"No idea. Nothing's worked so far."

"It's really a tremendous product. Inexpensive ... euphoric ... highly addictive despite rumors to the contrary. What a terrible blight."

"So terrible you let shitheads peddle it throughout your building, take a cut off every sale, and probably have all of your women hooked on it."

"Only most." The Chink glanced again at the bald woman. "I assure you, I have never held ... a vial to their tongue and made them partake."

"Are we done rehashing old history?"

The Chink tented his fingers for a moment. "How much did you love your wife?"

Clay clenched his teeth. "A lot."

"That's a very poor response. Try harder."

"I don't see what this has to do with anything. I didn't come here to talk about Terry. I came here to find out who killed her. How much I loved her is irrelevant."

"It is entirely relevant."

Anger burst through Clay, flaring like a pile of gunpowder exposed to a spark. "Just fuckin' tell me—"

The Chink brought his hand down hard on the desk, eyes blazing, and leaned forward. "Do not presume to give me orders in my place of business!"

Clay heard a movement behind him and knew that the tall woman had left her post at the window and was standing someplace much closer. He didn't turn around, but he could feel his entire body tense, waiting for an attack that didn't come. For a moment there was silence.

"It pains me to speak, and pains me very much to speak quickly," the Chink said. "Shouting is ... agonizing, and I will not abide it. If you can't remain civil and refrain from telling me how to conduct my business, then our conversation is over and I wish you the best of luck finding your wife's killers."

"Killers ..." Clay murmured, noting the plural. He wasn't surprised, really. Hadn't he already guessed at the truth? Hadn't he thought that Escobar had taken out the hit but not actually performed it? What he didn't know, and needed from this strange man in his green suit, were the identities of these two people. If he was going to get those, he was going to have to play ball.

He looked up and saw a knowing smile on the Chink's face. Glaring at him but holding his tongue, Clay made a gesture with his hand. *Get on with it.*

"How much did you love your wife, Mr. Foster?"

Clay sighed. "She was the only person I'd ever met who mattered. She taught me how to care about other people. The things they loved about me, that made me right for R-9? She undid a lot of that. I loved her enough that I wish every hour of every day since she died that I could go back and switch places with her. This place ... it doesn't even fucking deserve someone like her, but she showed up anyway, and all it could do was kill her. She was the best we had to offer and it killed her anyway."

He sat back in his chair, staring at the man in the green suit. The Chink made a waving motion and Clay heard the bald woman move back to her post.

"Tell me, do you wish to find the person who killed your wife, or the person who decided she was to die?"

"I want them both."

The Chink made a chortling noise. "That's an expensive proposition."

"I can pay—"

"No, you can't. At least, not the way you think. As mentioned, I have need of your talents, Mr. Foster, and it's because ... of them that I agreed to see you."

"Let's hear the pitch."

"I could provide many interesting projects for you. These projects would give you the opportunity to make a much more real, much more substantial difference in this city than your police work. I can give you the chance to put to use skills that have lain dormant for some time now."

"Skills like getting rid of people my employers don't want around anymore?"

The Chink smiled, tented his fingers, glanced out the window and back at Clay. He shrugged. "You are certainly capable of it."

"Look, you're right ... I can do a lot of things, but killing people on command isn't on the list anymore. I did my last of that at the end of the war. Don't tell me I'm the only assassin you can get your hands on." Clay glanced back over his head at the bald woman. "I doubt I'm the only one in this room."

"My bodyguard has talents, some of which overlap yours. Blending into a crowd is not on the list."

"You don't say."

"I can't send her to the places that I could send you. Work for me, Mr. Foster. That's what I'm offering, and in time you'll learn all there is to know about your wife's death."

"I'm not looking for a job."

"You won't at least consider trading your services on a case-by-case basis for information?"

"So you can jerk me around for as long as possible while Terry's case grows colder and colder? No fucking way."

A flash of genuine anger crossed the Chink's face. He stamped that emotion away and replaced it with something that looked like scorn. "Then why, Mr. Foster, should I have any interest in doing business with you?"

They sat there for a moment in silence. The man in the green suit seemed in no great rush, so finally Clay, who was tired of this stinking office, pushed forward. "Give me the name of the person who called in the hit. I can find out the rest on my own."

The Chink sighed. He looked unimpressed, unenthusiastic, uninterested. Disappointed. "No names, but I'll point you in the right direction for ... the sum you gave to the Brooklyn school system last year."

Clay didn't want to know how the Chink knew the amount of an anonymous donation. It didn't matter anyway; they had entered into the meat of it, the negotiations. He leaned forward. "I need a name."

"A name costs more. Not more than you could afford, perhaps, but I don't want any more of your money than what I've quoted. You've refused to offer your services, but I'm still helping you because you were so cooperative in answering my questions. You'll make the transfer here, and when I've confirmed the deposit, I'll give you not a name but an address."

"A place won't be enough."

"It will put you on the path, and it will cause you to become noticed by people who you may want to notice you, though their notice does not come without ... its own risks."

"How do I know what I'm getting? If I pay you and you tell me 'somewhere in Brooklyn,' that does me no good."

"I'm an honorable man, Mr. Foster."

"Give me the name of the hit man, at least."

The Chink reached back with one arm, scratched the rear of his head, yawned. "You will have to learn of that ... person ... yourself. I assure you that if you continue down this path you've chosen, you'll meet them in due time."

"The amount you're asking for should get me more than an address. I'll give you half of it for a location."

The Chink considered this, and when he spoke he drew his first word out in a long sound that was almost a sigh. "Three-eee-eee-quarters."

"Three-quarters for a location and *why* they want the drive. You said you couldn't tell me what was on it or where it was, but you didn't say anything about why they want it."

The Chink tapped his fingers together twice in a tiny gesture of applause, then leaned forward on his desk. "Very good. I accept your deal."

Clay reached into his pocket and the Chink's eyes followed the motion. There was a moment of tension, and Clay diffused it by laughing. "Your bodyguard searched me pretty good."He brought his tablet out of his pocket, moved his fingers through the holos, and let the device read his thumb and retina as he brought up his banking utilities. "When I make this transfer, is your Amazon back there going to step up and try to snap my neck?"

The Chink tilted his head, looked at the woman, and then back at Clay. "I don't believe so, but she has ... been known to surprise even me."

"I'm just thinking there's not much I can do if you decide to hold out on me."

"No, there isn't. Tell me, have you ever heard anyone in all of Brooklyn claim that the Chink had 'held out' on them?"

Clay had not. He tapped the button that would send the payment, closed the application, held the tablet in his lap. "It's done."

The Chink glanced down at a holo screen embedded in his desk, gestured above it a few times, and nodded. "So it is. Thank you, Mr. Foster."

"So, what do I get for that exorbitant amount of money?"

"Eight twenty-five Eighth Avenue, New York, New York," the Chink said.

Clay tapped the address into his tablet and glanced up. "My wife has never been to Manhattan."

"Neither have you."

"So why would someone on Eighth Avenue want to kill her?"

"Why indeed? Perhaps because the contents of her SynchDrive could put someone in that building in a very, very precarious position, were said contents ever to reach the right people."

Clay rubbed a hand across his face, glanced over at the woman—she was looking out the window, her back to them, apparently satisfied he was not a threat—and back at the man in the green suit. "That doesn't make any sense," he said. "She was a mid-level employee for a company that makes floor polish, for Christ's sake. She didn't even get to use the nice bathrooms."

"I think that things ... stopped making any sort of sense for you several days ago, did they not, Mr. Foster?"

"How am I going to get a pass into Manhattan? They don't hand those things out easily, not even to people with money. There's no way they're giving one to a Brooklyn beat cop."

"It does seem unlikely. My advice to you, Mr. Foster, is ... be resourceful."

Clay felt tired. He wanted to be away from this place and this strange little man who had helped him by giving him no help at all. Away from the stink and the light and the heat. "One more question," he said. "I want this one for free."

The Chink tilted his head, raised an eyebrow, made a gesture of encouragement.

"Where's the cleanest, quietest place a guy can get a bed in this shit hole you call an empire?"

The Chink broke into a tremendous grin and, despite the obvious pain it caused him, began to laugh.

CHAPTER 9

Jimmy

It was four in the morning when Clay finally reached his room. The Chink had directed him to a small building at the edge of The Hook, away from the central drag. The flophouse—Clay couldn't muster the charity to call it a hotel—was not entirely devoid of action. The bar on the main floor was nothing more than a series of boards laid across sawhorses and an old creaking bookshelf full of rotgut booze. A few drunks were clustered there.

A poker game was going at the only decent-sized table in the place, the men around it all three-quarters in the bag, squinting at their cards and slurring their words. They were playing with wads of crumpled bills, but Clay also saw what looked like an expensive and probably stolen tablet on the pile.

He tossed a few bills onto the counter. "I need a room, and send up a bottle of whatever passes for your best bourbon."

The bartender grunted acknowledgment, grabbed the money, stuffed it into a battered cash register. "Got a bottle of JD in back. Still sealed. That work?"

"Close enough."

The bartender set a key down in front of him. "Room twelve. You want a girl to go with it? You pay her separate. I recommend Jenny over there."

Clay looked over at the girl, who was short and black and round. She had her arms wrapped around one of the poker players. As he watched, the player leaned his head back, tongue extended, and the girl let a few drops fall from an Elixir ampule into his open mouth. "What is she, fourteen?"

The bartender glared at him. "I don't run kids."

"That's the right answer. Just send the booze." Clay headed for the stairs. He hadn't had sex since the night before Terry died. Hadn't really even given it much thought other than the brief flash with the bald woman. The idea seemed appealing in concept, but he knew he'd just be thinking of Terry. He wasn't going to fuck another woman with her on his mind.

Upstairs was pretty bad, but Clay had spent nights in bombed-out buildings where the staccato chatter of assault rifle bursts sounded out often in the night and the closest thing to a mattress was a threadbare jacket tossed on a gritty floor. Here the bed was gray and dingy, bowed in the middle from too much use, and covered with scratchy blankets that seemed to have been woven from fiberglass ... but it was still a bed, and no one outside his window was planning on tossing a live grenade through it. There was a rickety end table on one side of the bed, an equally ailing dresser, and at the far end of the room a cheap card table and a metal folding chair that looked fifty years old.

When the knock came at the door, Clay got up from the bed, where he had been sitting with his head down, thinking about Terry and about what he was going to do to the men who had killed her. Holding his gun in one hand, he opened the door with the other. A brown-skinned woman was standing behind it—another working girl, judging by her outfit—holding a tray, a bottle, and two glasses. Clay stepped back, opening the door fully, scanning her quickly for threats. There was nowhere in the skin-tight leggings or the barely there midriff to hide a gun or a knife, so he gestured for her to come in and moved back toward the bed.

"Put it on the dresser."

The woman shut the door behind her and did what she was told. He heard her set down the tray, heard the clink of a glass, the sounds of the bottle being opened and liquor being poured. She stepped toward him.

"You maybe looking for more than whiskey tonight, mister?" She put all the sultriness she could manage into the question, her tone low and husky.

I know that voice. Clay looked up, reaching out and taking the whiskey, paying attention to her face for the first time. He had seen her before, many times, the last one just recently. He brought the memory up: Kellen, leaning out the cruiser's window and threatening to take her in for solicitation.

"Hi, Janelle," he said, and the woman started, her eyes narrowing, and after a moment a look of recognition came to her face.

"Oh, son of a *bitch*! Where's your fat spic partner? He hiding in the motherfuckin' closet? You got no jurisdiction here. Don't even try to tell me you do."

Clay shook his head. "Relax. I'm not here as a cop."

"That right? You just come to The Hook for the fun of it?"

"What," Clay said, his voice dry, "you don't think this place is fun?"

"Man, I don't need this shit." Janelle stood with her arms crossed. She was tall, though not as tall as the bald woman at the Chink's place, with ebony skin and curly black hair that fell down to mid-back, held back with a single silver clip. She had wide hips and big, heavy breasts and was wearing tight-fitting, colorful synthetics that accentuated both.

"Sit down." Clay was too wound up from his conversation with the Chink to sleep right away, and having someone to talk to would be better than sitting here alone with his thoughts.

"I need to get back to work."

"Place seemed pretty dead."

"It's a goddamned graveyard. Ain't had no one all night, and if I don't bring Gregori a hundred dollars, I won't get my shit."

"I'll pay. Sit down. Have a drink. Plenty to go around. Consider it a talk job. You get those, right?"

"Not so much," Janelle muttered, but she did as she was told, grabbing the metal chair and turning it around to face him before dropping onto it. Clay gestured at the whiskey and, after a moment, she went ahead and poured herself a finger's worth. She sipped and grimaced a little but sipped again. Clay took a drink from his own glass, swallowed, and closed his eyes for a moment, enjoying the burn. Then he looked back at Janelle.

"Thought you weren't the soliciting type," he said and she frowned. Her face had not yet become gaunt and lined, like most long-term Elixir users. There were no blooms at the corners of her mouth—sores that appeared as the chemicals in the drug ate away at the soft tissue there—but there were bags under her eyes. She would have been beautiful without the drug. With it she was only average.

126

"Yeah. Listen, my man got a hole put in his stomach and then got burnt the fuck up, all right? I ran out of my supply in two days."

"Why don't you just quit it?"

"You think I'd be turning tricks if I could quit it?"

Clay shrugged. "Seems like you don't enjoy this life too much."

"No shit. I never fucked for money before two weeks ago, and I swore right up till three minutes before I did it that I never would. That shit has hooks, all right?"

"So I've heard. Why'd you start?"

"Everyone said it was okay. Like having a drink or smoking a joint. And it was! It was fine for so long. It was ... I could just take it, like at a party or with Arón, have a blast, go a week or two before the next round. No problem. Something ... changed."

"That so?"

"Took a lick one night, got so fucking high I barely remember what happened. I felt like I was the best, smartest, happiest person on the whole planet. Felt like I could do anything at all. It was like Elixir, only better. Amped up."

Clay nodded. "And the next day you wanted more, so you talked yourself into believing it was just because the trip had just been so good."

Janelle gave him a haunted look. "How did you know that?"

Clay had heard this story from too many junkies too many times. He knew all about what the Brooklyn PD called "the shift," the change that could happen to an Elixir user after a few weeks or many months. Strange thing was, the shift hadn't happened to *anyone* in the early days. It had only started happening to people after the drug had insinuated itself deep into every social stratum of the city. "How long before the other shit started?"

"What, the sweats and shaking? The puking? The feeling like if I didn't take another lick I might as well kill myself because my head was going to split open from the pain? Didn't take long. Elixir never did none of that to me before, but it does now. I have to have it every day now, and it barely even gets me off. Double, triple ... each time it's a little less good than the time before, but I gotta have it. It's like being trapped in hell until you get a lick."

Janelle flexed her fingers, looking for words she didn't have to describe the pain. Clay watched her, impassive, interested but not terribly moved by the story. Maybe it would have done more for him if it hadn't been the thousandth time he'd heard it.

"How'd you end up in The Hook?"

Janelle sighed. She took another drink of her whiskey—no grimace this time—and refilled the glass. "After Escobar got himself killed, what was I supposed to do? Got no money, got no place to stay. Nothing. Went looking for a dealer, figured I could pay with ... Well, turns out it was Gregori, motherfucker who owns this place. He said he was cruising Crown Heights for new girls, tells me to come on down to The Hook and get set up. Free room, cheap food, Elixir every day. So here I am."

"Here you are." Clay kept his tone light, but Janelle still bared her teeth.

"So what happens now? This the part where you swoop in and save my life? Whisk me off somewhere to get fixed up?"

Clay shook his head. "I don't think that happens much outside of stories."

"Right. So ... what? You want to fuck? Sit around drinking whiskey and telling old stories? It's your dime, Mr. Policeman."

He wanted to fuck her. Wanted to tell her to take off her clothes, get down on her knees, and put her cunt in the air so he'd have something to look at while he finished his whiskey. He could imagine spreading those long, thick legs wide to find the pink slit between them, then licking her big, brown nipples while he filled her with his cock.

He wanted to, and maybe if Terry had died three years ago instead of three weeks ago, he might have. Instead Clay gave Janelle two hundred dollars and sent her away to get her drugs. He locked the door behind her, sat down in the metal chair, poured himself a second glass of whiskey, and downed it in two gulps.

He thought about Terry, images of their sex together flashing through his mind. Before he even knew he meant to do it, he was jerking off standing up, reliving in his head the time she had lain on the bed, spread open for him, and masturbated herself to orgasm while he watched. He thought about how her voice had sounded when she'd gasped, the way the muscles around her pussy had contracted over and over as she climaxed, and then he was spilling his sad and lonely come all over the floor of this shitty no-name brothel.

Afterward, he had thought the anger might dissipate, but it didn't. It roiled around inside of him worse than ever, raging like a fever, a sickness that no amount of drugs or nanotreatments could cure. Terry was gone, taken from him forever, and he still didn't even know who'd killed her. He thought about the Chink, who had punished him for not wanting to become a hired gun by giving him nothing more than an address and some vague information. *When this is done, I might just come back for you and your bald bodyguard.*

Clay filled his glass again, drank it down again, set it on the nightstand. The whiskey burned in his nose and throat, drowning out the stench of The Hook, and that was good. He lay back, closed his eyes, and was granted a tiny miracle: sleep came rolling over him like a thick bank of fog, and Clay let it happen.

* * *

An hour later, maybe less, someone put the heel of their boot to his door and sent it crashing inward. A hulking silhouette charged into the room, surprisingly fast for its bulk, and swatted Clay's gun away as he brought it up from under his pillow. Clay squeezed the trigger involuntarily and a shot rang out, the bullet punching a chunky hole in the drywall. Clay felt the man grab his wrist and jerk, and he knew he could either cede his grip on the gun or have his bones snapped. He chose the former, dropping the weapon and bringing his free hand up to grapple with the man.

They wrestled, struggling for the advantage. The man let go of Clay's right wrist, and then hands wrapped around his neck. He tried to pull them away but couldn't; the guy was too strong. Lying on his back in a pair of skivvies, Clay was not in the right tactical position to grapple with this burly motherfucker. He was going to have to play dirty.

Clay jammed his hands forward and up, seeking the soft spots of the man's eyes, and dug his thumbs into them. The thug roared, pulling backward, his grip on Clay's neck loosening. A voice from the hall shouted, "Hey, Jimmy, whaddafuck?"

Great. Two meatheads. Clay kicked out, connecting squarely with Jimmy's jimmy, and when the man pulled backward, hands going to his crotch, Clay shoved him. Caught off balance, Jimmy fell backward off the bed and landed on the floor with a crash.

Now his buddy was coming into the room, but where Jimmy had been surprisingly quick for his size, this guy was a moose. All lumbering, ponderous bulk. Clay grabbed his gun from the bed, swung it around, and put three bullets in the center of the moose's chest. When he turned back to his first attacker, Jimmy had already regained his feet and was charging again.

Clay was still sitting—not the best position from which to mount an attack—and Jimmy was much faster than his recently deceased friend. Clay fired once, a wild shot that passed harmlessly over Jimmy's head. Then the goon was on him again, and Clay took the hit with his shoulder, letting the force bowl him over and out of the bed. They landed on the floor, shards of wood driving into Clay's back. He jammed his knee into Jimmy's gut and used the man's momentum against him, flipping him sideways. Clay rolled with him and landed straddled atop him. He hauled his fist back and slammed his knuckles down four times into Jimmy's throat.

He could have smashed the man's windpipe in and left him lying there to suffocate, but he wanted a few answers first, so he pulled the punches just enough to avoid murdering a second person in that room. As the blows landed, all the fight went out of his assailant, and Jimmy made a strangled sound of agony. Clay stood up, making his way rapidly back to where his gun had fallen. He grabbed it, turned around, and leveled it at the man on the floor.

"Christ, don't shoot me!" Jimmy wheezed, still holding his throat.

Clay reached out and flicked on the light. The man on the floor was huge, and most of the bulk was muscle. Cords of it stood out, thick and ropy, on his neck and arms. He was wearing a pair of stained short-sleeve coveralls that made him look like a mechanic, except the stains were dark maroon. His face was bright red, a vein throbbing in his forehead, sweat beaded up and dripping into his buzz-cut black hair.

"Why the fuck *wouldn't* I shoot you?" Clay said. "You just busted into my room and tried to strangle me, you piece of shit. Who sent you?"

"Please, man ... it was just a job, all right?" Jimmy seemed to be regaining the ability to speak as the pain and constriction in his windpipe decreased. When he threw a cagey glance at the door, Clay snapped his fingers.

"Hey, eyes over here, and *fuck* your job. Answer the question."

"Word came down from Ty at the Starfish."

Clay shook his head. "No. Whoever Ty at the Starfish is, he's taking orders from someone else. He doesn't decide to put a hit out on a random person he's never even seen before. Try again."

"Man, I don't fuckin' know who Ty got it from."

"Hope you're right with God, then." Clay aimed the pistol at Jimmy's head.

"Okay, all right, Jesus *Christ* will you put that shit down?! Ty usually ... I mean, not always, but the word usually comes from the Chink. From that fucking bald ninja bitch he keeps up there with him."

"That's better." It made more sense, but was it too easy? Clay had wondered how the Chink would handle rejection. This was one possible answer, but Escobar had seemed obvious, too, had made sense, and that had been wrong.

"Can I fucking go?" Jimmy said, pulling himself up to his knees, and Clay shot him in the stomach. The slug hit him like a charging bull, doubling him over even as it threw him backward, and when he uncoiled it tossed blood up in an arc that sprayed from floor to ceiling. He ended up on his back, legs sticking out, an expression of dumb, uncomprehending shock on his face.

"Guess it depends on whether you can crawl." Clay set the gun on the top of the dresser. Keeping his eyes on the man on the floor, he began to dress.

"Oh, Jesus!" Jimmy was rolling on the pitted, gouged floorboards, clutching his stomach. "Aww, Christ, I'm killed. You fucking killed me!"

Clay cinched his belt. "It'll take hours for you to bleed out, Jimmy. Crawl the fuck out of here and find a hospital. How's your insurance? They have good medical care in The Hook, right?"

"Are you fucking *shitting* me?!" Jimmy cried. Blood burped and gurgled up from the wound in his stomach when he did this, and he groaned, beginning to cough.

"Oh ... so they don't. Well, shit, Jimmy."

Jimmy bared crimson-flecked teeth at Clay. "I hope you burn in fucking hell, you rich piece of trash!"

Clay grabbed the gun, strode over to the man, aimed at his skull. "Fuck it, then. If you're not going to crawl, I'm going to put you out of your misery right here on the floor."

The hulk below him let out a little shriek and covered his head with his arms, as if that would do a bit of goddamned good. Then he reached out, digging his fingernails into the wood, and began to haul himself toward the exit.

"Thatta boy," Clay muttered. He grabbed the last of his stuff and made his way over to the room's single window. The wooden planks below, suspended over the roiling black water, looked clear. Behind him, Jimmy was slowly dragging himself away, and when Clay glanced over he saw that the man was leaving a bright red smear on the floor. "If you make it, tell Ty at the Starfish to do a little research before putting someone like you on someone like me. Coming bare-handed? That was fucking stupid."

Jimmy didn't seem to be paying attention. He was pulling himself over his companion's body, grunting with the effort, wheezing out occasional obscenities. Clay could hear cautious footsteps in the hallway; apparently someone had decided that the shooting had stopped for long enough that it was worth investigating. He thought there was about a 70 percent chance that Jimmy would make a full recovery. The thought just warmed his heart.

Now, then. The Chink. Had he sent these boys, or did someone just want to make it look like that was the case? Clay didn't know, and right now, short on sleep, his head aching from the whiskey and the fight, in a place he didn't know and surrounded by people he couldn't trust, there wasn't much choice. He was sick of this shit. He wanted to know the truth, about this attack and about Terry. If that meant storming the Chink's fortress, well ...

"Fuck it," he muttered. "We're going to find out."

Clay unlatched the window, hauled it open, and stepped out onto the fire escape. No one shot at him. That was a plus. From there he made his way quickly down to the grimy walkways below. Walking steadily, dealing with the muck on the boards, Clay headed for the Westin and his second meeting of the night with the Chink.

CHAPTER 10

A Piece of the Puzzle

The gorilla doorman stood up as Clay stepped inside, clearly reading the intent on his visitor's face. "You're no longer welcome here, so why don't you turn the fuck around and—"

"I hear you're fast as hell with that piece," Clay said. He saw the guard's eyes go wide, and the man began to draw. Clay pulled his own gun from behind his back and fired. The bullet caught the guard in the thigh just as he pulled the trigger, and Clay felt the wind as the slug passed less than four inches to the right of his head. The guard fell sideways with a yowl but had the presence of mind to hold on to his gun and pop off another shot even as he was dropping. This one was nowhere near on target, and when the man hit the ground, Clay put a second bullet into him, this time in the right shoulder. Now the guy let go of his gun.

"That *was* fast." Clay stepped forward.

"What do you want?" the doorman said through clenched teeth.

"I'm here to see your boss." Clay reached down and grabbed the spare gun. "I don't give a shit if he *wants* to see me or not. I suggest you lie here quietly until I'm out of sight and then fuck off to get patched up."

The man was silent, gritting his teeth against the pain. Clay stood up, pointed both guns down the hallway, and began to make his way toward the room with the monitors. The scar-faced attendant must surely have been aware of his presence by now.

The man behind him shouted a parting comment. "The Chink will eat your fucking liver!"

Clay didn't bother looking around. "I know."

Bulldog had decided to split town; the booth was empty. *Must've been feeling too old for this shit.* Clay glanced in at the screens and could see guards mobilizing near the body scanner. Four of them. He could tell by the way they held their weapons that none had formal training and was glad for it.

Clay was halfway to the detector room when the building lights flared, the red glow replaced with a sudden brilliant white light. A shrill ringing alarm began to sound, and Clay heard shouting coming from the casino floor. People would be evacuating, no doubt, and more guards would be mobilizing. Time was now his enemy; the more of it he spent, the better-organized the forces arrayed against him would be. He didn't know how many men the Chink had, but he knew it would be more than the four at the metal detector.

He turned the corner, crouched low with his guns held out, and heard a shout. A shotgun blast thundered like a special delivery from Thor, and a section of the wall to Clay's right disappeared. Clay swung his head in the direction the shot had come from, found the man with the gun—who was, in fact, a raven-haired, shrieking harpy of a woman—and shot her in the arm. She went down, and Clay, still running forward, shot the guy standing behind her who was just beginning to raise his gigantic hand cannon. This one wasn't so lucky, and the bullet hit him right in the chest, throwing him backward.

Two down. Clay heard a pistol fire and felt searing heat in his left arm. He swung his gun around and fired one shot without aiming. It hit the detector and Clay heard the *pang-eeeeen* sound of it ricocheting off somewhere. The two men standing next to the machine ducked. Clay came to a halt, leveled his gun, and shot one of them in the left side of his gut. The man went down with a scream, and in the process of falling clutched at his buddy, who had regained his composure and was an instant from shooting Clay in the face. The bullet instead hit the ceiling four feet above Clay's head.

"Ah, Christ, Bill!" the last man standing said, bringing the gun back down, his expression one of pure misery. He knew he wasn't going to get another shot off. His face said he was waiting for Clay to take him out, and Clay didn't disappoint him, aiming at the man's knee and firing. The final guard fell, dropping his gun as he went. Clay didn't think the guy would ever walk without a brace again.

Clay glanced down and saw that the earlier bullet had only grazed him, plowing a hot and bloody groove into his bicep. Lucky. He made his way through the detector, checking on the four as he went. The man he'd shot in the chest was dead. The other three were alive, and the woman was trying to drag herself back to her shotgun. Clay grabbed it from the floor and, when she clawed at his leg, gave her a kick in the chops for her trouble. He collected the other weapons, tossing those he couldn't carry back into the hall from which he had come. He reloaded his own pistol, the best weapon of the bunch by a wide margin, and took the combat shotgun the woman had been using. He shucked it one-handed and the spent shell hit the floorboards and clattered away.

The room was hazy with gun smoke, the scent of expended powder overwhelming. It took him back to his time in the trenches, early in the war, when whole swaths of Missouri forest had stunk like this after periods of mortar bombardment. There was a single archway before him that led to the central room of the casino, where the tables and the bar probably now sat empty. Behind cover, there would be men with guns waiting for him to come through.

There wasn't any choice, so Clay went forward at a run. At the arch, he dived, twisted in the air, and landed on his shoulder. He rolled once, guns outstretched, and came to rest against the heavy wooden leg of a craps table. Without waiting, he thrust upward, pushing against the underside of the table with his back and shoulders, and upended it. The table fell with a thud, chips and dice and drinks crashing to the floor. Clay dropped down behind the table again and waited for the fusillade of bullets that was surely headed his way.

Nothing. Not a single shout, not a single blast from a shotgun, pistol, or assault rifle. There was no noise in the room except the blaring alarm, and after a moment more, that also cut out. As the ringing in his ears subsided, Clay heard a hissing static noise, and after a moment the Chink's cracked voice, calm and reasonable, addressed him.

"Mr. Foster, you're committing suicide. Please consider your actions."

Could the man hear him? Clay gave it a shot. "I don't take it well when people put out a hit on me!"

Over the PA, the Chink snorted. "If I had wanted to kill you, why would I have waited to do it?"

"Maybe you hadn't made up your mind."

"I wouldn't have let you leave were I still undecided. Come upstairs, Mr. Foster. Let's talk a bit more."

"That sounds even more like suicide."

"If I wanted to kill you I would ... release the chlorine gas primed to pump into the vents above you and watch you asphyxiate in agony on my floor. More compelling to me would be discussing why, exactly, you've decided the men who attacked you were acting on my orders."

"They told me they were!"

"I have a general rule against guessing, but I'll allow myself a small exception in this circumstance. I would *guess* that the ... men who assaulted you received their orders from a man named Tyrone, who owns a detestable brothel not far from where you bedded down for the night."

"They said he gets his orders from you, so I decided to come find out, and your ape at the front door told me I wasn't welcome. Things ... escalated."

"They did indeed." Clay could hear genuine mirth in the Chink's fractured, rasping voice. "I didn't give any orders to Tyrone this evening. I believe we're both being targeted by a common enemy. Come upstairs, Mr. Foster. We have more to talk about, and at any rate it's either that or I'm afraid I'll have to release this gas. I can't have you running around shooting ... any more of my employees or guests. Michelle will meet you at the staircase."

Michelle. The bald Amazon, of course, standing at the staircase waiting for him. What if there was no gas? What if she meant instead to assassinate him? It was impossible to read the truth in the Chink's ruined voice through a buzzing

PA system without the benefit of visual or other nonverbal cues. He could only go with his gut.

His gut told him to be careful but that nothing the Chink had said rang false. It was very possible the ducts could release chlorine gas, which would sink to the floor and murder Clay while leaving everyone on the upper stories untouched. It was even more possible that the two thugs who'd attacked him while he was sleeping had been working for someone else. It was almost guaranteed that he'd been played in some way, by some unknown adversary far from this building. He'd come back to this place wanting answers; now he had his chance.

"I'm coming out."

"What an excellent choice." There was a click as the Chink disconnected. Clay rose up on his haunches and glanced over the edge of the table he was sheltered behind. Michelle stood at the far end of the room by the stairs, arms crossed, black eyes staring as if she could bore a hole through the table and into Clay with her mind.

She didn't take a shot at him, which he'd thought a real possibility—she had no gun with which to do so. Clay stood up and began crossing the casino floor. It was strange to see in full light. Shoddy. The dirt and imperfections normally hidden by the dim red lighting were now on full display.

"My employer is waiting for you," she said in the same dead voice as he neared. "He has instructed me to tell you that in a gesture of goodwill, I am to forgo collecting your weapons or otherwise hindering you. However, I will stand at your side throughout the conversation with him."

Clay raised an eyebrow. "He must have a lot of faith in you."

Michelle stared at him with her ebony eyes. "I have broken better men than you, Officer Clay Foster. If you displease my employer in any way, I will handle you as I have handled all others who have made that mistake."

Her tone never changed as she delivered this threat. No emotion ran across her face. She might as well have been reciting from an academic paper. Without waiting for his response, she spun and began to climb the stairs. Clay, who had no idea if this boast was true and didn't really care, followed.

* * *

"What an interesting night this has been."

The Chink was regarding him with sparkling eyes and a small smile on his face, as if the events of the last half hour were amusing to him. For his part, Clay felt little guilt over his actions. Those who chose to work as guards in a place like The Hook were rarely without sin, and it was unlikely Clay was the first man at whom they had ever fired a weapon.

"Can't argue with that." Clay glanced over at Michelle, who was proving true to her word, standing a pace away to his left with her arms crossed, eyes blank, staring at the wall.

"You're an impetuous man at times, Mr. Foster. You should ... consider your actions more thoroughly."

It was true, but Clay didn't really feel like admitting it. "Was I just supposed to head off and never find out whether you'd sent them?"

The Chink favored him with that broad toothy smile. "Perhaps not, but you might at least have made the effort of bribing or threatening Tyrone for information."

"You knew they were coming for me before it happened, didn't you?"

"Of course I did."

"How long before?"

The Chink merely smiled.

"So you let them come … Why? Why not tip me off, if you're so worried about my safety?"

"If you'd been murdered by two thugs who between … them share perhaps half a functioning brain, Mr. Foster, then it would certainly have made it obvious that you were not the man I needed. I thought this would be a good test, but I *had* hoped you would verify your sources before charging headfirst into my casino, waving your guns around. My surgeon is going to be very busy this morning, and it took a good deal of persuading to convince Michelle not to remove your head from your shoulders."

Clay shrugged. He glanced again at Michelle, who was still staring straight ahead, and looked back at the Chink.

"Her presence makes you uncomfortable," the Chink said.

"Everything about this makes me uncomfortable."

"That is another way in which you are exceptional, Mr. Foster. Most … people who come here to see me become convinced that Michelle is nothing more than a personal consort. They cease to notice her at all. You will not make that mistake."

No, he most definitely would not. Everything about the woman shrieked danger to Clay, especially her seeming lack of concern. She made him edgy in a way that few other human beings were capable of. He wanted to be away from this place, so he got down to business. "Why am I here? What do we have to talk about? Our business is settled."

"Mr. Foster, you have injured four of my people, killed one of them, and scared away my clientele. That last represents a good deal of money."

Clay shook his head. "If you're looking for reimbursement on your nightly take, you're looking at the wrong guy. You've already got enough of my money."

"We established that your money is not what interests me."

"We've also established that I'm not going to become a hired killer."

"That's what caused you to wonder about my involvement, is it not, Mr. Foster? You believed that I was so deeply hurt by your rejection of an offer I never actually made, nor had any intention of making, that I might have decided to have you killed."

"Even if you weren't going to ask me to kill for you, whatever you wanted would've ended with me hurting people."

"And clearly you're ... concerned about hurting ... people." The Chink's face took on a pained expression. He coughed twice into a handkerchief, grimacing, and took a swallow of port.

"Not if they deserve it."

"Mr. Foster, I've invited you up here to converse not because I enjoy our talks so very much. They are, as you ... can see, quite uncomfortable for me. Well, then. This attack on you was also an attack on me. Our mutual enemy hoped to eliminate you and, had it worked, would most likely have spread information that I had ordered the assassination of a police officer."

Clay leaned forward. "If this person is our enemy, then why won't you tell me his fucking name?"

The Chink looked unimpressed at the interruption and waited a moment before continuing. "Perhaps aware of your impulsiveness, they also planned that, should you survive the attack, you would then seek revenge on me ... which you did. This was supposed to result either in your death in my casino or the even more advantageous but highly improbable outcome of my death at your hands."

"Why is this person so hot to go after you?"

"I believe I'm an impediment to their long-term plans."

"How so?"

"Mr. Foster, because we share a common enemy does not mean I've become an information dispensary. I have a ... new proposal for you. A deal, if you will."

"How do I know you didn't order the hit just to convince me that we have a mutual enemy?"

The Chink shrugged. "You can choose to believe what you like. Does it change anything? I am willing to give you more than I was before this action against you occurred. Do you want it?"

What was there to lose? "Let's hear the offer."

"You're in need of a pass to Manhattan. I'll provide you with one. This pass will be issued by the City Council of New York, via their police department."

"Is this going to be some kind of forgery bullshit?"

The Chink took a sip of port, cleared his throat, held his hands palms up for a moment. "Does it matter, Mr. Foster?"

Clay considered this, found that it did not, and moved on. "What keeps them from coming after me in the interim?"

"Nothing. They have swung and missed, and may swing again. You must not breathe a word of this to anyone, not even your partner. Our enemy doesn't know that I am aware of their plans against me. If they knew, you and I would both be the target of ... an individual whose name I can't give you, because I don't know it. This person does not seem to exist and works very hard to keep it that way."

"Someone that good ... that's who killed Terry, isn't it?"

"That's extremely likely."

"So how does this enemy not knowing about your plans keep me safe?"

The Chink nodded, as if he approved of the question. "If it appears to them that I sent you away with no information, why go to the trouble of finding more hit men?"

"Why not just send the assassin?"

The Chink tilted his head. "Will you be so easily snuck up on unawares by an assassin, Mr. Foster?"

"No, and why risk it if I'm not a threat, right?"

"Precisely. This was a matter of convenience. You were simply a tool with which they could try to hurt me."

"All right, I get it. What's my part of the deal? What am I supposed to do for you?"

The Chink leaned his elbows on the desk, put his hands together, and rested his chin on his knuckles. "I will provide ... you with a SynchDrive. Once you've gained entry at the address I've given you, choose any terminal in any room above the fourth ... floor and mount the SynchDrive for fifteen seconds. You'll do this first, before pursuing any other activity, in order to maximize your chance of success. Complete this task and I'll consider all outstanding debts paid and our relationship ended."

"What am I supposed to copy onto the drive?"

The Chink laughed his creaky, painful-sounding laugh. "You have it the wrong way, Mr. Foster."

Of course. "What am I supposed to do once I get inside? How do I find out who's responsible?"

"A second SynchDrive, placed in the right computer, may bring a tremendous amount of clarity to your situation."

"The right computer …"

"I would suggest, Mr. Foster, that you … work your way to the top."

Clay didn't trust this man. The plan seemed too facile, too convenient, as if there were unfortunate truths the Chink wasn't bothering to tell him. Still, this was all he had, and if the people responsible for his wife's death were indeed in Manhattan, he had no other or better way of getting to them.

"Fine. If I can prove they killed Terry, I'll get them out of both of our lives for good."

The Chink tilted his head. "I thought we'd established that you would not kill for me, Mr. Foster."

"Their deaths won't have anything to do with you," Clay said.

The man on the other side of the desk closed his eyes. Smiled. Nodded. "Then we have an accord. I think now you should … make your way back to your home. The sun's coming up, and by the time you can reach the subway, the trains will be running again. I think we've established that The Hook does not have your well-being in mind. Michelle, please give him the drives."

Clay stood and turned to Michelle. She held out her hand, and in it were two SynchDrives.

"The red drive is ours," she said. "Use it on any terminal above the fourth floor. The blue drive is yours to do with as you wish."

"How do I know that it won't send off everything on my tablet as soon as I stick it in there?" Clay said, glancing back at the Chink. The way a SynchDrive ordinarily worked was to automatically download any new data in certain folders that the user pre-cleared for backup and then wirelessly synch it to the company's private cloud using a proprietary encryption algorithm. Clay had no doubt that the Chink possessed the resources to modify his drive so that it could harvest information from folders that the user had never selected to be included.

The man in the green suit smirked. "You don't. I advise you to remove any information you might consider sensitive before inserting that drive into your tablet, Mr. Foster."

"Right," Clay said, turning back to the Amazon and taking the drives from her outstretched hand. "Thanks. Sorry you didn't get to break me."

She wasn't looking at him but rather over his shoulder, at the Chink. Her eyelid twitched once, and then she turned those impossible black eyes away from them both and went to stand again by the window.

CHAPTER 11

The Island Fortress

The walls surrounding Manhattan were eighteen feet tall and six feet thick, angled outward and topped with razor wire and surveillance equipment. Armed guards patrolled them at all hours. They were made from layer upon layer of sturdy sheets crafted from a composite of titanium, granite, and silicone laid over a honeycomb of spun carbon fiber. The material was resilient, heat-resistant, and had tremendous give if impacted—it would distribute the force throughout its entire structure. The walls could withstand a direct hit from a bunker-busting missile or a tanker-size fertilizer bomb.

Clay had never seen them up close; the nearest he'd ever come was halfway across the Brooklyn Bridge, where a hasty barrier of concrete and chain link had been erected, bisecting the pedestrian walkway. Vehicles coming from Brooklyn had to use the Manhattan Bridge, where they were required to pass three checkpoints. The first was located at the entrance in Brooklyn, the second at the wall itself, and the third at the point where the bridge connected back to the land, in Chinatown.

It had been eight days since his visit to The Hook, and no further attempts had been made on his life. It seemed as if whoever had ordered the hit on Clay at the hotel had since decided he was not a threat. Most likely he was no longer of enough significance to be worth killing.

His efforts to locate Terry's SynchDrive had proved fruitless. Whatever she'd done with it, she hadn't left any kind of clue at all, and it wasn't anywhere in their house or in her personal effects from the office. Clay had even called her parents in Rochester and had them search the place, saying that the drive contained vital financial information. They had been unable to locate it anywhere in their home. Clay wasn't surprised.

He had initiated the procedure to have the backed-up data transferred to him from the SynchDrive's provider as soon as he returned from The Hook. After sending them countless documents to verify that, yes, he was the Clay Foster listed as her beneficiary, they'd finally transferred all her encrypted data. Using her passphrase to decrypt the files, Clay was soon faced with an unfortunate truth: there was nothing there of any importance. The drive's wireless connectivity had been turned off or disabled weeks before Terry's death. Everything that was backed up was mundane—photos, personal documents, financial data. Whatever had gotten Terry killed, it was still on that drive, and nowhere else.

Because the drive was off, it couldn't be tracked. Somewhere in Brooklyn there was a piece of silicon and aluminum the size of a bottle cap that held the key to his wife's death. Searching for it any further was pointless; the drive wasn't a needle in a haystack, it was a single atom of needle in a haystack.

"Papers, officer?" a pleasant voice said, jerking Clay out of his reverie, and he glanced up at the woman standing to his left. He was seated with the rest of his fellow officers on a police bus, and two agents from the second checkpoint were working their way down the rows, one from the front, the other from the rear. They were both female, dressed in navy blue uniforms of slacks and short-sleeve button-down shirts, each with a too-precious little hat perched on the side of her head. The hats looked to Clay like big, blue versions of the vegetable dumplings he sometimes got at the Korean place by Prospect Park.

"Right here." He held out his tablet. The Chink had kept his word: less than twelve hours after visiting The Hook, Clay had received notice of his appointment to a group of consultants being brought in to educate the NYPD on Elixir. The next day he had been hauled in front of Chief Baker. Furious that Clay had been put on the list, Baker had made his disgust clear without ever stating it outright and had followed that up by intimating that Clay had bought his way in. It was no secret within the department that Clay had wealth.

Clay had stayed silent and let the man carry on. He wasn't sure where the vitriol was coming from, but it didn't matter; for all his power, the chief hadn't been able to do anything more than fume. Clay's record was spotless, and now that he was on the list, there was no real way to object to his placement there. Clay had already received a communication from Manhattan's chief of police commending him on his exemplary record and expressing hope that together the two cities could find a way to combat the Elixir threat.

The woman glanced over Clay's electronic documents, nodded, and held out her scanner. Clay pressed his thumb to it and looked down at the screen so it could read his retina. Once she was sure of his identity, she gave him a smile, thanked him, and moved on to the man sitting to his right, a fat detective named Anderson who worked in the Commercial Crimes Unit of the Southern Precinct, down near the flooded remains of Coney Island.

Everyone checked out and they were soon moving again, passing through the thick walls and entering the city proper. There was murmuring on the bus; none of these cops had been through the walls since they'd been built, and few were old enough to remember the island as it had been when entry was available to all. As they descended into the city, all eyes were glued to the bus's windows.

The final checkpoint was smaller than the others and involved only a cursory check of the driver's information. A quick swipe or two on the tablet and they were waved through, briefly joining the traffic on Chinatown's main drag. Carts lined the street, piled high with steaming food, exotic produce, Asian technology, designer handbags. In the past, these would have been knockoffs, but Clay thought it likely that those days were gone. There was wealth here, and some of the most impressive technology he'd ever encountered was on display. He saw a man on the corner holding up a gigantic sign, written in hanzi, with extendable myoelectric arms that gave him a reach of more than eight feet.

The bus turned left and headed down Bowery, toward the NYPD headquarters at the base of the now-defunct Brooklyn Bridge. They passed dozens of government buildings, and what impressed Clay most was not their size or the grandeur of their architecture but simply how clean they were. This city was rich. It had always been a center of wealth, but now it was rich to its very bones, the poor all but eliminated from its boundaries. There was no more readily visible proof of that fact than the lack of graffiti on the building's faces, of garbage in the street, of Elixir addicts sleeping off their licks in a nearby gutter. The place was practically shining.

The fat cop, Anderson, grunted, slapping Clay's shoulder and pointing. "Goddamn, look at that." He needn't have; the statue rising up from the NYPD courtyard was impossible to miss. Thirty feet tall and gilded with gold, it showed a strong-jawed, square-shouldered officer in full uniform, cap smartly placed on his head, staring out with a look of perpetual vigilance. At his knee and slightly behind, safe and protected, stood a small girl. The words *Fidelis Ad Mortem* were emblazoned in two-foot-high letters on the pedestal below the man.

"You know many cops who look like that?" Clay asked.

Anderson snickered. "Having a hard time thinking of any."

"Maybe they breed 'em better here in the big city."

"Well, I'm sure us backwoods yokels wouldn't know anything about that."

"No doubt."

The bus turned, descending into a massive underground parking lot. They passed civilian vehicles, squad cars, SWAT vans. On the bottom floor were spaces marked for visitors, including ones designed to accommodate larger vehicles, and their bus pulled into one of these. Near the front, Deputy Chief Amanda Warren, who'd been tasked with leading this crew of consultants, stood up.

She was a short woman with cropped auburn hair, a pale complexion, and a deep, purple scar running in an ugly zigzag from forehead to chin. The scar had come from a burglar she'd surprised on patrol one night early in her career. He'd gotten far worse than he'd given; even with blood pouring into one of her eyes, Warren had shot him twice and left him wheelchair-bound for life. Clay knew little else about her except that she had a reputation as a hard-ass, relatively honest cop who put in the hours, put in the work, and expected her people to do the same.

"Listen up," she called, and the driver tapped her on the elbow and handed her a small microphone. She thanked him and began to speak again. Her voice echoed throughout the bus."I know a lot of you have opinions on our good friends at the NYPD that you're just dying to share."

There were laughs at this and more muttering, and Warren glared out at her men for a moment before continuing.

"First off, I don't think I need to remind anyone that you're here as representatives of the Brooklyn Police Department, and you're expected to behave in a courteous, professional manner at all times. We know goddamn well what these people are up against when it comes to fighting Elixir. Privileged assholes or not, these men and women are cops, and what we know can and will save cop lives. Anyone here think that's a bad thing?"

No one did.

"Good. We're going to share what we know, and we're going to do it without complaint. I've spoken with Inspector Dennis Haley, who's running the NYPD side of this little get-together, and with the chief of police here, Officer Andrew Bartolo. They've assured me that their people will treat us with the respect we deserve, but should that not be the case, you're expected to take it with dignity and restraint. Behave like a fucking grown-up and bring the issue to me. Haley's people don't want to piss him off. He's a tough son of a bitch."

"Just like you, ma'am," someone called out, and there was laughter.

Clay saw Warren suppress a smile. "Now, I know this is the first trip to the island for basically everyone here. You'll have plenty of time to explore, and your passes are good everywhere in the city, so you don't have to worry about straying too far afield. That said, if I hear about a single one of you ending up drunk and disorderly and causing trouble for our hosts, I will personally make sure that you're busted down a level and that you get the most pig-shit assignments possible for the next two years. Any questions?"

People seemed pretty clear on that one. Clay didn't even hear any muttering.

"All right," Warren said. "Let's get out of this bus and show these folks what they're in for, and how the pros deal with it."

The other officers made positive noises, and there was a smattering of applause. Clay was unmoved. It was a good speech, but the Brooklyn PD's answer to dealing with Elixir, so far, had been to flail about helplessly as the drug consumed their city. All they could teach the NYPD was how junkies would behave, how to spot the signs of addiction, and how to deal with the pimps, pushers, and petty thieves who were going to flood their streets if the drug took hold.

What they couldn't do was explain how to get someone to stop taking Elixir, even after their third time through detox. They couldn't explain how to combat the surreal way in which the drug went from being the sort of thing a wealthy socialite could drop at a party and then not think about for a week, to a wicked grinning baboon hanging from that same person's back, its claws dug so deeply into the body that removing them might well kill the host.

If the drug had really come to Manhattan, it was only a matter of time before the city began to rot from the inside. Clay didn't believe there was anything he or the NYPD or anyone else could do to stop it.

* * *

Inspector Dennis Haley had been a basketball player talented enough to be picked up late in the draft by the pros and had earned his permanent Manhattan residency by spending a couple of years warming the Knicks' bench before washing out of the league. Dark-skinned, he had a broad nose and intense brown eyes. At six foot eight, he towered over everyone else in the room, and he had a hard, imposing manner to match his athletic build. Now in his early forties, his face was beginning to show frown lines, and there was a good bit of gray in his short brown hair.

"It's a pleasure to meet you all," he said once they had been shuttled into a conference room. His expression was severe, but Clay heard genuine warmth in his voice. "I used to love playing in Brooklyn. Great town. I hate what's happening there and hope you'll believe me that I've lobbied to extend support out past the walls. I also hope you'll understand why we're pushing so hard to keep Elixir out of our city."

This introduction was met with general murmurs of approval. Haley didn't waste more time on pretty words, signaling instead to an officer at the door. Five lieutenants from Haley's team filed in. The inspector introduced them and sat them down by the podium. They didn't look like the statue out front; they looked like regular cops, guys who did a job and then went home to their wives and kids and didn't worry too much about *Fidelis Ad Mortem*. Clay couldn't say why, but this made him feel better about the whole consultation exercise.

Once his lieutenants were seated, Haley continued. "We asked Chief Baker to provide us with a group of men and women who've worked in all areas—vice, narcotics, homicide, you name it—so that we can get an idea of how the drug has impacted your work. Deputy Chief Warren assures us you've all spent plenty of time dealing with Elixir and its effects. Over the next few days, we'll be doing a series of exercises and Q&A sessions designed to get our teams up to speed. After that, it'll be four or five weeks of putting together action plans and holding training sessions. What I'd like to do first is get to know each of you a bit, what your departments are, what your experience is. Let's go around the room and do a brief introduction ... I'll be taking notes."

Clay was fourteenth out of twenty-four officers, not including Deputy Chief Warren. When it was his turn, he kept his summary quick and succinct.

"Officer Clay Foster, Patrol Services. I've been on the force six years. Before that I was in the war. Regular army and some classified service. I spend most of my time now dealing with Elixir in one way or the other ... If it's happening on the street, it's usually because someone's either been licking or is trying to get there."

There were some chuckles at this, and a few nods.

Haley moved his fingers over his tablet and glanced up at Clay. "Some pretty impressive stuff on you record, Officer. I see you caught a big fish up in Crown Heights not so long ago."

"It was kind of a catch-and-release, given the way Rikers works." There was even more laughter at this, but Haley didn't join in. Deputy Chief Warren was glaring at him, so Clay continued. "Not trying to be glib, sir. We worked hard to get the guy behind bars."

Haley nodded. "I understand, Officer. We've got our share of overcrowded prisons on the island, too. Never a good thing to see someone who belongs there end up going free after a token amount of time."

"It was not a career highlight," Clay said.

This time Haley did smile, briefly. "Thank you, Officer."

The second highest-ranking person in the room, from Brooklyn's end, was a man named Jacobs, a sergeant. Most of the men were either regular officers—guys who worked the streets like Clay—or detectives who spent most of their time on specific cases. As Haley mentioned, all of them had plenty of experience dealing with Elixir. Clay couldn't think of a Brooklyn cop who didn't.

After the introductions, there was a lengthy Q&A. The lieutenants, working from their own notes, picked particular officers and asked them questions, getting a feel for the men and what they had to offer. Some of the Brooklyn cops were half-worthless as speakers, inarticulate and unable to express what they had seen and done, but Haley didn't seem worried about this. Clay understood; not every man performed well when singled out like this. Some of the officers would no doubt fare better when put into a smaller, more informal group.

After two hours, they broke for the day, not wanting to exhaust the Brooklyn cops or flood those from the NYPD with information. It was nearing five in the afternoon anyway, and shifts were going to end soon. Haley thanked them for their time and told them taxis could easily be caught out front.

As they were shuffling out, Haley tapped Clay on the shoulder and asked him to hang back. Once the room had emptied, the inspector pointed to a couple of chairs and they sat down.

"Classified service, huh?" he said.

Clay nodded."Yessir. One regular tour, then training, and then a whole lot of stuff I'm not allowed to talk about."

"Past the perimeter?"

Clay hedged. "There wouldn't have been much use for someone like me on the line. They had me all over the place."

Haley gave an impressed frown. "Navy SEALs here."

"No shit. Thought you were a basketball player."

"I was. Came out of Navy at twenty-one, spent five years in the league, then went into SEAL training to help with the war."

"Twenty-six is old for that. Guess you were in the right shape for it, though."

Haley smiled. "I did all right."

"I heard you guys basically saved Maryland and Delaware by yourselves."

"That's the story the brass likes to tell," Haley said. "Me ... I'd probably give *some* of the credit to the citizen groups that sweated and stank and bled with us out in those marshes for five solid months."

Clay nodded. Some of the best people he'd worked with during the war hadn't been official soldiers at all but simply people who'd felt compelled to take up arms to protect themselves and their loved ones. That this was also true of some of the best people he'd fought *against* had become increasingly apparent as he spent time behind enemy lines.

"Officer—"

"Clay, sir, if you don't mind."

"All right, if you'll call me Dennis." Haley took a breath, tilted his head, regarded Clay for a moment. When he went on, his voice was guarded. "Clay, if asked by a neutral third party, would you claim that this group of men and women is the best Brooklyn PD has to offer?"

Clay laughed a little. "Honestly, I don't know these guys. Pretty sure there's no one here who's outright owned, if that's what you're asking, but there's no one here without some dirt under their nails, either."

"So why do you suppose they got chosen?"

"I'm guessing it's a reward for guys who've … made Chief Baker's life easy. Bunch of light duty—short hours, lots of time off here in Shangri-La."

Haley nodded. "Deputy Chief Warren provided me with dossiers. The 'getting to know you' routine was mostly about seeing how much of what was said matched up with them. For the most part, it was pretty close. You stood out."

"I didn't match up?" Clay asked, raising an eyebrow.

"Oh, you matched fine, but there's a whole lot you didn't say, and you're not being entirely truthful now, either. There's no dirt under *your* fingers. You're riding a six-year clean sweep from IA, you've never taken a shot at anyone who didn't ask for it, and your marks on everything from fitness to how promptly you file your reports are exemplary."

"That's all just Army training," Clay said. "Didn't think most of that was worth mentioning, and I'm not really into thumping my chest about how many bribes I've turned down."

"Does it embarrass you? Being a good cop?"

Clay shook his head. "No, but it puts the ones who aren't quite so clean on edge. I don't blame them. I don't know how it is here, but over there ... you gotta live. You got bills to pay, kids to feed, a wife who's probably out busting her ass, too. So when the guy in the Audi slips you a couple bills because, yeah, you're giving him a ticket for speeding but maybe you'll decide not to notice that the passenger seat's occupied by a sixteen-year-old working girl ... you take it."

"Except *you* don't."

"I have advantages they don't have."

"Money, right? It's easier for you to be clean."

Clay thought of Escobar and the way the man had shrieked as the flames consumed him. He wondered how clean Haley would find that. "I'm no angel."

"No cop is. Why haven't you gone for lieutenant? Or at least detective?"

"I like the beat. I like my partner. I've thought about lieutenant ... Not sure they'd pass me."

"Forgive me for being blunt, Clay, but you're not well-liked in the department, are you?"

"Not by the beat cops, but I do all right with everyone else. Well, almost ... I don't always play politics very well, so some of the top brass doesn't love me either."

"Your partner's a beat cop and he likes you."

"Kel's not real dirty, either, but he's so goddamn personable that no one minds. They think I'm an asshole. Full of myself because I can afford to stay clean."

Haley made no comment.

Clay grinned a little. "They're probably right."

"No one likes the clean cop, maybe," Haley said, "but the beat cops don't have anything to do with making lieutenant.

The people who make that call will respect you, because it gets easier as you go up in rank. On patrol, you're down there in the thick of it, and not taking the money makes the others nervous. As a lieutenant, that's less of an issue—you're not out there every night. They don't know what you're doing or not doing. As an inspector or a deputy chief, the things that were liabilities on patrol become assets. You should think about moving up. You've got the right record."

Clay nodded. When this was done, when he'd gotten to the people responsible for Terry's death, he wasn't sure there would be a place for him with the Brooklyn PD. He wasn't sure there'd be a place for him anywhere by then, but he'd long since ceased worrying about that. "I'll take it under consideration, thanks."

"Good. Tell you what ... there's a place not too far from here that serves up a hell of a burger. Expensive sons of bitches, and it's hard to get in if you're not connected, but they're worth it. Terrific beer lineup, too. They still get stuff from Oregon and Chicago. You have any plans this evening?"

Clay, who couldn't exactly tell this man that he planned to make a surveillance sweep of the building he was intent on breaking into, said he did not.

Haley nodded. "I'll treat ... if you let me pick your brain on this Elixir shit for an hour or two."

Clay hadn't had beer from Oregon in six years. It was almost impossible to find and difficult to re-create due to the particular climate in the area; you couldn't grow the right hops anywhere else. That and an excellent burger seemed particularly appealing.

"You're on. Long as I get to ask some questions about your city in the process."

"Fair deal," Haley said, and he stood, motioning toward the door.

* * *

"We could probably get you a permanent pass."

Clay hadn't expected it, but somewhere along the line this casual dinner had evolved into a full-on recruitment pitch. The inspector had decided early on that Clay was the best of the bunch and could be a prime asset for the NYPD.

Clay glanced up. On one of the holo screens, the Yankees, mired in a three-years-and-running streak of mediocrity, were getting beaten up by the Indianapolis Astros. Clay winced as one of the Yankees' players batted into an inning-ending double play. He'd grown up adoring the players from the early thirties teams, a group of scrappy, home-grown kids who'd brought a few division championships and one World Series win to the Bronx. The thought of a pass that would allow him into the city to catch a game was tempting, even if the team was still rebuilding its farm system and needed another couple of years to contend.

Haley followed his glance and grinned. "We get a lot of tickets, too. Yankees, Giants ... I go to Knicks games all the time."

Clay glanced over at him. "If Deputy Chief Warren knew you were trying to poach her people, she might have something to say about it."

They were on their second beer. The burgers were long gone and had been every bit as good as advertised. Beef and lamb and veal, topped with bacon, blue cheese, and a house steak sauce that Clay would've bought by the bottle. It was hard to find this kind of quality in Brooklyn even in the ritzy places. Getting it in a neighborhood burger joint, even an exclusive one, was impossible.

Haley gave him a sidelong grin. "Frankly, I don't want most of her people. They've got things to contribute to this project, but there's no one else on that list with a record anything like yours. They're regular cops. A little lazy, a little dirty, a little undisciplined. I've got a thousand of those already."

"I'm a pretty regular cop." Clay knew the defensive tone of his voice proved the words a fat lie.

"Bullshit," Haley said, not unkindly. He took a swig of beer, looked up at the game, gave a slow shake of his head.

"Jesus Christ, Vasquez can't hit."

Clay blew air through pursed lips. "Can't field either. I swear to God, if he'd just get a body in front of the ball ..."

"Good thing we're paying him forty-eight million a year, huh?"

Clay nodded. Took a long, slow drink to buy time, came up with an excuse. He turned to Haley. "You can't have me yet."

"At least there's a *yet* in there. Why not?"

"You know about my wife. It must've been in the dossier."

Haley nodded, favoring Clay with a sympathetic frown. "I do. Fucking shame, losing someone like that. My husband ... I can't imagine it."

Husband. That caught Clay off guard, even though same-sex marriage had been legal in the country for decades—one of many factors that had led to the war with the USS. He tried not to look surprised, saw Haley's smirk, and knew he'd failed. *That's right*, the man's eyes seemed to say. *I'm ex-Navy, ex-NBA, a police inspector, and married to a man. That a problem?*

"Right ... How long you been with him?" Clay asked, but he knew it had been a while. The ring on Haley's hand was tarnished and scuffed and scratched, the yellow-gold sub-layer showing through the white-gold coating. A ring that had seen the years go by.

"Married twenty years this August," Haley said. "Four years before that. He stood by during the whole SEALs thing. Could never really believe that ... but he's still here."

Clay mused on this. "We made it to ten—seven married— before Terry ... fell. You've been with your guy a long time, so maybe you'll understand this. Terry loved Brooklyn as much as I do. I want to see what I can do to help it. I can't come running to the bright shiny city that doesn't really need my help. Not yet."

It was a lie, of course, or at least half of one, but he thought he'd sold it well. It was true that he cared about Brooklyn and that Terry had, too, and a part of him did balk at fleeing behind the walls while his city died. But the real reason was simple and uncluttered by emotion: Clay was probably about to become a wanted man in New York.

Haley seemed to buy what Clay was selling. "I understand, but you're wrong about New York not needing you. Queens and the Bronx are a mess, and Manhattan ... the cracks are starting to show. They'll spread fast. Clay, I don't mean to be a downer, but what are you going to do for Brooklyn? Elixir's got that city in a death grip, and I don't think one good cop can pry it out, especially not with that gang of crooks you call a city government. Here in Manhattan, there's still time."

"There's still good in Brooklyn. There's still plenty of people worth saving, plenty of reasons not to abandon them."

Clay meant it. Brooklyn was descending into addiction, crime, and prostitution. Downtown was a corrupt, blackened heart thumping out an arrhythmic beat at the center of the city. Still, there were good people there, and plenty of them, making their way through life as best they could. They deserved to be able to walk down the street at night without having their throats slit and their pockets rifled.

"I'm not denying that Brooklyn deserves better." Haley stared into his beer for a time before looking up at Clay. "I'll shut up. If our positions were reversed, I know all it'd do is piss me off if you kept badgering me. Just know that the door is open to you and Officer Ruiz. It'd be a better life and a chance to effect some real change. You wouldn't believe the resources we have. The money in New York is like nowhere else."

"I saw the statue." Clay tried to keep the bitter tone from his voice but was not entirely successful.

Haley gave a short disgusted laugh. "That thing's a fucking embarrassment. Wasn't the chief's idea. That one came right from the mayor."

"Not surprised. Can't imagine any cop would want it out there."

"It looks good on the news when they show the building. That's the point of everything in New York now ... to look good on the news. With D.C. bombed to shit, Chicago on fire half the time, and Boston mostly sunk, what's the U.S. got left? Philly's broke. Pittsburgh's broke. It's just New York—we're the shining jewel to show that America's all right."

"Even though we lost two-thirds of America ten years ago," Clay said, nodding. After the South had seceded, the western states had grown tired of providing resources and soldiers for the fight. They'd seized the opportunity to withdraw from the union as well and had proceeded to harry both armies along their borders. Eventually, the U.S. had settled with them in order to focus solely on the United Southern States, which had begun attempting not just secession but invasion.

"Right. The AFS, those bastards, may have three of the four strongest cities in what used to be America, but it's still numbers two through four. They don't have New York."

"They can have L.A.," Clay muttered. He'd been once and found it a sprawling, filthy nightmare baking under the hot desert sun.

Haley laughed. "San Francisco has its charms. Played a few games there before the West broke off."

Clay hadn't been. Couldn't say. He shrugged and drank his beer, watching the screen.

"Well, think about it," Haley said after a time.

"I will. I appreciate it. I'm just not sure I could make the jump right now even if I wanted to. There's too much I'm still trying to do for Terry."

"Do you think you're doing what she'd want?"

Clay wondered if the man had any idea how close to home that question hit. He pondered in silence for a while and finally spoke.

"Doesn't matter. It's what I have to do."

CHAPTER 12

The Encounter

The Manhattan Water and Power building rose up before him like a twisted steel delusion, all glimmering metal and sparkling glass, its form a structural impossibility made real by the marvels of engineering. Less than five years old, the skyscraper had been built with the latest in ultra-strong materials, its bizarre arches and spirals created with the aid of complex mathematical algorithms designed to ensure integrity in a structure that looked spun-sugar fragile. Critics could argue whether it was art or not, and would probably be doing so for the next hundred years, but it was a technological miracle and Clay thought it was pretty goddamn amazing.

Eight twenty-five Eighth Avenue. This was the building the Chink wanted him to infiltrate. Clay had looked it up on the Net, of course, but if there was a connection between the largest utility company in the Northeast and his wife's murder, he hadn't discovered it. The Chink had said that their mutual enemy was involved with this address, however, and recommended Clay "work his way to the top." That meant the executive suites, and that narrowed the list to but a few names.

It was eleven thirty on a Friday. He'd been in New York for two weeks, and he'd been to the building before to study the comings and goings of those who worked there. He'd also spent hours on the Net getting intimately familiar with its layout, its maintenance access shafts and hallways, and the location of certain vital offices. He had begun to form something of a plan and thought that through improvisation and a touch of good luck, he could manage to get where he needed to be.

Brand-new building, brand-new security. Clay wasn't getting in through the front door without an invite. Even the maintenance staff had to go through the standard thumb and retina scan. These could be faked, but not with the resources Clay had on hand. He had to get by the scanner entirely. The way to do it was the same way that had worked for thousands of years: bribe the doorkeeper.

Figuring out who that was hadn't been hard, just a matter of watching the shift changes and doing some facial lookups in the NYPD database. There was a guy, Tom Aiken, who worked eight to four on weekdays, monitoring the scanner. Much of the time, he was the only man in the room, and while the entrance was under video surveillance, it wasn't monitored with vigilance. If someone was watching, it only had to *seem* like the device had read Clay's print and his eye. That would probably be enough.

Clay had tracked Aiken one night to a little bar in Chelsea, near the water, where the drinks were mostly synthetic and laced with endorphins and other feel-good additives, some of questionable legality. Clay hadn't given a shit about the drinks—on the vice scale, this was barely enough to get a frown, let alone a fine—so long as it meant he could talk to his man alone. Neither had he cared that the bar was a notorious cruising spot for gay men, except that it meant he would need to pick up Aiken before anyone else did. This had proved none too difficult; the bar had been practically dead on a Tuesday night, which had made it easy to sidle up to Aiken, order a drink, and get the man talking.

Aiken hated his job, and so Clay had made him a simple proposition: half the man's yearly salary delivered to his bank account that night and another half after Clay was finished in the building. Aiken had pondered it for a while, sipping his drink. They had retired to a rear booth and probably looked like they were laying the groundwork for a tryst.

"No one gets hurt," Aiken had said. "Right?"

Clay had shaken his head. "No one. I have absolutely no intention of getting violent in the middle of the MWP offices. I need some stuff from a computer, that's all."

"Mmm. I don't want my name used, either."

"If they catch me, they'll know who was on shift when I got through," Clay said. "I won't give them your name, but—"

"I'll handle that. I've got administrator access."

"I don't suppose I need to tell you that if any word of this gets out, or if you decide you don't want to let me in after all, I'm pretty capable of making problems for you."

"Please. I don't give a shit about those pompous holier-than-thou bitches or whatever corporate espionage shenanigans you're up to. You should see what I pay to live in someone's closet ... and can I even get a cost-of-living increase the last two years? I think not. You want in? Pay up and I'll get you in."

So Clay had, and now it was time to put Aiken's statement to the test. He headed for Forty-ninth Street, where the crew entrance was. He'd secured a pair of coveralls from another employee late the previous evening, this time swiping them from the man's locker at a local gym, leaving the guy's jeans and T-shirt alone except to stuff a few bills into the pocket. He had also taken the man's badge—this guy worked the late shift and wouldn't be in to report the loss until long after Clay was finished.

The man's hair in the picture was jet-black, so Clay had dyed his own. The dye would wash out before he was due back at the NYPD headquarters on Monday, but the fact that his facial features were nothing like in the picture and his skin two shades lighter was a mild issue. It wouldn't stand up to close scrutiny, but Clay intended on avoiding any such occurrence. Getting up close and personal wasn't the goal of this particular mission.

He'd studied the traffic patterns and knew that no one came through the security checkpoint at this hour of the day unless they were running severely late. He stepped through the door and took the stairs. Head down and moving fast, he strode through the tiled hallway and into the security room. He glanced over without lifting his head, saw that Aiken was sitting behind the glass wall, manning the security booth, and kept moving toward the scanner.

"Morning," Aiken said through the intercom. "Step in, do your thumb first ... you know the drill."

"Just hurry it up already." This was a predetermined response meant to identify him in case Aiken had any doubt. Clay stepped into the machine. He hovered his thumb over the pad, keeping it at least half an inch from the surface. After a moment, the light went green; Aiken had manually authorized him.

"Eyes." Aiken was affecting an impressive tone of bitchy disinterest. Just a guy who hates his job buzzing in a guy who's late. Clay had to suppress a smile. He stared into the lens, but Aiken never turned it on. After a moment, another light went green.

"You're clear. Have a *lovely* day."

Clay stepped through, coveralls on, badge around his neck. It would open most of the doors in the facility for him. All he had to do was take the quickest route to the ones he needed and do what he had come to do. He was in.

* * *

Part of him wanted to rush up to the penthouse offices, hold a gun to the head of the first person he saw, and demand to know why Terry was dead. For a moment, Clay almost surrendered to the impulse. Even had that been the right move, and it surely wasn't, he didn't have a gun. He'd come with only his tablet, a few useful pieces of equipment, and the Chink's SynchDrives. He remembered his promise to the information broker; before he allowed himself to hit the executive suites, he would find an open terminal. Clay was many things, and not all of them good, but he was not a man who went back on his word.

The Chink wasn't the only one with toys, however. Clay had brought with him a device that had been sitting in an evidence locker for months, not bothering anyone, just waiting for him to spirit it away. Burglars used them all the time. The rumor was that they'd been developed by a technologist in The Hook who'd come to a bad end when he'd tried to use one of his devices to rob a casino. They'd fed pieces of him to whatever lived in the waters below the walkways.

About the size of a dollar coin—back when they'd made them—the thing was nothing special to look at, just a small gray piece of plastic with a peel-and-stick backing. All Clay had to do was attach it to any box on the building's fire system, and with a command from his tablet he could trigger the alarm. An evacuation should ensue, the people in the building following a routine established by the drills they dealt with every six months.

The maintenance entrance he'd come through led below ground. Once through security, Clay followed a hallway to a central location that contained a gigantic freight elevator and two other lifts designed mainly for human beings. From this core, which existed on every level, various maintenance access routes were available. There were several halls leading to staircases and a series of air shafts and vents, some of them large enough to accommodate a person.

Clay had little use for the vents. His intent was to take an elevator to the sixth floor, which contained several offices full of MWP peons and virtually no one of any real import. It was almost noon. By the time he got to the offices, vast swaths of employees would be at one of the building's six cafeterias or eating lunch outside the office.

Once he found a terminal farm, he just had to gain entry, stick the SynchDrive into the first computer he saw, and be done with it. By the time the terminal's operator returned, Clay would be long gone and whatever data-gathering worm the Chink had loaded onto the drive would have infiltrated the network. Clay was sure that MWP's encryption and security were world-class. He was equally sure that the Chink knew exactly what to expect and had already devised a way around it.

Clay hit the button and stepped into an alcove. He waited there for the elevator, listening for the sound of anyone approaching. He didn't want to be caught here by any legitimate maintenance workers who might know he didn't belong. When the elevator doors opened, he waited a moment to be sure that no one was exiting and then stepped in. "Floor six."

The elevator made a soft chime and the doors closed. As it began to ascend, Clay busied himself with his tablet, hoping that anyone who entered might not notice he didn't belong, but it proved an unnecessary precaution. Shortly, another chime indicated he'd arrived at his destination.

The central maintenance core on this floor had lower ceilings than the one in the basement but otherwise looked identical. Basic drywall, synthetic tiles, exposed ductwork, cheap paint marred with the chips and scrapes of passing equipment—it would have been at home in any New York structure built in the last hundred years. Whoever had designed the place wasn't worried about impressing the help.

The access hallway led into a lobby between two large offices. There were two chairs there, upholstered in lime-green leather, and a plastic table with a few brochures on it. Above them was a large flat holo screen playing a promotion video on a loop. A chirpy blond woman displayed what seemed like about eight hundred perfectly white teeth while extolling the virtues of the great Manhattan Water and Power.

The entire north wall was clear synthetic glass. As he neared it, a single frosted stripe materialized in the glass, a warning to keep oblivious people from walking right into it.

Past that, Clay could see a terminal farm, one of hundreds in the building, at which nameless drones spent their lives doing whatever it was that drones did in these places. Few of the terminals were occupied, but there was a receptionist he was going to have to deal with. Clay pressed his pass to a black plastic plate on the wall and a section of the glass slid open.

"Hi there," the receptionist said. He looked to be in his early twenties, with tan skin, perfectly trimmed brown hair, and dark eyes. They guy was beautiful, well-proportioned, built. He had to be working here between modeling or acting gigs.

"Hey, how's it going?" Clay asked, affecting a genial tone.

"Oh, I'm great. TGIF, you know what I'm saying?" The man laughed. "Here to fix something?"

"That's right."

"Super-good! I'm supposed to log it. Can you put it into terms that a *total* tech-phobe can understand?"

Clay forced a laugh and went ahead with his plan, citing a common problem in his own office back at the precinct. "Got a report of a charge plate not working over in Section D, I think."

"Ugh, those things go out all. The. Time! Can you believe it, with what they paid for this place? Don't even get me started on the toilets. Do you know which terminal?"

Christ. Clay scrambled. "Not sure ... ah ... Whoever took the call, they didn't write anything down. Can't trust anyone to do their jobs, you know?"

"Oh, honey, you are preaching to the *choir* over here. But listen, maybe you want to come back when folks aren't at lunch? Then we can find out who called with the problem."

"I've got a detector. Built into my tablet. I'll just go down the row, no problem."

"Oh, fantastic. Just about set here, then. What's your name, my man?"

Clay had memorized the name that went with the badge he'd stolen. He hoped the receptionist didn't know the guy. "Nick Lowe."

"All right, Mister Nick Lowe, you are good to go."

"Thanks, man."

The receptionist chirped some pithy good-bye as Clay turned and headed into the terminal farm, annoyed with himself. He should've known the name of an employee who worked in Section D and was at lunch. He'd let the fact that this was an office building and not a drug den or an enemy encampment get his guard down.

Clay supposed he'd have to deal with the receptionist again when he returned, but at least he wouldn't have to make up any more lies. In the meantime, he tried to put the screw-up out of his mind. He found Section D and turned in to it. The first cubicle was unoccupied. Taking the SynchDrive from his pocket, he checked to make sure the terminal was merely in standby and not disconnected. It was live. Clay paused for a moment, thinking.

So ... do you think the Chink's telling you the truth or just using you to plant this thing on the network?

It wasn't the first time he'd asked himself that question, but the answer had never changed: it was the best lead he had. If the Chink proved treacherous or false, there was going to be a hell of a reckoning in The Hook when Clay got out of here. He'd burn the place to its foundations to get at that croaking little man. In the interim, he could only trust that the guy had made a fair deal.

Clay bent down as if to inspect the charge plate on the desk's surface. He slipped the drive into the mounting device on the side of the terminal. If the cube was under video surveillance, someone would have to be watching pretty damn carefully to have seen the move. The drive lit up, the red casing glowing a bit. As it did its thing, Clay took his tablet out and passed it over the charge plate as if inspecting it. He counted a slow fifteen out in his head, giving the drive more than enough time to do its work. When the count was done, he ejected the drive.

Almost before he had stood up, his tablet chirped. Clay tapped and dragged, pulled up the messaging interface, and glanced at the anonymous text he'd received.

> *Thank you, Mr. Foster. All debts paid in full and our working partnership is now concluded. Please discard the drive. Beware of arachnids.*

Clay had no idea what that last line meant, and that fact made him very nervous. He glanced around but couldn't see anything that looked remotely like a spider, and so he put the phone back into his pocket, tossed the drive into a trash can, and left the way he had come.

"All set," he said to the receptionist as he passed, not stopping his stride, hoping to avoid another long discussion. "Have a good weekend."

"You know it, my man!" The guy tossed him a wave before turning back to his screen. In another moment more, Clay was back in the maintenance hallway, headed for the elevators. The first part of the plan—the easy part—was done. Now it got hard. Now he headed for the upper suites to get some answers about Terry.

CHAPTER 13

The Woman in the White Suit

The eighty-fourth floor of Manhattan Water and Power was a tribute to two things: opulence and electricity. The walls were gray marble streaked with white and lined at about six feet with glass tubes through which blue arcs flickered, lending a cool glow to the stone. Above him hung suspended hundreds of old-fashioned filament light bulbs, the kind that had long ago been outlawed in most places. The wires inside them glowed hot and orange, the warmth of the light contrasting with the cool of the walls. Clay couldn't see the ceiling, but below him was an intricate parquet floor made from interwoven slats of blond and red wood. The MWP logo had been inlaid in the center of the lobby area using large pieces of translucent acrylic behind which more blue lighting glowed.

There were several leather chairs and a sofa scattered around the lobby, all of them black, slung low, reflecting a retro design sensibility that echoed the Scandinavian heyday of the early part of the century. Holo screens were hung at intervals along the walls, broadcasting the same propaganda he had seen below, though someone had muted them. The narrator on screen made a sweeping gesture, displaying those shining teeth again, before stepping aside to reveal the site of a future fusion plant. Below her were words *Cleaner Than Coal, Safer Than Fission, More Reliable Than Solar or Wind.*

Elena Reyes, the COO and best-paid executive in the United States, was responsible for the daily operation of the company. She shared the floor with three others. There was Allen Burke, chairman of the board, in his late eighties and not active in the company's day-to-day operations. His office stood empty much of the year. Janette Moore, the CFO, put in long hours at her desk six days a week. She had come from the finance industry and helped Reyes reshape the company into a global force. Finally there was Alex Szarka, the CEO and son of the company's beloved, long-deceased founder. His father had taken MWP from a family-owned energy redistribution center on the Upper East Side to the largest and most powerful utility company in the Western Hemisphere in just twenty short years. Szarka's apple had fallen unfortunately far from his father's tree; the man had a reputation for laziness, spending much of his time strolling the building, chatting with underlings about politics, finances, or the local news. Approaching fifty and early retirement, he was a figurehead. Reyes represented the real power in the organization, and Clay planned to start with her terminal.

He stood looking out from a crack in the door, not yet ready to step into the lobby. Unlike on the other floors of the building, there was no central maintenance hub—perhaps low-level employees weren't allowed on this floor unless there was an emergency. Clay had been forced to climb stairs from the previous floor and open a hidden panel in the wall. He had an excuse to be here if needed, had complete knowledge of the layout, and had a course of action planned.

Clay took his tablet out and brought up the interface to trigger the fire alarm. The plan was simple: set off the alert, wait for the offices to clear out, and then get inside. It would take at least twenty minutes for the fire department to get in and kill the alarms and quite a while longer to determine what had triggered it. Clay had attached the device not at the central core but in a random maintenance hall halfway up the building. It would be an hour or more before the tower was cleared for repopulation. He'd be long gone by then.

Clay swiped at his screen and keyed in the trigger code, cocking his head and waiting. Just as he was beginning to fear that the little gray box had been a dud or that it didn't work with this type of system, he saw a bulb on the wall begin to strobe. It was followed by an obnoxious buzzing noise played at earsplitting volume. Clay clenched his teeth.

Less than a minute passed before Clay, already wishing he had brought earplugs, saw a group of people emerging from the offices. The receptionist, a woman in her mid-twenties, came first. After that he saw a rotund man who must have been Alex Szarka, the CEO, and right behind him was Janette Moore, shouting at what appeared to be nothing and gesturing furiously over a tablet screen as she walked. After a moment, Clay realized she must have been using one of the new cochlear phone implants, effectively giving her an earpiece without requiring her to wear one.

"I didn't even think this place *could* catch fire!" the receptionist cried as they moved past him toward the bank of elevators, a note of fear in her voice.

"It can't," Szarka said, his tone warm and comforting. "Don't worry yourself, Eva. It's strictly a precaution. This building is fireproof. Now let's get on the elevator and—"

"Stairs," a commanding voice shouted over the din, and Clay saw Elena Reyes turn the corner. She stood perhaps five-five and was wearing an impeccably tailored suit of browns and creams with a pair of leather flats. Her brown hair had been straightened and cropped at the shoulders, and there was a simple ruby pendant around her neck. Her face was intense, not angry but focused and alert. She was striding forward with the air of someone who had somewhere to be, even if somewhere was the curb outside.

"What's that, Elena?" Szarka called, and the woman jabbed a finger at a metal door next to the elevators.

"You can't take the elevators during a fire. They head for the bottom and open up."

"We have to walk down eighty-four flights of stairs?" Szarka said, looking mildly appalled.

"Be thankful the elevators will work on the way back up," Reyes said. "Come on."

She strode forward, grabbed the door, and held it open for them. Szarka looked in Clay's direction, and even though he was standing in darkness, the door barely cracked, Clay could have sworn the man spotted him. For a moment it seemed as if their eyes locked, and Clay found himself holding his breath—he couldn't close the door now or the movement would surely be seen.

Then Szarka turned, put a gentle hand on the receptionist's shoulder, and headed with her into the stairwell. Moore, the CFO, was still shouting at what appeared to be no one and working with her tablet.

"Janette!" Reyes snapped her fingers.

The woman glanced up, saw the door being held, and nodded. "Sorry," she said, and then, "What? No, not you, idiot.

You wouldn't catch me apologizing to you at your funeral. Shut up and keep hunting down that data."

Moore disappeared into the staircase. Reyes glanced behind her for a moment, as if looking for someone else, but no one came and she soon entered the stairwell. The door closed behind her. Clay waited a few seconds more and then made his way into the lobby. The braying alarm pounded in his temples, but he forced it out of his mind and got going, using his access badge to open the door to the office suite.

Reyes's office was at the end of the hall, taking up the southeast corner of the building. Clay's maintenance pass was supposed to give him full access, but he was prepared to kick in the door if he had to. It turned out not to be necessary; Reyes hadn't locked it, and it glided open at his touch.

The room couldn't rightly be called cavernous, but only because fully half of the walls were glass from floor to ceiling, at least fourteen feet tall, letting sunlight stream in and offering a breathtaking view of the city. Clay could see all of the New York's landmarks, old and new. Out past the East River, the bay that had once been Greenpoint and Long Island City glimmered in the sun, a few skeletal remains of buildings still poking from the calm waters.

The other two walls of the office were wood-paneled and boasted several original works of art. Reyes's gigantic desk was stationed in the corner, pointed at the windows and looking out over the city. It was faced by three black leather chairs and was the most modern thing in the office, made of metal and acrylic, lined with glowing blue lights like the hallway outside. Her terminal sat at the center on a tall stand, and Clay saw that it had been designed to be used while Reyes walked on a treadmill that was parked under the desk. There were no decorations save for a single framed photo of a woman who might have been Reyes's sister, though the resemblance was not close enough to be sure.

The alarm was still screeching in the hall, but at least it was quieter in here. A light above the door was alternating white and red flashes, but with the amount of sun streaming in it was barely noticeable. Clay imagined that by now most of the people in the building would be in the staircases, headed for the street, probably grumbling about this unplanned interruption. He stepped onto the treadmill, which wasn't running, and moved to the terminal, taking out the Chink's second SynchDrive.

"I think that's about enough, Officer Foster."

He turned expecting to see Elena Reyes. What he got instead was Tom Wolfe with tits. The woman standing before him was maybe thirty, trim and fit, wearing a full southern dandy's outfit—pants, shirt, vest, jacket, all of them gleaming white. Black tie. Black and white tuxedo shoes. Her hair was pulled up under a white homburg hat with a wide black band around its crown. She looked the very picture of an 1800s Kentucky colonel … except she was female and wearing a pistol slung low over her right hip. She hadn't drawn it, not yet, but the fingertips of her left hand rested gently on its edge, the nonchalance of the pose betraying the truth: this woman was a coiled snake waiting for an excuse to spring.

She knew my name. Clay felt a wave of hopeless frustration roll through him. He took a few steps backward and climbed off the treadmill to stand next to the desk.

"How long have you been tracking me?" It couldn't have been since his arrival; they never would've let him send the Chink's worm spelunking in their network.

"Oh, it's been a while." There was the slightest ghost of a Carolina accent to her speech. *While* came out just a bit like *wall*. This woman must have emigrated north sometime after the war. It was uncommon—the majority of southerners were firmly ensconced in the USS, and there hadn't been many visas available to people on that side of the conflict—but it wasn't completely unheard of.

"Long enough to do a face lookup, anyway."

The woman smiled at him, just so pleasant, as if they were having a nice conversation in the park. Her eyes gave him nothing, though. "That's right."

There was something familiar about her, about the way she held herself, the way she looked at him. Even her smile made him think of something, someone, from some time before. "You have me at a disadvantage, miss. I don't know your name."

"Why don't you call me Olivia?"

"Even though that's not your name."

"Oh, a girl can't just hand her name out to every strange gentleman she meets. I'm sure you understand." *I'm* came out as *Ahm*. Clay was sure of it: this woman had grown up in North Carolina.

"Well, Olivia ... here we are."

"Indeed. I have to frisk you now, Officer. I hope you won't take it the wrong way. Please stand still, because if you move I'll shoot you in the leg, and I wouldn't want to stain the wood."

She stepped forward and Clay felt himself tense involuntarily. She noticed, stopped, waited for him to suppress it. This one was a pro. Clay forced himself to relax, and Olivia strode forward again. As she extended her right hand out to begin the pat-down, he noticed two things. First, she kept her left hand on the gun, another sign that she knew what she was doing. Second, there was a small stylized tattoo of a spider on the back of that hand. It had a red stripe on its abdomen. *Beware of arachnids.* Would've been nice of the Chink to give him some idea what he was up against.

"Nice tattoo."

"Thank you." Olivia patted him down quickly, working with expert efficiency even with a single hand, removing his tablet from him before stepping back. "Redback spiders are real bitches. Take off the badge."

Clay did as he was told. Olivia took the badge, backed up a few steps, and glanced at it.

"Well, I'm sure Mr. Lowe will be happy to have this back. Or did you buy it off him the way you bought entry from Mr. Aiken?"

Clay shook his head. "Stole it. No idea who the other guy is."

"That's a terrible, transparent lie. You've cost Mr. Aiken the job he so hates, and Mr. Lowe will need to be very convincing to keep his. But no matter."

"Doesn't matter to me at all."

Olivia gave him a toothy smile. She stepped over to a small pad on the wall and tapped it a few times. The alarms stopped. "That's so much better, don't you think? You can come in now, Ms. Reyes."

Elena Reyes stepped through the door, looking at Clay with interest. He could discern no immediate malice; her expression more closely resembled that of an entomologist who's encountered a particularly fascinating though somewhat perplexing specimen.

"Hello, Officer Foster."

Clay was already tiring of the pointless formality, but he played along. "Ms. Reyes."

She stepped farther into the room, coming to stand next to Olivia. "If you wanted something from me, it might have been easier to schedule an appointment."

"I didn't think you'd be interested."

"I'm *very* interested in you. Why don't you sit down? We have a few questions. Olivia?"

The woman in the white suit strode quickly forward and rearranged two of the leather chairs so they were facing each other. She pulled the third behind one of them, and Clay understood; she would sit to his rear with her hand on her gun while they had this little chat.

"There's no reason for that," Clay said, gesturing as Olivia sat down in her chair.

"I've done my research," Reyes said. "You're a dangerous man even without a weapon. Sit down, Foster."

There was a note of comfortable command in her voice that grated against Clay. "I'm not one of your peons."

"What you *are* is in no position to argue with me. You've no jurisdiction in this city, you're breaking and entering, and you were about to engage in theft. Sit down or I'll have Olivia put eight million volts through you."

"Zap!" Olivia said from behind him, and Clay glanced over his shoulder, glaring. She gave him another sweet smile that didn't touch her eyes and held up a small black box with two metal nubs protruding from it. Clay turned back to Reyes, clenched his teeth, and nodded. He moved to the chair and sat down.

Reyes stepped over, lowered herself into her seat, crossed her legs, leaned forward a bit. "Why are you here?"

"Pretty sure you know the answer to that."

Reyes frowned. "Pretty sure you should answer the question."

Clay, with no real options available to him, decided on honesty. "Someone in this building had my wife killed because of something she knew. Right now, I'm thinking it was you."

Reyes tilted her head, raising her eyebrows. "Did I, now? Is that what the Chink told you? That disgusting cockroach, holed up in his sodden dung pile across the bay, points his finger my way and you come running ... for what? Were you here to kill me, Foster?"

"I was here to gather evidence."

"And you believed I'd have a folder labeled *Police Officers' Wives to Murder* on my work terminal?"

"Anything's possible."

"What did the Chink have you do for him? What was the price of his garbage information?"

"I paid in cash."

Reyes contemplated this. Shook her head. "No, that's not all you paid. You've been lied to and betrayed, Officer Foster. It's going to cost you very dearly, and I'm not talking about more cash."

"Is this where you have me killed, too?"

"Why it is that you're so ready to believe that a person in my position would be ready to kill a ... I'm sorry, I don't even know what your wife did."

"She was a chemist. A lab technician at Shun Ten."

"So, I would kill a chemist ... or have her killed, at any rate. For what?"

Clay leaned forward in his seat. "Why don't you tell me? I'm tired of this."

"I'm sure I have no idea." Reyes kept her voice cool. "Really, Officer Foster, if you're stalling for time, be assured that neither the fire department nor the police will trouble us up here. I can keep you as long as I like before sending you off to be stripped of your temporary pass into our city and shipped back to Brooklyn for discipline."

Fine. "She got her hands on some data that you didn't want her to have, and you killed her to keep her from making it public. Well, I'm sure you didn't do the work personally. I assume the lunatic behind me did it for you."

"I see. And you've seen this data?"

Was there an edge in her voice, a forcefulness to the question that was more than necessary? It was hard to tell. The woman was so goddamned smooth. Clay tried to string her along. "Maybe."

"I don't think you have," Reyes said. "I think the Chink told you things that he knew you wanted to hear and you ate it right up. Very well, believe what you'd like. It's irrelevant to me. Here's why you're still sitting here, Officer Foster ... I need to know why he sent you to my office. I'm quite sure it wasn't to gather data from my terminal, because even had I called in an execution order on your wife, I certainly wouldn't have left evidence on a company machine. No, he had you do something else in this building first, didn't he?"

"I really couldn't say."

Reyes shrugged, shaking her head. "Fine, then. We'll play this game. Why you remain loyal to a loathsome criminal who's sent you on a life-ruining mission, I have no idea, and I don't really care. If you won't tell me what you've done, then things will have to get a great deal more unpleasant."

"I can handle unpleasant."

"I do hope so." Her voice was dry, with just the slightest sarcastic edge to it. Clay turned in his seat to watch as she stepped to her desk and tapped at the terminal. Glancing over the screen, she met his eye and sighed theatrically. "Honestly, all of this over a missing SynchDrive."

Clay tilted his head. "I never told you her SynchDrive was missing."

He saw it then, all the proof he needed, passing over her face in a single instant. A widening of the eyes even as her mouth compressed to a thin line. Then she swallowed. "I'm certain you mentioned it."

Reyes had gone back to her calm, cool expression, but everything had changed, and everyone in the room knew it.

"Sure I did," Clay said, smiling a little. "Sure I did."

There was silence for a time. Clay sat, feeling the twin stares of the two women, one behind him, one to his left.

Finally Reyes spoke. "You're very calm."

"I'm waiting to see what happens next. Does your cute little bodyguard here put a bullet in the back of my head? Or do you take me somewhere else before you kill me?"

"I'm not having you killed. What we'll do is take your tablet—that belongs to me now—and anything else you have on your person. Then Olivia will escort you to Sublevel B of the parking garage. I think you'll find, much to your dismay, that the security cameras don't work well in that part of the building. Not very well at all."

"I guess that'll be convenient for whoever you've hired to beat the shit out of me," Clay said.

Reyes gave him a predatory smile, all teeth. "We're going to have your legs broken. Well, not broken, really ... *Shattered*, I think, would describe the outcome better. I don't know if you'll ever walk again, Officer Foster, after we drop what's left of you in The Hook. I don't believe the Brooklyn PD has managed to hold on to its pension fund, not while Chief Baker and Mayor Alvarez sell the city off in chunks to fill their own pockets, but since you're a man of means I'm sure you'll be able to afford a very nice wheelchair."

Clay was about to call this smarmy woman a worthless murdering cunt when he heard the sound of the gun being pulled from its holster

"It's time to get up now, Officer Foster," Olivia said.

It was all Clay could do not to leap from his chair and attempt to strangle the Reyes woman to death, gun or no gun. He could picture the grin on her face, the light in her dark eyes. Goddamn him for getting caught like this, for ending up powerless when faced with the two people in the world he most wanted dead.

In the end, he controlled himself. He stood slowly, never taking his eyes off of Reyes. For her part, she met his gaze, the slightest hint of a smirk on her otherwise impassive face.

Okay, fine. When that bitch behind me gets close ...

But Olivia didn't get close. "Put your hands behind your back. Ms. Reyes will be putting a band around your wrists. If you even *shiver* while she's near you, I'll shoot you in the head. Do you believe me?"

Clay did. He put his hands behind him, thinking rapidly, trying to find the exits. There weren't any, not up here. Even if he was able to get behind Reyes, put an arm around her throat, and use her as some sort of shield, there were eighty-six floors to cover. By the time he reached the bottom, even in an elevator, there would be security waiting for him, and, of course, this woman would pursue him the entire way.

Reyes opened a drawer and pulled forth a small piece of cord that Clay recognized from his police work. Woven from synthetic fiber and capped with a hard polymer block, the devices had replaced plastic zip-ties as temporary restraints in the early part of the century. They didn't cut up the prisoner's wrists and were next to impossible to break. Once they were on, Clay was going to be trapped.

"Make a run for it." Olivia's voice was the merest whisper, so light that Clay, less than five feet away, could barely hear it. "Now's your chance!"

Oh, how good that sounded, and if not for the tinge of gleeful malice that came through even in that hushed tone, he might have done it. He could hear in her voice how badly she wanted the excuse to pull the trigger, how much she hoped he would take her wicked advice.

Clay wasn't enthusiastic about getting the shit kicked out of him and even less so about spending the rest of his life in a wheelchair, but he was not going to die by being shot in the back while running away. He stood his ground.

"Pussy," Olivia murmured as Reyes returned, and Clay could see the smirk on her face without turning to look at her.

"If you want to tell me what the Chink sent you here to do, this would be your last opportunity," Reyes said. She slipped the tie around Clay's wrists and cinched it tight, and that was it. There was nothing he could do now except hope that an opportunity to run like hell presented itself at some point during the journey to Sublevel B.

He'd meant to kill the two people responsible for his wife's death—the one who'd done the killing, and the one who'd ordered it—but now what Clay wanted was so much more. He wanted to see this woman ruined, her empire crumbling around her, her days spent in a cramped prison cell. He wanted justice for Terry, not simply cold revenge. If he got out of this, he would make it his mission to expose whatever information it was that Terry had dug up on this woman and to make sure Reyes was still alive to face that exposure.

"Let's just get on with it, you murdering bitch."

Reyes walked past him, opened the door to her office, stood by it. "What a fascinating imagination you have, Officer Foster. I wish you very many pleasant days to come."

The last line dripped with sarcasm, but Clay had no response to it. Olivia approached him—he could hear the soft tapping of her tuxedo shoes—and pressed lightly on the back of his neck with the muzzle of her gun.

"Ten hut, soldier! Head for those elevators."

With nothing left to do but follow orders, Clay began to walk forward. He passed Reyes, who gave him a parting smile that was about as false and unpleasant as any Clay had ever seen, and then he was in the empty hall. He heard Reyes close the door behind them.

"What a fun afternoon we're going to have," Olivia said. "I'm so glad you came."

"None of this makes any goddamned sense," Clay muttered, mostly to himself. "What the fuck do you even need with a SynchDrive full of test results?"

He heard laughter behind him. It should have been a pretty, sparkling sound, like a shower of jewels on a bed of harp strings, but something about it sent shivers running down his spine.

"Oh, Officer Foster. Kendra really was so very disappointed when you couldn't find that drive."

It clicked. This woman had seemed so familiar even though he'd never before in his life encountered anyone, male or female, who went around in that kind of outfit. Now he understood. Kendra. Goddamn, what balls.

"You came right up to me in my house," Clay said, not turning around. "You put on a Northeast accent and a suit that doesn't make you look like an insane person, dyed your hair, and came right back to where you murdered my wife and looked me in the eye and lied about working with her."

"And you never even *checked*!" Olivia, or Kendra, or whatever the hell her name was, exclaimed. "What sort of a police officer *are* you?"

It was true. He'd meant to check—she'd sold herself perfectly, but he'd still meant to check on her just to be sure— but his planning for The Hook had gotten in the way. He'd let Kendra and Shun Ten Industries slip from his mind.

Olivia gave a wistful sigh. "If only you'd shot me with that gun you were holding in your ridiculous little canvas purse."

Clay had nothing to say to that, and in fact did not trust himself to speak at all without saying something that would get him shot, so he stayed quiet. They reached the elevators and Olivia pushed a button, and then she came up behind him, pressed the gun into his back, and leaned in very close.

"Her hair smelled like orange blossoms," she whispered into his ear, and somehow that changed things, made the truth more real, more concrete. This woman had killed his wife, and those words were meant to let him know it, beyond a shadow of a doubt. In that moment, Clay had never hated anyone or anything more. The hatred was like a veil thrown over his eyes, turning everything not red but white. He understood for the first time that it was truly possible to be blind with rage.

Then like a lover she nuzzled him and took his earlobe between her lips for a moment and stepped back, laughing some more.

The elevator chimed and the doors opened. Clay stepped inside and the woman who had murdered Terry followed.

CHAPTER 14

A Friend in Need

"Hello, boys," Olivia said as the elevator doors opened.

The three men tasked with crippling Clay were leaning against the concrete wall. Two of them—one white, one Hispanic—boasted enormous beer guts. The third, also Hispanic, was younger and in better shape. All three were broad-shouldered and muscular. Clay guessed their combined weight at something approaching eight hundred pounds. All were dressed in dark jeans and black T-shirts. Next to them, on the ground, was a blue canvas duffel bag.

Clay thought the two with the guts were in their forties. The white guy had a long scraggly beard, going gray, shaggy brown hair, and a shapeless nose that had been broken more than once. The other one had cauliflower ears, a long black ponytail, and a rib cage that stretched a 2X shirt nearly to bursting. His face was scarred and pitted with the ghosts of what must have been a righteous acne problem in his youth.

Those two had a sort of "been there, done that" look in their eyes that told Clay this was just another job for them, like a plumber's thousandth leaky sink. The other one was the guy Clay was really worried about; he was twenty-five at the oldest, taller than the other two, and his muscle hadn't started running to fat yet. He was going to hit like a bullet train, and he looked amped out of his mind on what Clay guessed was a combination of excitement and some kind of drug—not Elixir, maybe meth. His eyeballs were practically bugging out of their sockets and he was grinning with anticipation.

The space around them was all poured composite, the walls lined with long strips of LED lighting, a few vent shafts, no windows. It looked like any other underground parking garage, but there weren't any cars visible, just a big, empty expanse. The only exit Clay could see was a solid eighty yards away, a ramp leaning up to the next level. The three men were between him and it, but Clay still felt a sliver of hope. These guys weren't built for speed. If he could catch them by surprise somehow, get around them, he could outrun them. The key was the gun. If he could get it away from the woman in white, even for a short time, even cuffed like this, he might have a chance.

"Ms. Olivia," the guy with the ponytail said, and the deferential note in his voice seemed very out of place.

"This awful man upset Ms. Reyes terribly," Olivia said. "Get moving, awful man."

She shoved Clay in the back and he stumbled forward. Ponytail didn't move out of the way but instead swung his fist hard into Clay's gut. Clay went to his knees, breath gone, fighting to keep from puking.

"Get him up on his feet." The playful teasing note had left Olivia's voice entirely and the words came out like chips of ice, terrifying in their sudden deadly seriousness.

Someone grabbed Clay by the hair and yanked upward, and he snarled in pain, forcing himself to a standing position, guts still roiling. He spun to face the man who'd done it and found himself nose-to-nose with the youngest of the three. This close, Clay could read the burning desire for violence in the kid's eyes, in the awful grinning rictus on his face, in the entire set of his body. His aggressor's black hair had been buzzed nearly to nonexistence, and Clay could see beads of sweat standing out on the red-brown skin of his scalp. He was flushed. Mottled. Tweaked out, excited, and ready for the real work to commence.

"*Voy a matarte y chinga tu madre.*" The kid's breath smelled like road tar.

"That so?" Clay slammed his head forward, using the hard ridge of bone at his brow. His aim was a little low—he'd wanted to hit the kid's nose—and he felt teeth shatter and dislodge, felt the kid's lips pop like fat, greedy leeches, bloated and straining against their skins. The kid stumbled backward and fell to his knees, hands clasped over his mouth, giving a keening howl of agony. Clay's forehead was lacerated from the broken teeth and had to be bleeding, but all he could feel at the moment was grim satisfaction.

"Mother*fucker!*" Ponytail shouted, and he swung with his meaty left hand. Clay saw a big gold ring coming for him out of the corner of his eye and ducked sideways, not avoiding the blow but at least lessening its impact. The punch caught him in the temple instead of breaking his jaw, and white spots burst across Clay's vision like fireworks. He stumbled sideways, and something hit him so hard in the side that he heard his ribs snap. A bright bolt of agony streaked through him and he cried out, almost losing his footing. No, damn it. If he went to his knees again, they would never let him back up.

Clay spun, putting his back to the kid, who was still on his knees and wailing into his hands. The garage exit was to his left, still eighty yards away. He saw that the guy with the beard had hit him with a baseball bat. The duffel bag was open now, and Clay could see another bat, a couple of knives, a ball-peen hammer, and what looked like a cattle prod. Jesus Christ, all this right here in the *parking lot*? And the NYPD was worried about Elixir?

Olivia stood with her arms crossed, observing the fight, gun at her hip, the intent expression on her face like that of someone watching the last moments of a particularly close sporting event. She had removed her hat, holding it in her right hand, and let her hair down. The image of that woman standing there, in that place, with that suit on, was baffling to Clay in his present circumstances.

"Fuckin' get up, Lu!" the guy with the ponytail shouted at the kid with the broken teeth, and after a moment the kid struggled up, stumbled drunkenly over to the duffel bag, and brought out the cattle prod and the other baseball bat. He swung around and staggered up, spitting blood and broken teeth onto the pavement. His face was a mess, his neck and hands stained crimson. The blood had formed a long, dark *V* on the front of his shirt. He tossed the baseball bat to Ponytail and slurred something unintelligible at Clay through his mangled lips. Might've been Spanish, might've been English, didn't really matter. The meaning was clear.

The guy with the beard gestured, and they spread out, flanking him, driving him back toward the wall. Clay saw Olivia following, staying close. Whether she was enjoying what was happening or not was impossible to say; her expression of intent concentration hadn't wavered.

The white guy was now on Clay's left, the ponytailed man on his right, and the kid with the cattle prod and the busted mouth directly in front of him. They were slowly tightening the half circle they'd built around him. Clay was not looking forward to getting into cattle prod range, but there was nowhere else to go, and with his hands tied behind his back, he was at a severe disadvantage, limited to using his feet and head as weapons. He glanced behind him, looking for something he might use to cut the tie at his wrists. There was nothing back there but smooth composite.

The guy with the beard, seeing Clay look away, shouted, "Get him!" and charged. The other two, taken by surprise, stood flat-footed for a moment before joining him, giving Clay a little working space. He rushed the man who was charging him, juking at the last moment as the guy swung his baseball bat, avoiding the blow. Clay brought his knee up and drove it into his adversary's bulbous gut. The guy made a coughing, whoofing groan and went to the ground. Clay lifted his leg up again and brought his foot down hard on the back of the man's head. The bearded man flopped once, like a gutted fish, and lay still.

The kid with the cattle prod was almost on him, spraying out wet and bloody Spanish profanities, swinging his weapon two-handed over his head like a sledgehammer. Clay counted his blessings; someone who wasn't an idiot would have led with the prod's pronged end, stabbing forward as if wielding a rapier, and probably would have connected. The genius in front of him hadn't thought of that, which let Clay sidestep and avoid the attack. The cattle prod hit the concrete tip-first. Clay stomped down, hoping to snap the thing in half, but the kid was quick and hauled it out of the way in time.

Clay heard footsteps to his right and brought his shoulder up instinctively, saving himself some pretty severe skull trauma at the hands of Ponytail, who had swung his baseball bat with all the force of a major-league hitter seeking a home run. Clay's shoulder took the blow instead. "Fuck!" he shouted and danced backward, narrowly avoiding tripping over the bearded guy. Having acquired some distance, he stopped moving, and the group came again to a temporary standstill.

"Am I going to have to get involved here, Pastor?" Olivia asked in a flat voice. She was standing a few feet behind the kid with the mashed lips.

"We got this," Ponytail said.

Olivia's intent, almost angry expression hadn't changed since the fight began, but now she flicked a quick glance over to the thug, curled her lip in a brief sneer, and made a scoffing noise. "He has his hands tied behind his back and he's already killed one of you."

"Gonna pay for that, motherfucker," the kid said, the first clear words he'd delivered in English.

Clay spit. "I think I'll break one of your shins next."

The kid almost took the bait. Clay saw his eyes go wide and knew he would've charged if the other man hadn't called out, "Hold up! Lu, you fuckin' shithead, he'll just do you like he did Teddy."

The two men exchanged a glance and began again to advance on Clay, who was out of room to back up. He waited, watching the tip of the cattle prod, making sure he knew exactly where it was. That thing would put him on the ground in an instant, and on the ground he might as well be dead. Lu and Pastor would not break him fast now. They'd take their time, drawing it out as retribution for their dead friend.

Elixir

Just as Lu got within striking range with the cattle prod, Clay feinted left. The kid took the bait, lunging forward with the prod toward the space he thought Clay was headed for, but Clay shifted direction back toward Pastor, whose eyes popped open in surprise. These guys were obviously used to overwhelming an untrained and probably helpless opponent, getting him down, and then doing their work while the man lay curled up on the ground. Fighting someone who was much quicker and had real combat training seemed a new experience for them.

Pastor didn't have time to raise his baseball bat before Clay hit him, shoulder lowered like a football player. The hit caught the man off-balance and he staggered backward, throwing his hands out for balance and losing his grip on the bat. Clay heard it clatter to the ground and he spun again, felt Luis's hands grab at his shirt and miss their hold, and shoved his way past them. He had a clear line of sight to the exit and, goddamn it, he was going for it, gun or no gun. It was the only chance he had.

Clay tensed his legs and propelled himself forward, beginning the sprint. That was when Olivia, standing to his left, dipped her hand to her hip and pulled her gun. Jesus Christ, she was fast. Faster than anyone Clay had ever seen, like a trick shooter out of some ancient Western. Her hand snapped forth like a snake ambushing its prey, the gun sounded, and the bullet bounced off the pavement less than a foot in front of Clay's feet. He came to a skidding halt.

"Oh, Officer Foster, that's definitely not how this plays out," Olivia said, and she smiled at him. Clay thought it was the most sincere expression he'd seen the woman make, a malicious look of enjoyment that made it very clear who was in

207

charge. All of this was simply theater for her amusement, and it didn't matter what he did to her bumbling thugs; this woman was blindingly fast even while maintaining pinpoint aim. He wasn't going anywhere.

Then something hit him in the back like a shell from a howitzer, and time skipped a beat. When next he was aware, he was on his knees on the concrete and his back felt like someone had coated it in kerosene and lit it up. The cattle prod—while he'd been marveling at Olivia's speed, the kid had come up behind him and jabbed him in the back with it. Now he was down and it was all over. Clay turned his head in time to see a big black boot coming down, and there was a sickening wet crunch inside his head as his nose broke.

Clay fell to his side, instinctively turtling, pulling himself into as much of a fetal position as he could with his arms bound, trying to protect his head and neck as the beating began in earnest.

* * *

When they took their first break, Clay was still conscious. He'd lost track of the individual blows, but he didn't think they'd broken anything more than his nose, a few fingers, and a couple more ribs. Clay was aching all over, lying panting on the concrete, his face covered with blood and spit and snot. He felt like a piñata, and he knew this little fiesta was just getting rolling. Stomping on his bound hands, kicking at his arms and legs with their steel-toe boots—even the hits with the bat were little love taps compared with what was coming next.

As if to prove this point, Clay saw both men turn from the duffel bag and stand, each carrying a knife roughly the size of Rhode Island.

"Remember not to kill him," Olivia said. "Oh, and make sure to leave an eye so he can still look in the mirror."

She was leaning against the wall, arms crossed again, watching with a small smile on her face. Clay tried to tell her to go fuck herself. His ears were full of a high-pitched whine that drowned out his own voice, so he had no idea what the words sounded like, but if they'd come out as anything other than a gargling rasp, she didn't react.

"What about his tongue?" Pastor said. "We owe him something for Teddy."

"I can't see why he'd need it," Olivia said. Clay groaned, kicked with his legs, wedged them against the concrete, and tried to shove himself toward the exit. It was still about two hundred feet away. Might as well have been two million. Clay closed his eyes. He tried to pull Terry's face up in his mind, and the first image he got was his wife's lifeless body lying on that metal table in the morgue, eyes black and puffy, forehead scraped down to the bone. A wave of despair swept over him.

This is how it ends. This is all I could do for her.

Pastor grabbed him by the hair and jerked his head back like a man getting ready to cut a pig's throat. "Open wide, *mamon*."

Clay clenched his jaw tight, eyes still closed, not fighting, expending all his energy on picturing his wife again, the way she was meant to look. He wanted that image in his head when these motherfuckers pried his mouth open and cut out his tongue, wanted to remember to the end why he was here, what he had done this for. He felt a cold metal blade press against his lips and drew them back in a grimace, teeth still clamped together.

"Pry 'em open!" Pastor said to the younger guy, Luis, and Clay heard the kid's knife clatter to the ground. A hand wrapped itself painfully around his lower jaw, pulling downward. The top of the knife began to twist and turn, seeking entry, scraping against his teeth. Clay heard himself making growling noises of helpless rage. He could feel his jaw weakening, could feel the knife beginning to slip between his teeth. In a few moments more, they would carve his tongue off like a slice from a roast.

In those final moments, he brought her forth, whole and alive like he wanted, so real he felt he could open his eyes and still see her. There she was in her wedding dress, hands resting on his chest, eyes open and locked with his. His favorite memory. Christ, how he missed her.

That was when Clay heard tires screeching through the ringing in his ears. The sound came from one level above, and as it echoed down through the garage, Pastor and Luis stopped what they were doing. Clay's eyes shot open and he saw Olivia bolt toward the elevators and disappear into the stairwell. The two thugs, much less quick and apparently not gifted with the woman's sense of self preservation, were staring at the ramp. Luis had taken his hands away from Clay's jaw, allowing him to turn his head. He did so and saw a thing of such beauty that it rivaled the image of his wife that he'd only just summoned up.

Two NYPD patrol cars were barreling toward them, lights flashing blue and red on the gray concrete walls. They covered the distance in a matter of seconds and came to a screeching halt just as Luis and Pastor were getting to their feet. Two uniformed officers leaped from their passenger-side seats and leveled their weapons at Clay's assailants.

"Drop the fucking knives and put your hands in the air!" one of them shouted, and that was enough to send Luis, already hyped up on drugs and the pure adrenaline that came with getting ready to cut someone's tongue out, off the deep end. He shrieked some mushy oath at the cops and charged, knife held above his head two-handed, like a man about to plant a stake in a vampire's chest. He made it about three steps before the cops opened fire and cut him down, filling his chest with bullets. Clay saw bloody chunks blast out of the back of the kid's T-shirt in at least half a dozen places.

Pastor shrieked, a noise of pure anguish, and Clay understood immediately from the tone that the guy had just watched his son get gunned down in the middle of a parking garage. He wanted to shout at the officers, tell them to keep this one alive, that they needed any information they could get on Olivia and Reyes, but he couldn't summon the energy to try. Even if he had, he doubted they would have heard or understood, especially with Pastor howling like some kind of goddamned werewolf and waving his knife around.

"Drop it!" one of the cops shouted again. "Drop it or I *will* shoot!"

"I fucked both your mothers in the ass!" Pastor told them and stepped forward. Three seconds later, he was lying face down in an expanding pool of blood. Clay could hear cautious footsteps approaching him.

"You okay, buddy?"

Clay wheezed out a laugh. "Been better."

He heard another door open, heard more footsteps, saw black shoes stop close to his face. With a great effort, Clay turned his head and looked up. It seemed to take a while; the officer before him was about thirty feet tall. At last Clay got to the man's face, though it seemed now that a dark gray fog was descending over everything. After a moment, he realized he knew this cop.

"Clay, my friend," Haley said, "I do believe they call that 'the nick of time.'"

Clay put his head down, closed his eyes, and went somewhere else.

* * *

Clay came to in a squad car, leaning against the door, and found that the blood on his face had dried and he was stuck to the window. It took him a few attempts to pull free, each sending excruciating bolts of pain through his broken ribs. He must have said something, or made a noise, because Haley swung his head around, looking back at Clay from the front seat.

"Still with us, Officer?"

They were moving down a wide four-lane avenue—Clay didn't know which one. The siren wasn't on, but they must've been using the flashers; the drivers of cabs and other vehicles were grudgingly moving out of the way to let them pass.

"Yes," Clay said. "Yes, I—ah, goddamn it."

He spit a tooth into his cupped hands, stared at it for a moment, and carefully put it into his shirt pocket. He heard Haley give a short incredulous chuckle. "Jesus Christ."

"Yeah." It wasn't the first tooth Clay had lost. A hit from the stock of a rifle had previously cost him four. Maybe they'd be able to put this one back, maybe not. Didn't matter. Oral surgeons were goddamned artists with the new polymers that companies were coming up with, now that all of their R&D departments weren't legally mandated to focus on the rising oceans. In most ways, Clay's false teeth were superior to his real ones.

"We're taking you to a hospital," Haley said.

Clay grunted, shaking his head. "They can get to me there."

"Maybe you missed it, but we did a pretty good job of making sure 'they' won't be getting to anyone anywhere."

"No, not them. Those assholes ... not the problem. People I'm worried about are still out there."

"Listen, Clay, I have no idea what you're talking about. We got an anonymous call that you were being beat to shit in a parking garage. We responded. Turns out the caller was right. You want to clue me in?"

Clay tried to make his brain work. "I pissed off some people."

"And we'd like to arrest them."

Clay shook his head. "Forget it. It's complicated. Who the fuck would call about ... Could you trace it?"

In the forties, Brooklyn had installed autotracers that could pinpoint the location of every call coming into the precinct to within a few feet of its origin, usually in less than a second. The tech was widespread, and there was no doubt the NYPD used it as well.

"Encrypted," Haley said. "It told us the call was coming from northern Alaska. Voice was all messed up, too."

"That's expensive equipment." Clay had had his own call with a messed-up voice not so long ago. Interesting, but not something he wanted to share with Haley right now. He stretched and grimaced. Now that he was waking back up, the various cuts and bruises and breaks were beginning to clamor, each demanding his attention with increasing fervor.

"I'll start rounding up all the millionaires in the city. Hope you've got a few years."

Clay had an idea for a millionaire they could start with, and he almost said her name before realizing it made no sense. Why would Reyes order him beaten and then immediately call it in to the police? But who else would have done it? No one had known he was down there except for Reyes, Olivia, and the three thugs.

He worked it over in his mind for a time, staring out the window. Finally he sighed. "I have no idea what the fuck is going on."

"Let us get you some help, Clay. You took a hell of an ass-kicking. I'm surprised you're awake."

"If you want to do me a favor, drop me in a random spot near a liquor store and let me disappear with a bottle of whiskey."

"Cut the bullshit. I'll post a guard if you want it, but I'm not taking you anywhere but a hospital."

Clay hadn't been in a hospital since his time in Virginia. He wasn't looking forward to visiting one now, though the prospect of painkillers was deeply enticing, but Haley's voice made it clear there would be no arguing with him.

"Post two guards." Clay knew it wouldn't be enough if Olivia decided to move against him. He wondered if he could persuade someone to get him a gun to keep under his pillow, and thought it unlikely.

For a time they rode in silence. Clay watched the buildings go by, marveling even in his discomfort at just how goddamn clean the city was. Maybe in the last century New York had been a cesspit, and maybe Queens and the Bronx still were, but Manhattan looked better than anywhere else he'd ever been. Parts of it seemed almost to glow. He wished Terry could have seen it.

After a while Haley turned to him again. "Whoever it is you think ordered this beating ... do I need to worry about you waging some kind of war in my city?"

"It doesn't matter. Forget it."

Haley raised an eyebrow, and Clay saw that the man wasn't going to forget anything that had been said in this car. He regretted bringing it up in the first place, would never have mentioned anyone but the three thugs if he hadn't been coming out of battered unconsciousness. There wasn't a scrap of proof he could provide about Reyes, and now Haley had to worry that as soon as Clay had healed up, he was going to embark on some bloodthirsty campaign of revenge.

It was the right thing to worry about.

CHAPTER 15

Inwood

Haley had kept his word, posting two guards outside Clay's room at the hospital. He'd assured Clay they were trustworthy, which hadn't done much for Clay's sense of security. He'd seen Olivia acting, had himself been fooled by "Kendra," and knew that if she wanted to gain access to the hospital, she'd be able to do so. From there the two cops would barely be a speed bump.

The doctors had set his fingers and nose, wrapped his ribs, and put about a thousand pounds of salve on his cuts and abrasions. He hadn't been able to look at any of the nurses, couldn't meet their eyes, had felt a tremendous wave of relief each time they'd left. Christ, all he could think about in this place was Terry.

No one killed him on the first night, which Clay had spent fighting the painkillers in his system, trying to stay awake and mostly failing. He had twice woken shouting out, waving his aching arms at imagined aggressors. Both times the room had been empty and he'd had to endure an embarrassing visit from the cops outside. They'd been courteous, but Clay could tell they didn't understand why they'd been ordered to protect a man who refused to disclose who'd had him beaten.

In the morning two new guards were swapped in. Clay didn't interact with them. Didn't do much of anything, really, except sleep in fits and starts. It felt safer during the day, which wasn't saying much. Clay wouldn't feel safe again until he was certain Olivia was dead. That woman was a viper.

The second night was better. The nanotreatments had already done enough work that Clay had refused his pain medication, and while the dark hours weren't comfortable, he didn't mind. It made it easier to stay awake. Clay spent the time going over and over the events that had happened at MWP in his head. Who had known? Who had made the call?

He'd ruled out Aiken. The man in charge of the security booth wouldn't have had any way of knowing that Clay was getting the shit kicked out of him. The receptionist from the sixth floor, the one who looked like a model? That made no sense either. But there hadn't been anyone else. The Chink? Had the worm that Clay had installed given the information broker access to the building's security feeds? But no, Reyes had told him she was shutting those feeds. The Chink's worm couldn't deliver data that wasn't being streamed to the network in the first place.

It was past midnight when it hit him, and as soon as the name came into his mind, he could see how all the pieces fit. The money, the scrambling equipment, the access to the security feeds, the knowledge of Clay's presence in the building and what Reyes would have done to him. There had been a moment, after he pulled that fire alarm and the executive offices were emptying, where Clay was sure he was about to be caught. A moment when MWP's fat figurehead of a CEO had seemed to stare right at him.

He'd thought it simply a coincidence after the man had moved on but now believed otherwise. Alex Szarka had seen him, understood his purpose, and decided not to alert the others to Clay's presence. He had done that, and later, when he came to realize what was happening in the building's parking garage, he had called the police. But why? Why let Clay in, and why bail him out afterward, unless ...

"Maybe the motherfucker's not quite as clueless as he's been letting people think," Clay muttered.

He picked up the new tablet that Haley's people had brought him, but what good would it do? It wasn't like he could simply look up Szarka's contact information and give him a call. The man's number was surely unlisted, and Clay had no police business he could use as an excuse to call for a lookup. Haley wouldn't have it. No one Clay knew would have it.

Except the Chink.

"Great. Wonder what he'll want for it this time."

Sighing and rolling his eyes, Clay began keying in a message.

* * *

Clay left the hospital at seven in the morning against the advice of his doctors and against the requests of the two police officers who had, an hour earlier, replaced the men who had stayed with him through the night. They wanted him to remain until they could get in touch with Haley, but the inspector was proving hard to track down. After thirty minutes of waiting for them to get their shit together, Clay gave up, went to the front desk, and signed himself out. He walked into the early morning sunlight with the two cops following behind him, still protesting.

"We're going to have to take you in," one of them said, and Clay turned, one eyebrow raised. The man's face was ruddy, flushed with the embarrassment of having his authority ignored and the frustration of spending the last thirty minutes getting the runaround on the phone.

"What are the charges?" Clay's pass was still valid, no one had filed any complaint against him, and he had signed all the paperwork for his discharge. "Is there some kind of Manhattan law that lets cops detain someone in a hospital against their will?"

The cop stammered, trying to find an answer, and couldn't come up with anything.

His partner shrugged. "Whatever, man. We can't hold him if he doesn't want to stick around."

"Which I don't," Clay said. "I need to get the hell out of here. I'll call Haley myself. There's a better chance he'll want to talk to me, anyway."

"Why don't you go back to Brooklyn?" the first cop said. "Go back to your shit precinct with the rest of the losers."

Clay gave him a broad grin. "Afraid your boss will figure it out?"

"What's that?"

"That guys from a *real* city might make better cops than a couple of assholes whose big bust this week was giving a jaywalking ticket to a rich old lady?"

"Hey, fuck you, man!" the second cop said.

Clay turned to him."Come to Brooklyn sometime. See how long you last. Until then, thanks for the bodyguarding, and go fuck yourselves."

Clay walked. He listened to their footsteps to see if they were going to come after him for that last comment, but they let him go. The streets were busy with morning commuters, and within a few minutes he'd lost himself in the crowd. He kept his head up, staying alert; there was still the possibility that Olivia had been watching him this entire time, waiting for him to leave the hospital. He didn't think she'd attempt an up-close assassination with this many witnesses, but it wasn't hard to imagine a rifle pointed at his head from any one of the thousands of windows he was passing. He had to get off the streets and find a better place to hole up.

The nanotreatments were doing their work, and in another couple of days his bones would be healed, his bruises and scrapes gone. Already he felt much better, but he still ached all over, especially his ribs. Just breathing was uncomfortable, and if he forgot himself and turned too quickly, a jolt of pain would blast through him. He needed more time.

Clay stopped at a bank and transferred a large quantity of funds to what criminals called a "disco card"—it worked like any other banking card but wasn't tied to any fingerprints or retinas and was disconnected from the cloud. The cards were legal but risky. Lose it or have it stolen and the money was gone. Clay knew that Reyes could have his Manhattan pass revoked and perhaps also freeze access to his accounts, so he had to take the risk. He was surprised she hadn't done it already.

Clay grabbed a coffee from a street vendor and paired it with a bagel. He paid the man and kept moving. Manhattan had nothing that remotely resembled the seedy flop in which he'd stayed, briefly, in The Hook. More was the pity; that sort of place was exactly what he needed right now. Any hotel in this city would want two forms of ID, at which point he might as well launch signal flares and perhaps telephone Reyes to let her know where he was.

Why hadn't they come for him at the hospital?

That was the biggest question, and Clay didn't have an answer for it. There was no question that Olivia would've been able to neutralize the two cops outside his door, but she hadn't come. No attempts had been made on his life, and Clay had no idea why. If the situation had been reversed, if it had been Olivia sitting helpless in a hospital bed without so much as a pistol for protection, he'd have come for her.

Clay headed down into the subway. It would be much easier to tell if he was followed in the confined space. He supposed it was possible that Reyes had access to the city's ubiquitous cameras, and if that was the case, they'd be able to track him any time he showed his face in public, but he thought it likely she would need to file a criminal case against him to have that option. If she'd done that, the officers who'd tried to detain him at the hospital would have brought it up.

No one was following him. He spent two hours moving from train to train, taking a random path around the island, watching the faces of those in his car and those getting into and out of the cars around him. If there was anyone trailing him, they were better at it than anyone he'd ever encountered, and as much respect as he had for Olivia's abilities, he didn't think even she could've stayed with him while simultaneously avoiding his gaze for this long. Not unless she was a shapeshifter, anyway, because dyeing her hair wasn't going to do it anymore.

Clay didn't have access to any scrambling tech. He had switched off his tablet in order to prevent tracking, and he wasn't thrilled about contacting Haley on a standard vidphone, at least not until he'd learned more. He didn't want to go back to the inspector until he could lay it all out. He doubted he could convince the man, but he was going to try. Haley would be a powerful ally if he could be made to believe that Elena Reyes was the type to order the murder of a cop's wife.

He didn't want to call Haley, and he didn't want to spend a lot of time in highly trafficked places, so Clay took a train north, as far as he could go without leaving the island, and got off at the Dyckman Street Station, in the neighborhood of Inwood. Far removed from the bustle of the city and populated mainly by people who worked farther south, it was one of the least crowded areas of Manhattan during the day. It was here he would try for a hotel room.

There wasn't a whole lot of choice. Inwood was still largely residential, and the only lodging available was a cheap chain motel on the edge of the Harlem River. The clerk was maybe twenty-two, black, with a pleasant grin that revealed bad teeth. Tall, skinny, and gawky, with a suit half a size too big for him, he looked like a high school kid who'd borrowed his dad's dress clothes for a formal.

"Help you?" he asked, trying unsuccessfully not to stare at the bruises and cuts on Clay's face.

Clay tried on a friendly smile. "Definitely. I need a room. And before you ask, yes, I'm okay. Got hit by a car riding my bike, but ... well, you should see the car."

The kid—his name tag read "Jeff" and said he was a manager, which seemed impossible to Clay—chuckled a little at that. "Man, wow ... that sucks. All right, sure thing. I just need an ID and a bank card for deposit."

"How much will it cost me to, uh ... dispense with the formality of all that?"

Jeff looked utterly confused for a moment, and then something seemed to click. "Oh, uh ... no, I can't ... I mean, the system won't even print a key without them."

"You're a manager, right, Jeff? Don't tell me you don't have an override."

"I don't want to get involved with anything, you know? It's nothing personal."

Clay shook his head. "There's nothing to get involved with. I'm in the city for business, right? But I figure, why not also have a little pleasure while I'm here? But the old lady, she's not so understanding. So I got one of these."

He set the disco card down on the counter. Jeff's eyes flicked down to it and back up.

"So I'm thinking, let's skip the ID and the charges that'll show up on my statement. You got a girlfriend?"

"I do," Jeff said.

"Bet she'd love a night out on the town."

Jeff narrowed his eyes a bit. "It'd have to be a pretty good night. Wait ... are you a cop? Is this some kind of setup?"

"It'd be a real nice night. And I *am* a cop, actually, but not NYPD. I got nothing to do with anything. I just want a room. I might call some ... company, later, and I need a place to entertain them."

Jeff looked both ways, then back at Clay, his mouth a tight line. "Look, unless you got, like, a thousand bucks for me, forget it."

"Will a thousand get it done?"

The kid's eyes widened. "You serious?"

"You set the key on the counter, I swipe my card, you see the cash come through, I take they key. All right?"

It was all right, and in the end Clay found himself in Room 304, as safe as he was going to get on this island without somehow mutating his DNA. He sat down to check his messages and saw one in particular that interested him greatly. It was encrypted at a level that was only supposed to be available to police and government agencies, but it had come from neither.

> *The man you are looking for can meet you this afternoon at a location of your choosing. Give an address. Make sure your reply is encrypted, lest your visitor be much younger and much blonder than you'd like. —C*

Well, all right. Clay glanced at the motel's stationery, found the address, and sent it to the Chink along with his room number. A few moments later, another message came through.

> *2 PM. Listen for three knocks. You now "owe me one," Mr. Foster. Don't think I won't collect. —C*

No, he had no illusions about that. Sooner or later, the Chink was going to ask him for something. What it was and whether Clay would be willing to deliver, he didn't know and wasn't enthusiastic about finding out. Still, it was something, which was better than nothing. It was, of course, possible that the Chink was ratting him out and by doing so settling whatever feud it was he had with Reyes, but there was no other way to get to Szarka.

Clay glanced at the clock and saw it was noon. His stomach rumbled. The bagel and coffee were long used up. He wanted to take a shower, but lunch seemed an even better idea. Order in or risk going out?

"Fuck it. Let's take a walk."

CHAPTER 16

Benefactor

Clay had been out of the shower for about ten minutes when someone knocked on his door. The rapping came at exactly two in the afternoon, a confident noise, three solid taps in rapid succession. Clay found himself wishing for the gun he'd left in the safe at his previous hotel, but he couldn't exactly go there now to pick it up.

"Step back from the door," he said as he crossed the room and looked through the peephole. A single rotund figure was standing with his back to the far wall, eyebrows raised, looking slightly amused. It was either Alex Szarka or a remarkable body double.

"Are you armed?"

"I am not." The man's voice was barely muffled by the cheap motel door.

"All right." Clay opened the door. The two men eyed each other.

"Pleasure to meet you," Szarka said at last.

"Get in. Stand with your back to me and don't move."

The man's look of amusement grew, but he did what he was told, and Clay shut the door behind him and threw the deadbolt. "I don't believe I've had this done since I attended my last rock concert, some years ago," He said as Clay frisked him.

"Not taking any chances," Clay said. The man was clean, and that was a good sign. "Go sit on the chair at the far end of the room."

Szarka again obeyed orders. Clay stood in the entryway, arms crossed, looking at him.

"I am not an enemy, Mr. Foster." Szarka smiled. He was short and heavyset, with thick, curly dark hair, porcine jowls, and a Stalin mustache underneath a bulbous nose. His eyes were tiny black pinpricks under heavy brows, set far apart on his face. He was wearing a suit that must have cost him tens of thousands of dollars.

"Maybe you're not. How would I know?"

The man shrugged. "If I were, would not the wisest course of action be simply to blow open your door and come through, guns blazing?"

He had a point. Still ... "Maybe you're trying to get some info out of me. Maybe you think I know where the drive is."

"I don't need that information from you," Szarka said. "Please sit down, Officer. You've been injured and I doubt that you've healed enough yet for standing to be terribly comfortable."

He hadn't, and his ribs were aching, but Clay wasn't sure he wanted to get off his feet just yet. "No offense, but friends of Elena Reyes don't exactly put me at ease."

Szarka gave him a bitter smile. "Then it will be a great relief for you to know that Elena Reyes is in no way any friend of mine, and it's due to a true, deep desire to see her life destroyed, as she has destroyed mine, that I am sitting here."

Clay studied him for a moment longer and then sat on the edge of the bed, still a healthy distance from Szarka. He didn't think this man was any physical threat, even in his own limited physical condition, but it never hurt to be cautious.

"Thank you for trusting me," Szarka said.

"I don't know that we've gotten that far yet, but we'll see. Did anyone see you at the front desk?"

"No. There was no attendant and I didn't ring the bell."

"Good. So let's get to it. Why'd you call the police when Reyes was having me beat up in the parking lot? It *was* you, right?"

Szarka leaned back in his chair. "It was. When I saw you hiding there—and for that you can thank the expensive ocular implants which correct my ever-degrading vision—I understood your intent. Not the specifics, of course, but surely you had come to do *something* untoward up in those offices. I decided not to stop you, at least not right then. I knew that Olivia was still up there and that you wouldn't get too terribly far with her around, which gave me the time I needed to find out who you were. Once I gathered that information and determined that we are very likely on the same side, I checked the video feeds to see if I could locate you, saw the beating taking place, and called the police."

"Reyes said she shut off those feeds."

"She did. I have a private set of which she's unaware."

That was one mystery solved. Clay moved on to the next. "You said that you're on my side, which means you're against Reyes. You run the company. Why not fire her?"

Szarka grimaced. "I am the majority shareholder of the company, it's true. My father set it up that way, against the protests that I was equipped with neither the talent nor the desire to manage a corporation of this size. Those protests were not ... unreasonable. If not for Elena's abilities as a businesswoman—and they are immense, do not doubt it— Manhattan Water and Power would have foundered. Her vision has taken it to places beyond anything even my father could have imagined."

"Being willing to have your opponents murdered probably helps."

Szarka nodded. "Yes. And I would be rid of her if it were that simple. It is not. For one thing, I need the approval of our board of directors, which they would never give. For another, she has leverage that could be used against me."

"She's blackmailing you?"

"In a sense. It's never been spoken, but it doesn't need to be. You're familiar with Elixir from your line of work, I assume?"

"Way too familiar."

"As am I, on an entirely different level. Intimately familiar, to my everlasting regret."

Szarka couldn't meet his eyes now, and after a moment Clay understood. "You're hooked. You're a licker."

The man nodded, jowls quivering, and for a moment Clay thought he was going to start sobbing. Instead he took a breath and looked up. "I want you to understand that I am not ... For all the money in my life, I was never one of those rich children who fall into drugs or other reckless behavior. My father, rest his soul, raised me to be better than that. It ... She ..."

The man couldn't finish. Clay could hear agony in his voice. Despair. Shame. "Reyes is responsible, isn't she? Somehow she got you hooked?"

"She exploited my trust!" Szarka cried, and now there was a whining, wheedling note in his voice that Clay didn't like. He sounded like a child trying to get out of something.

"Doubt she held you down and dropped the stuff into your mouth."

"It was early on, before the drug's strength was known. She told me there was no addiction rate, that it was no more harmful than alcohol. We were having martinis. She offered and I accepted. She did it *with* me, goddamn her, from the very same ampule, and it was fine. It was all fine, for months, and then ..."

"And then it wasn't." Clay had heard this story from a hundred junkies. A thousand. It was all fine until it wasn't. Some switch had flipped for Szarka, just as it had flipped for all the rest.

"I need it every single day, and Elena knows it. She has exploited this need. It's very difficult to get Elixir in this city, even now, but not for her. She supplies me with what I need, and I make no trouble as she maneuvers me into early retirement, assumes control of my shares, and takes my company from me."

"Until she ends up blowing everything on Elixir, or dropping too much and dying."

Szarka gave a grim shake of his head. "She's not addicted. I've seen her take it many times, but she's never gone over the edge. She's never moved to *needing* it."

"Everybody does eventually. She will, too."

"What's the longest period you've heard of between use and addiction?"

Clay shrugged. "I don't know ... eight months? Maybe ten for a super-casual licker?"

"Elena's been using Elixir multiple times a week for at least two years. Far longer than I have, far longer than *anyone* has without making that move. I told her it would happen and she laughed at me. Said I understood nothing. Somehow, she can use it at her leisure without the switch ever flipping."

"That's impossible. How could she do it?"

"I don't *know*!" Szarka slammed his fist on his meaty thigh, clenched his teeth, and looked out the window. "The drug is doing nothing to her, even as she snaps up land in Brooklyn that has been absolutely *blighted* by Elixir."

This was news to Clay. "Why's she doing that? I guess she could sell it back someday if the city turns around, but ... does she really need more money? She's about to force you out and become the richest person in the country. What else does she want?"

Szarka favored him with a grim smile. "Power. Isn't it always about power, once wealth is no longer an issue?"

"So why doesn't she fucking run for mayor?"

Szarka gave a disdainful chortle. "Mayor? What power does the mayor have? Mayors answer to the people, and every four years they need to sing and dance and beg for another run. Egomaniacs run for mayor. The powerful control their worlds in much more subtle, much more real ways."

"What does grabbing up parts of Brooklyn that've been turned into a hellhole give her, then?"

"She plans to finish the consolidation of power that the war started. She wants to make New York its own superpower, the center of the United States and the largest, strongest city on the planet, and she wants it all to run on my—her—electricity.

Manhattan Water and Power, with Elena Reyes at the helm, will provide the beating pulse for the city that proves a model for the rest of the world."

Clay raised an eyebrow. "I still have no idea how buying out Elixir dens in Brooklyn helps with that."

"She wishes to bring Brooklyn back to New York. Manhattan's boundaries are overflowing, and it cannot continue to exist behind its walls if it wishes to expand. Brooklyn can contain the overflow, and she will own that land. Brooklyn can also house future reactors and an unprecedented power distribution system that will make Manhattan Water and Power the largest and most important distributor of electricity in the world. The infrastructure is already there, waiting for her. The fusion reactors on Long Island sitting dark, delayed by the war. The transatlantic cables that terminate in the bay ...

"This is a *global* play. Entire governments will be beholden to a company that, thanks to my retirement and subsequent surrender of my shares, she will own 67 percent of. Enough not only for majority control but for absolute power to veto or force through her plans regardless of the board's objections. In effect, she will re-privatize the company. Sitting in her walled fortress, she will build an empire."

Clay made a low whistle. "This lady is out of her fucking mind."

"She may be, but it doesn't matter. She will sit back and watch Brooklyn crumble just to try."

"How did you figure all of this out?"

Szarka gave a slow shake of his head. "I told you Elena holds no great respect for me. This has proven something of a blessing. She suspects me of no treachery because she doubts I would be clever enough to pull it off. She's wrong. It has taken me months to piece this information together through slow and very careful accessing of records, acquiring certain encryption keys, and overhearing conversations that I was, of course, not intended to overhear."

"And you kept it to yourself ... Why? Take this drug shit to the press, man! Let them know that she's a licker. Nail her to the wall."

Szarka raised one bushy eyebrow. "You've met the woman in the white suit."

"Give me a fucking break. You're New York royalty. You're sitting on a fortune that you couldn't spend even if you tried. Whatever Reyes is paying that chick, you can afford to pay her more."

"If you knew her at all, you would understand." Szarka sighed again. "There is no amount of money in the world that will deter Olivia once she's been set on someone. She's chosen to give Elena her loyalty, and that choice is absolute. It's not about money ... If I tried to bribe her or hire her away, she would take such affront that she'd probably kill me on the spot. The possibility of my violent death at the hands of that woman is horrifying, and for a long time I was paralyzed by fear of her reprisal. As I sank deeper into my addiction and all my attempts to conquer it proved futile, I came to realize that greater risk must be endured."

"Fantastic." Clay's ribs were hurting and he wanted to sit in a chair with a back, but the bed was the only option in the room. "If Olivia's that into knocking people off, why didn't she come for me at the hospital?"

"The police showing up at such an unexpected time has made Elena a bit gun-shy. I believe she's pulled back on any activities until she can determine what happened."

"Are you safe?"

"I believe so, but it doesn't matter. We must act now. I've begun to assemble the evidence against Elena, and I am not alone. An associate of mine contacted you, in fact, not long ago, before he was forced into hiding."

"What? Who?"

"I won't reveal his name just yet, but he told me that he called you and arranged to meet at a park near your home."

"No shit? I thought that was just Olivia getting me out of my house so she could toss it again and try to find my wife's SynchDrive."

"That would have been a waste of her time. Your wife hid the drive somewhere far from your home."

"So where is it?"

"I don't know, b—"

"Jesus Christ ..."

"But my associate does. He may even have the drive on him, but he can't do anything with it, because we need something from you."

Clay nodded. "You need me because I'm the only person left alive who knows her encryption key."

Szarka smiled at him. "That's entirely correct, though it's not the only thing we need you for."

"Well, before I sign up for anything else, why don't you tell me what the fuck is on this drive and why it's so important."

Szarka didn't look put out by this demand. If anything, he seemed pleased. "The drive contains a very large quantity of data harvested from Anuhya Imran's archives, and those of various others, by your wife, at my associate's behest. There is likely to be all sorts of interesting and valuable information within, but one item in particular is vital to the cause. It is the chemical code for a counter-drug, one meant to neutralize both Elixir's effects and its addictive qualities."

"A cure."

"Exactly that. The Elixir addict takes this drug and Elixir loses its hold over them."

"Why the hell would Imran have a cure for Elixir in her archives? Shun Ten's not a pharmaceutical company."

"I'm afraid I don't know the answer to that question. My associate has all of the information and can tell you more."

"So someone just takes this drug and no more shakes? No more pain or nausea? No more cravings?"

"I believe so. Of course, they also lose the benefits—the euphoria, the energy, the feeling that all is well in the world. These are strong draws, and some will, to be sure, choose to continue their addiction. Your work will not be ended, Officer Foster, but many would gladly be rid of their need for the drug even if it meant losing access to its positive effects. I am one such addict."

"You seem pretty stable compared to most of the lickers I've known," Clay said, but was that true? Brooklyn Heights had been full of well-to-do addicts who had managed to keep the drug's hold on them from completely destroying their lives, at least so far.

"I'm careful and regimented. I take the drug in the early morning hours and proceed about my day when the effects have worn off. This has worked for me, but time is growing short. I now often wake two or three hours early, craving my next dose. These cravings will grow worse and become physically painful, and I will begin taking the drug earlier. Inevitably as the window continues to shorten, I will double up, taking two doses per day. This is the same process you've no doubt observed many times.

"It happens much faster with the addicts you deal with because they lack the knowledge, desire, and willpower that I have. A typical Elixir user would be—what was your term?— 'licking' three times a day by now. I'm not, but I'll get there, and by then I'll have been forced into retirement. Elena will either blackmail me or reveal my problem to the board and force them into a vote of no confidence. It was the unstated threat of the latter that compelled me to execute the legal documents that will give her all but a nominal portion of my equity upon my departure."

"Well, fine, so I've got the encryption key and you've got the guy who knows where the drive is. Take me to him, we go get it, and—bam—you're cured."

Szarka shook his head. "My apologies, but he is extremely averse to meeting in person. Additionally, when I said the drive contained data on the cure, what I should have said was 'half of the data.' The other half is somewhere else."

"Where's that?"

"We're hoping the answer to that is on your wife's SynchDrive."

Terrific. "All right. What else has to happen?"

"My associate is a journalist who was working with your wife. He can't take this story public until he understands the link with Reyes. She had your wife killed—why? We have to know. If he begins giving information out in pieces as he continues the investigation, he'll be dead before the week is out. It has to happen all at once, a simultaneous publication and data release to dozens of media outlets. A tidal wave of evidence that will engulf Elena and make it impossible for her to buy her way out of prosecution ... Even then, Olivia must be dealt with."

Clay thought it over. At last he leaned forward, looking Szarka in the eyes. The fat man stared back, unafraid to meet his gaze, and it was this as much as anything else that convinced Clay of the man's sincerity.

"Two things. You give me two things, and I will open up the data that you do have, go get you the rest of what you need, and take care of that bitch in the white suit."

Szarka nodded. "I'm listening."

"First, I want to meet this other guy. In person. Tonight."

"He really—"

"I don't give a shit. Talk him into it, bribe him, point a gun at the back of his head, whatever ... I don't care, but I'm not giving that encryption code to anyone without looking them in the eyes first."

Szarka looked unenthusiastic, but after a moment he took a breath and assumed a calm businesslike air. "I'll make it happen."

"Good. Second, when all this is finished and the information is out there and the cure is being synthesized, I want you to use all of your money, your power, your political clout to make sure this stuff gets into the hands of *everyone* who needs it. Here and in Brooklyn and anywhere else in the entire world where there's so much as one ampule of Elixir. No saving it for the rich people, no sitting behind your big walls and pretending everything is fine while the rest of the country burns, and no charging people out the ass for it. Everyone gets the cure. Everyone. We clear?"

"Like Waterford crystal, Officer. I will gladly take up the task of providing the cure to the entire city, the entire country, and the entire world. That would be a fine legacy, no matter the cost."

Could Clay trust him? Didn't matter—this was the best shot he had, and he was going to take it. If Szarka tried to go back on his word, to monetize the cure or otherwise profit from it, Clay would expose him. He hoped he wouldn't have to do it, didn't think he'd have to, but he knew that Terry would have wanted the cure to be available to anyone and everyone, and he was prepared to do whatever it took to finish what she'd started.

"All right," he said.

Szarka stood up, and Clay did the same. The two men shook hands, and Szarka headed for the door.

"Ten thirty p.m.," Szarka said. "The parking garage behind Port Authority. Third floor, space E84, black Cadillac Z-Cell. You'll be picked up by my driver. Don't engage him, just get into the car. He'll take you to a safe place."

"Safe assuming Olivia's not already watching us."

Szarka gave him a thin smile. "Were that the case, I think we'd both already be dead. Good afternoon, Officer Foster."

Szarka moved his ponderous girth through the door and it closed behind him. After a few moments, the immensity of what was happening seemed to come crashing down on Clay, and he moved to the chair Szarka had been sitting in. *Holy shit.* For a time, he sat, hands on the armrests, staring at the bare motel wall.

Terry, why didn't you tell me? I could have helped.

But she hadn't told him, and he hadn't been able to help. Terry hadn't known the stakes of the game she was playing, and she'd paid the highest price for it. Now there was nothing left to do but try to make things as right as they could be.

CHAPTER 17

Union City

When the driver took him into the Lincoln Tunnel, Clay very nearly protested. They were heading for New Jersey? Clay had no idea if his Manhattan pass was still valid. New York didn't bother checking them on departures, but if Clay tried to come back in with a defunct ident, he'd be refused entry. His enemies were here; he needed to be here, too, at least until he could be sure he had another way onto the island.

In the end, he held his tongue. Sitting in the plush leather seats of the Cadillac, feeling tremendously out of place in a pair of beat-up jeans and a T-shirt, Clay watched the lights of the tunnel go by. It was almost eleven at night and traffic was thinning. The Cadillac rolled along in near silence, its heavy shocks absorbing potholes and surface changes without complaint.

The driver looked to be in his early thirties. He was thin almost to the point of being gaunt, with sunken cheeks and a high brow capped by short blond hair. When he glanced at Clay in the rearview mirror, Clay saw that his eyes were an almost colorless shade of light blue. He was wearing a tailored suit and a black tie, and he gripped the steering wheel at ten and two with long, elegant fingers. As they came out of the tunnel, the driver touched his fingers to his right ear and, after a moment, spoke softly.

"Yes, Mr. Szarka. No, we've just reached New Jersey. All right. Flower Hill. Yes, sir." He touched his ear again, apparently ending the conversation.

Clay doubted that most of the traffic leaving Manhattan ever really saw New Jersey, at least not the part of it that lay just to the west of the Hudson River. The people in those cars would travel right from the tunnel to the highway, and from there on to parts less blighted. Clay's driver instead turned and headed north along Park Avenue, first into Weehawken and then into Union City. Clay had never been here before and wasn't sure he would ever want to come back; New Jersey looked like a fucking war zone.

The area had been hit particularly hard by the floods, and the lowlands between Hoboken and Newark were now brackish, disease-ridden swamps. What was left was filthy and battered, left to rot by fleeing inhabitants, filled with derelicts and burning trash can fires. It was like a caricature of the 1970s, the way people who weren't actually from the area had thought of it. Gangs had claimed Union City and its surrounding neighborhoods decades before Elixir had hit the scene. The drug had barely changed a thing in this place. It was business as usual.

The Cadillac caught stares as it went by, but not ones of jealousy or hate. Apathetic curiosity was as much as anyone seemed able to muster. For the most part, they were staring because it was something else to look at beyond the ruin they saw every day. These streets weren't dying—they were dead— and the only inhabitants left were carrion feeders. Men and women as roaches, subsisting on detritus. After Manhattan, it was startling, like a move from the lush hillsides of Maui with the broken, jagged landscape of Mars.

They turned west on Forty-eighth Street and from there made their way into what looked to Clay at first like a park. When he saw the headstones, lined up in their neat little rows, he laughed to himself. This was some real skull-and-bones bullshit they were playing here. Midnight meetings in the cemetery.

Szarka was standing by a particularly large and ostentatious monument, dressed more casually than he had been earlier. He was wearing dark blue jeans and a shirt of silvery material that flowed around his bulky frame. There were gigantic sweat stains around his armpits and at his neck. A satchel of burnished leather was slung over his shoulder like a purse. The car pulled to a stop before him and the driver flicked off the headlights and sat back, not speaking. Clay opened the door and stepped out.

"Officer Foster," Szarka said.

"Clay's fine. Listen, if I can't get back into Manhattan, I'm not going to be much use to you. We couldn't have done this on the island?"

"My associate won't set foot anywhere in the city. He's convinced that doing so would prove fatal. There are few eyes indeed that spend any time looking toward Union City."

"That still won't help me if they turn me away at the checkpoint."

"Elena has made inquiries about having your pass rescinded, but they've been met with substantial resistance. It seems almost as if her own network is fighting her in this regard. The message is destroyed before it's ever sent out. I have heard that it's a source of substantial confusion and frustration among the technology team."

The Chink. Had to be. "That's handy."

Szarka smirked. "Indeed. Even were the request to go through, I fear she would be loath to attempt an explanation as to why a decorated Brooklyn police officer was infiltrating her offices, particularly as it might lead to questions about why that police officer was found in the midst of a savage beating in her parking garage."

"She trapped herself."

"For now, yes. In the future I imagine she will remove her enemies to a less central location before setting her thugs on them. As it stands, you may continue to come and go as you please."

"Speaking of, how'd you get out here if you lent me your driver?"

"I took a car service and had them drop me a few blocks from here. I wanted to come out ahead of time and brief my associate. Shall we go meet him?"

"Let's do it."

They walked north through the rows of graves. It was sticky-hot out, and big beads of moisture were hanging on to the grass. Clay's shoes were soon soaked. At the north end of the cemetery was a wide band of trees. Clay could see a figure under one, and as they got close the man slapped at his arm. "Son of a bitch! The mosquitoes here are like vampire bats."

"You were the one who chose to meet directly next to thirty miles of shallow swamp," Szarka said. "It was also your choice to stand under the trees. It's better out in the open."

"Fuck that. Do you know how dangerous this is? And you're standing around in a shirt that's visible from space. You're insane. Is this Foster?"

"No, just some random hobo he found wandering around," Clay said.

The guy in the shadows gave a scoffing laugh. "Right. I'm Luke. I work for the People's Voice."

Clay chewed on this for a moment. "I have no idea what that is."

"Figures," Luke said. "Fucking Brooklyn ... The People's Voice is only the biggest independent online news outlet in New York."

"Online and independent? So, what, there's like six of you?"

"Man, fuck you. We've brought down titans over there, all right? And there's eight of us."

"Eight." Clay glanced over at Szarka, who looked pretty serene for a man who might soon liquefy entirely in the heat. Feeling tired and still aching, Clay ran a hand through his hair, squeezed his neck, looked back at Luke. "Well, that's fan-fucking-tastic, because we have a titan that needs bringing down. You're claiming to be a journalist?"

"That's right."

"Good. Why'd you never meet me at the park? It was you who called me, right?"

Luke nodded. He stepped forward a little, enough so Clay could see his face. The man was tall, black, gawky, and a bit hunched, as if ashamed of his height. He had a long face, clean-shaven, with a too-small nose and wide lips that he kept licking. His puffy brown eyes flicked back and forth, scanning for danger, and he kept rubbing his hands together. He was doing some kind of shitty ninja impression, dressed from head to toe in tight black clothing.

"I was gonna meet you. Seriously, I didn't mean to leave you hanging, but just as I was getting ready to head out, our detector software goes berserk and we realize there's some kind of worm in our network. It's just mowing through our security, and it's downloading every goddamn thing it can find … so long as it's stuff about me. Totally ignoring everyone else. Soon as our data guy Seth told me that, I was fuckin' outta there. I'd only been working on one thing for weeks."

"What was that?" Clay asked.

"Your wife."

There was silence, and then Luke's eyes went the size of hubcaps.

"Not that I was, you know … *working* on your wife. I mean, I was working on the stuff she was feeding me. On the data. The shit about Imran and MWP and fucking Elixir. Far as I know, your wife was a nun. I mean, probably not because nuns can't get married, but I never saw her naked or anything. I mean, I never saw her at *all,* actually, so I couldn't have—"

"You should probably just stop talking," Szarka said, not unkindly, and Luke snapped his mouth shut, looking mortified.

Clay shook his head. "Right. How the hell did you ever get in contact with her? And how'd you know that story about her and that guy Halstead?"

"Halston. She told me that in case I ever needed to prove I knew her to you … and to make sure I knew it was really you I was talking to. Listen, she came to us. We got a lot of good press a couple years ago when we outed that councilman who was bringing those little girls to that … that shack of his. So we get this encrypted e-mail that says it has information about a massive cover-up. It gets sent over to me because I usually cover corruption angles, and for a week I ignore it. Conspiracies in the city are like flies on shit, you know? Thousands of 'em buzzing around. But she mails again and this time she attaches just a little clip, like eight seconds, of two people talking about ... well, I didn't even know what. Big chemical terms being thrown around. Just audio, but, man, it's obvious they're talking about fabrication and they know their shit, and you can tell by the tone of their voices that there's no way they'd be talking about it out loud if they knew they were being recorded.

"So pretty fucking soon, she's sending me reams of data. Most of it's bullshit, right? She knows that, but what she shows me is ... Buried in there is all this stuff that makes no sense. It doesn't relate to anything else around it. Chemical signatures she says are all wrong, test batches that are contaminated in ways she says would never happen. I ask her what the fuck I'm looking at and she tells me, 'Those are components of Elixir.'"

Clay slapped at a mosquito. "How would she know that?"

"Man, I asked her the same fucking question. So that's when she sends me the whole story. She's working late one night, running some tests. Gets everything set up, gets it running, and goes out to get something to drink from the break room. On the way she passes Imran's office and hears a voice. It's low, but it's obviously pissed off, and she can't help but listen a little."

Terry knows the voice she's hearing. It's Dr. Imran who's hissing words out that don't make any sense in a tone Terry's never heard the woman use before.

"You never told me it would be habit-forming!"

Shun Ten doesn't make any products that are habit-forming. They don't even make products meant for consumption. Confused and concerned by the anger in the doctor's voice, Terry leans in closer, listens carefully.

"No, you've made me into a criminal!" Imran shouts.

There is a pause, and Terry realizes she is listening to a phone call. A person on the other end of the line must be speaking.

"This is unconscionable. I can't stand for it and I won't continue working with you on this ... this poison."

Another pause.

"I won't go alone. No, but ... No. I ... How can you do this to me? After all we went through together, I—"

There is a final silence, and then a crash makes Terry jump. Imran has hurled something at the door and it's shattered, little pieces dropping to the thin industrial carpet. The phone. After a moment more, Terry hears Imran get up to retrieve the pieces. She decides that this would be a good time to leave the hallway and quickly heads back toward the lab.

It will be ten days before she convinces herself to break into Imran's computer and learn more about what the doctor is doing, and two weeks before she realizes just what it is she's uncovered. In five weeks she will have filled her SynchDrive to brimming with data. In eight weeks she will be dead.

"That's how it went," Luke said. "We were almost there. Everything was all good at first, and she was sending tons of stuff. Last thing I got was part of a call she actually managed to record ... It's all fucked from bad decryption, but here, listen."

He held up his tablet, and both Clay and Szarka leaned in. At first there was only static, but after a moment a voice emerged, robotic and breaking up.

"... and I can't exactly send Elixir component reports to Manhattan Water and Power, now, can I?"

Another voice, equally broken, cut in. "Don't ever ... name again. Do ... understand what's happening ..."

There was another long burst of static and then a quick back-and-forth of fragmented dialogue, the two warbling robot voices going back and forth.

"... no one is going to ..."

"... someone is ..."

"... reason to suspect ..."

"... don't call ... again ... number. .... Wish you ... pleasant days to come."

The transmission ended. Something about that last line nagged at Clay, and in a moment more it came to him. He pointed at Luke's tablet. "Play that recording again. Just the end of it. Just the last sentence."

He did as he was asked, skipping past the initial static and dialogue. The last line from one of the two robotic voices echoed out from the machine.

"... don't call ... again ... number. .... Wish you ... pleasant days to come."

I wish you very many pleasant days to come. The exact same sentence Reyes had used when dismissing him in her office not four days earlier.

"That's Reyes," Clay said. "That is Elena fucking Reyes on the phone with Anuhya Imran, discussing the production of Elixir."

Szarka looked confused. "What?"

"That last thing she said ... it's exactly what she said to me right before she had Olivia escort me out. *I wish you very many pleasant days to come.* It's a dismissal, the thing she says to someone when she thinks it's the last time she's ever going to talk to them."

"Why in God's name would Elena be involved in a phone call like that?"

Clay ran a hand over his stubble, staring at the wet grass, thinking it over. Something tickled at the back of his mind, but every time he tried to bring it forward, it seemed to disappear. "I don't know. Yet. But that's her. Luke, was there anything else?"

Luke lifted one hand, palm up, in a gesture of apology. "That was it. After that she started refusing to transmit data. She burned out the transmission chip in her drive, and she wouldn't send me anything, no matter how secure the connection. She wanted to meet in person and go over everything together. I think she knew someone had gotten wind of things. Maybe she was even worried that I was setting her up."

"So where's the drive, then?"

Luke reached into the pocket of his jeans and brought the drive out, holding it up. Clay could see that part of it had been burned away, as if with a soldering iron. "Like, two days after she stopped picking up her phone, it shows up in my mail. No note, no information, just a drive, but I know it's hers. Unless someone else had *Foster* engraved on a crypto-locked, burned-out SynchDrive and sent it to me."

"It's hers," Clay said.

"I figured she'd call me and set up a time to meet, but then ..."

Clay felt his jaw clench. "Goddamn ... Imran, that piece of shit. She came to the funeral. Told me how sorry she was. Was she involved?"

Luke held his hands out, palms up. "No idea. Probably not? I doubt she has any clue that Terry was murdered. No one knew what your wife was doing. Hell, it took me a few days to figure out what had happened, after she stopped answering contact requests. Wasn't really surprised to find her in the obituaries, not after she went dark like that. Never bought that it was an accident. I knew right from the start someone had found her out. That's why I tried to meet you."

Clay was staring down at the grass again, deep in thought. Why hadn't she told him? Why had she tried to do this by herself? Had Terry been protecting him? That didn't make sense; she hadn't known about Olivia, at least not in the early going. She must have been keeping it from him for some other reason.

Something came to him then, out of the blue. A different question, but related, and equally important. He looked up at Luke. "How the fuck did my wife manage to break into Imran's archives? That shit must have had some serious encryption on it."

Luke shifted from one foot to the other, looking not at Clay but past him, and sucked at his teeth for a moment before responding. "See, I asked her that too."

"Judging by the way you're squirming, I'd say you got an answer."

Luke sighed. "Look, man, even in great relationships there are going to be some secrets."

Clay cracked his knuckles. Luke stared down at Clay's fists for a minute, then glanced up. "On the other hand, if you want to know, who am I to stop you, right?"

"Right. Whatever you know, I'd like to gently encourage you to share it. Now."

"So, your wife had access to military-grade decryption software. Stuff that was ahead of the curve ten years ago and still pretty fucking good now. She told me they gave it to her in Virginia, during the war."

What? "That doesn't make sense. She was a nurse's aide. Handing out pills and taking temperatures and shit. Why the fuck would she need that kind of tech?"

"That I do not know." Luke looked at Clay's hands again. "Seriously. She told me the USA had given her some tech and trained her to use it and that she'd left it lying in a box in your basement until she overheard that phone call ... That's all I know."

Clay's stomach hurt, like someone had wound up and slugged him there. Terry was a chemist, not some kind of secret agent. What the fuck was going on? "I'm going to ... file this, I guess. Get back to it later. If I find out you're withholding info from me, though, I—"

Luke held his hands up. "Dude, I'm a journalist. You're some kind of fucking war hero, and I'm sure you could break my arms before I even got a punch in. I am not even close to that stupid."

All right, then. Clay turned to Szarka. "How'd you get involved?"

Szarka put his hand into his pocket, drew forth a handkerchief, and mopped his brow. It was a pointless endeavor. The sweat was replaced before he could get the cloth back into the pocket.

"By the time all of this had happened, I had long since come to understand most of the particulars about my unfortunate situation. I knew I was addicted to the drug and that Elena was using it to extort me. When Luke reached out to me, I sensed an opportunity."

"I was actually looking to widen the net," Luke said. "Terry had found a connection to MWP, so I started at the top. It's his company, right? So I sent a feeler, just saying that I'd been provided with some interesting anonymous data about MWP. I wanted to see how he reacted."

"Don't lie to the man," Szarka said. "You wanted to meet so you could get your pickpocket companion from your absurd tabloid to steal my phone and try to break into it."

"Well ... that, too."

Szarka grinned. "We scheduled a lunch and spent that time feeling each other out. It became apparent to me that Luke was sincere, if at times overzealous, in wanting to root out corruption. I resolved to help him. The next time we met, he returned my phone."

"There wasn't a single thing on it," Luke said. "Nothing about any of this stuff, anyway. Couple vids of, like, half a dozen naked girls rolling around on his bed, that kind of thing, but nothing about Elixir or Reyes."

Clay glanced sidelong at Szarka, who gave a small shrug. "Wealth has its privileges."

Luke made an involuntary motion with his hand, as if brushing something away. "Anyway, we met a few more times before I told him what was going on. That was around the time Terry got, well ... killed, I guess. Alex probably saved my life.

When I saw that the worm was targeting me specifically and got the fuck out of the offices, I called him. He sent me here. It's a shithole, but I'm still alive. Woulda contacted you but I didn't know how to do it without them finding me. We've been working on breaking your wife's encryption, but her fucking passphrase is really strong."

"Yeah, that was the point," Clay said. "We didn't want random assholes breaking into our data. If you'd just mailed me the thing, I could've accessed it a long time ago."

Luke rolled his eyes. "Right, sure. And then either Olivia puts a knife in your throat and snags the drive or you take it to your boss like an asshole and fuck everything up."

"You're right, I'd never have thought of posting a story about it on a site no one reads."

"Fuck you. Eighty million visits monthly."

"How many of those are from your mothers?"

"Man, I've had about enough of this guy's bullsh—"

"We can dispense with the pointless antagonism," Szarka said. "Everyone here is on the same side. We wish to see Elixir cured, Elena removed from power, and her bodyguard ... removed entirely."

"Preferably with a nuclear strike," Clay muttered. He turned to Luke. "So we have the drive and I have the key and you have the means to distribute whatever's on it to eighty million visitors and bring down another titan. That's the plan, right? Finish what Terry started?"

"That's the plan."

"So why the fuck are we standing in a graveyard in Earth's Asshole, New Jersey, instead of doing those things?"

"We can decrypt the data now," Szarka said. "That's good, but this data alone will not provide the cure, nor will it take care of Olivia, and we still don't know how Elena is connected to all of this. Why did she set Olivia on your wife in the first place?"

Clay considered this, and in that moment the tickle that had been sitting there in the rear of his brain leaped forward, connecting two more dots, and all of a sudden the whole of the picture seemed to swim into view.

"Holy shit," he said, and the two men both glanced at him, near-identical expressions of confusion on their faces.

"What?"

"Reyes. Jesus Christ … *that's* why she's never been addicted and never will. She's sitting at the top."

Szarka's eyes narrowed. "I'm not sure I understand … Why would she never become addicted?"

Clay's heart felt like it was going to leap out of his chest. Of course. Here at last was a central piece of the puzzle, to which many others connected. Why would Reyes never become addicted? Why indeed?

"Because it's her fucking drug," he said and glanced over at Luke, whose eyes had gone wide. They were darting back and forth, not focused on Clay but distant, and Clay knew the man was putting the pieces together in his mind. "You see it, right? She thought this thing up and had it made. It can be completely decentralized because she doesn't give a shit if the money gets back to her. She doesn't even *want* it to. Maybe she had it built first as a way to control people like Alex, but it's gone beyond that now … It's the blight. It's Brooklyn."

"Why use a drug?" Luke said. "Why not pollution or some shit?"

"Pollution is expensive." Szarka looked like a man who'd just taken a solid hit to the jaw. "You have to pay to clean it up.

But with a drug, people pay *you*, if not for the product then certainly for the cure. It makes sense, Clay. The ability to take Elixir whenever she wants and never have a problem … it's because whatever component creates the addiction isn't present in her doses."

"That's why she had to have Olivia kill Terry. Not because of her plans to take your job but because Terry had evidence that Elena Reyes is at the top of the pyramid. It's her fucking drug."

Luke pulled his tablet out and slid the SynchDrive into its receptacle. "Let's decrypt this shit right now and get it backed up. What's the data key?"

The key was thirty-two characters long and made up of a pattern of numbers, letters, and characters that he and Terry had chosen at random. Clay gave it to Luke, who tapped them in.

"All right, and the passphrase?"

"It's from a poem." Clay recited it:

> Yet fill my glass: give me one kiss:
> My own sweet Alice, we must die.
> There's somewhat in this world amiss
> Shall be unriddled by and by.

"Nice," Luke said. "Who's that by?"

"No idea."

Szarka chuckled. "Not the scholar that your wife was, are you, Clay?"

"I got through high school," Clay said. "That was pretty much a miracle. Went right from there to the Army. They don't read a lot of poetry on the front lines."

"Too bad. It might have helped."

He shook his head. "Whatever. Did it work?"

"Yeah, it's all here. First half of the cure, bunch more component data, and ... fuck yes! Test batch results from a factory in Queens called Envision Chemical, owned by Alexander Wihone. Her notes say they're tests on the other half of the cure. The component list must be in that place, somewhere."

Clay grimaced. *Great, more crossing in and out of Manhattan.* "Why the hell are they making a cure? What good does that do Reyes?"

Szarka coughed. "She can't attach her name to the drug, but she can most certainly attach her name to the cure, and the obscene profits that will come with its production."

"Christ. Anything else?"

Luke was still scrolling through the drive's contents. "Looks like more encrypted calls, too, and I bet I know who from. Those things take weeks to break cleanly, but I'll get started tonight. This garbled shit won't cut it."

"You're going to back that up, right?"

Luke nodded. "Double-secure encrypted connection to a private, equally encrypted, distributed cloud backup. Best tech that Alex's money can buy."

"Good. What's next?"

"Next, you visit Envision and find the rest of what we need to synth a cure. I keep gathering data. Alex heads back to MWP and keeps watch from the inside. We have to tie Reyes to this."

"They're not going to let me waltz into a production facility and start stealing data," Clay said.

"How many times have you been stopped from going where you wanted to go?" Szarka said.

"Not many. Is it guarded?"

Szarka shrugged. "Who can say? Security may be light. The chemicals Wihone's company makes are likely worthless until combined with others, and anyway, no one knows he manufactures an Elixir component."

"Right. No one wants to bust up into a place that mostly makes industrial adhesive or whatever," Luke said.

Szarka nodded. "Elixir isn't Elixir until it's mixed, and that happens at other locations. The people doing the mixing don't know where the components come from. This is by design. The drug doesn't become a target for theft or violence until an individual dealer combines components at a distribution site."

"Places like Escobar's joint in Crown Heights," Clay murmured.

"I don't know him."

"Doesn't matter. He's dead."

"God*damn*!" Luke cried, slapping at his arm and leaving a red-brown streak of mosquito and blood. "Let's finish up and get the fuck out of here."

"Give me the factory address." Clay took out his tablet. "And give me your Synch name. I'll add you to my list, and then as soon as I get the data from the workstation at the production facility, my drive will upload it and you'll get a notification."

Luke gave him the necessary information and Clay entered it into his tablet. Then he looked up. "Now give me Terry's SynchDrive."

"Why?" Luke said.

"Because it's my wife's, and she's dead, so that makes it mine."

"What do you want with a broken SynchDrive, man?"

"Why do you care?"

Luke considered the question, then shrugged and held the drive out to Clay. "Whatever. I got everything I need."

Clay took the device and slid it into the spare receptacle on his tablet. "Time to make a run to Brooklyn, I guess."

"You may not even need to come back to Manhattan," Szarka said. "At least not until you have to testify. Of course, if you desire, I can very easily ensure that your temporary pass is made permanent. You'll be a hero in my city and in your own, Clay."

"I've been told that before," Clay said, thinking of the man who had recruited him away from the regular Army and into the R-9 program. What a hero they'd made of him. "I'm not interested in any of that. I want the woman who killed my wife dead and the woman who gave the order ruined and in prison. After that's done, whatever."

"Speaking of ... how you going to deal with Olivia?" Luke asked.

Clay had been considering this very question. He spoke slowly, feeling out the plan even as he articulated it. "There's a man in The Hook who knows who she is, or at least knows about her. Cryptic motherfucker and not always helpful, but if he can help me track her down, tell me where she lives or at least give me some info on her movements, we might have something. I think I can convince him that it's in both of our best interests. He might already have decided that, actually ... He set up the meeting earlier today."

Szarka looked unconvinced. "I know who you're talking about but can't fathom why he would help us further. I've offered him money in the past, but all he wanted was information that I was unwilling to assist him in gathering."

"Yeah, that's his deal, but after my little chat with Reyes I know a few important things, one of which is that she knows who he is and *really* doesn't like him. Removing her from the picture benefits him. I think …" Clay laughed a little, giving an incredulous shake of his head. "I think I'm about to offer the services that I refused to sell him in the first place."

"Assuming he helps us, how do we proceed?" Szarka asked.

"After you guys get out of here and are home with the data, preparing your big exposé, I'll focus on her. Shouldn't be too hard to figure out what happens from there. Either I disappear or she does."

"What happens if you fail to find her?"

"Then I'll make myself seen. Make a few accusations, get things out in public that her boss wants kept private, and she'll come for me. She's probably already coming for me. I don't know why she didn't try to take me out at the hospital."

Luke looked up from his tablet. "What happens if she kills you?"

Clay shrugged. "Then you're stuck in this shithole and Szarka loses his company, which is what was going to happen anyway before I showed up."

"So all of this is riding completely on you."

"That's right."

"And if you fuck up, I'm probably a dead man."

"That's right, too."

"No offense, man, but … you got any friends that wanna help out?"

Clay thought he might. "We'll see. Anything else?"

"Nah. I'll wait till you guys are gone and then head out."

"There's really no reason for that," Szarka said. "We're quite alone here. I can offer you a ride."

Luke looked appalled. "No way. Less people see my face, the happier I am. Just go, man. It'll make me feel better."

Szarka seemed about to protest. Clay held his hand up. "Let him do what he wants. Come on."

He turned and began to walk. After a moment, he heard Szarka begin to trudge after him, wheezing a little in the hot, humid air. He thought about Olivia, the woman who had killed his wife. She was out there somewhere, probably feeling safe and secure, confident that Clay's attempt to gather data from Reyes had been thwarted. He hoped she felt safe. Hoped she felt content. It would make her slow. Inattentive. Lazy.

Moving through row after row of the dead, Clay began his plans to add one more to their number.

CHAPTER 18

Chase

"Grand Central Station, Jeffrey," Szarka said as they slid into opposite ends of the Cadillac's rear seat, and as soon as they'd closed the doors, the car began to move, rolling along the crushed gravel toward the cemetery's entrance.

"You're putting me on a train?" Clay said.

"You have no car and they don't allow taxis into Brooklyn. I think it would be wise for you to get out of Manhattan immediately. I don't think your hotel room is tremendously safe."

"Probably not. My commanding officer is going to be pissed. I'm supposed to be in meetings tomorrow, not—hey, is this guy okay? You told me not to talk in front of him."

"Jeffrey has been with me for many years. He's trustworthy, but the less he knows, the better it is for him. I'm not worried about any betrayal, only that he's able to claim ignorance on as many details as possible should he become wrapped up in our little ... adventure."

"Right, well, anyway, Deputy Chief Warren will have my ass if I don't show up tomorrow."

Szarka considered this. "When all is said and done, I think she'll forgive you. Is there somewhere you can go in Brooklyn once you've completed the next task?"

"I'll probably head for The Hook. At least if they come for me there, I'll be on turf that's hostile to everyone. Our mutual acquaintance might even offer a safe harbor."

Szarka made a noise of approval. He reached forward and tapped on the burled wood paneling of the console between the two seats to reveal a small compartment. Inside there was an etched-crystal decanter and two matching glasses.

"This is very good scotch. Would you care for some?"

Clay considered, shrugged, nodded. "Sure, what the hell?"

Szarka poured and they sipped at their liquor in silence for a time. The man hadn't been lying; the whisky was very good indeed, nuanced, with enough smoke to be interesting but not so much that it overwhelmed everything else going on in the glass.

"What are your plans when this is done?" Szarka asked.

Clay had no idea. He couldn't imagine continuing to live in the big brownstone in Brooklyn Heights, even if everything went perfectly and he ended up both still alive and still a cop. He couldn't picture living without Terry at all. It was like his life had been in suspended animation since her death. The single driving force in his world now was the intense desire to put his hands around Olivia's throat and watch her eyes as he choked the life out of her. Other than putting Reyes in a cell for a very long time, he'd never planned beyond that point.

"Back to being a police officer?" Szarka prompted and glanced over at him.

"I don't know. I really don't. Whenever I think about what comes after, it's just this big blank. I still ... There's a part of me that still expects that when I get home, Terry will be there waiting for me."

"It passes in time."

"How would you know? Aren't you confirmed bachelor Alex Szarka, with his bedroom full of naked chicks half his age?"

"Those events are exceedingly rare. I did not lose my wife, Clay, that's correct. I never had a wife to lose. I lost my sister, two years my senior and the greatest friend I've ever known, the woman whose two children are the legal heirs to my fortune. She was thirty-four when it happened, and I don't believe I felt … right … again for at least two years."

"That's not the same," Clay muttered, sipping his scotch.

"Isn't it?"

"Not unless you were fucking her."

"I see. Is *that* what you miss?"

It wasn't, or at least it was only a single star in an entire galaxy of things he missed about Terry, and Szarka's voice said he knew it.

"I miss everything," Clay said.

"That doesn't change." Szarka finished off his glass with a large gulp, grimaced a little, poured more. "Missing them never goes away, but expecting them to be there behind every closed door … that fades in time."

The car made a left, and Clay glanced out the window, realizing for the first time that they weren't anywhere he had ever been before. He didn't know where they were going, but it was most definitely not back toward the Lincoln Tunnel. Based on the position of the walled city across the Hudson, in fact, they were heading north. Clay opened his mouth to ask about this, and as he did so he saw the driver, Jeffrey, glance back at them in the rearview mirror. There was a look in his eyes that stopped Clay cold, something calculating on the surface but below it a lot of panic just barely held in check.

Clay sat up straight. "Shit."

Szarka glanced over at him. "What is it?"

"Stop the car. Motherfucker ... stop this car right now!" Clay wished he had a gun, wished like hell he hadn't left the stupid thing in the safe back at the hotel two days ago when he'd made his ill-fated entry into the MWP tower.

"Foster, what are you ... Jeffrey, do as he says."

"I'm sorry, Mr. Szarka," their driver said, and the panic was evident in his voice. He actually sped up a little. "I'm sorry!"

"Jeffrey, what have you done?"

"They went after my little girl!" The man wailed, and now he was positively tear-assing it down the street.

"Oh, for fuck's sake." Clay was staring ahead now. Three blocks up the street, there was a line of cars waiting. Men were standing in front of the cars, five or six of them, and Clay had no doubt that each was armed. He grabbed at the handle, ready to throw himself into the street if he had to, but Jeffrey had locked them in and disabled the buttons on the rear doors.

"Jeffrey, you must stop the car!" Szarka shouted.

"They're going to cut off her hand!" Jeffrey kept the pedal down.

They were two blocks away, and Clay was perhaps another five seconds from reaching forward and snapping the man's neck, even if it meant a wreck. He had no doubt whatsoever that whatever deal Jeffrey had made with these people for his own life, it meant nothing to them; this was a hit squad. They were going to open fire on the car and everyone in it. Elena Reyes was done fucking around.

To his right, Szarka was bent over, rummaging through his leather satchel, fat fingers moving frantically. In a moment more he found what he was looking for and drew it forth: a gorgeous, immaculately kept six-shot revolver that looked older than God. The thing must've been worth a small fortune. Szarka held it between two fingers like a dead fish, extending it wordlessly to Clay, the expression on his face conveying that he had no idea how to use it and no desire to learn.

Clay had both the training and the stomach. He snatched the gun from Szarka's hand, thumbed back the hammer, and leaned forward, pressing the muzzle just behind Jeffrey's right ear. "Stop the fucking car or I put your brains out through the windshield!"

Jeffrey took but a moment to process this and then slammed on the brakes. If he'd meant to disarm Clay, he was very nearly successful, but Clay managed to retain his grip on the gun.

"Unlock the doors. *Do it!*"

"My baby girl," Jeffrey moaned, but he reached down and pressed the button. Clay heard the doors unlatch and saw Szarka throw his open and begin to scramble out.

"Stay low!" Clay shouted at him, but the man was in a panic, not paying any attention.

"Oh, God. Oh, please, God." Jeffrey had his eyes closed, was repeating these words in a litany. Whether he was praying for his daughter or himself, Clay didn't know.

"Get out of the car, asshole."

"But—"

"You wouldn't even be the first person I've shot in the head in the last three *weeks*. Get out!"

Jeffrey's hand scrabbled at the door and opened it. He didn't so much step out of the car as slide sideways, falling onto the asphalt with a grunt. Clay glanced up and saw the men who intended to kill him running toward the stopped Cadillac. He leaned out the window and fired three shots. The men scattered, taking cover behind garbage cans and doorways. There were a few pops as they returned fire. One shot hit the windshield in front of the passenger seat and went right through.

"Are you fucking serious?" Clay muttered. How was it that a man of Szarka's wealth and power was driving around so unprotected? Was Manhattan really that safe?

He threw his door open and jumped from the rear seat, stepping over Jeffrey, who was still on the ground hiding from any stray bullets. Clay considered stomping the man's head flat and decided against it. Jeffrey had betrayed his boss, but at least he'd had a reason beyond greed to do it.

"Szarka!" Clay screamed.

A bullet bounced off the car not six inches from his head and whined away into the night. Clay had a moment of uncanny memory—it seemed for a brief flash that he was in a Missouri forest and not an empty street in New Jersey—and then came back to reality. He hauled himself into the driver's seat and threw the car into gear.

Through the spider-webbed glass of the windshield, Clay could see that the men were making their way forward again, staying on one side of the street or the other, moving from cover to cover. They were almost atop him. He stomped on the pedal and the Cadillac surged forward. Damn thing must have had a whole rack of Z-Cells under it to produce that kind of torque.

In a few seconds he was past the men, who in their excitement converged once again in the street, firing after him. Clay brought the car around in a screaming, fishtailing 180-degree arc, tires smoking. Without hesitation, he hammered on the pedal with his foot and the car leaped forward like a jungle cat springing from the bushes, intent on taking down some unsuspecting prey. The men held their ground long enough to put a couple more holes in the windshield—neither of them in front of Clay's head, fortunately—and then scattered to the sides. Clay saw that Jeffrey, too, had crawled out of the way and was huddled in the doorway of a condemned tenement.

Szarka was running down the sidewalk in the same direction Clay was now headed, gut bouncing in a way that would have been comical in other circumstances. Clay caught up, rolled down the window, shouted, "Get in the fucking car!" and, when Szarka looked over, slammed on the breaks. The car came to a halt and Szarka made a sharp turn, heading for the rear passenger door. As he did so, there was another series of pops, and the Cadillac's cracked rear windshield disintegrated. Clay felt something hot and wet bloom on his right shoulder and looked down to see that he had been grazed. His T-shirt was soaked with blood.

Szarka pulled himself into the car, gasping, choking, wheezing. He sounded like someone who'd run for thirty miles, not three blocks, and Clay wondered if the man was going to have a heart attack in the backseat.

"Stay low!" In the rearview mirror he saw a few more muzzle flashes before the men turned and began running back toward their own cars. "Stay low until I tell you it's safe. And next time spring for the armor plating and bulletproof glass, you sheltered asshole!"

"Guh!" Szarka managed, which Clay decided to take as acceptance. He stomped on the pedal and the Cadillac took off again, headed south. It was hard to see with the shattered windshield refracting the streetlights into a million tiny points. Clay wished he had time to stop and kick the windshield out. He didn't; the men behind them would reach their cars in mere seconds. He had to get out of their line of sight.

Clay hauled the wheel to the right, turning west, clipping the curb as he did so. The car bounced hard, but the shocks handled most of it. At the next street he turned left again—north—and after that west a second time. Like this, he took a zigzagging course through the streets. Clay didn't know this area, didn't know where he was going, but he knew that if he stayed in a straight line the hit men would catch up to him. He was pretty sure they had more bullets than the three that were left in his gun.

"Where ... we going?" Szarka was lying sideways on the seat, staying low, as Clay had told him to do.

"Away. You got any more bullets?"

"Think so."

Clay grabbed the gun from the front passenger seat and held it backward. He felt Szarka take it from him.

"Don't know ... how to load," the man wheezed.

"Jesus. All right, listen, there's going to be a—"

He was cut off as a car roared from a nearby alley and missed clipping the Cadillac's rear bumper by a matter of inches.

"What the fuck?" Clay shouted, looking into his rearview again. The car that had tried to hit him was not in pursuit. Clay turned, taking the corner with his wheels screeching. He was met with the sight of another car ahead, driving down the center of the street and aimed right at him.

"Christ, shit! Hold on to something!" Clay yanked the wheel hard to the left. The Cadillac fishtailed, but this time it was impossible to avoid some contact. The other car smacked into the back right panel, spinning them clockwise. Clay turned the wheel into the skid, felt the tires catch, leveled the car out. "You all right back there?"

"I dropped the gun." Szarka was still wheezing but could at least form full sentences now. "Bullets are everywhere."

"I'll try to keep it steady. Look, there's a little switch that covers the chamber. Hold it open, put the bullet in, spin the chamber. It's not hard."

Szarka didn't seem interested in responding. Clay could hear him rooting around in the back of the car. The other cars had closed the distance behind him and were almost in shooting range.

"They must be tracking us," Clay said. "This thing's a fucking deathtrap. We have to get free of it."

Szarka sat up "I have the gun, but we can't outrun them on foot."

"No shit. How many more bullets do you think you have?"

There was a pause as Szarka considered. "Twenty?" he finally said.

"Okay. Get six more bullets into the thing. Just flip the switch by your thumb and the barrel will spin."

Szarka did as he was told, fumbling a bit, cursing as he dropped bullets back onto the car floor. Clay glanced in the rearview mirror. He was outdistancing the other cars—the

Cadillac had a hell of an engine under it—but they were running out of straight road.

Szarka shoved the final round into the chamber and released the thumb lever. "Got it."

"Good." Clay slowed a little, letting the hit men close some of the distance. "Now empty it out the back windshield. Keep your head as low as possible. After that, find all of the bullets. Find every single one rolling around on the floor and all the ones left in your bag. Put them somewhere where they won't fall out."

"I don't know how to fire this—"

"Just point it and pull the trigger, motherfucker! Hold it tight and keep your wrist steady against the kickback. Do you want to live or should I just pull over right now and make a break for it? I bet I'm a lot faster than you are."

"All right! I just never thought—"

"Stop talking and shoot!"

Clay was angling toward the Hudson River. He was quietly thankful that it was the middle of the night in a downtrodden industrial area of the city. Apart from a few homeless people staring with confused curiosity at the cars screaming down the street, blowing through stoplights, he'd seen no one at all.

"Here goes ..." There was a report, loud like thunder inside the car. Clay's ears rang with it.

"Good!" he shouted. "More!"

Szarka squeezed out shot after shot, firing all six rounds in fairly rapid succession. When Clay could hear again, he noticed the man making a wheezing sound that he thought might have been laughter.

"Having fun back there?"

"That was ... extremely satisfying."

The drivers had pulled back a little and weren't returning fire, happy to let Clay and Szarka run out of road. There were no further turns available, and directly ahead the street ended with a short strip of lawn. Past that there was a massive chain-link fence, eighteen feet tall and stretching out in either direction to meet the edges of the buildings that lined the road. Behind it were crates, barrels, and what looked like construction equipment.

"Sit up and put your seat belt on! Fast!"

"Oh, God!"

Clay heard shuffling, the sound of a belt spooling out, a click."Here we fucking go!" He pressed down on the accelerator. The strip of road ahead of them rapidly dwindled to nothing. They hit the curb, the front end of the Cadillac shooting up into the air and coming down on the soft grass. In the bouncing light, Clay tried to aim for what looked like an area behind the chain link that housed a pile of what he hoped were empty orange barrels. That seemed like their best bet.

They hit the fence at almost eighty miles per hour, the Cadillac tearing through it like a baseball through wet paper. There was a cacophonous thunder as they hit the barrels, sending them flying like startled birds. As they cleared this first obstacle, the car twisted and bucked, barely slowed, plowing now into what seemed like thousands of road signs standing in rows. Clay heard one of the tires go with a sharp report like a gunshot and the car listed to the right. He fought against the wheel, trying to keep his course straight, and in a minute more they came through the forest of bright yellow signs and into a large and open expanse of asphalt. Clay slammed on the brakes and the Cadillac came to a screeching, shuddering halt.

"Out!" Clay unbuckled himself and threw the door open. Whether the hit men could really track the car didn't matter; he had no time to change a tire.

"Where are we going?" Szarka was scrambling to exit the vehicle, clutching the gun in one hand and his leather satchel in the other.

Clay glanced around and saw ahead of them a darkened warehouse surrounded by the hulking shadows of construction machinery. He pointed. "There."

"And then?"

"You need to shut up and do what I tell you. Give me the gun."

Szarka didn't look happy, but he handed the weapon over without a word.

Clay checked the chamber, saw that it was empty, held out a hand. "Bullets. All of them."

Szarka dug into his pocket and pulled out the rounds. He held them out to Clay, who grabbed first one handful and then a second, stuffing them into his own pocket. It wasn't optimal—if he was going to have to use an antique revolver, a speed loader or two would have made life a lot easier, but this would have to do. His service pistol, clip-loading and capable of firing twice as many rounds in half the time, wasn't going to magically teleport from the hotel.

He gestured to their left. "I need you to run as fast as you can. When you get to the warehouse, wait for me at the first window you see that looks like it can be broken."

"I don't—"

"Fucking *go!*" Clay shouted, motioning with the gun. Szarka stared at him for a moment, his expression indignant, the look of a man not used to being given commands. Then he pressed his mouth into a thin line, nodded once, and took off. Clay began reloading the gun. He could hear the shouts getting closer as the men worked their way through the barrels. He had to get to cover. From there, he could begin the process of picking them off, which was the only way he and Szarka were going to survive the night.

He needed the fat man alive. Crippled as he was by the hooks Reyes had in him, Szarka could still move mountains with nothing more than a phone or tablet. He could get Clay through Manhattan and into Brooklyn and then back to finish the job. He could provide capital if it was needed. He could keep Luke alive and funded, assuming Reyes's people hadn't already gotten the twitchy journalist. He could even help placate the deputy chief, who would be ready to have Clay hauled back to Brooklyn and put behind bars after what was about to go down.

These men weren't going to let him escape, so they had to die. In the dark, they would be vulnerable, and Clay knew how to take advantage of that. He had years of training to draw on, and he was not afraid. There were at least twelve bullets. That was more than he needed. Clay finished loading the gun and jammed it into his waistband. He spun on his heel and took off after Szarka, headed for the shadows.

CHAPTER 19

Hunters Hunted

Szarka was doubled over, hands on his thick thighs, gasping for air. He was standing in the dark by a large unlit window that looked in on what Clay thought was a small office built into the southwest corner of the building.

"If we break ... into this building it ... will bring police."

Clay tapped the window and frowned. Composite. No one used glass anymore, which was going to be a problem. "I don't think we'll be able to, anyway. Shit. What do I do with you?"

"Do with me?"

"I need you out of the way. I need these guys spread out so I can pick them off, and I need you to not get found."

Szarka looked around, still panting. "If I had the ability to disappear, I would have done so quite some time ago."

"Wouldn't matter, with you breathing like that. Come on, follow the edge of the building."

They moved deeper into the inky shadows, so dark that it was almost impossible to see what was in front of them. They could hear shouting behind them as the men conducted their search. Szarka came to a stop. He was no longer gasping, but each breath was still loud and wheezing.

"If we go further I'm going to brain myself," he said. They were between pieces of hulking machinery, cut off from the warehouse's exterior lights, and the tiny sliver of moon overhead gave them virtually nothing to work with.

"Yeah, it's too dark." Clay needed elevation, a way to survey what his quarry—men who still thought of him as prey, which was exactly what he wanted—were up to. On his left was a massive dump truck, and Clay was struck by an idea.

"Come here." He moved around the rear of the truck, hands out, navigating by touch as much as sight. There were nothing but vague silhouettes to be seen here at the rear of the warehouse, and the looming equipment didn't help.

"What are we—"

"Feel this?" Clay grabbed the man's hand and brought it forward, pressing it against the back of the truck. There were bars there. "That's a ladder. Climb. Inside the truck. It'll take them forever to think of looking for you in there."

"How will I get out?"

"We'll worry about that once they're all dead."

Szarka considered this for a moment in silence.

"Look," Clay said. "Their plan, right now, is to find us and put a whole bunch of bullets in us. Both of us. Reyes knows now that you're in on this, and she's cleaning up her loose ends. I'm going to make sure she doesn't get what she wants."

"I don't understand how Elena figured out—"

"She shut off the video feed to the parking garage. Who's the only person who has a private feed, could've seen that I was getting the shit kicked out of me, and called the cops? She knows it was you, and she probably figured out you've been snooping around. Anyway, it doesn't matter. They're going to kill us unless we kill them first. If you have a problem taking orders or with me doing what I need to do, now's the time to say so."

Szarka shook his head. "I'm not going to protest."

"So fucking climb."

He did as he was told, and when he had swung his heavy legs over the edge and lowered himself down, Clay climbed up as well. Glancing over, he could barely see Szarka's bulky figure sitting at the bottom, some eight feet below.

"Not a sound until I identify myself, all right? Not even if it takes till dawn."

"Very well. How will I know it's you?"

"I'll tell you my wife's name was Terry."

"What if they know that?"

Clay rolled his eyes. "You really think they're going to guess the password that quick?"

"I suppose not."

"Right. No more sound."

Clay hauled himself up and perched on the edge of the dump truck's giant metal receptacle, some twelve feet in the air. He couldn't see any of the men he was hunting, not yet, and they had stopped making noise.

The warehouse was two stories tall, nothing more than a huge box made of sheet metal. The roof was still ten feet above him, and though it would have given him the best possible vantage point, Clay didn't see any realistic way of reaching it. For that matter, he wasn't goddamned Batman. There was no way to attack his enemies from that height other than shooting at them, and that would alert the others to his presence. He didn't want to use the gun at all if he could get by with his hands.

If he'd been fully healthy, Clay would've leaped to the ground. He was still aching from the earlier beating, though, so instead he used the ladder. Back on ground level, he began to move slowly forward. His eyes were adjusting to the dark now, and he could see more of what was around him. He wondered if the men had split up. Probably. If they were smart they would be working in pairs, but he hadn't known many smart hit men.

As if to confirm this belief, he saw a solitary silhouette cross between the rows of machinery, perhaps ninety yards ahead of him. Clay increased his speed, moving forward, wanting to get behind the man. In a few moments more, he could hear footsteps and, incredibly, the man grumbling to himself about the heat. Glancing around the corner, he saw that the man had stopped and was down on his hands and knees, peering under the body of a bulldozer. There was no one else near him, and no one in the other direction. Elation surged through Clay. If these guys were this dumb, it'd be a piece of cake. Clay rounded the corner and charged the man, moving lightly on his feet and making little noise.

The guy didn't hear him until it was far too late. By the time he looked up from what he was doing, Clay was already there. Clay drew his foot back and kicked like a soccer player making a shot on goal, his foot connecting with the hit man's lower jaw. The guy's teeth came together with a sharp, flat crack, and Clay saw a fleshy blob—he thought it was the tip of the man's tongue—go flying. The hit man didn't even make a noise, just crumpled and fell flat on his face, out cold. Clay knelt down, feeling in the dark with his hands, and found the man's gun and an extra clip.

"Hey, what the fuck?" someone shouted from behind him, and Clay got moving, leaping forward and running at top speed. He heard footsteps as the man gave chase, and in another moment they were joined by a second set of feet. Someone fired a shot and Clay heard it bounce off a piece of metal by his head. He reached a gap between two bulldozers, turned to his right, kept moving. The space was barely enough for one man, which meant the two goons pursuing him would need to enter single file. He swung around the edge of a bulldozer and turned a one-eighty, crouching and leaning out from the metal just enough to see who was coming.

The two men pursuing him weren't much better than their friend had been. If there was a hit man school somewhere, Clay doubted they'd finished at the top of their class. They both tried to turn into the narrow path at the same time, and one of them swore as his hip bounced off the metal and he lurched sideways. There was a comical flailing of arms, like something from an ancient silent film, as the two figured out who was going to go first. When they'd done so, and the one in front was halfway into the gap, Clay raised the pistol he'd lifted from the first guy and put a round into this new one's face.

"Holy shit!" the man behind him cried as the one in front went down, and he began to turn. Clay shot him twice, hitting once in the side and once in the neck. The hit man dropped, kicking his legs and gurgling as blood flooded his windpipe.

Clay got up again, not wanting to stay near the place where the shots had sounded. Three down, but how many were left? Had there been five or six? He tried to think back to what he'd seen when they were racing along with Jeffrey still at the wheel of the Cadillac. He thought it was five, but that wasn't good enough. He had to assume six.

Clay could hear shouting again as the remaining hit men regrouped. He wondered if they would stick together this time. If the rest of them were as bumbling as the first three, that might actually make his job easier. Why hadn't Reyes sent Olivia? Maybe she had. Maybe Olivia was there in the shadows somewhere, waiting and watching, hoping that Clay would take out these lesser creatures and give her an excuse to get her hands dirty.

Ahead of him there was a large, triangular tower made of metal bars. At its top, far too high and narrow to reach by climbing, a red light blinked next to a large dish. Clay had no idea what sort of signals the dish received and didn't really care. What interested him was that this tower could give him access to the tops of several tractor trailers parked in a long row. High ground would give him an advantage, and with the odds still being at least two to one, Clay was looking for advantages. He grabbed one of the bars, braced his foot against another, and began to climb.

There were eighteen trailers lined up in a row, their cabs detached. Upon reaching the top, Clay spun and headed back toward the voices. He was hoping to come upon the men unawares, in a group, and rain bullets down on them. Clay didn't care if these men lived or died, but he wanted them to be disabled and no longer interested in pursuing him or Szarka.

"Shut up!" someone shouted. "Both of you shut your fucking mouths. They'll be listening."

So that made six after all, and at least one of them had half a brain. That was disappointing. Clay paused in his advance, listening for footsteps, but if the men were on the move, they were walking carefully.

Clay began to move forward again, making no noise of his own, staying near the edges of the trailers where they would be reinforced and less prone to bowing inward under his weight. There was a dim glow coming from a large bulb on the far corner of the warehouse, and he saw a shadow cross not far ahead. It was a brief flicker, but it gave him some indication of their location. He stepped carefully across a gap between the trailers and continued his progress.

He'd nearly reached the point where he'd seen the shadow when another voice called out, this one higher-pitched and excited.

"There he is! Paul, the motherfucker's above you!"

Clay swiveled his head around and located the source of the voice. The man who'd sounded the alarm was short and wiry, possessed of a shaggy mane of dark hair. He was standing by the bodies of his friends, gun out, and he didn't wait for his companions to act, hauling his weapon up and triggering it five times in rapid succession. Fortunately, in his excitement, he neglected to take any kind of real aim, and only one of the bullets was anywhere close to true. It barely nicked Clay's leg, punching through a loose fold of fabric without touching the skin. It was the second shot to hit him without doing any significant damage that night, and Clay was thankful for his luck. Three inches to the right and the bullet would've taken out most of his shin.

He could hear shouting now as the other two men struggled to find a vantage point from which they could see Clay. The man who'd shot at him was running forward and raising the gun again, and Clay decided not to press his luck. He brought his gun up, leading the man a little with his shot, and fired. The bullet caught the hit man in the left shoulder and he spun with a howl, dropping his gun and clapping his hand to the wound.

"There he fuckin' is!" shouted a voice to his right, and Clay acted on instinct, leaping from the trailer as a hail of gunfire filled the space he had just been occupying. He landed and rolled, cursing as his still-healing body protested against the action, holding tight to the gun. The extra clip in his pocket jabbed him hard in the thigh, and he felt Szarka's revolver fall from his waistband, heard it go clattering across the pavement.

Clay regained his feet, raised the gun, blew half the shaggy-haired man's face off. He spun and aimed at the first of the two men coming around the trailer's corner. The hit man pulled up short, eyes going wide, knowing what was coming but too bulky, too slow, too far into his movement to stop it. Clay pulled the trigger.

Nothing. The gun gave him nothing but a harsh clicking, scraping noise. Something had snapped inside it. Fucking Korean pistols. The hit man's terror swung in an instant to a kind of vile glee, fat lips spreading into a wide toothy grin. He raised his gun.

"Sucks for you, shithead," he said as his partner came up beside him.

"Sure does," Clay lowered his head. "Do it, I guess."

"Bullshit. You think I'm going to make it that easy? You fucking killed four of my friends."

"Three. One of them's still alive." Clay kept his head down, not out of fear or even deference but because he was calculating exactly how many steps he would need to make before he could dive and reach the six-shooter, which was lying halfway under the tread of a bulldozer. "He's just missing some taste buds."

"Man, fuck you," the second hit man said. He was tall and thin, Abbott to the first guy's Costello.

"Yeah, sure, fuck me." Three steps. He would need three steps to get enough speed for the dive to the gun. Would they be slow enough to give him three steps? Clay thought that they might.

"You got zip-ties?" the fat man—Clay could not stop thinking of him as Abbott—asked his buddy.

"Fuckin' right I do," Costello told him.

"Go put 'em on."

Costello lowered his weapon and then, like a fool, gave Clay his chance, stepping right in front of Abbott's gun and looking down, digging in his pocket for the plastic ties they planned to use to bind Clay's hands.

Clay leaped forward, taking three large strides, and he was already on the third before Abbott even cried out a warning. As Costello looked up, an expression of dumb surprise on his face, Clay made his dive. He was in the air as Abbott brought his gun up, aiming around the still-bemused Costello, and by the time the man fired, Clay was scraping the shit out of his elbows on the asphalt. The bullets bounced off the metal two feet above him as his hands touched the cold, beautiful lifesaving metal of the pistol.

Wrapping his fingers around the wooden grip, Clay rolled sideways and saw that Costello was just now figuring out that he should be shooting. He began to raise his gun and Clay thumbed back the hammer and pulled the trigger.

The six-shooter delivered. Compared with the Korean pistol, the report seemed like it could split the Earth in half. There was a rumbling thunder as the noise reverberated off the trailers and construction equipment. The bullet drove

Costello's entire face inward and blew it out the back of his skull in a great gout of liquid, black in the dark. Costello dropped, revealing Abbott, who was now soaked in his friend's remains, his eyes wide, shocked *O*'s.

I might have to get me one of these. Clay shifted his aim and fired again. The report rang out and Abbott flinched, but he didn't die; the bullet had missed his head by a fraction of an inch.

"You fucking *shit!*" he screamed and took another shot. Clay felt the bullet hit him, a white-hot poker driven suddenly into the meaty part of his thigh, and he roared out some profanity of his own, returning fire even as his leg buckled and he fell. This time the shot was true, and it vaporized a good portion of Abbott's right shoulder. The hit man shrieked and turned, as if it had suddenly occurred to him that he'd left the stove on, and began a shambling run up the pathway between the machinery. On the ground now, Clay took his time, aimed the six-shooter, and shot the man in the back of the head. Abbott, dead like his friends, dropped first to his knees and then forward onto his face and lay there in a spreading pool of blood.

"Goddamn." This was a problem. The shot in the leg hadn't hit his femoral artery, at least, and that was a big plus, since bleeding out on the pavement in front of some shithole construction warehouse in New Jersey was not on his to-do list, but he couldn't exactly leave a chunk of lead in his leg. Had the bullet come out the other side? He was going to have to move to be sure.

Clay drew his leg up a little, and that was bad. Gritting his teeth, he grabbed it with both hands and hauled upward. That was a lot worse. Clay looked up and swore at the moon. The moon didn't seem to give a shit, so when the pain lessened a little he looked back down to assess his wound. The bullet had entered about six inches above the left knee and traveled directly through. At least that was some luck.

His pant leg was soaked with blood and he needed to get pressure on the wound. He wasn't wearing a belt, but Abbott was, lying less than four feet away. Clay pulled himself over to the body, teeth clenched, avoiding the pool of blood, and reached underneath the prone form. He unhooked the belt and began sliding it out. A moment later, he'd looped it around his leg and pulled it tight. This resulted in another burst of profanity directed upward, but afterward the throbbing seemed to relent a little. It was time to try standing up.

That activity took him five minutes. He crawled to the bulldozer, hauled himself up using only his arms—which were not happy about this treatment mere days after being pummeled by steel-toe boots—and then got his good leg under him. Once standing, he had to take a moment to adjust. His leg was throbbing, sending jolts of pain through him so excruciating that his vision went gray with each one. He was close to passing out, and the world had taken on a strange, fuzzy, surreal tone. Clay glanced up, and for a moment he thought he saw, perhaps fifty yards away, an ethereal figure bathed in a white glow, watching him. The features were indistinct, but the silhouette was female.

"Terry?" he said, and then a much worse thought came to him. Not Terry, no, but possibly—another wave of gray swept over him. When it finally passed, he felt better, but the ghost figure had gone, if it had been there in the first place. Jesus, was he hallucinating? That was a bad sign. Clay closed his eyes and forced himself to wait until the pain had dissipated a little and the dreamlike feeling had passed entirely.

Once it had, he enacted a couple of tests to see how much weight the hurt leg would hold. The answer was: not much. So he stuck near to the construction vehicles and equipment as much as he could while he made his way back to Szarka, using it for balance as he hopped along.

At last, he reached the dump truck and spoke his companion's name. There was no response, and Clay grinned. "Good man. But it's really me. My wife's name is Terry."

"I heard a good deal of shooting." Szarka's voice reverberated as it drifted up from the dump truck.

"Things got a little hairy. Do you think you can get out of there on your own?"

"No, I believe I'll need your help."

Just another fun moment in a night full of them. Clay grabbed the ladder and pulled himself upward, letting his bad leg dangle. When he reached the top, he peered over. Szarka was on his feet and staring up.

"That sounded laborious. Are you injured?"

"Shot in the leg. Let's get you out of there so we can get me some bandages."

"Have you taken care of our enemies?"

"All six of them."

"That's … just remarkable."

Clay shrugged. "It's what I was trained to do. Listen, here's how this is going to work. I'm going to brace myself against the ladder and hang my arms down. You're going to get a running start and jump, pushing off the wall with one foot. I'm going to grab your arms and haul upward, and we're going to get you to a point where you can get a leg over the side. All right?"

Szarka looked skeptical, but he nodded. He walked to the far end of the dump truck and turned. "Ready?"

Clay shifted his good leg, sliding it through a rung so he could pull with the thigh, and nodded.

Szarka did not start from a dead halt with particular grace. His approach was slow and clumsy, but he picked up speed near the end and proved surprisingly good at planting his foot and launching off of it. The first time was actually the closest of the first five, and if Clay had been able to use both his legs, it would have been over. Clay thought they had it anyway when Szarka brought a foot up and got the tip of it over the edge, but it slipped off and the momentum of his thigh falling down caused him to sway, costing Clay his grip on the man's arms. Of the next four tries, none were quite as good.

Clay let Szarka rest for a moment to catch his breath, then said, "Last try. If this one doesn't work I'm going to have to break into the cab, hotwire it, and dump you out. That will take a ton of time, and I don't know how much longer we have before the police decide that, yeah, we're in Union City but they still should probably investigate all that gunfire at the warehouse."

Szarka nodded. "Getting picked up by the police would be a setback."

"Even worse than getting shot in the leg. You ready?"

"Yes, all right. Yes."

"Any time."

Szarka took a deep breath and began lumbering forward again. The man was obviously not used to physical exertion but was giving it his all, running as fast as his legs could move him. He caught the wall perfectly and launched himself into the air. Clay grabbed his forearms and hauled like a man trying to boat a marlin. Szarka kicked out, swinging his foot up. He was not limber, and for a second Clay was unsure it would reach, but then the entire foot, including the heel, made it over the ledge. Clay switched one hand from the man's arms to holding that foot, keeping it from slipping. Szarka, grunting, his shining silver shirt now soaked with sweat and covered with grime, worked his way over. When it became obvious the man was going to make it, Clay let go and made his way down to the ground. Szarka followed a few moments later, panting.

"Nice job," Clay said and grinned.

Szarka gave him a rueful smile. "I'll pay for it tomorrow. Something went, in my back, on that last one."

"Yeah, well, we can compare who's worse off in the morning. Right now I need bandages, disinfectant, and painkillers."

"Are you able to walk?"

"Not far, but we're not going far."

"Where *are* we going?" Szarka asked as Clay began to limp along. After a moment he lent his arm as a stabilizer, and Clay took it gladly.

"We're going to stop by two of the dead guys and find one with car keys. It's ... not pretty, and it's going to get worse, because we'll need a piece of them to bring with us in case their fob's biometric."

"A piece of them ..." Szarka sounded less than enthusiastic.

"You don't have to watch." Clay really didn't give a shit what Szarka thought about it. They needed a working vehicle right now, one that didn't belong to Szarka and wasn't likely to be traced by yet more thugs. If getting a car meant cutting the finger off a dead man, well, Clay had done worse.

"You've saved my life several times this evening, I think," Szarka said. "I won't watch, but neither will I object."

"Fair enough. Let's go get this over with."

* * *

The third car they tried opened up as they got close to it, and Clay was glad he'd brought one of Costello's fingers along, as the vehicle almost certainly would've remained locked otherwise. The fob contained a short-range detector and would pass the unlocking command to the car only if it was in the presence of its owner's DNA. This had proved a largely reliable system, though it did occasionally lead to someone's having fingers or hands cut off by people who wanted car.

"Nice ride," Clay said. It was a Mirae, a Korean luxury brand that had arrived about six years ago with the boast that it had the most comfortable interior of any car on the market. The latest ads featured beautiful people in little or no clothes, looking shocked, apparently caught in their cars at or near the point of intercourse, with the words *But It Just Felt So Good* prominently featured. The brand's stock had risen meteorically since the ads' debut.

"It certainly won't look out of place in Manhattan," Szarka said.

"Right. You drive. I'll sit in the back. My leg hurts a little less if I keep it straight. I'll find a drugstore on my tablet."

"Reyes might be tracking your—"

"If she can get through the encryption I use, she deserves to catch me. It's government shit, not cop shit."

Szarka considered this and seemed to accept it. He helped Clay into the car and then sat in the driver's seat. "What should we do about Jeffrey?"

Clay glanced over at him, raising his eyebrows. "I don't think he's a danger to us at this point."

"No, I meant … are we just going to leave him stranded in New Jersey?"

Clay gave an incredulous laugh. "You want me to go back for him? I thought I did more than I needed by not shooting that motherfucker in the head. He drove us right at six guys who intended to fill that car with bullets, and they weren't gonna worry about aiming around him. We already saved his life. I'm not rewarding him for trying to help them kill us."

"If they're threatening his child, he can hardly be held responsible for his actions."

"Bullshit. You're always responsible for your actions. He made a choice. He could have come to us for help, but he chose to sell us out instead. As a reward, he gets to walk his ass back to the tunnel and try to get through it on foot. He's got a pass, right? They'll let him in."

"Do you really believe Reyes or Olivia will allow him to live after failing them?"

"Do I look like I give a fuck?"

Szarka was silent for a moment, obviously displeased with the situation and trying to think of a counterargument. At last Clay got impatient.

"Can you at least drive while you're thinking about how to rescue the guy who tried to get us killed? This hole in my leg isn't exactly comfortable."

"Forgive me for caring about a man who has worked in my service for more than a decade." Szarka made no move to start the car.

"Look, get me to New York and then you can come look for Jeffrey all you want. The two of you can reconcile and go out for burgers. It'll be a love story for the ages. Just get me across the fucking bridge."

Szarka's head snapped up and Clay understood that, somehow, he had just given the man ammunition for argument. He rested his forehead against his hand, waiting for it.

"Jeffrey is a registered driver," Szarka said.

"What an exciting fact to know," Clay muttered.

"That means he can bring passengers in and out of Manhattan and, more importantly, present their credentials for them. Tell me, Officer Foster, do you expect our traffic stop to go well with your leg soaked in blood and my outfit covered in grime?"

"Seems unlikely. That's why we need to stop somewhere and—"

"If we're sitting in the back of a Mirae K3 with a licensed driver at the wheel, we'll barely get a glance before being waved through."

"No," Clay said. "You're asking me to trust someone who just tried to get us both killed. Why wouldn't he just call them up when we got wherever we're going and tell them where we are? What the fuck is *wrong* with you, man?"

"I told you, there were extenuating—"

"And I told *you* that's a load of horse fucking shit!"

"We don't have time for this!" Szarka slammed his fist down on the wheel. "Reyes has already sent six men to kill us.

Who knows what others may be on their way? Who knows when the police will show up? Who knows where Olivia might be? Perhaps she is already hunting Luke down and murdering him. I must get in touch with him and help him remain safe. I must get you into Manhattan so you can hole up and get healthy. I don't have time to drive around what's left of New Jersey with you, Officer Foster, looking for an all-night clothing store in order to replace your blood-soaked pants!"

"Jesus Christ ..." Clay put his hand to his forehead, tried to think through the pain. What Szarka was saying made sense, at least until they got into Manhattan. After that they could reevaluate. "All right, fine. Fucking whatever. I'm going to have a gun on him the entire time, do you understand that? The entire fucking time. If he takes a single turn that doesn't look right, I'm putting a bullet through his head."

"Yes, yes," Szarka said. "Do what you feel you must."

"You want to call him or what? I doubt he's still huddled in a doorway somewhere."

Szarka touched his earlobe, activating the embedded communication device there. "Call Jeffrey," he said and then sat, waiting. Someone must have answered on the other end, because Szarka began to speak.

"Jeffrey. Yes, it's Alex ... No, I understand. No ... they're dead. All of them. Officer Foster is quite something ... No, I've convinced him that you might yet be of use to us, and that leaving you stranded in New Jersey is a poor idea ... No, of course we can't *trust* you. Foster will have a gun aimed at you for the entirety of the drive ... Yes, well, it's a bit late for regret, isn't it?"

"Just a bit," Clay muttered, and Szarka shot him a look.

"Do you know where they're holding your daughter? Do you have some sort of contact? ... What? For God's sake, why didn't you ... Hold on."

He turned to Clay. "They don't have his girl. It was merely a threat, not a kidnapping."

Clay was surprised to feel his jaw actually drop. He hadn't thought that was a real thing that happened. "Are you serious?!"

Szarka had turned his attention back to the conversation happening in his ear. "Jeffrey, if you'd told me, I could have helped. I can *still* help. I can wire you enough funds to take your entire family anywhere in the world and keep them there as long as you need ... Of course I would do that ... Yes, even now ... Yes, tonight ... Yes, of course." Szarka's cheeks reddened. "There's really no need for all of that. Where are you? ... Very well, we'll pick you up ... No, not the Cadillac. They've been tracking it. We've acquired another vehicle. A Mirae. Black. Watch for us ... Yes, Jeffrey ... No, not forgiven, but this is a start. Good-bye." Szarka tapped his ear again, leaned back, sighed, and glanced over at Clay.

"That guy's an idiot," Clay told him.

"He was frightened and not thinking well."

"And an idiot. You didn't answer my question before. How do we know he won't sell us out again?"

"We don't. Do you have a better idea?"

Clay didn't, and after a moment he shook his head. "Where is he?"

"Thirty-sixth and Park." Szarka started the car and stepped on the gas, rolling into the street and signaling a left turn. "How's your leg?"

"Feels like someone's going at it with a hacksaw. Don't worry about me."

They drove in silence for a time. Szarka sighed, tapped the steering wheel with his fingers, looked over at Clay. "We're being hunted now. Both of us."

Clay nodded. "You blew your cover by getting me out of the end of that beating."

"You wouldn't have been much use to me crippled."

Clay grunted laughter. "Not saying I don't appreciate it, just that you're in a precarious place now."

Szarka nodded. "I won't be going home any time soon. Not until Olivia is dealt with."

Olivia. Clay wondered where the woman was, why Reyes had entrusted his and Szarka's murders to hired goons, and when the other shoe would drop. He supposed he would find out in time. Hopefully, he wouldn't be crushed beneath it.

Of course, it occurred to him, maybe there was another reason for her absence. Maybe she'd had another errand that night. "You need to call Luke. Like right now."

"Indeed. I hope—there's Jeffrey."Szarka pointed.

Clay followed the gesture and saw a man in a dark suit sitting on a crumbling set of brick steps. His eyes were sunken into dark circles and he was staring out into the street with a forlorn expression. He looked like a man who'd been doing some soul-searching and wasn't terribly happy with what he'd found.

Szarka pulled the car up and Jeffrey glanced over at them. He stood and made his way toward them as Szarka put the car in "park" and stepped out. Clay stayed where he was, unable to walk and not particularly interested in greeting this man anyway.

Szarka and Jeffrey exchanged words and shook hands. Then Szarka turned to the car and Jeffrey followed. The fat man opened the passenger door and got in. Jeffrey sat in the driver's seat. He glanced over at Clay, who returned the gaze.

"Uh ..." The man seemed to have no idea where to begin.

"Just fucking drive."

Jeffrey put the car into gear and got it moving. "Listen, about all this—"

"Clay is fully aware of you situation," Szarka said. "I wouldn't waste time apologizing, as I don't believe he has any intention of accepting the apology. I'll locate a pharmacy at which you can acquire the goods we need to patch him up."

"And my family?"

"I'll wire them fifty thousand dollars right now. You can confirm the wire and give instruction to your wife once we're past the checkpoint. Your daughter will be safe."

"What if they've taken her already?" Jeffrey said, and Clay stirred. His leg hurt like a motherfucker, and he really wasn't in the mood for this.

"Then she'll lose her hand and it'll be your fault," he said. "How's that sound, Jeff? You could've gone to Alex straight from the start and spared all of us this grief. Now it might be too late. How you gonna feel every time you have to look at that stump, man?"

"Jesus," Jeffrey said, his voice choked. A traffic light in front of them turned red and they slowed to a halt. Clay glanced around, looking for figures coming toward the car, or vehicles trailing them, any indication that Jeffrey had sold them out again, but the streets were empty.

"This is unnecessary." Szarka's voice was full of reproach. "Officer Foster is angry because he has a bullet in his leg—"

"That's one reason."

"But needless antagonism aside, there's very little likelihood that anything has happened to your daughter. You did what you were told right up to the point that Clay held a gun to your head. Why would they punish you or your family when you made every reasonable attempt to fulfill your bargain with them?"

"I don't even know who *they* are," Jeffrey said. "Who knows how crazy they might be?"

"I know who they are. I'm going to tell you, but I have to call someone first. He may be in danger." Szarka tapped his ear. "Call Luke."

"They had the car traced," Clay said, "Why didn't they just go after us at the cemetery?"

"Perhaps it was too open," Szarka said. "Too easy for one or more of us to escape. Better we be delivered in a neat little packa—Luke. Yes, it's Szarka. We've been compromised and attacked by Olivia's men ... No ... No, I ... Luke, stop talking. Stop. Get out of wherever you are, right now. Don't use your car. Do you still have the cash I ... Good. Buy something tonight and get away from Union City ... Yes, that would be a good destination. Send me an encrypted e-mail when you arrive ... Yes, all right. Good luck." He touched his ear and turned to look at his driver. "With that done, I believe it's time to make a co-conspirator of you, Jeffrey."

Jeffrey considered this for a moment, the look on his face that of a man unsure just how much he really wanted to be a co-conspirator. Szarka gave him time, looking at his driver, a sly grin on his face, and Clay understood what the man was doing. He was trapping Jeffrey. Once the driver knew what they were up to, he became a liability to Reyes whether or not he alerted her to Clay and Szarka's location.

Clay caught Szarka's eye. Gave him a grim smile. Nodded. *Good man.*

Jeffrey saw this and sighed, seeming to understand that he had no choice. As the car moved along the empty streets, Szarka began to talk. Clay could see signs for the Lincoln Tunnel. For the second time that night, they were headed for Manhattan.

CHAPTER 20

Safe House

"This apartment has been with my family for at least thirty years," Szarka said. "If Elena Reyes knows about it, then I'm afraid there's nothing more I can do for us. It's never been held in my name, nor in any of my relatives' names. My father acquired it through clandestine means."

"Bought it for his mistress, huh?" Clay said.

"One of them," Szarka said with a grim, thin-lipped smile.

"It's a nice place."

The small vestibule had marble floors and white, wood-paneled walls. The style was from some period in European history—Clay didn't know which—and had gone through a revival in the early twenties. It looked outdated again now, but the apartment itself was in immaculate shape.

"Why's this place so clean if no one uses it?"

Szarka slipped off his shoes. "A service comes through once every few months to take care of dust and cobwebs."

"That means Reyes could get to people who know about this place."

Szarka clapped him on the shoulder. "When I began to gather information on Elena, I let the original crew go and

301

brought in a new group that I pay only in disco cards. They don't know my name, have no idea that I would be here now, and aren't due for another visit for at least six weeks. Relax, my friend."

Relax. Sounded easy, but with so many people involved in this, the possibility of treachery or simply a cataclysmic fuckup gnawed at him. There wasn't much he could do about it right now, so Clay moved on, following Szarka.

Past the entry, the place opened out into a grand receiving room, off of which led three hallways. This room had wooden parquet floors and the same white walls, and at its center was a gigantic Oriental rug in red and gold. The furniture was white leather, worn a bit here and there but clearly cared for. Clay half-sat, half-fell down on one of the two gigantic couches and propped up his leg, grimacing. The painkillers had taken care of the worst of it, but he wasn't going to be comfortable for a while. They hadn't wanted to stop at a hospital, which meant no nanotreatments.

"You're going to get blood on that," Jeffrey said. He was standing beside Szarka at the entrance to the room, looking around. His voice was full of distaste, and he was looking at Clay with a prissy expression that made Clay want to leap from the couch and ram his fist down the man's throat.

"Oh, shit, am I? How fucking *common* of me."

Jeffrey opened his mouth to respond to this sarcasm and Szarka put a hand on his shoulder. "Jeffrey, please … That sofa is neither young enough to be worth anything nor old enough to be worth anything. Let him rest." He stepped into the room, beckoning Jeffrey to follow, and they sat down. Szarka let out a deep sigh as he sank into the leather, and then he leaned forward to inspect the decanter on the table, wincing a little as he stretched his back. "I think this is bourbon." He pulled the top and sniffed at it. "No, rum. Not-so-good rum, but rum nonetheless. Gentlemen?"

"I'm in," Clay said. He wasn't really supposed to be drinking alcohol on top of the painkillers, but fuck it.

"Sure," Jeffrey said. He was looking off to the side, out the floor-to-ceiling windows that opened up on Amsterdam Avenue. They were on the Upper West Side, near the old Museum of Natural History, which had been closed down after a bombing in the thirties and had never reopened. Jeffrey looked far less distraught than he had earlier. Finding out that his wife and baby girl were unharmed and on their way to Boston had improved his outlook dramatically.

The driver had been dumbfounded when he first learned that it was Elena Reyes who had blackmailed him into betraying Szarka. It had taken a full explanation of her reasons, including the painful admission from Szarka that he was addicted to Elixir, to convince Jeffrey of the truth.

Szarka handed them each a glass with a generous helping of rum in it. "*Salud,*" he said and took a long drink. Clay and Jeffrey raised their glasses and each drank as well.

"We need a plan," Clay said.

Szarka swallowed his rum. "I plan on sleeping."

"Me, too," Jeffrey said quietly.

"That's terrific, but I'm thinking longer term than that. We're going to be here a while. I can't go raiding Brooklyn drug factories with a hole in my leg. Plus, I'm covered in blood, you're covered in dirt or tar or whatever the fuck that is, and even Jeff here's not looking so great after rolling around in the street dodging bullets."

Szarka nodded. "I have few articles of clothing here, and none that would fit either of you, but you can at least shower. There are four bedrooms and three full baths. Jeffrey looks the most presentable of the three of us. In the morning I suggest we send him out for clothing and other supplies. I will be ... incapacitated for a few hours when we first get up."

Clay glanced over at him. "You have everything you need here?"

"I've anticipated needing this space for quite some time, as my investigation of Elena became increasingly dangerous. It's stocked for a month or so, but we must finish this. I can't get what I need in this city without Elena's help, and she ... I can't tell you how much I detest even speaking about this."

"Then let's drop it."

"Thank you."

"How fast do you think you can have those nanotreatments delivered?"

Szarka had connections that would allow him to obtain the treatments without a hospital stay. Properly administered—and Clay knew well how to do so after so many years in the field—the treatments would reduce a catastrophic injury like a bullet wound to a few days' annoyance. That was good. After taking a beating one day and then having to stitch his leg up by himself in the back of a moving car less than three days later, Clay was ready to feel whole again.

"Tomorrow afternoon."

"Good. I'll need three, maybe four days before I can head to Brooklyn. We should spend them doing something useful."

"I'll be working with Luke, transferring him as much data on Elena as I can acquire from my archives. I can only assume that since she's aware of my interference, she's taken steps to secure her own data, but I have a great deal stored in a great many places of my own."

"You've really been working on this for a long time," Jeffrey said. "Christ, Mr. Szarka, I can't tell you how sorry I am. I just ... screwed it all up."

Clay shifted position on the couch. "Reyes did that. You fucked up a little piece of an already fucked-up situation. Hell, it kind of helped—we know Reyes knows now. So relax."

"This from the guy who an hour ago was telling me to imagine my daughter's arm ending in a stump."

"How about we put a bullet in your leg and see how pleasant you are?" Clay said.

"I'll pass." They drank in silence for a time.

"So, the plan," Szarka said.

"You handle nanotreatments and getting ready for Brooklyn," Clay said. "This asshole handles clothes, food, and other supplies. And booze. This rum's all right, but it's not whiskey. I like Maker's Black, Jeff. Alex here likes that twenty-year Highland shit with the silver thistle on the bottle."

"My name is Jeffrey, so that's what you can call me," Jeffrey said, shaking his head and looking disgusted. "And I know what Mr. Szarka drinks. What do *you* do for the next four days, other than bleed on his furniture and insult people?"

"Heal up. That and I'm going to get in touch with a dear, dear friend in The Hook. I think he and I need to rekindle our relationship. There's a certain spider-tattooed lunatic out there who needs some serious investigation."

Jeffrey looked confused.

Clay waved it away. "Don't worry about it. Less you know about her the better. She's going to be dead soon anyway."

"You really believe you can kill her?" Szarka said.

"Yes. Anyway, what's she done? She's fast on the draw and she managed to kill an unarmed chemist. Big fucking deal."

"I don't think I need to tell you that those are the least of her ... professional accomplishments."

Clay leaned his head back and was amused to realize he was exhausted. Why this should surprise him, given that it was nearly six in the morning and he'd been shot not three hours ago, he couldn't say. "Let me worry about Olivia. You worry about the rest."

Szarka looked troubled. "There is ... one final item that we still need to discuss."

This was news to Clay. He raised an eyebrow. "What is it?"

"We need someone to actually synthesize the cure once we have the data."

Clay set his rum on the table, scrubbed a hand across his face, looked back up at the older man sitting across from him. "You didn't think this was something I should know?"

"I didn't expect it to be an issue. If you acquired what we needed, I thought I could handle contacting her and getting her to agree."

"Her?"

Szarka sighed. "The most qualified person, a woman who would have both an understanding of the drug and access to equipment needed to synthesize a cure at least in experimental doses, would be Dr. Anuhya Imran."

Clay felt his jaw clench and forced himself to stifle a curse. *Imran? The bitch whose stupid greed had cost Terry her life?*

"You've got to be kidding me," he said at last.

Szarka made a face as if he'd bitten into a lemon. "Luke and I were hoping not to involve you in this, but now ... with Elena aware of our plans, we can't afford to wait until we have the data. We need to secure Imran's help as soon as possible."

"There has to be someone else. Someone out there who can make this shit who isn't the one responsible for putting Elixir on the streets and getting my wife fucking killed."

"She is a talented chemist and she knows more about Elixir, its actual chemical composition, than anyone else alive, even Elena. She doesn't have all the puzzle pieces, but we can deliver them to her, and there's no one in a better position to quickly and efficiently assemble them. She can even commandeer Shun Ten equipment to quickly make a proof of concept cure."

"That's what this is about, isn't it?" Clay said.

Szarka leaned back on his sofa, sipping his rum, looking at Clay with a sort of serene curiosity. "You believe I'm in a rush because I'm desperate for the cure?"

"Fucking right I do."

Szarka shrugged. "Perhaps I am. Does it matter? We're up against a wall here, Clay. If you'd have it be someone other than Dr. Imran, tell me who makes more sense and I'll endeavor to recruit them."

Clay chewed his lip, thinking, but nothing came. Terry might have had a list of chemists, but Terry was dead, killed for spying on the woman he was now going to go ask for help. It tore at him, but there was nothing to do about it.

"We might find her highly sympathetic," Szarka said. "She didn't sound happy with Elena on the recording, and Luke said she had no idea that your wife's death had anything at all to do with her."

"Luke's an idealist kid who wouldn't know what Imran is or isn't aware of any better than I'd know what the Queen of England's pussy tastes like."

Szarka gave him an unimpressed glance. Jeffrey was sitting, legs crossed, with a tight offended look on his face. Clay wanted to tell the man to fuck off with his attitude. Instead he sighed, rolled his eyes, threw one hand in the air, and took a slug of his glass of rum.

"Fine, whatever. We'll stop at her place before we hit the processing facility. That work for you?"

"It does."

"You got anything else you want to tell me? Any more revelations?"

"I do not."

"All right, then."

Szarka nodded and upended his glass, finishing the liquor in one large swig. He set it on the marble coffee table and yawned. "Gentlemen, there are doors all along the western hall that lead to bedrooms. Mine is at the far end. You have your pick of the other three. Good night."

Jeffrey watched him waddle off and then returned to staring out the window, sipping at his rum. "That guy's too nice for this stuff."

Clay glanced over at him. "Yeah, it's too bad he's not more of a shithead."

"Are you being sarcastic?"

Clay shook his head. "No. A bigger shithead would've noticed Reyes was an amoral climber hell-bent on taking his job and had her booted long ago."

"Guess you're right."

Clay shrugged, finished his rum, set the glass down. "Doesn't matter now."

Jeffrey looked up at him, "You should probably get some sleep, too. Get healing."

"There is no fucking chance I'm leaving you to sit out here and call your friends again ..."

Jeffrey gave a disgusted sigh. "Why would I do that? What would be the ... the goddamned purpose, now? Unless you win, I'm a dead man. Wasn't that the point of telling me everything? I failed to deliver you and Alex, and now I know all about Elena Reyes and the great Elixir conspiracy. The first thing Olivia would do when she was done gutting the two of you is snap my neck."

His voice was bitter, filled with distaste and self-pity. Clay wanted to sock him in the eye. Instead he said, "There's nothing you can say that would make me trust you."

"No? Well, I don't think you have a choice, Officer Foster. Those nanotreatments need four days to do their jobs. Either you stay up the entire time or sooner or later you have to take your eyes off me. Do you think you can go ninety-six hours without sleep while healing up from being shot?"

Clay considered this. What was the right play? He couldn't trust Jeffrey's honor, but could he trust the man's self-interest? "Look me in the eyes."

Jeffrey looked over at him, raising an eyebrow.

"Szarka might be too nice for this shit, but I'm not. If *anyone* shows up at this apartment because of you, they'd better kill me. If they don't manage to, I will hunt down your beautiful baby girl and I will do a lot worse than take her hand, and I'll make your wife watch. Do you fucking understand me?"

Jeffrey bared his teeth. "You don't need to threaten me."

"Don't give a shit. I'm doing it anyway. Do you believe me?"

Jeffrey stared at him for a moment longer, mouth pressed into a thin line. "I believe you're a loathsome enough person that you would actually hurt an innocent little girl, yes. Is that what you want to hear?"

"That'll do. So, you going to call anyone while we're asleep, Jeffrey?"

"I'm going to sit here and think for a while and then I'm going to go to bed. I won't be calling anyone until this is all done."

That'll have to be good enough.

Clay stood, wincing at the ache this caused in his leg, and began to shuffle for the closest bedroom.

* * *

The Chink gave them everything there was to be found on Olivia. The man had agreed to help them only after Clay had secured a promise from Szarka that Manhattan Water and Power would, after Elena Reyes was gone, work to strengthen The Hook's power grid without any attempts to legitimatize it or bring the flooded neighborhood back into Brooklyn proper. Szarka had sworn to make it happen, provided the Chink would agree to pay for the power being delivered, and the Chink had accepted and gone to work.

The total amount of information available on the woman in the white suit filled four paragraphs in an encrypted e-mail. She was in her late twenties or early thirties, spectacularly fit and agile, and broadly known for her speed both with her hands and on foot. She was a masterful gunman but preferred a blade for up-close work and carried both on her person most of the time. Her hand-to-hand style bore no resemblance to that which USS soldiers had employed during the war.

Her Carolina accent was real, or at least the one she preferred when not playing a character, but she was a capable mimic and spoke at least three languages conversationally. She held citizenship in both the USS and the United States—though whether the latter was acquired legally or not the Chink could not determine—and could move between the two countries at will. She was loyal to Reyes and Reyes only, for reasons she had never divulged. Whom she had served or what she had done before coming north, no one knew. The spider tattoo was a mystery, as was the reasoning behind an assassin's wearing such a conspicuous mark.

One of the paragraphs mainly consisted of unfounded rumors, including the widespread but unproven belief that she was a lesbian and an often-echoed rumor that where the woman's vulva should have been, there was only a set of teeth. Popular though it might be, Clay doubted the veracity of the latter. He didn't give a shit about the former.

By all accounts, she was also a ruthless sociopath with psychotic tendencies. She could hold herself in check when necessary, but the woman was at her most content when the time came for her to get personally involved in the torture and execution of other human beings. She usually became very chatty while doing such work, and that was the closest thing to a weakness the Chink had been able to locate.

"She is a monster," Szarka said when Clay shared the information with him. "I once saw her break a man's fingers, one after another, by bashing them with a paperweight while security held him down. He had stolen some money from petty cash, and he kept apologizing, begging her to stop, promising to pay back double, triple, quadruple what he'd taken. All the while she kept that same smile, that same voice, but her eyes …"

Clay knew the type. He'd seen them in the Army from time to time, smiling away even while performing some heinous act, and always with that same thirsty, raging look in their eyes, like they were feeding on what they were witnessing. He was not like them; Clay could kill without concern or regret but took no pleasure in the act. Where Olivia enjoyed it, Clay simply didn't care.

Jeffrey proved trustworthy. He ran errands, bought clothes and food and alcohol, even cooked a couple of surprisingly good meals in the apartment's vast kitchen. Clay set him up with encryption not available to the general public that allowed him to contact his wife and verify that she and their daughter were safe.

Clay healed. Szarka's contacts had come through and provided him with plenty of nanotreatments, and the microscopic machines had gone to work on Clay's damaged leg just minutes after injection. A wound that would have taken months to heal had been reduced in four days' time to little more than a blemish. He thought that nanotreatments were one of the greatest inventions of the twenty-first century. For localized non-lethal wounds that weren't absolutely time-critical, you couldn't beat the stuff.

They'd kept mostly to themselves, holed up in relative safety. Clay had sent an untraceable message to Deputy Chief Warren telling her that he was alive but in tremendous danger and that he was taking shelter in Queens. He doubted she would organize a manhunt, but if she did, he didn't want it to happen in Manhattan or Brooklyn. Warren responded saying that he'd been suspended indefinitely from the Brooklyn PD, stripped of his access to their servers, and that it would be a miracle if he ever regained his job. Clay didn't bother replying. He'd expected all that.

He had also contacted Inspector Haley. Clay had written and rewritten the message, trying to determine how much detail was too much, whether he should reveal the full scope of Reyes's involvement with Elixir. Finally he'd stopped short of explaining everything to the man, wanting to do it in person, and said only that he'd discovered a tremendous conspiracy that involved Elena Reyes. Clay believed he could convince Haley of the truth, especially if he could show some of the documentation that had been on Terry's SynchDrive, but he couldn't risk sending that information along. Haley would have to wait until they could meet in person.

The inspector had responded with five words—*tell me when and where*—and Clay had been glad to see them. He'd replied that he would make contact again soon, with the passphrase *Bronx Bombers* to verify his identity if the communication was unencrypted, and left it at that. When he was back from Brooklyn and preparing to go up against Olivia and bring Reyes to justice, he would meet with Haley and secure his aid.

Clay also engaged in one final parlay with the Chink, this time offering a singular exchange. In the future, when all of this was clear, he would perform one mission of the Chink's choosing, as long as didn't required him to take any lives. He would do it without asking questions, and without consideration of whether the consequences would affect his work as a police officer, if indeed he was ever able to return to the force. In return, he wanted a clear answer to a single question: why had the U.S. government given Terry technology capable of breaking high-level encryption routines when she'd been in Virginia acting as a nurse's aide?

The Chink accepted the bargain and answered the question in the same communication. "You could ask the Colonel that gave you your missions in North Carolina about Operation Exodus, or you could visit this interesting data store and look it up yourself, using the following log-in credentials and security token."

The link took him to a darknet site, a nonpublic part of the web accessible only to those with the proper log-ins. Hidden behind the wall, Clay found a store of information, rumors, and off-the-record conversations on a wide variety of missions undertaken by the United States government before, during, and after the second civil war. Clay had no idea who maintained the site, and would never know—the Chink's e-mail had specified that the credentials were good only for a single access, and the data was displayed with a proprietary module that prevented downloading—but the sheer quantity of data was mind-boggling. Three of the six missions he'd performed in North Carolina were cataloged, though none of them were the last one. Only two men on the planet knew those details, and Clay was certain that the other one would die before letting them slip.

Clay didn't have the time to browse idly. He found the entry for Operation Exodus and began to read. It was a lengthy collection of documents, interviews, and recorded phone calls, and it took him more than two hours to get through the whole thing. When he was done, he closed the darknet link, put his tablet to sleep, and stared at the wall for a time, thinking. So that's why she'd done it. Not out of fear for him or for herself but simply because she'd been ashamed and hadn't wanted him to find out a truth for which he'd have forgiven her within seconds of her admitting it. Terry had kept what she was doing hidden simply to preserve the halo she knew he'd always seen above her head, to keep even the slightest hint of tarnish from it.

She hadn't known the stakes. She hadn't known about Olivia or just how ruthless Elena Reyes really was. Now she was dead because she'd kept her activities from Clay, so that he wouldn't learn that for two years she'd filed regular reports to the government about the soldiers in her care. The brass had wanted to be sure that the men coming from the front lines, particularly special cases like Clay, could be trusted to return to civilian life.

Terry had, in exchange for money to help her struggling parents, been trained to break into soldiers' communications and forward them to the Army. Operation Exodus had been implemented in just about every hospital in every state. Terry was but one of many, and as soon as she'd realized she was falling in love with Clay, she'd bowed out of the program entirely. The government had accepted her reasons and told her they intended to collect their equipment but had never followed through on it. Bureaucracy. It had come with them to Brooklyn and sat in a box, unused, until Terry grew suspicious of Anuhya Imran.

Clay wanted to hold his wife tight and tell her he forgave her, but there was nothing left of Terry to hold. There was only ash and dust, sitting in a pewter urn on the mantel, in the dark, back in Brooklyn Heights, and Clay could speak forgiveness to those ashes all he wanted, but Terry would never hear it. She was gone.

* * *

It was a Tuesday night when they made the trek through Manhattan, down to the Lower East Side and across the bridge into Williamsburg. The place had been transformed over the first half of the century into a glass-tower wonderland. Once the domain of broke artists and filled with industrial buildings, later a bastion for the young and hip, it was now the sort of place affordable only to those with real money. An entire generation of entrepreneurs' children, kids who'd grown up fat and lazy on their mothers' and fathers' stock option money, called Williamsburg home. Most of them were badly hooked on Elixir and frittering their trust funds away at an appalling pace.

The rising waters had made a peninsula out of the neighborhood, sinking the Navy Yards, most of Greenpoint, and parts of Bushwick. This only increased the exclusivity of the area. Some of Brooklyn's finest and most corrupt politicians and businesspeople maintained residences here. The rest lived in Clay's neighborhood.

Doctor Anuhya Imran lived in an apartment she had once shared with her city councilman husband and two children, before the latter had grown up and moved out and the former had left her to shack up with a campaign adviser. It was all very sordid, and Clay had heard about it from Terry even before the scandal hit the papers. Imran had been open about it, even making jokes, but her work had started to slip and she'd become forgetful. Scatterbrained.

Clay might once have had some sympathy, before learning the truth about his wife's death and the doctor's involvement with Elixir. Now he wanted to get this over with as quickly as possible, secure her agreement, and get the hell away from her before he did or said something stupid.

They pulled into the visitors garage below a stark, jet-black building that stretched at least thirty stories into the air. Even through the Mirae's insulated interior, Clay could hear the sound of fans running, sucking the stink of car exhaust and the Brooklyn air away from the underground facility. He opened the door and glanced at Szarka.

"You coming?"

"I think that would be best, don't you?" Szarka said, his voice dry.

"Probably." Clay got out of the car. Jeffrey would wait for them there until they returned. During his years of service to Szarka, the man had developed a patient serenity that was impressive.

Szarka exited the vehicle and stood next to Clay. Ahead, there was a bank of elevators, and the two men began moving toward them in unison. Up above, they would find the doctor, their key to curing Elixir.

CHAPTER 21

The Doctor

Imran lived on the twenty-third floor and had given Clay a guest access code. He had contacted her and set up the meeting, saying only that after going through the box of items from Terry's desk, he had found a few things that belonged to the doctor and wanted to return them in person. Imran seemed to have accepted the lie without question. When they stepped into the hallway that stood between the two apartments that took up the entire floor—*Jesus Christ, these places must be gigantic*—Clay stepped forward, Szarka behind him, and rang the bell for 23-A. They waited a moment, and then the door clicked and swung inward.

Anuhya Imran was in her early fifties and gifted with an exotic beauty that was so stunning it seemed to stop Clay in his tracks every time he saw her. He didn't know if it was surgery or makeup or nanotech—perhaps some combination of all three—but the woman didn't look a day over thirty, and frankly she looked pretty goddamned amazing for thirty. She had thick raven-colored hair that fell to her shoulders in loose curls, large eyes with dark irises, high cheekbones, a prominent nose, and full red lips. Her skin was dark brown,

319

the color of a fine maduro cigar, and when she smiled at him, her teeth were straight and so white they shone even in the dim hallway.

"Hello, Clay. It's nice to see you," she said, her voice soft and warm. She glanced over his shoulder, noticing Szarka, and her smile flickered only momentarily. "Who've you brought with you? I don't believe I've had the pleasure ..."

"Anuhya, this is Alex Szarka. He's the CEO of Manhattan Water and Power."

It took only a moment for it to sink in, but when it did, Imran's smile left completely. There was the briefest flash of what looked like terror in her eyes, and Clay prepared to stop her should she try to slam the door, but the look was quickly replaced with something more like calm, quiet despair. Imran closed her eyes, put her head down, breathed deeply. Then she looked up at them.

"So you know, then." There it was: there could be no other reason why Clay would have brought someone from MWP to her home. Imran knew it, had realized it in that brief instant, and seemed to have made her peace with it. "Are you here to arrest me, Officer Foster?"

"Not unless I have to." There was no value in letting her know he'd been suspended from the force. Better she think he still had some sort of authority left.

"I see ... and why have you brought Mister ... I'm sorry, was it Szarka?"

Szarka stepped forward, nodding. "It was, and it's a pleasure to meet you, ma'am."

Imran gave him a halfhearted smile. "I wish I could say the same, but I fear tonight may not go well for me. Will you come in, gentlemen? I might as well be a good hostess. I suspect we have a great deal to talk about."

Clay met her eyes. "Anuhya, do I need to warn you not to make any rash decisions?"

"With one glaring exception, I'm not the rash-decision type." Imran sighed, turned, and motioned for them to follow. "Please take off your shoes."

They did so and followed her down a wood-paneled hall that led into a massive kitchen that opened onto an even more massive living room. The rooms were sleek and streamlined, with furnishings of polycarbonate, dark wood, steel, and leather. One wall was made up of windows. Another contained a gigantic holo screen on which the news was playing, muted. Imran snapped her fingers at it and the picture disappeared.

"Nice place," Clay said.

"Yes, thank you. My ex-husband was tremendously proud when we first qualified for this building. Now, he ... well. Would you two like something to drink? I have wine, or sparkling water, and I believe there is some whiskey around here somewhere."

"I'm good." Clay leaned against the countertop, watching her as she poured herself a generous glass of red wine.

"Mr. Szarka?"

"Sparkling water, please."

She handed him a glass and gestured toward the couches. "Please, sit."

"You first," Clay said, and this earned him a frown. He simply stared back, and after a moment Imran clenched her teeth and moved to the living room.

"I don't know how you think I could run on this floor, in these socks, even if I wanted to." She sat down. "But if you're quite certain I'm not about to make a mad dash for the door, perhaps now you're ready to join me?"

"I was more worried about you pulling a gun from some kitchen drawer and shooting me in the back." Clay crossed from the open kitchen to the living room and sat down facing her. Szarka sat to his left.

"I detest firearms. I've never even seen one in real life, other than in police holsters. I wouldn't know what to do with a gun even if I owned one."

"Good to know."

There was a moment of silence as the three contemplated each other, and then Szarka took a breath. "Ms. Imran ... Doctor ... we need your help," he said.

Imran raised an eyebrow. "That's not what I was expecting."

"Me neither," Clay muttered. He hadn't expected Szarka to broach that topic first. "Let's rewind a bit. When did you first get involved with Elena Reyes?"

She shook her head, looking at the floor, and sighed. "Second grade. We were seven years old."

"Were you making drugs for her then, too?" Clay was unable to keep the acid note from his voice, and this earned him another glare.

"Elena was my best friend. We were never in trouble, never did anything except play by the rules, run circles around the others in our classes, and ace everything they threw at us. We were two public-school kids in a world that was falling apart, and we held on to each other."

"So, how'd you get to this point?"

Imran put a hand to her forehead. She reached forth with her other hand, took her glass of wine, and downed two large swallows before setting it back down on the coffee table in front of her. "I don't know."

"Reyes contacted you, asked you—"

"No, I contacted her."

Clay tilted his head. "What, you called her up and asked her if she had any plans to build a drug empire?"

Imran shook her head. "For God's sake, Clay … you can't possibly—"

"So, what happened?"

"I was going to lose this place. We never did pay off the mortgage like we always said we would, and the agreement that allowed me to take possession of it also required me to assume the debt. Shun Ten is a lucrative job, and I thought I could consult, but nothing seemed to work out. I was having trouble concentrating. I …" She trailed off, seeming very interested in her fingernails.

"You weren't dealing well with the dissolution of your marriage?" Szarka said. He knew about it; everyone knew about it, a fact that Clay could see pained the woman. She looked up at them, eyes dry, her expression nearly serene, and shrugged.

"Douglas began seeing other women in the first year of our marriage, and I became aware of it sometime in year two. We had several fights—screaming matches, to be honest—and each time he would promise to reform. I quickly realized that the thrill of convincing yet another young woman to part her legs was something he would never be able to give up, and after a time I accepted it. I accepted him for what he was. I raised two children with him, let him think I believed his lies, and thought that would be enough."

"But it wasn't," Clay said.

Imran frowned. "Clearly not. He left me for an idiot. I think that was what upset me so much for so long. She couldn't even win him reelection. I'm not sure that woman could have successfully managed George Washington's campaign, and they wanted to make that man *king*."

"If you're hoping a sob story is going to make up for—"

"Don't you dare!" she said, her eyes blazing. "I called Elena to see if Manhattan Water and Power had any need of chemistry consulting. Z-Cell refinement, wastewater treatment ... anything. She said she had a project in mind that she'd been meaning to contact me about. I didn't know what I was doing until it was too late."

"You must have had some idea."

"In the early going it was all just theoretical. She had formulae from some other source and wanted to know if they could be broken apart. All I had to do was ... borrow time on Shun Ten's sequencers and get her the data. The amount she offered was exorbitant, and when I asked why, she told me she was protecting against industrial espionage. If she paid me more by far than the work was worth, it was less likely another company would lure me away."

"So you weren't the one who came up with the drug?"

"Certainly not."

"Do you know who did?"

Imran shook her head. "Elena is a tremendously wealthy woman with uncountable connections in nearly every powerful country around the globe. Does it really matter which she tapped to create the early formulae? By the time I was involved, it had been broken down into components. I was working on only a few of them."

"And you never got curious?"

"Of course I did, eventually. I sat down and really looked at what I was sequencing. I called her on it and she lied to me, told me it wasn't going to hurt anyone, that the drug was being manufactured as a competitor to medicinal marijuana, that it was going to bring comfort and solace to desperate people."

"You had to have known it was addictive."

Imran shook her head. "The parts that do that are manufactured elsewhere. I never touched them. I didn't even learn about them until much later."

"Why didn't you go to the police after that?"

"I … I was afraid. I've built my whole life here. I didn't want to get in trouble … I just wanted to keep my house, and there was so much *money*, and it was so easy to tell myself that it was their choice. That the people taking the drug were responsible for their own actions. That it wasn't my fault."

"Great. So the whole rest of the city can burn, right? As long as you get to keep your fucking slate countertops?"

"Can we keep this civil?" Szarka said.

"I would appreciate—" Imran began.

"My ability to stay civil disappeared around the time Elena Reyes had my wife thrown off our balcony." The words came out like chips of dirty ice. They tasted foul in his mouth.

Imran reacted as if she'd been slapped, eyes going wide, the color draining from her face. For a moment her mouth worked as if she were speaking, but no words came out. Clay gave her the time. To his left, Szarka shifted his weight and glanced out the window, looking uncomfortable. At last Imran spoke.

"That's impossible." Her voice was tight and croaking, as if someone had locked her throat in a vise. "Clay, no."

"I've met the person who killed Terry. You know who I'm talking about."

Imran didn't answer but wouldn't meet his gaze, either, and Clay knew he was right. This woman was well aware of Olivia.

"Did you know, Anuhya? Did you know that Terry was about to blow everything wide open? Did you look the other way when it came time to get rid of her, like you did with Douglas and his women? Like you did with Reyes and her drugs?"

"I had no idea!" Imran cried, and now there were tears sparkling in her eyes. "Oh, no ... You must think I'm a monster!"

Clay didn't say anything. Imran put her fingers to her eyes, brushed away the tears, looked straight at him. "I never knew that Terry's death was anything other than an accident. I swear that to you on my soul."

"Your soul's not—"

"On my *children's* souls, then! At first I was willfully ignorant, and then later I was ... willfully deluding myself. After that I was just afraid. Afraid of what Elena has become and of that ... that woman she keeps around. Olivia. She's like a big, mean dog straining on its leash. You can see in her eyes that she wants to bite."

"That she does," Clay muttered.

"But I never knew about Terry! I never had any idea she was in danger. I wouldn't have let it happen. I would have done something ... anything."

"Would you? She was about to send you to jail. Would you have gone? There's still time. We could make a few phone calls."

"I thought you weren't here to arrest me." Imran stiffened a little in her seat.

Szarka leaned forward. "Doctor Imran, we have one half of the formula needed to fashion a cure for Elixir, are in pursuit of the other half this very evening, and with your expertise could begin manufacturing on a trial basis in mere days after acquiring it."

Imran looked taken aback. "A cure? How did you—no, I don't want to know how you got it."

"You didn't know she was making a cure?" Clay said.

"No, I haven't been involved in that. I just run the tests each week when she sends me new data. But that's wonderful. I just … Do you understand the danger you're putting yourself in?"

Szarka sighed. "We do, but it must be done. Clay's tasks are to acquire the other half of the cure and to handle Olivia. My task, and that of a few others, is to attempt to bring Elena Reyes to justice. We need you, both to build the cure and to provide testimony."

"Oh, no, I couldn't … She's my best friend! Or she was. I can't send her to jail."

"Your best friend threatened to have you killed!" Clay cried. "I've heard your half of the conversation—that's what she told you, right? That if you went to the police, she'd set Olivia on you?"

Imran nodded, looking miserable.

"Whatever you two once meant to each other … those days are gone. She will *eliminate* you the moment you're not of use to her anymore. Don't you understand? That's where this is going no matter what you do. You *know*. You think she's going to let you live?"

"Clay, please." Szarka kept his voice calm.

Even in his anger, Clay appreciated the tone. It was that of someone who has sat through board meetings, negotiated with tough clients, and understands that the open hand often gains more than the closed fist. Clay had never been able to keep his hands open for very long.

Szarka turned to Imran. "Anuhya ... may I call you that?"

"Certainly."

"You have become involved in something terrible. I understand that. I've dealt with similar occurrences in my life. Whether or not you willingly provide testimony against Reyes is something you will need to work out with the police and your lawyers. But you have the power tonight to make a decision that could help tens of thousands of people. Perhaps more."

Imran was chewing her lip. She took another big gulp of wine, looking out the window. "I'm so afraid of what Elena might do to me ... or to my children."

"Rightly so, but that's where Clay comes in. He neutralizes Elena's most immediate threat while the evidence we're gathering does the rest. By the time we've fashioned a cure that can be widely distributed, Elena will be in jail and will have much bigger things to worry about."

"You have a chance to make up for what you've done," Clay said. "All the people you've hurt, all the lives you've helped destroy. We're giving you that chance instead of hauling you into jail and letting you rot. Make a fucking choice."

Imran gave him a cool glance. "I don't need a lecture on the useless destruction of lives from a civil war veteran."

"Tell us what you need, Anuhya," Szarka said, his voice calm. Jesus, he was playing the good cop so well it was easy to forget that he wasn't one. "What can we do to convince you?"

Imran contemplated her glass of wine for a long while and then drained it in a single gulp. She looked not at Clay but at Szarka when she spoke.

"If it goes poorly for me in the end, will you tell my children that I tried to do something to put things right? That when I realized what I'd been a part of, I was horrified, and that when a solution presented itself, I did what I could?"

"Of course," Szarka said.

"Maybe we can build a statue, too," Clay muttered.

Imran ignored him. "Bring me the data and I'll formulate your cure, Mr. Szarka. It won't make up for … for Terry, or for the others I hurt, but it's a start."

"Thank you," Szarka said. "It means a great deal to both Clay and me."

The trio made their way back to the front hall. There, the two men put on their shoes, and Szarka stepped out through the door and into the hallway. Clay turned to Imran. "Terry would want me to apologize for the way I treated you."

"But you wouldn't do it on your own, would you?" Imran said, and when Clay shook his head, she gave him a small, sad smile. "I deserve your wrath, Clay, and while I know it won't help anything, I want you to know how sorry I am for everything."

Clay nodded. She was right: it didn't help anything. But he believed her. "If you help us fix this, I'll try to keep you out of jail."

Imran's jaw clenched for a moment. Then she nodded and closed the door, leaving them to the task at hand.

* * *

"You going back to Manhattan tonight?" Clay asked after they had reached Bushwick.

Sitting beside him in the back seat of the Mirae, Szarka shook his head. "Every time we have to pass a checkpoint, it's an opportunity for our whereabouts to become known. We shouldn't return to Manhattan until all three of us are finished here. Jeffrey and I will find a diner. Additionally, I'm hoping to find a replacement for a stolen car that belongs to a dead man."

"There are still chop shops on Atlantic that'll sell you a cheap junker for cash. Get something inconspicuous. It'll probably still run on gas or electric, though, so you'll have to watch your fuel. Not too many stations around anymore."

Z-Cells hadn't really taken off until the end of the war, even though the ban on building gas-powered cars had been in effect since the thirties. Up until then electric had been the principal alternative, but Z-Cells were a better choice. They lasted for thousands of miles without needing a charge, and the principal distributors—Manhattan Water and Power one of them—had worked out a month-by-month pricing structure that was accessible to the average man. It occurred to Clay that he was, in fact, still paying Szarka and Reyes every month for his own Z-Cell, even though his car was sitting useless in a garage in Brooklyn Heights.

They were on Broadway now. The Envision factory, which took up an entire block between Atlantic and Herkimer, was close. Clay had spent the last several days preparing to enter it. He wasn't expecting much trouble. It was principally involved in producing components for eye cream. The Elixir production was a little side business the owner had started up after one of Reyes's many intermediaries had gotten in touch. It was just a way to make an extra buck, and the guy probably had no idea that the particular chem he was sequencing was being mixed into the drug that was destroying Brooklyn.

It was close to midnight. The plant didn't run a third shift, which meant that for the next five hours or so, it would be empty of everyone but the security guards. There were half a dozen of those, all supplied by a firm in Queens, none of them ex-military or ex-cops.

The building was three stories tall, and he could safely ignore the first. It was entirely taken up by the production lines, long conveyor systems that began in a sterilized clean room and ended at a machine that labeled the bottles and sorted them neatly into boxes. The tech had barely changed in fifty years, with the exception of a slow winnowing of the human element; the process was now almost entirely automated.

Above the processing floor were two stories of offices. Somewhere within them was the owner's terminal, and on that terminal was the data they needed to finish synthesizing the cure for Elixir and to free New York, Brooklyn, and the rest of the country from its deadly grip. Clay had studied the architectural plans, but none of the offices had leaped out as being terribly large or impressive. Nothing screamed "boss" to him. He'd have to hunt it down manually, searching for a terminal that would accept the log-in credentials he'd gotten from the Chink.

He'd acquired a new bag and had in it his tablet, which was populated with both his SynchDrive and Terry's. The bag also held Szarka's antique six-shooter, two dozen extra bullets, and a special toy Szarka had set him up with. The device could be held to just about any mag-lock on the planet, and given enough time, it would disrupt the field. Unless the door was additionally secured with a traditional lock, it would pop right open. Manufactured by hand in Indonesia, the devices were deeply illegal, carrying a felony charge and a mandatory two-year prison sentence just for possession. How the man had obtained it, Clay didn't ask.

"Pull over and drop me off here," Clay said when they were four blocks away.

"Yes, sir." Jeffrey had unconsciously slipped back into driver mode, and Clay laughed a little. The car pulled to one side and came to a halt.

Clay glanced over at Szarka. "Go to Jimmy's Auto Repair on Atlantic at Dewey. Tell the guy at the counter that your car has a broken fan belt and you don't want it anymore. He'll get what you mean."

"He won't care that it's—"

"We've busted that place for moving illegal vehicles, like, thirty times. He won't care. He'll pay you in cash or trade. Pick something old, boring, and nondescript. Meet me back here at this corner. If I'm not here by three, get the fuck out of Brooklyn and let me worry about finding a ride."

"You're certain?"

"I've got people here who I trust. If something goes wrong at the plant, I'll get to them, or I'll be dead and it won't matter anymore. I don't think you're going to bust in there yourself."

"Most likely not. Very well, Officer Foster. Good luck to you."

"Thanks." Clay opened the door. The heat and the stink came blasting in like tainted wind from a giant's asshole, assaulting him with something that approached physical force.

Christ, he'd forgotten it was like this. How was it that Brooklyn smelled so much worse than Manhattan?

As if echoing his thoughts, Szarka gave a disgusted groan and muttered, "How do people live here?"

"Not everyone's born with a trust fund." Before Szarka could respond to this, Clay stepped out onto the street and closed the door. He tapped the roof of the car a couple of times, turned, and headed toward the facility. Behind him, he heard the car roll off.

Once he got used to the smell, Brooklyn felt pretty much like he'd remembered. Like a terminal cancer patient, the city was carrying on. Traffic still filled the streets, even at midnight, and there were people in the fast food shops and all-night drugstores he was passing. Some of them probably lived totally normal lives. Many more probably hustled to make ends meet, performing various acts of questionable legality, from petty theft to running drugs in small quantities. Heavy Elixir addicts were still the minority, but the numbers were only growing, and it wasn't going to stop so long as the drug retained its built-in switch that allowed users to enjoy it for months before craving it.

No one bugged Clay. He was dressed in thrift-store clothes and hadn't shaved in three days. He didn't look like a cop, and he didn't look rich. There wasn't any point in mugging a broke-looking, well-built guy in his thirties. There were much easier targets to be had. A few people asked him for cash, but not many. Panhandling was a dying art in a world that had left change behind and was rapidly doing the same with paper bills.

The processing facility was a massive thing of cinder block and sheet metal, square and bulky with small windows lining its second and third stories. There was a small parking lot on the left side, and that edge of the building was lined with docking bays, all locked tight. The only other visible entrance on the ground floor was at the front, a set of double doors made out of transparent acrylic. Even could he have broken through the material, Clay would merely have set off alarms and alerted the entire building, and probably the Brooklyn PD, to his presence.

Clay had other ideas. The chain-link fence around the perimeter was fifteen feet tall and topped with razor wire, and the front entrance to the driveway was closed off, but according to the plans, there was an opening at the rear, barred only by a single swing-arm gate. The goods manufactured here weren't high-value, and there wasn't much risk of a break-in. The purpose of the fence was mainly to make the place look secure from the Atlantic Avenue side, where thousands of cars and people on foot passed by it daily.

Walking casually, projecting the air of a man doing nothing out of the ordinary, Clay made his way down the street, following the long side of the building, keeping his head down and staring at the pavement. Places like this were lined with cameras, and while he doubted that the owner had sprung for expensive facial recognition tech like MWP had, he didn't want to take any risks.

The security building next to the gate was small and ramshackle, sitting on a tiny lot full of refuse and patchy grass that hadn't been mowed in weeks. There was a flickering light coming from inside. Probably a guard watching television, maybe a Yankees game. The concept felt almost foreign; it seemed like a hundred years since Clay had thought about baseball. A sudden longing for a burger and a beer and a ballgame—any game, even one where their fifth starter, Tony fucking Nicolo, was getting shelled again—swept through him.

Clay ambled up to the gatehouse and tapped on the window. The guard, a guy who looked fifty going on three hundred, looked up. He had a chin for each of his three days of beard stubble and greasy dark hair streaked with white and kept long, the better to comb it over a massive bald spot. The man slid the window open.

"What?"

"Hey, sorry," Clay said. "My GPS thinks I'm in fuckin' Queens and I'm just looking for ... 835 ... Man, I can't even pronounce this street. Here, do you know what this is?"

He set his tablet on the little shelf under the window. When the man stood up, rolling his eyes, and leaned forward to look at it, Clay reached forth, grabbed him by the head with both hands, and slammed the man's forehead down against the steel window frame. The guy struggled, and Clay yanked his head back up and brought it down again. This time the guard went limp, and Clay let him slide to the floor. He grabbed his tablet and stuck it back in his pocket.

"Sorry, buddy." The guard wasn't going to wake up any time soon, and when he did he was going to have two black eyes and a hell of a lump on his forehead, but Clay was pretty sure he'd heal up all right. He walked around to the rear of the building, intent on entering and taking the man's keys, only to find it locked from the inside. Great. The window at the front was too small for him to climb through without significant difficulty, and breaking the door down wasn't worth it. He'd just use the cracking device Szarka had given him.

Clay moved on, walking through the gate and heading for the dumpsters at the rear of the building. The back door was to their left, a big steel thing covered with fading, peeling red paint. This entrance was used by the maintenance staff and wasn't alarmed. Clay could crack the mag-lock, open it up, and walk right in. From there it was only a matter of avoiding the guards until he found what he was looking for.

The mag-breaker was a tiny piece of plastic with a single red LED bulb, powered by a miniaturized Z-cell that could provide more than a hundred thousand hours of continuous use. He held the breaker against the magnetic lock and watched as the light began to blink, first slowly and then speeding up. The device was doing its work, detecting the lock's unique electronic signature and running disruption routines. In a few moments more the light went solid. Clay gave the door a gentle tug, and it swung open. He was in.

CHAPTER 22

The Hard Truth

Clay had been inside the Envision production facility for twenty minutes and had yet to encounter a single guard. Twice he'd seen flashlights moving far down a hall and had ducked into a nearby office, but both times the patrol route of the men with the lights had moved away from him. He had no idea how thoroughly they inspected each office as they passed, but he guessed the answer was "not very."

These were standard rent-a-cops. They had no reason to expect a break-in and had no motivation to do their job with extreme vigilance. They weren't thugs or murderers or criminals, nor did they have any real loyalty to the company; they were just regular men and women collecting a paycheck, and Clay didn't want to have to break anybody else's face if he didn't have to.

The process of finding the right terminal was proving incredibly tedious. Each system had to be yanked out of sleep mode and scanned for user credentials. So far he hadn't found any accounts that matched Johnathan Wihone's name, and he was getting annoyed. The process was taking too much time;

Clay hadn't forgotten that his last attempt at industrial espionage had nearly cost him his ability to walk.

He'd started on the top floor and was now nearly done with that level. He was scanning perhaps the fifteenth terminal he'd encountered when he heard a buzzing noise from the floor below. There was some exchange between a few of the guards—too far away and too muffled by the floor between him and them to understand—but Clay could tell by the tone that this was some exceptional event. Frowning, he finished up with his current terminal, another dud, and slid out of the office and back into the dark hallway. He could hear the two men talking at the far end of the hall and crept closer to catch them in the middle of their conversation.

"… fuckin' weird lately, is all."

"No, yeah, I know. It didn't used to be like this."

"Checking in on us on patrol and shit? Like we're kids?"

"Right? It's eye medicine. Who the fuck is going to steal eye medicine?"

"Ain't even the good shit, neither. It's store brand!"

There was laughter and shuffling noises as the men moved to split up. Clay was prepared to leap into the nearest office, but his caution proved unnecessary. Neither man was moving toward his hallway. He moved back up the hall to the next office in line, reached out and turned the knob, found it locked.

Fucking finally. Clay's picks were with his gun in the hotel safe, back in Manhattan. He hadn't dared go looking for them while resting up at Szarka's apartment, and Jeffrey hadn't been able to procure a replacement set. Kicking in the door would make too much noise, and for a moment he was stymied. He considered moving on to the next office and hoping for the best, but the locked door spoke to him. He didn't think it was a coincidence.

Clay glanced up, thinking, and saw his solution above him. The entire floor of the building was actually a single large space; the walls rose to the ceiling but not into it. The offices were effectively large cubicles with doors on them. The ceiling itself was built from aluminum frames and white drop tiles. If he could access the adjacent office and reach the ceiling, he could pass over the wall and into the locked office.

Backtracking, he entered the office he'd just left. The ceiling was eight feet above the floor, and Clay would need to access it right at the edge of the wall, as the tiles wouldn't hold his weight. The most obvious choice for a climbing platform, the desk, sat in the middle of the room. It was a bulky metal thing but not heavy, and Clay was glad to find when he pushed on one corner that it slid on the industrial carpet.

Working as quietly as he could, he removed the holo monitor and lightkeys from the desk, along with the occupant's pictures and a stack of technical manuals that seemed to relate to the production line below, and set them on the floor. Whoever came in tomorrow was going to be deeply confused, but by that point Clay would be long gone.

With the desk cleared, he began to pull it toward the wall. It made a light scraping noise against the carpet, but Clay didn't think any guard would hear unless they passed directly next to the office, and even then they might miss it if they weren't paying attention. Still, he was glad when he reached the wall without any interruption, and he quickly climbed onto the desk. Removing the ceiling tile was a piece of cake, and in another moment his suspicions were confirmed: above the wall there was more than a foot and a half of empty space. Easily enough to crawl through.

Standing on the desk, Clay could just reach into the ceiling and over the wall to grasp the edges of a tile that rested above the locked office. Carefully, quietly, he removed it and set it on the desk. Then with a little hop he boosted himself up and into the space he'd made.

Only once he was hanging there, his abdomen resting on the part of the ceiling that touched the wall and could thus support him, did he realize the rest of the problem: there was no way to maneuver himself into a feet-first landing. Clay knew how to make an eight-foot drop, land on his feet, and roll with barely a sound. Doing it on his hands, however, was going to be difficult. He glanced around, but a pair of aluminum braces and a pipe prevented him from swinging his legs to either side. And there wasn't enough vertical space to pull them up under him.

Well, here goes nothing, then. He pushed forward with his hands, bending at the waist and pressing his chest against the wall, slowly moving downward. The plan was to inch forward as far as possible until he felt his center of gravity shift. With his arms fully outstretched, this might cut the eight-foot drop to as little as five feet, and at least he would be landing on industrial carpet set atop concrete floors, instead of creaking hardwoods.

After another few inches, he was able to bend his knees, swing his legs up, and plant his feet against the room's true ceiling, which was also made of concrete. He could feel the muscles in his abdomen beginning to complain at the strain this put on them, and the ghost of the bullet wound in his leg wasn't thrilled either, but he ignored them both. This approach allowed him another six inches before he recognized that to move any farther he would have to straighten his knees, and the moment he did so he was going to slide forward and into the room.

Taking as deep a breath as he could, holding his hands out before him with fingers splayed, Clay let himself fall forward. He hit the carpet with a hard jolt that ran through both arms, tried to take as much of the impact as possible with his muscles, and rolled forward in a somersault that was only halfway controlled. One foot swung too hard and thudded against the carpet, but the descent had otherwise been quiet. Clay pulled himself quickly to his feet and hunkered there for a moment, listening, but there was no hint of any reaction from elsewhere in the building. After a few seconds more, he stood up. He glanced at the door, confirming that it could be easily unlocked from the interior. At least when he left, he'd be able to just walk out.

This office was close to an exterior light, and its blinds were open, which made it easier to search than most of the others he'd so far explored. At one end there was a couch with two chairs facing it, which was unusual. The desk was covered in picture frames, most of them digital, displaying flats and holos, stills and vids, the images mainly of two young, adorable kids with dark tan skin and brown hair. There was a plaque on the wall, and Clay stepped forward to read it. Softball league championship, 2052. Johnathan Wihone. That was his man.

Clay stepped around the desk and leaned over it, looking at the terminal. It wasn't anything special: a holo monitor, a set of lightkeys, and the small peripheral interface into which a SynchDrive could be slotted. Clay pulled his drive out of his tablet, leaving Terry's in there, and slid it into the machine. The terminal came to life, projecting a welcome screen. After a moment, the Chink's data-mining software, set to start up when the drive was mounted, began its work. There were a few visible glitches on the holographic screen as the program sought to gain entry, and then the entire screen blinked and the GUI came up. The background image was another shot of Wihone's impossibly cute kids.

The SynchDrive wasn't big enough to suck down the hundreds of terabytes of data stored on the machine's drives, and its wireless connection wasn't fast enough to transfer the data in real time—he'd be here all night—so Clay would have to do some sorting. He opened another one of the Chink's programs, this one built for rapid data analysis, and gave it a few parameters that would match the formula he was looking for. Then he brought up the file management interface and began flipping through storage bins, flicking his hand to move them one by one over the program. One after another, the program flashed red "not found" text, and Clay brushed them aside.

The application had just gone green and informed him of a match when all the lights in the building went on. The change sent a surge of adrenaline rushing through him, and he jammed his hand into the messenger bag, pulled the six-shooter and leveled it at the door. With his left hand, he gestured for the terminal to begin copying the matched folder's contents to the SynchDrive.

The building's PA system crackled a little as someone activated it, and the voice that echoed out from the little speaker above his head filled him with instant, abject loathing.

"We know you're skulking arooound up there," Olivia crooned in her singsong voice. She punctuated this by slamming whatever it was she was using to broadcast back down into its receiver.

Goddamn it, how had they known? Had Jeffrey sold them out again, or had they managed to place some kind of tracking software on the tablet the NYPD had given him after Reyes confiscated his own? Clay had no idea and supposed it didn't matter. He glanced at the progress meter. Sixty-five percent. Jesus, why was it no matter how fast these things got, people just kept making files that were bigger and bigger? He resisted the urge to shout profanities at the machine, drumming his fingers on the table and thinking about escape routes. The window was out; the sides of the building would offer no handholds for climbing. He was going to have to make it back through the production facility.

There was conversation coming again from the floor below him, and one of the voices was rising, getting angry. It was cut off by a single flat crack. Someone had shot the man who was shouting. Clay had a pretty good guess who *someone* was. Other people were shouting now, too, but another muffled report seemed to quell whatever petty rebellion was rising. Clay heard a woman's voice—couldn't make out the words— shouting orders. They would be coming for him, now and coming quickly. He glanced at the screen. Eighty-eight percent.

"Come the fuck on!" The tablet was sitting there on the desk. He snagged it and tapped out a quick message to Szarka, which he didn't even bother to encrypt: "Get out of Brooklyn."

The device would be useful in another way: if he got the SynchDrive into it, he could monitor the whole uploading process. It would take maybe twenty minutes to transfer this amount of data wirelessly, and with the level of encryption he was using there was no chance at a partial transfer. They had to have it all to have any of it. The encryption hashes wouldn't match up otherwise.

Ninety-six percent. Clay could hear voices at the far end of the building. He didn't know how many people Olivia had with her, but it wouldn't take them long to sweep this floor. He had perhaps three minutes to—

"Check Wihone's office first!" Olivia shouted from somewhere way too close, and at just that moment the drive's internal LED flashed, indicating that the data had transferred. Clay yanked it from the receptacle, slammed it into the tablet, and tapped "yes" when the dialog came up asking if he wanted to copy the data on the SynchDrive to the tablet and all other available devices. He then swept the tablet into his bag. He moved around the desk and broke into a dead sprint, pistol held in a death grip, hitting the door with his shoulder.

The door, a flimsy thing made from two thin sheets of composite with about an inch of open air between them, cracked and splintered, flinging wide. No one was in his way, but Clay as much sensed as saw two goons to his right, perhaps ten feet away. Even as his momentum carried him to the far wall, he spun and fired a shot in that direction, not hoping to hit anything, just buying time. The two guys dropped to the ground as Clay bounced off the wall, turned, and ran in the opposite direction.

Someone fired a gun, and a section of the wall to Clay's right exploded in a blast of chalky white powder. He heard Olivia curse as he ducked around the corner. "If he leaves this

building, it better be because every last one of you is dead!"
she shouted.

Clay was happy to let her take her anger out on her men.
He sped down the hall with long rapid strides, moving as
quickly as he could. He needed to get out of the facility and get
lost in the streets of Brooklyn, needed to give the SynchDrive's
wireless connection time to do its work. Without the data, his
personal revenge against Elena Reyes and her bodyguard was
pointless; now that he knew what Terry had died for, it was no
longer enough to simply kill those who had caused her death.
She'd set out to expose those who'd created Elixir and deliver a
cure to the world. He was going to make that happen.

But, goddamn it, they weren't going to make it easy. Just as
Clay got within a few yards of the door, it burst open and three
men in black suits came through. They saw him and shouted,
raising their weapons, and Clay dived forward. He hit the
short-fibered carpet with his elbows, feeling them burn as they
scraped along the synthetic loops, and kept the gun pointed
up. One of the guys, faster on the draw than the other two,
fired a shot that went over Clay's head.

Five shots left. Clay fired once, putting a slug into the belly
of the man who'd been first through the door. The guy fell
backward into the other two, arms flying up in the air, gun
falling to the ground. Clay rolled and came up on his knees. He
took advantage of their momentary confusion to steady his
aim and fire rounds three and four. Each hit its mark, one in
the arm of the second man and the other in the leg of the third.

Now all three were on the floor, and Clay shoved himself to
his feet. He took a running leap and cleared the writhing mass
of limbs, barreled into the stairwell and very nearly fell down
the concrete steps. He grabbed the metal railing with his left

hand, and his momentum swung him around so that he could see back through the door and down the hallway. Olivia and two other men were pursuing at a full run, and she raised her gun one-handed without breaking stride and fired a shot that passed close enough to Clay's face that he felt the wind of it. Christ, she was good. Most people couldn't hit the broad side of a barn when running like that.

Clay spun and began to descend the stairs three at a time. It was a valuable talent, though he'd been expected to use it in pursuit of terrorists, not fleeing from hit men. They'd spent hours drilling it into him at the military base in Pennsylvania, officially listed as abandoned and known to its occupants only as "the facility." Clay could make a pretty good pace, but he'd trained with a guy who'd been able to descend five or six stories in mere seconds. Clay's talents lay in other areas, and he found himself wishing now for his rifle and a little distance between him and the people behind him. The idea of putting Olivia's head in his crosshairs was very appealing, but the quarters were too close, and anyway it was back in Brooklyn, safely stored away. All he had was the revolver. They hadn't been able to get any other firepower in Manhattan, not while trying to stay hidden in Szarka's safe house.

Clay skipped the second-floor landing and headed right for the first. He wasn't going to get out from anywhere above street level; there weren't any external fire escapes on this building, and the window would have given him a sixteen-foot drop onto solid asphalt. He could *probably* have managed that, but there was no guarantee, and if Olivia found him hobbling with a broken ankle or a torn ACL, she wouldn't hesitate to gun him down. He'd do the same in her place.

He was nearly at the bottom when they burst into the stairwell above him. Olivia leaned out over the railing, gun pointed down, and fired three blind shots. Two of them blasted holes at Clay's feet. The other hit the metal railing by his arm, made a high-pitched sound as it bounced, crossed his body, and drove through his left bicep. A searing, burning pain tore through him and Clay shouted profanity. He brought his own gun straight up and fired one of his last two rounds, hoping to catch her in the face. He wasn't that lucky, but at least she withdrew. Clay exited the stairwell and came out into the massive production line that took up the facility's ground floor.

His arm was pouring blood, so there was no point trying to hide. They'd track him down in seconds. No, what he needed was cover, and there was precious little of it to be found here. Most of the line was made of skeletal machinery and conveyor belts. There were huge gaps where a well-placed bullet—and Clay had no doubt Olivia could place her bullets well indeed—would find him. Across the room, Clay saw what looked like at least half a dozen men in dark suits spreading out and coming his way. The pain in his arm was making it hard to think, and for a moment Clay felt raw panic at the edges of his mind.

I really could've done without getting shot again. With that thought, his training kicked in, pushing the panic away. There was a pallet stacked high with packages of tiny glass bottles to his left, and Clay bolted for it and swung around behind it even as gunfire erupted from the group of men at the far side of the room. Glass shattered and sprayed, but none of the bullets made it through the layers of bottles and bubble wrap to reach him.

Clay switched the gun to his left hand, ignoring his raging arm, and grabbed a handful of bullets from the bag's pocket. He wasn't going to be able to take every one of these motherfuckers out, not from here, but he wanted to have more than one shot left. He flipped open the cylinder guard and quickly inserted five new rounds, the tips of his fingers burning against the hot metal. He transferred the fully loaded gun back to his good hand. The shooting had stopped, but he couldn't stay here. They would close in on him in less than a minute.

There was a big metal machine, at least eight feet tall and six feet wide, about sixty feet away from him, behind two conveyor belts. If he could reach it, he would be that much closer to the stairwell that contained the maintenance exit, from which he hadn't yet seen any guards or hit men emerge.

"You're really making this hard on yourself, Foster," Olivia said.

"Seems like you're the one doing that," Clay called back, and he rushed from behind the pallet and leaped over the first of the two belts. Olivia shouted something indistinct and there was more gunfire. Clay waited for the shot that would catch him in the shoulder, or the kidney, or the back of the head. It didn't come, and after a few more strides he vaulted over the second conveyor and slid around the side of the machine, bullets piercing it with deep metal clanking noises.

Olivia was directing her people. "Spread out. Take both sides."

"First person you send at me's getting a bullet in his teeth!"

Olivia's men must have hesitated, because when next she spoke her voice was dripping with sarcasm. "Aww ... did the bad man say something scary? Here's an idea, when he sticks his head out to look at you, *shoot him in the face!*"

Clay heard footsteps moving to flank him. He didn't stick his head out but instead chose to dart forward again. This time he would head for the wall, which he would follow until he reached the clean room about three-quarters of the way toward his exit.

The men began shooting as soon as he moved. Clay tried to stay low, stay behind the conveyor belt and at least use it as some sort of cover for his vital areas. If they hit a leg, then so be it, but he wanted to be able to talk if he were surrounded. The longer he could keep Olivia spouting her bullshit, the better the chance that the SynchDrive would finish its upload.

Nothing hit him, though a couple of the shots connected with the wall close enough to spray his face with painful shrapnel. Whether the men were awful shots or the assembly line provided better cover than Clay thought, he couldn't say, but he wasn't about to complain. The clean room's window was a few feet ahead of him now, and he raised the gun.

Hope that's glass. He fired three times, saw cracks splinter out from the holes, and was thankful for it. A more modern facility might have been built with polymer windows. The bullets would've gone through, but when he threw himself at the window, he would've simply bounced off.

Clay leaped into the air, and that was when he heard a gun go off, farther away than the rest. The shot was impossible, and perfect, and he knew even as the bullet hit him in the side that it had come from Olivia's weapon. Goddamn her.

Clay crashed through the window headfirst and hit the floor with a bone-rattling thud. The gun skittered across the tile floor and came to a stop in the corner. He lay there amid the tiny squares of glass, gasping, blood gushing from his pierced gut in what felt like a tidal wave.

CHAPTER 23

Clean Room

"You know," Olivia said, her tone indicating she was contemplating some deep and universal truth, "I really would've thought you'd have learned not to steal from my employer the first time."

Clay groaned, clutching his gut and rolling over onto his back. He stared up at her, coughing a little, trying his best to look unimpressed. *Buy time.* Sure ... how was he going to buy fifteen minutes?

"That was a hell of a shot."

She was standing above him, dressed in her white suit, still wearing her hat. Four men in black suits stood directly behind her, and he could hear others talking outside, on the production floor. It sounded like they were organizing efforts to assist the men he'd shot upstairs.

"It's a specialty of mine. I have others, too. We'll get to them." She turned to the men in the suits and made a shooing motion. "You guys can fuck off. Secure the perimeter or whatever it is you do."

They filed out. When the last one was outside, she turned back to him.

"So, why didn't you head for the hills like the idiot you're working with? The one from the People's Voice? We're going to find him, you know. It's only a matter of time before he does something stupid."

"Why would I go anywhere? I like it here."

"I guess it doesn't matter," Olivia went on as if he hadn't spoken. "We were going to hunt you down eventually anyway, but you made it a lot easier on us by coming here. I gotta admit, I was starting to regret not finishing you off at that warehouse in Jersey."

"What?" Clay didn't understand. She'd been there?

"It's funny, but I was *pretty* sure you saw me at one point. Couldn't help getting close. I wanted to see how you handled that shot in the leg."

It came to Clay then: the woman in white. The floating apparition he'd briefly mistaken for Terry's ghost before dismissing it as a product of his pain-addled mind. It had been neither. His other guess had been right after all.

"Thought that was my imagination. Why didn't you kill me?"

"Because it wasn't my bullet." Olivia smiled. The more he saw that expression on her face, the more Clay came to believe it was entirely a learned action. It never looked quite right, and it never touched her eyes.

"You didn't want to start with an advantage."

"Ex-*actly*. I was having so much fun watching you work against those goons, just waiting until you were done and really feeling like you'd conquered the world. It was going to be great, and then the last asshole left got off that lucky shot, hit you in the leg, and ruined my night."

"So you let us go."

"What were you going to do? Don't you understand? She's not afraid of you. You disappeared for a few days, but guys like you can't stay disappeared. You have to have your pointless revenge, just like with Escobar."

"What the fuck are you talking about?"

"We figured, why not leave a little incriminating evidence in your place while I was going through it? Nothing too obvious, just a little tease. That way, if anyone *does* decide to do an inspection, it'll point to a guy who already hates you and who was getting a little too goddamn big for his britches."

"Jesus." The fleur-de-lis. Clay closed his eyes for a moment. Not only had they tricked him, but he'd done their dirty work for them. "You used me."

"Worked out better than we could've possibly hoped. We figured you'd just rattle him, but you went above and beyond. Had to have your revenge, right? And now here you are, just like we knew you would be. Your fat-ass benefactor is pretty clever, but he didn't think of the facial scanners on the bridge. He's used to driving around in that Cadillac with the anti-scan windows, but—oops!—you left it in Jersey."

"How'd you know we were coming here?" Clay's side felt like Niagara Falls, but he knew better; the bullet had missed his kidneys, and his liver and was probably lodged somewhere in his intestines. He wasn't bleeding that badly. He had hours, possibly days, before the wound killed him. Keep her talking. *Keep her talking.*

"Look, it's not like we don't know what was on your wife's SynchDrive. You've got half of something. The other half is here. I mean, it's in a couple other places, too, but this was the obvious target. Let me guess ... fat ass wouldn't get involved without you promising to help him build a cure."

"That was the deal."

"Tough titties for Alex, huh?" Olivia knelt down next to him. She pulled at the left leg of her pants, raising it up to reveal that the black and white tuxedo shoes were in fact boots. Clay saw a bone handle sticking out, and Olivia wrapped her fingers around it, drawing forth nine inches of smooth, sharp steel. The knife glinted in the harsh lights of the clean room as she reached forward with it and tapped him on the chest.

"Here's what's going to happen. First, we're going to deal with you. Then we'll worry about fatty, and then the driver. After that we'll finish up with Luke. I am going to have so. Much. Fun!"

"It'll be like fucking Christmas, I'm sure." Clay coughed again. "But what about—"

"Enough. Do you think I'm going to sit here talking while that drive finishes uploading? Do you *really* think that, little man? What am I, a James Bond villain?"

"You sure dress like one," Clay said, and Olivia flicked her wrist. The tip of the knife went from resting against his chest to slicing an inch-long gash in his chin. Clay felt it scrape against his jawbone and sucked in air with a hissing noise.

"Let's get that drive." Olivia reached into Clay's messenger bag and retrieved the tablet. The screen was locked, but she tapped in the code without having to ask. Clay wondered how she'd obtained that little piece of information and decided it didn't really matter now.

Olivia stood up, glanced at the screen, and shook her head. "Sixty-eight percent. *So close!*"

"Fuck you."

Olivia pulled the SynchDrive from the tablet, dropped it on the floor, and crushed it under her heel. Clay saw the little blue LED fade into nothing, taking with it the last of his hope. He tried to sit up and felt pain rip through him. It made his arms and legs feel like marshmallows, soft and fat, unable to support any real weight.

"*Et maintenant, pour la bouquet final ...*" Olivia hauled her arm back and hurled the tablet hard at the linoleum floor. Even reinforced as the models given to police officers were, they weren't meant for that sort of abuse, and Clay saw the screen shatter and the casing blow into multiple pieces. He supposed some of the internal components might be salvageable, but that didn't matter. Nothing mattered anymore except the tiny piece of plastic he'd seen go skittering across the floor and wedge itself under one of the machines in the corner.

It was just a little thing, no different in most ways from the other pieces that lay scattered across the floor, but to Clay it was the most important object in the world. He tried not to stare, tried not to give any indication that it mattered, because if Olivia saw it in his eyes, it would be all over. He looked back up at the woman in white. She was holding her knife loosely in her hand, smiling down at him.

"All done! Now, listen, I've been thinking ... what about a deal? Maybe I leave you lying here bleeding instead of lying here dead."

Clay raised an eyebrow. "You couldn't have brought that up before you shot me?"

"You didn't give me time! See, working for Ms. Reyes is great, but I don't meet too many men, except for old, fat ones and weak little fuckboys who couldn't handle what I have to offer. I've got an itch I'd like to scratch, and you're just right, with your muscles and those rugged good ... Well, you're not *ugly* anyway. And you've got the whole brooding hero thing going. So sexy!

"I'm going to hold my gun against your neck, get you between my legs, and see if you can make me come. If you do, you win the prize! Maybe you'll even heal up and try to come get another piece of me ... one kind or another."

That hungry look had come into her eyes again, the one he'd seen when she'd arrived at his place, playing the part of Kendra, and taken too long shaking his hand. Clay didn't believe it. Not the desire, not the offer, not any of it. She wasn't letting him leave this room alive. Not a chance in hell.

"I heard you didn't swing that way. Figured you and Reyes were an item."

"Oh, isn't that always how it is? A girl shows a little aggression and they start calling her a dyke. What Ms. Reyes does on her own time is none of my business. The only thing she has in her pants that is of the *slightest* interest to me is her wallet, and even that's not really important. You hear anything else fun?"

"That you got a set of teeth up there. That a rumor, too?"

"Why don't you try and find out? Think you can do it, Foster? I know you've got a hole in your side, but it seems like you Army boys are *always* up for it."

Clay coughed. "What's the catch?"

"Why would there be a catch?" Olivia's voice was an ugly parody of innocence.

"Because you're you. What's the fucking catch?"

"Well, there is *one* thing." Olivia knelt down again, leaning over him. "When we're fucking, I want you to tell me I'm better than her. That this is the best you've ever had, that the bitch I threw off the balcony can burn in hell for all you care. That, compared to me, her pussy was a dirty sweat sock full of glue and sand."

She was in close now, her lips inches from his, voice barely more than a whisper. "You think you can do that for me ... soldier?"

Clay wanted to reach out, grab her by the throat, and throttle her to death. In those last moments, he wanted to stare into those big, blue eyes as the life left them and tell this woman that she would never mean to anyone what Terry had meant to him, that she was a worthless nothing who no one would mourn when he'd finished killing her. He wanted to do this so badly that he could feel his hands twitching, but he knew that if he tried, Olivia would quickly repel the attack, and so he forced himself to lie still, remain calm, wait for it all to be over.

"I'd rather fuck her now than you ever."

The look of hunger left Olivia's features in an instant, replaced with something between a snarl and a smirk. Clay wondered if the lust had been an act or if it was something she could turn on and off at will. Now there was only this expression that made him think of a cat toying with its prey.

"No reason to draw this out, then. Let's get on to the fun part."

"Can't wait," Clay said and coughed again.

"It's really only fair ... You tried to steal from us, so I'm going to steal from you. I think I'll start with your skin. Bit by little itty bit."

Oh, Jesus Christ. "You're going to get blood all over your suit."

Olivia leaned farther forward, so that her eyes were again only inches from his. She pressed the blade against his bare right arm and gave him the first grin he'd ever seen from her that looked real.

"Can I tell you something?" she said, her tone conspiratorial. "That's. The best. Part!"

And still grinning, eyes lit up with a kind of lunatic glee, she jerked her entire arm, and so began the acts of theft she'd promised.

* * *

Clay was having a hard time breathing. He wasn't sure if it was the bullet in his side, the rib Olivia had cracked when she'd kicked him after the third time he'd reached for the knife and tried to take it from her, or the many parts of his body that seemed to be screaming for his attention.

Olivia had started with the upper half, cutting Clay's shirt from his body. She'd taken perhaps a dozen pieces off of him since then, each about the size of an old silver dollar. They lay on the floor next to him in a loose stack, like wet pancakes drenched in crimson syrup. Olivia knelt above him, suit flecked with blood, soaked in the stuff up to her forearms. She was humming.

Clay hadn't screamed yet. He didn't want to give her the satisfaction but didn't think he'd be able to stop it from coming pretty soon. It seemed like each time she cut another piece off of him, it hurt worse than the last. His body was starting to clench in advance, and when she'd taken the last one, he'd felt his gorge rise as his stomach tried to loose its contents in protest. Clay was lying on his back and didn't really fancy drowning in vomit as Olivia stood above him and laughed.

The tiny piece of hope was still lying there unnoticed under the machine. Clay had no illusion that he was going to be able to get to it, much less get away, but knowing it was there helped. Maybe someday someone would find it. Maybe they'd get curious about what it contained. Maybe Terry would be avenged.

The knife came down again, and Clay thought this time he was going to scream. It was scream or puke, and of the two he preferred the former.

Goddamn, Terry, I'm so fucking sorry. He found himself hoping there was something after this, some place he might go and be reunited with his wife. Then he wondered if all the people he'd killed would be waiting there for him, too. What would they say to him? What would Terry say when she saw them all? When she saw that little girl?

"Oh, I want a nipple," Olivia said, mostly talking to herself, as if she'd nearly left the grocery store without picking up an item on her list. Clay bared his teeth at her, getting ready for it. The knife was moving toward him at a speed that seemed at once desperately fast and yet terribly slow.

The tip of the knife had just slid into the skin of his chest when the entire side of the building exploded. The blast blew in the rest of the windows of the clean room, pelting the two of them with glass fragments and smoking debris. Olivia was thrown sideways, mercifully taking her knife with her. Temporarily freed, Clay had a sudden, insane urge to take all the pieces she'd cut from him and try to stick them back in place.

What the fuck is going on? The thought was almost idle. What did it matter? He was lying on the floor bleeding to death, and now shit was blowing up. Did it really change anything?

Clay could hear men screaming now, some in pain, others in confusion or aggression. There were popping noises as people began firing their guns. A few feet to his right, Olivia was pulling herself to her feet. Her white suit, already splattered red, now also bore large smears of black soot.

"Goddamn it!" She sheathed the knife and pulled her gun from its holster on her hip. Her hat had come off and her blond hair was half-unpinned, unkempt, one strand of it sticking out to the side. There was a big, black smudge on her face, and she'd taken some kind of shrapnel to her left cheekbone. She looked out the now-shattered window and her eyes went wide. "Oh, you fucking meddling whore!"

Then she was sprinting out of the room, leaving Clay alone on the floor. For a moment he just lay there, wondering what the hell was going on. Then he forced himself to clear his head. Someone had given him a tiny window in which to act.

"You gotta do this." Clay clenched his teeth, put his arm down, and shoved himself to a sitting position. His gut shrieked in protest, and the rest of his body wasn't much happier. For a few moments he could do nothing more than sit there with his eyes closed. Then the pain receded just a bit, like a wave pulling back during what was still the peak of high tide, and he opened his eyes again. The piece of plastic ... had it been lost in the explosion?

It had not. It was still lying just under the lip of the machine, wedged between the wall and one of the device's legs, untouched and easily accessible. If God existed, Clay was pretty sure the guy didn't owe him any favors, so he was going to have to chalk this one up to dumb luck.

Get to it. That's step two.

He didn't want to think about steps three through infinity, so instead he braced himself for another round of pain and leaned forward, pulled his legs under him, and got up on his hands and knees. Shirtless and covered in sticky, drying blood, Clay began to crawl.

His abdomen felt as if someone were stabbing it with a pitchfork, his whole upper body as if it had been lit on fire, and his arms as if he'd spent the afternoon power-lifting. It didn't matter. There was nothing to do but press on. Either he escaped now, in the chaos, or he was going to die here at Olivia's hands. Grimacing, Clay crawled along, ever closer to the machine. Outside, the gunfire continued, seeming to come from every direction, as if two small armies had engaged on the production floor.

At last, after what might have been two minutes or two hundred million years, he got there. Clay leaned his forehead against the metal for a few seconds, its cool touch like the caress of a lover. Then he breathed in, opened his eyes, and reached forward with his hand to pick up the thing for which he'd made this agonizing journey.

Terry's SynchDrive was in no worse shape than it had been that morning. The wireless connection was burned out, so it couldn't transmit data without being inserted into a terminal or tablet, but it still contained what he needed. When he'd plugged his own SynchDrive into his tablet, it had begun copying the data to Terry's drive even as it endeavored to send the data wirelessly. It had failed at the latter, but the internal connection was much faster, and Clay was sure that more than enough time had passed.

With Terry's SynchDrive, there was still a chance. He still had the second half of the data they needed to synthesize a cure. Now what he had to do was get out of here, get cleaned up enough to pass the checkpoint, and get the hell back into Manhattan as fast as he could. Szarka and Jeffrey were in grave danger, and Luke wouldn't be far behind. Time was now at an absolutely premium.

He put the drive into the pocket that wasn't soaked with blood and reached up. Grabbing the edge of the conveyor belt, Clay began to pull himself to his feet.

CHAPTER 24

Reunion

The good news was that it was easier to walk than crawl. It put less pressure on his core and brought less agony from the bullet wound. The bad news: it made him more aware of the dozen other holes the bitch in the white suit had carved into him.

Clay was standing at the door to the clean room, looking out through its tiny window, left arm wrapped around his gut. In his right he held Szarka's six-shooter, reloaded and ready to go. Bending down to pick *that* motherfucker up hadn't been fun, but he'd done it. He was going to need it when it came time to carjack someone, assuming he got out of this building alive.

He couldn't see much from his vantage point. The room was still full of smoke, and the angles were bad. Mostly he could see two guys in black suits using a part of the assembly line as cover, occasionally leaning out and firing a round or two. Clay thought he was probably going to have to kill them. They were between him and the maintenance exit, which still seemed the most logical way out of the building. He couldn't imagine the front door was unguarded.

Step eight ... Clay almost laughed at himself; he couldn't really remember if the last step had been seven or not. *Shoot those guys, then use their cover.*

There wasn't anything to do but go for it, so Clay turned the handle and opened the door. One of the two guys turned to look at him, and Clay shot the man in the face from twelve feet away. This got the attention of the other gunman, who began to spin to make visual contact with this unexpected assailant. Clay pulled the trigger again and the six-shooter roared in his hand. Jesus, it was so much louder than the modern pistols almost everyone was using.

The bullet hit the man in the side of the neck, punching right through, and blood began pouring from both holes like a fountain. He grabbed his throat with his hands, eyes going wide, and fell sideways. Writhing on the floor, he made gurgling noises like a partially stopped drain. Clay hobbled forward, still clutching his stomach, and took position behind the machine. The man who was drowning in his own blood pawed ineffectively at Clay's shoe, but Clay ignored him.

Glancing out around the machinery and through the smoke, Clay saw forms moving. The volleys of small-arms fire were slowing, and he thought many of the people in the building must be running out of ammo. There was a hole in the far wall the size of a van, chunks of concrete, insulation, and drywall strewn before it like Mardi Gras vomit on a sidewalk. There wasn't any cover in this area, and it was empty except for a single body, a man wearing jeans and a ratty T-shirt—not one of Olivia's people.

To his right, near the front door, two men in suits lay on the ground in pools of blood. Past them were several more pallets full of bottles, and it was behind these that much of the

Elixir

attacking force seemed to have taken cover. At least the men and women leaning out from behind them to take an occasional shot at the far side of the building didn't look to be wearing suits. It was hard to tell with the smoke.

Clay was about to turn away when an eddy in the gray veil before him brought a momentary improvement in visibility, and what he saw stopped him in his tracks. He hadn't expected ... but what *had* he expected? He hadn't lent an ounce of thought to the question of who these new entrants into the fight might be, but he hadn't expected to see a tall, bald woman in black combat fatigues standing among their ranks. She turned and met his gaze, and in her ebony eyes he saw a kind of vitality that had never been there at any point during his visit to the Chink's casino, as if a part of her were alive here that had not been, there. She gave him a brief nod and pointed emphatically at the door that led to the maintenance stairs.

Clay gave her a salute, acknowledging the command, wondering what the hell the woman—what had her name been?—was doing leading this rescue attempt. He was about to follow her orders and head for the door when he heard a female voice shout something, and there was a sudden hail of bullets sent in the direction of the bald woman and her men. Olivia's men were charging at her order.

Acting on instinct, Clay brought up his revolver and fired as the first of the men came into view. The bullet missed, and before he could take a second shot, he managed to rein himself in. This wasn't his fight, not anymore. His job was to get the data in his pocket to Szarka and Luke. After that he could hole up, heal up, and take another stab at ridding the world of Olivia, but for now all else was secondary. As if to confirm this, the Amazon woman shouted his name and pointed again. Clay got moving before the advancing force noticed him, hobbling along toward the door. Behind him, there was gunfire. Screaming. The sound of glass shattering.

He'd nearly reached the door when he heard Olivia's voice behind him. "You don't walk out of here that easily, Foster. Turn around or I'll shoot you in the back."

Clay stopped and stood still for a moment, thinking. He was gut-shot and carved up like a Christmas ham. He needed medical attention—surgery, this time. Nanotreatments weren't going to cut it.

"Around!" The chirpy, lilting note was gone entirely from her voice. Whether it was an act meant to make her victims uneasy or how she really was when relaxed and in control, Clay didn't know, but it seemed that when things reached a certain level of gravity, the woman in the white suit was capable of putting her playful approach to psychopathy away.

Clay turned, wincing, and looked up at his opponent, standing before him covered in blood and soot, holding her gun at arm's length. He didn't like looking down the barrel of that thing, but if this was the end, he was going to meet it with whatever amount of dignity he could muster. He forced himself to straighten up. Behind Olivia, people were dying. Clay couldn't tell who was winning that fight and wasn't sure he cared.

"You're going to have to kill me," he said. "I'm not letting you take any more pieces."

"I will do whatever I want. Your friend in The Hook thinks he can spring you, huh? He ruined my fun, and I'm going to eat his fucking heart for it, but first I'm going to finish teaching you your lesson. You think it's bad now, big man? We haven't even warmed up. When you're cursing your wife for the thieving cunt that she is and begging me to kill you, then maybe we'll think about whether to let you die or not."

Clay tried to lift his revolver, thought he'd done a pretty good job at doing so with speed, and was dismayed when Olivia snapped her wrist sideways like a striking snake and fired her own gun. She never even took her goddamned eyes off of him and still managed to shoot the pistol out of his grip while it was half-raised, like they were in some kind of western. His hand went instantly numb, and Clay had to glance down to make sure he still had all his fingers.

"You know what makes me sad, Foster?" Olivia took a few steps toward him. "I had to shoot you because you were running away. I wanted to go with the knife right from the start, up close and personal, see if your training was everything it's supposed to be. I know where you came from, what you can do ... Never did get to go against one of you R-9 boys in the war."

"You never fought in the fucking war. You're too young."

"Oh, honey, I killed my first soldier when I was fourteen. They started me on dogs. That was when I was five. Now hold still ... I'm going to cut both of your Achilles to make sure you don't go too far while I help my boys finish taking out the fucking trash."

Olivia crouched, keeping her eyes up and her gun raised, reaching with her left hand to pull the knife from her boot. She had just pulled up her pant leg when Clay saw someone emerge from the smoke behind her. He shifted his eyes up to see who it was and knew instantly that he'd made a mistake in doing so. The woman in the white suit registered the change of focus and leaped into action.

The Chink's bodyguard—*Michelle. Her name is Michelle*—raised her gun and aimed it at the back of Olivia's head, but as she pulled the trigger, Olivia dived sideways, reaching back behind her to fire a shot of her own. Michelle's bullet plowed a hole into the linoleum floor, just missing Olivia, whose own shot was also amazingly close. The bullet hit a pipe just above Michelle's head, and it began to spew water. The bald woman ducked, giving Olivia time to scramble around the corner of the clean room. Michelle saw this and made her own running dive. She slid on the floor and took cover behind a bulky steel machine as Olivia reached back around the corner and fired a shot. Michelle's slide left a great red streak behind her. Clay didn't think it was her blood.

"Go, Foster!" the Amazon screamed. It was good advice, so Clay took it. He turned, the machine to his back and preventing Olivia from shooting him again, and began to shuffle his way along the last few feet of space between him and the maintenance exit. Behind him, he heard the sound of the battle raging on.

* * *

"Oh, fuck me," Kellen Ruiz said. "You stupid bastard ... what are you *doing* here?"

What Clay was doing was bleeding on Kellen's doorstep. He was going to have to apologize to Angela about that, sometime after he finished bleeding on her couch.

"I need help," Clay said.

"You need a fucking field surgeon! Jesus Christ, bro, you're gonna die right here on my porch. Why aren't you in a hospital? What the fuck is going on?"

"No time. Kellen, listen, I need clothes and painkillers ... and I need to get cleaned up enough to get through the checkpoints back to Manhattan."

"Are you shitting me? Clay, man, what happened? Why are you standing at my door in the middle of the night, no shirt on, with big goddamned chunks taken out of you and ... is that a bullet hole?"

Clay nodded and shrugged. How the hell was he going to explain all of this? It would take hours, and he didn't even have minutes. He settled for the facts. "Elena Reyes and her psychotic bodyguard did this to me. Kel ... please. I gotta sit down."

"Okay, bro, let's ... Hang on a sec." Kellen turned back into the house. "Angela, get the kids back in bed. Do not come downstairs, you hear me? Not for any reason, not till I say it's all right."

Clay heard Angela start some protest at this—she was not and had never been a woman prone to taking orders from her husband—and then she must have thought better of it, because she silenced herself. Kellen turned back to him. "Come in."

"I'm going to get blood—"

"All over the fucking place? Yeah, I got that. Officer Clay Foster, you are fucked up *royale*. Stand in the goddamn hall until I can put something on the couch, all right?"

Clay did as he was told, standing in the vestibule, swaying a little. He could hear Kellen muttering to himself in the kitchen, and after a moment his partner came back out holding what looked like a massive plastic tablecloth. He headed for the living room, motioning for Clay to follow, and draped it over the couch.

"Sit down. Try to ... Man, even your shoes are full of blood."

"Good thing you have hardwoods." Clay groaned as he sat down. His side didn't feel like it was gushing blood anymore, maybe because he'd run out of blood to gush.

"Stay there and try not to fucking die on my couch. I'll get the kit."

Kellen headed upstairs. Clay leaned back on the couch, resting his head and closing his eyes. He was exhausted, and the idea of sleeping was deeply appealing to him at the moment. That was no good, so he forced himself to lift his head up and open his eyes.

He hadn't needed to jack a car. Fortunate ... since he'd left Szarka's gun somewhere in the facility. There had been a Ford Z-Cell sitting in the parking lot—someone had driven it right through the gate—with the keys in it. Clay had heard sirens as he slid into the driver's seat: the Brooklyn PD finally responding to the miniature war happening on the corner of Atlantic and Havens.

Once clear of the parking lot and the police, he'd taken a moment while stopped at a red light to evaluate his wounds. At first he'd intended to head straight for Manhattan, but he realized there was no way he was going to make it through the checkpoint. Kellen's house in Bedford Stuyvesant was closer and safer than his own, and so he'd made the choice. He hated doing this, arriving shot and cut up at almost five in the morning, but there wasn't any better option.

"Okay, let's get to work," Kellen said, returning to the living room. "I'm thinking bullet hole first, unless you have any better ideas."

"Yeah, bullet hole first. Listen, it's still in there."

"I ain't trained to—"

"I'm not asking you to. We're not going to take it out."

"Are you crazy?"

"Kel, listen to me. There's not much time. People are in a lot of danger and I need to keep moving. You're not a surgeon and neither am I. I need painkillers, alcohol, and cloth to wipe up blood. If there's a hemostat in there, give me that, too."

"The fuck is a hemostat?" Kellen was digging through the kit.

"It helps clotting. Might slow things down."

"Jesus fuckin' ... You want sutures? This thing set me back a ton, but it comes with, like, every goddamn thing."

"No point. I'll just keep bleeding inside."

"Right. Okay, here. Painkillers. Narcotic or ..."

So it went. They did the best they could, hastily cleaning and bandaging the wounds to keep them from bleeding through whatever new clothes Kellen was going to provide. Clay was glad that Olivia hadn't made it to his face other than the slice on the chin, which didn't actually look too bad once the blood was gone. In clean clothes, he could probably pass for normal.

His wounds were burning and his gut ached like someone had sunk a hot poker into it. Clay slammed back two grams of ibuprofen with a shot of whiskey and asked for clothes. Kellen went upstairs to see what he could find and to reassure Angela that everything was all right.

"I'm shorter and fatter than you," Kellen said when he returned. "So it's gonna have to be shorts with a belt and a big T-shirt. Ain't got nothing else that'll fit."

"It's fine, Kel. Thanks." Clay stood up, clenching his teeth against the pain, and began pulling on the T-shirt.

"You gonna tell me what the fuck all is happening?"

"It's Reyes. It's all Elena Reyes, from Manhattan Water and Power."

"I've heard of her." Kellen's voice was cautious. Disbelieving.

"She's at the center of everything. Elixir, Terry, everything. And what I need to nail her to the fucking wall is on this SynchDrive, but it's burnt out and can't ... Jesus, Kel, I need your terminal. Shit! It could've been going this whole time!"

"Hold up. What's on that drive?"

"Data that shows what Reyes is doing. And the other half we need for the cure."

Kellen narrowed his eyes. "What are you talking about, exactly?"

"Kel, there isn't any goddamned time. I need your fucking terminal! I need to transfer this shit."

"That thing is not going anywhere near my terminal." Kellen's voice was calm and low, almost casual, but there was a note in it that caused Clay to stop frantically looking around for the terminal and turn back to his partner.

"Why not? Man, we can put her—"

"Listen to me," Kellen said. "Listen real careful, Clay. I love you. You're my brother, and I love you, and I'm sorry as hell about what happened to Terry, all right? But what you're doing, right now, right here? That's putting my entire family at risk. My wife, my boy, my baby girl. You just brought whatever this shit is that you have going with Elena Fucking Reyes into my house. Right into my house, right where my family sleeps."

Clay stared at him, at a loss, unable to come up with a response. After a moment, Kellen continued, still speaking in that same low, careful voice.

"If you transfer that shit from my terminal, they will be able to trace it back to me forever. If any part of this insane plan you've got goes wrong and you end up dead in a ditch somewhere—and sorry, bro, but that seems *real* fucking likely right now—then whoever did this to you, they're going to show up at my house next. You think I'm going to let you do that? Come on, man."

"I need your help," Clay said.

"I've given you plenty of help. Cleaned you up, patched you up, gave you clothes. I'll clean the blood off my porch and my floor, no complaints. I'll give you food if you want it. Booze. Water. Whatever you need to get on your way, but you need to get on your way. Get those shorts on and get your ass up out of my house."

Clay felt anger rising within him, bubbling up like boiling water in a dangerously thin pipe, ready to burst forth and scald whoever might be nearby. He tried to hold on to it, breathing as deep as his broken rib would allow. Christ, after everything else that had happened tonight, now he had to deal with this?

"I'm trying to finish what Terry started. She *died* for this."

"And I'm making sure Angela doesn't."

"What the hell, Kellen? You're my partner."

"That right?" Kellen snapped. "Last I was told, you were kicked off the force for whatever shit you've been doing over in luxury land, so I had to hear from Chief Baker that I didn't have a partner anymore. If I *did*, I know damn sure he wouldn't bring a fuckin' bomb into my house while my kids are sleeping there, but that's what you just did."

"No one's going to hurt your kids."

"This is supposed to be reassuring coming from the guy who's sliced up like deli meat? What do you think this is, Clay, a buddy movie?"

Clay unbuttoned his bloody jeans and pulled them off. Putting on Kellen's shorts, he gritted his teeth against the pain and the anger he could feel inside of him. "All right, whatever. I'll do it myself. Do you have a gun? Something that can't be traced?"

"Clay ... no, man, I don't keep black market weapons lying around my house. Will you *please* let me take you to a goddamn hospital?"

Clay shook his head, cinched the belt around his waist, and pulled on the T-shirt, moving slowly, fighting the agony in his gut. The only thing that mattered to him now was finishing this thing. Everything after that was a great black void, inscrutable to him. He made his way to Kellen's front door. "You should burn those clothes."

Kellen put a hand to his forehead. "Jesus, what a mess."

It was, but there was nothing to be done about it now, so Clay left him standing there like that and headed for the car. He would get to Manhattan, meet Szarka at the safe house if he could, and they would use the terminal there to transfer the data. After that, maybe he'd think about risking a hospital. He had to try to get better. Olivia had still never taken him when he was fully healthy. She was faster than him, and a better shot with a pistol, but he was stronger and had plenty of skills of his own. He didn't know if he could take her, up close and personal, but he hoped he'd get a shot.

He put the car into gear and got moving. Off in the distance, past the river, glittering and shimmering like something out of a fairy tale, Manhattan waited for him.

CHAPTER 25

Second and Second

"Can I see your CityPass, please?"

The woman in the booth was tall and tan and had raised an eyebrow briefly when Clay rolled down the window to look at her, revealing his cut-up face. She'd recovered quickly and assumed a professional air. Now, here it was: the moment of truth.

Clay leaned out the window and gave his most winning smile. "I walked down the wrong alley a couple hours ago and got beaten up pretty good. They took my tablet. Nothing's open ... Couldn't get a replacement. Could you look me up with a thumb scan?"

"Oh, I'm so sorry! Sure." The woman held the device out, and Clay pressed his thumb against it. The light went green and she took the scanner back, looking at the screen.

"Oh." She frowned.

"What's up?" Clay asked, still smiling, trying to appear nonchalant. If the pass had been revoked, he would have to come up with another plan.

"Well, you're clear. The history says you were locked out for a while, but someone overrode it, and now everything's good.

It's just ... I've never really seen anything like this. There's a note on your file, but it doesn't make any sense to me and I don't know who put it there."

Clay frowned. What the hell was going on now? "What's it say?"

"Uh ... well, it says to read it to you, actually. 'Full count, two-hole, second inning. *Fidelis Ad Mortem*' ... There's no digital signature. I didn't even know you could *do* that."

"What does it mean?" Clay had an idea but didn't want to reveal that to this woman.

"I'm not sure, sorry. I guess ... you're probably fine to move on. I'm going to call ahead to the other checkpoints and let them know you're coming so that they don't keep telling you about the note."

"Okay, thanks."

"Have a good day!" She smiled at him and hit the button that raised the gate. Clay drove forward, crossing a service road and taking the on-ramp to the Manhattan Bridge.

The message had to have come from Haley. He would have the access to override the lockout, and he knew Clay was a Yankees fan and would get the coded message. *Fidelis Ad Mortem* was easy, the motto of the NYPD. Was Haley saying Clay could trust him? Did it matter what Haley had to say? What was the right call?

It was the baseball stuff that really mattered. A full count meant three-and-two. Was that an address? Thirty-two? The two-hole meant the second batter, and then there was the second inning ... Second Avenue and Second Street? That sounded possible.

"Christ," Clay muttered, drumming on the steering wheel. What was the call? Try to make it across the entire city to

Szarka's apartment or head for Haley's location, which was much closer?

Clay wished he still had his tablet. He could just head for a hospital and let the thing upload while he was driving. But his tablet had been destroyed. Maybe he could get another in Manhattan if anything was open, but more likely he would have to wait a couple of hours, and that might end up with him sitting dead in this car outside an electronics shop.

No, it would have to be Haley. He had no choice. Even the crosstown trip seemed like too much. He would head for Second and Second. Assuming he could pass the other checkpoints, that was. Someone had locked him out once already, however briefly, and if they were watching the thumb scans, they might do so again just in the few short minutes between the edge of the bridge and the Manhattan Wall.

The attendant at the wall was male, forties, short and round and surly. He had a walrus-like mustache and beady eyes, and he peered at Clay with suspicion. "So you're the guy with the weird note on his profile, huh? Why'd they lock you out earlier?"

"No idea," Clay said.

"Right. What's with the gash on your face?"

"Cut myself shaving."

"Yeah? You shave with broken glass a lot?"

"All the time. What are you, the NSA? I'm a U.S. citizen with a valid pass, and I'm also a cop. You're keeping me from getting to HQ because I have a cut on my chin?"

The guy rolled his eyes. "All right, all right. Jesus. It's my job to ask questions when people look suspicious. You look suspicious. That car's not even registered."

Clay hadn't even thought about that. He shrugged. "I forgot."

"Yeah, or maybe you bought it from some chop shop in that shit-hole city of yours," the guy said, and before Clay could respond, he snapped his window closed. The gate ahead of Clay began to rise.

"And fuck you, too, asshole," Clay muttered. He resisted the urge to jam on the pedal and peel the hell out and instead calmly accelerated. There was still one more checkpoint, and he didn't need the guy calling ahead to recommend further harassment.

The last checkpoint was a breeze. He touched his thumb to the scanner, they waved him on, and he was in. Clay let out a breath of air that he hadn't realized he'd been holding in. The pain in his abdomen was a dull ache now, helped by the painkillers and sitting still, but he felt weak and shaky. Sick. He'd lost too much blood.

Clay found himself wishing for the days when Internet cafes had still existed, before wireless connectivity had become ubiquitous and driven them out of business. Driving across the city in morning traffic to get to the safe house and access its terminal would take an hour at minimum, and there wouldn't be any stores open at which he could get a new tablet for at least two hours. He had to find a way to finish this fast. Haley might be the answer.

The intersection on the corner of Second and Second was only a few blocks from where the bridge dumped out on Canal Street, and Clay got there quickly. Number thirty-two sat on the northeast corner, an ancient-looking building of two stories, each at least twelve feet high, made of red brick. In some distant past it had housed a film company, but it looked long-closed now, and the windows were boarded over. There were signs announcing its imminent destruction to make way for the sort of luxury condominiums that had already taken over most of the neighborhood.

Clay turned onto Second Street and pulled the car over to the curb in front of a no-parking sign. Maybe it would get towed. Who cared? It wasn't his, and one way or the other, Clay thought, this would be his last stop. If he came away from this building, it would be to collapse on the sidewalk and beg passerby for an ambulance.

He got out of the car, grimacing as he made the effort to stand, and looked up at the building. If there was any activity happening inside, he couldn't see it. The front door had multiple locks on it, but there was a utility door to the left with no visible obstructions. Clay moved forward, tried it, and found it locked. He glanced around, looking for any other way in, but the building was a solid brick wall at the ground level except for the two entrances on Second Street. Had he made a mistake? His lock picks were long gone, and with the sun coming up, trying to use them in a wide open space like this would've been a tremendous mistake.

He was about to return to the car when he noticed the graffiti. Really, it should have jumped out at him right from the start, given how clean the rest of the city was, but because the building was older, vacant, and run-down, it hadn't seemed out of place. It was a simple, small tag, but he doubted very much that it was a coincidence. It read simply "Bronx Bombers." It was the same phrase he'd given Haley as a proof of identity, and Clay was not surprised to find that the brick below it was loose. With a little effort, he was able to pry it away, and behind it there was a single key.

He knows I'm in trouble. Playing it safe.

Clay grabbed the key and tried it in the lock. It turned easily, and the door opened. Inside, it was dim, with a single bare bulb hanging from the ceiling. Someone had turned it on. The place was mostly empty but had pretty clearly been a maintenance room at one point. There was a huge plastic sink at one end, stained and cracked and pulling from the wall, and on the floor along the opposite wall were the remains of a wooden workbench. Trash and filth he didn't want to think about, aged many long years, was scattered around, the product of squatters, back when Manhattan had allowed undesirables to exist within its limits.

There was no indication of where he should go or that anyone else was even in the building, but the unlocked door said he wasn't alone, and there was only a single exit from this room. Clay took it and found himself in a stairwell. The entrance to the main part of the first floor was locked.

"Fucking great," he muttered, eyeing the stairs, and then got started climbing. It was a slow, arduous process, and it wasn't doing anything good for his wounds. A red spot was developing on his shirt, which meant that the gut wound had bled through the heavy layer of bandages he and Kellen had wrapped around his torso. When he got to the top he was exhausted, taking short, sharp gasps, and for a moment he could do nothing more than stand with his head bowed, hand on the railing, struggling to breathe.

"What a mess," Kellen had said, and boy was he right. As bad as it had gotten in the war, and it had gotten pretty bad, it had never been like this. His body had never taken this much punishment, and he'd been younger then and in even better shape. Clay was still fit, but not like when his strength and agility had been key to his daily survival. Not like that night in the swamp when he had run for what seemed like hours and, after taking a shotgun blast to the hip and stabbing to death the man who'd done it, struggled on for hours more.

He exited the stairwell and emerged into a wide hallway. It was dark in here, thanks to the boarded windows on his right, but some light filtered through. Several doors lined the left side of the hall, but most appeared to be locked, and a few had been boarded up completely. One was plastered with a faded sign that read "Caution: Live Wires."

Clay could see a door at the far end of the hall that was cracked open, spilling light out onto the dusty wooden boards. There were footsteps in the dust leading to it. Haley's? Or could someone else be here? It was hard to think clearly. He made his way along the hallway, left hand against the wall for support. At last he reached the end and pressed on the door. It opened with creaking hinges, and a jolt of adrenaline ran through him: someone who was not Haley was sitting in a chair at the other end of the room, looking right at him.

When Clay realized who it was, relief flooded through him. He would have known immediately, but the man was sitting far in the back, past the orb of light on the floor, mostly in shadow.

"Szarka," he said. "Haley got in touch with you, too?"

The fat man didn't answer, and in another moment Clay understood why. The black shirt Szarka was wearing was in fact a white shirt saturated with blood. The man wasn't looking at anything or anyone; he was staring dead ahead, eyes wide and frozen. Clay knew that if he gave that broad forehead a gentle shove, Szarka's head would loll back and expose a wide cut across the jugular vein. Someone had slit his throat, and Alexander Szarka would never be answering anyone again.

"Fuck!" Clay spun, but it was too late. Someone was racing up the hallway, and he just couldn't move fast enough to do a goddamn thing about it. He heard the door slam against the wall and felt a pair of hands hit him in the back, shoving hard. He stumbled into the middle of the room, off balance and still in mid-twist. His feet tangled, and for a moment he came close to falling, and that probably would've been the end of it, but Clay still had enough of his agility left to recover, and he came to a stop, hunched over against the pain, legs spread wide.

"Hello, sunshine," Olivia said when at last he looked up to meet her eyes. Her voice was husky and seductive, and the grin she gave him made her look like a great white shark. There was a jagged gash running in a crooked zigzag down the left side of her face, and a patch of her blond hair had been torn out at her forehead, leaving only a bloody circle the size of a dime. She didn't seem particularly bothered by these injuries.

Clay took as deep a breath as his guts would allow and let it out in a sigh. "I was *really* hoping the bald chick killed you."

The door had bounced off the wall and come nearly to a close behind her, and for a moment Clay entertained the idea of somehow circling around Olivia and making a break for it. Maybe he could—

Then the door opened again, and Haley stepped through and came to a stop behind Olivia, his face an expressionless mask. He closed the door completely, folded his arms, and stared at the two of them. Clay was silent, but felt no confusion. He'd understood the truth from the start: here was another man owned by Reyes, another little piece of the army she commanded throughout the city and beyond.

"When did she get her hooks into you?" he finally asked.

"Not long. Elena and I first spoke around the time you were waging war over in Union City."

"What's she giving you? It's not the cure. You're no licker. Is it just money?"

Haley shrugged. "Does it matter?"

It didn't. He was trapped, and Clay found he barely had the energy to care anymore. All he felt was a sort of mute sadness that the whole thing had come to this. He wanted to sit down. He wanted a glass of Maker's Black, probably the last he would drink in his life. He wanted this to be over.

"You know what you *should* have done?" Olivia said.

"Enlighten me."

"You should've gone home. You know, the big old building you shared with your pretty little wife? I was busy with the Chink's sexbot—who ran away like a little bitch, by the way. You might've had time to plug in that other SynchDrive and upload all the stuff you stole."

"I thought you hadn't seen that."

Olivia made an incredulous scoffing noise. "Oh, I see just about everything. Just hadn't *gotten* to it. I was having too much fun with you. Wouldn't you feel so much better right now if you'd gone home, thinking you'd stopped the bad guys even though you were about to die for it?"

"Figured you'd look for me there."

"I did! But you went somewhere else and managed to avoid dying at home. How nice for you. Do those cuts sting? I'm so terribly sorry."

"Do you ever shut up?" Clay said.

Olivia gave a short, sharp laugh. "Only when I'm working." Her eyes glimmered with a cold, hard light.

"You're not working now?"

"This is play." She put her gun back into its holster. "Think you're up for it, Mr. R-9? That's a big hole in your side."

Clay glanced down, then back up at her. "Honestly? I really don't think I'm up for it."

Olivia grinned again and took two more steps toward him. Clay took two back, glancing over his shoulder. There wasn't much point in retreating; a few more feet and he'd be sitting in Szarka's lap.

"Poor Alex," Olivia said. "He should've just done what Ms. Reyes told him. She might even have shared the cure with him eventually, once everything was all set ... if he made it that long."

"But he wouldn't let you blackmail him, so you cut his throat. Did you kill the driver, too? Where is he?"

"No idea. He's a loose end, but I'm good at those. I'll get to him."

She stepped forward again and this time Clay held his ground. She was directly under the bare, hanging bulb now, and her white suit glowed, even smeared as it was in black, bloody grime. She was smiling her fake shark's smile, teeth bared in what looked more and more like a snarl with each passing moment. Clay thought he was probably experiencing the last few moments of his life. He didn't think he would survive an assault long enough for her to torture him any further. This came as mild consolation to him, and he laughed out loud at the absurdity of it.

"This funny to you, big man?" Olivia took two long rapid strides toward him.

Clay took a swing—what else was there to do?—and she ducked it handily, bringing her fist up and into his gut. Clay screamed in agony and went to one knee, gasping and retching. Olivia stood over him like a conquering warrior, a sick, angry grin on her face. Haley still had his arms crossed, was still observing with a dispassionate expression, as if watching a rigged prizefight with a predetermined outcome.

"Why'd you stop laughing?" Olivia said.

Clay coughed up blood and spit it on the ground. He closed his eyes. "Just fucking kill me, then."

"Kill you? Sweetheart, we have to start all over again. I'm going to call some doctor friends right after I take that SynchDrive out of those ridiculous shorts you're wearing. We're going to get you all patched up, and then we're going to have some more fun together. We had a thing going between us. Couldn't you feel it?"

"Christ," Clay muttered.

"The Chink screwed it all up, that shriveled piece of shit. Do you know why he talks the way he does? I came to him first, you know, after I crossed the border and moved up to this freezing hellho—"

Enough with this babbling ditz act. "No one gives a fuck about your life story!"

Olivia was in motion before he'd even finished the sentence. She grabbed his head and brought it down against her knee. Black spots with strange, pulsing golden rings around them burst into Clay's vision, and a wave of nausea rolled over him for a minute. He dry-heaved once, both hands on the wooden floor.

"If you interrupt me again, I'm going to go to your ex-partner's house and murder one of his kids," Olivia told him, but she had indeed dropped the ditz act. "Do you want to pick which one? Which kid do you think Kellen Ruiz would rather see dead, in his most secret heart? The boy or the little baby girl? I bet it's the girl. He's a fence-hopper, right? They're pretty into the whole lineage thing ... He'd want to keep the son."

"You're out of your fucking—"

"Blah blah blah. You're going to listen to my story and you're going to fucking like it. When I first got here, I went to see the big king shit out in that fucking sewer he calls a home, sitting at his desk flanked by two huge gorillas in suits. I could tell right from the start that he wasn't going to be able to appreciate my particular talents—he doesn't have the ambition—but I laid them out for him anyway. When I was done, he looked up at me and he said, 'Whores should talk to the bartender downstairs,' and gave me this big shit-eating grin.

"The two meatheads went down so easy it was like killing big retarded babies. It wasn't even any fun, and it was over so fast that the Chink hadn't even moved from his desk. I came around the side to have a little chat. The silly little man had a teeny knife hidden under his desk, and he tried to jab me with it, so I put it into his windpipe. Then I told him I was going to leave him alive so he could think about how he'd made the biggest mistake of his life. Now he has to live knowing I'm out there somewhere and someday, when the timing is *just* right, I'll pay him another visit. He knows, and *that's* why he sent you, not to help with your little revenge fantasy but try and save his own bony ass."

"Fascinating," Clay said.

"Isn't it? Give me the SynchDrive now, Foster."

"You know you're going to have to take it from me."

"No, I want you to give it to me. Shall I convince you? I can think of so *many* fun ways." The chipper, ditzy note was creeping back into her voice.

Clay looked over her shoulder at Haley. He was frowning now, arms still crossed, head turned away from what was happening in front of him.

"Dennis ... there's still time to do the right thing."

Olivia laughed. "The right thing is to stand there like a good boy, and he knows it. Why would he turn down everything we can give him just to get himself killed?"

"Because he's a good man. He knows what's—"

"I got a husband with leukemia," Haley said, still staring off at the floor to his left as if it fascinated him. "He can't work. Got two little girls, a mountain of bills, an apartment I'm about to lose. I got—"

"What you *got* to do is shut the fuck up," Olivia said. "Shut up and do what you're told, *boy*, and we'll make sure your two nappy-headed little brats still have a place to sleep."

Clay kept his eyes on the inspector. "You're a cop. Don't let her do this. We can stop them right here. I have everything we need. We just ..."

He took an instinctive step toward Haley, and Olivia called his name. Snapped her fingers at him. When Clay turned his head to look at her, she took a step forward and swung her fist. Clay put a hand up to ward off the blow, and that was when things became chaotic. He heard the sound of movement from behind his assailant. Olivia heard it, too, and in an astounding move of dexterity used the momentum from the punch she was throwing to instead begin to turn around. Clay would have been amazed both by her agility and her instincts had he been capable of summoning up any strong feelings through the fuzz in his head.

She almost made it, but even fast as she was, she wasn't able to spin and raise her gun quite quickly enough. A shot went off, and something warm and wet sprayed in his face. Clay heard Olivia scream and saw her go stumbling away to the side, heard her collapse in a heap. He looked up, bewildered, and saw Haley standing over him, glaring at Olivia's crumpled body. The inspector held out his hand. "That's two you owe me."

"Goddamn." Clay felt lightheaded, confused, unable to process what was happening. Lifting his arm and taking the hand held out to him seemed an impossible task. He tried anyway, and the act cost him his sense of balance. The world seemed to tilt suddenly, and he heard Haley call his name as he fell sideways and crashed to the wooden floor.

Haley knelt next to him, asking if he was all right. Clay wanted to tell him to go finish the job he'd started with Olivia. To make sure the shot had been good. To make sure she was—

Olivia came snarling into his field of vision, eyes blazing, left hand held to her chest as blood poured forth from it. Clay felt a grim satisfaction at this even as she drove the butt of her gun down against Haley's right temple once, and then a second time, before pulling it back in a wide arc that whipped blood across the room and kicking him in the shoulder. Haley went sprawling, and Olivia gave a shriek of rage and hate and pain that sounded like nothing a human could possibly make.

Clay had rolled onto his back and was scrabbling with his hands, trying to find purchase, but Jesus Christ, he could barely feel his fingers and his arms were so goddamned weak, and now it was too late. Olivia dropped down hard, one knee landing on each of his arms and pinning them down. She straddled him in her dirty, bloody white suit, the light above forming a corona around her ragged, filthy blond hair. She pressed the gun to his forehead.

"You're dying. I don't have time to fix you up anymore, thanks to your friend over there, but I'm not letting you go gentle into that good fucking night."

She shifted her weight. There was pain for a moment as her knee drove into his bicep, and then it slipped off, falling to the floor, leaving his right arm free. Clay glanced over at it, feeling detached, almost like he was floating even though he was pinned to the floor. His fingers were lying loose on the ground next to her pant leg, which had pulled up, revealing the boots she wore underneath.

Revealing the knife she had jammed into the boots she wore underneath.

"I snapped her fucking neck before she ever went over the rail." Olivia's lips and teeth were coated in blood now. "Your dumb cunt wife never even noticed I was standing right behind her, and she died before she even hit the ground."

I need you to work for thirty more seconds, Clay thought at his arm. It twitched a little. Blood was dripping all over him, but Clay knew the wound wouldn't kill her, and she needed to die. If she didn't die, both he and Haley would, and so would Luke, and it would be over. Elena Reyes would win, and Terry's death would mean nothing, and goddamn it, that wasn't happening. He wrapped his fingers around the hilt of the knife.

"Does that make you feel better?" Olivia screamed at him and raised her gun. She pointed it between his eyes. "Does it?!"

Christopher Buecheler

"Not really," Clay said, and he jerked his arm, giving the motion all of his remaining strength. Olivia had time to turn her head and raise her shoulder—Christ, even with a bullet in her chest she was fast and her instincts were so good—but Clay had anticipated this and changed his angle. He twisted his wrist at the last moment, avoiding her shoulder, and drove the blade into her windpipe, right out through the other side. The strike pierced her carotid artery, and when Clay tore backward, ripping the blade out and cleaving through her trachea, blood jetted forth like a fire hose, coating his face, his clothes, the floor, everything. Olivia dropped the gun by his side and brought both hands to her neck, toppling over, hissing and gurgling like a fountain running low on water.

Clay forced himself to roll sideways. He couldn't sit up, exactly, but he managed to curl forward and brace himself on his left shoulder. He picked up Olivia's gun and aimed it at the woman thrashing on the ground in a pool of her own blood. Olivia seemed to realize what was happening. Her movements slowed, and after a moment more she propped herself up on both arms, looking up at him, her face a mask of gore, eyes like big blue oceans, blood pumping from the ragged gash in her neck.

She grinned at him, the shark's grin, wide and dangerous, but the grin never touched her eyes. In those, there was only a boundless, depthless hate.

Clay shot her. The bullet hit her forehead and tore off the back of her skull. Clay watched the mad hate die in the woman's eyes as she fell forward onto her face, watched her body twitch its last twitches. The gun fell from his fingers and clattered to the floor, and Clay was amused in a detached way to see that it was this noise, and not the gunshot itself, that caused Haley to stir. The man shoved himself to his knees, groaning, and surveyed the scene in front of him.

"I don't know what the fuck just happened, but well-done."

"You got a tablet?" Clay's voice was a cracked and broken thing, and it seemed to come not from within him but from down a long dark hall.

"Shit, right, let me call an ambulance." Haley began digging in his pocket.

"Haley, I need you to ..."

But Christ, could he *trust* Haley? The man had shot Olivia, sure, but all he had to do was deliver the SynchDrive to Reyes and he was still a hero. He could easily claim that Clay had been solely responsible for what happened to the woman's bodyguard.

"Need me to what?" Haley sounded like he cared. Like he was ready to do whatever was right, leukemia be damned.

It's either trust him or die here and accomplish nothing. Clay coughed blood onto the floorboards. "Take this down. Do it now."

Haley reached into his pocket and pulled the tablet out. He tapped at the screen a few times and nodded. "Give it to me."

"Doctor Imran. She worked with Terry at Shun Ten and will be able to put together the cure."

"Got it. Now let's—"

"Not done. You need to find Luke Eyenga, too. The People's Voice. He's on the run right now, but you'll find him. I'll give you his SynchName. Find Luke, find Imran, and get them what's on the SynchDrive in my pocket. You'll need the keys. You ready?"

"Ready."

Clay gave him the SynchName, then the data key. He waited for Haley to type them in and then spoke Terry's passphrase:

> Yet fill my glass: give me one kiss:
> My own sweet Alice, we must die.
> There's somewhat in this world amiss
> Shall be unriddled by and by.

"All right," Haley said, and before Clay could tell him not to bother, he was calling the paramedics. "I need EMTs, now. Bullet wound to the abdomen, among other things. Thirty-two Second Avenue at Second Street. Top floor. Come in the maintenance door, and hurry it the fuck up."

Clay laid his head back on the floor as Haley hung up. "It's over. Thank you."

Haley looked at him for a long moment and then sighed. "Elena Reyes was going to give me the John Wihone bust. She was going to give me that production facility. I'd discover the 'mastermind' behind Elixir, and with it the cure. This would be in a couple of years, after I'd made deputy chief and she had all of her ducks in order. I'd be a hero, a shoo-in for chief of police, a cornerstone in her glorious new regime." He looked over at Clay, shook his head, shrugged. "I got here after Szarka was … after she did that to him. I want you to know that. I didn't know about him until I walked in after you arrived. She told me to stay in the old electrical closet until you'd come through, and then to guard the door. After that—"

"After that it would all be easy," Clay said.

Haley nodded. "All I had to do was let that lunatic finish up with you and walk away from this building. Then I started thinking about those people who fought with us out in the swamps in Delaware, ordinary citizens who were out there getting shot up in the muck side by side with me and my men. Those are the people Reyes is ruining with this drug. If it was just rich assholes, maybe I could've done it, but—"

"But you couldn't." The room was getting dark, and Clay was having a hard time keeping his eyes open. Everything felt warm and soft now. The planks he was lying on were like down comforters atop a plush mattress.

"I'll get this stuff where it needs to go," Haley told him.

Clay nodded. "Take Reyes down, make the cure, and you're still a hero."

He reached out his hand and Haley took it. They sat there like that, for how long Clay didn't know. He could hear his own breath growing shallow. It was a strange experience. He thought about how he'd explain it to Terry and then remembered that Terry was dead and for the first time in his adult life felt tears prick at his eyes.

"Fuck, I miss my wife."

"She must have been a hell of a woman," Haley said. "Hell of a woman to be worth all of this. Keep those eyes open, Foster. Stay here."

He couldn't. The paramedics were coming through the door now, shouting orders, and Clay didn't want to close his eyes. He was afraid to do it, afraid that the vision waiting there for him would be of Terry's cold dead body laid out below the precinct, but he couldn't keep them open any longer. They closed of their own accord.

It wasn't his wife's body in that coroner's office that was waiting for him. Neither was it that old image that had always been his favorite, her atop him in her wedding dress. Instead he saw Terry standing on their balcony in a pair of old jeans and a ratty T-shirt, curly red hair falling like waves out behind her, reaching up on tiptoe to water her stupid spider plant. Hearing something behind her, she gasped, startled, and turned to see who had crept up on her.

And then she smiled that big beautiful smile that had taken hold of him forever at the VA hospital in Virginia.

"Where have you been?" she asked.

"It doesn't matter."

"Can you stay?"

"I don't know, baby. I don't think so."

Terry considered this. Nodded. Hit him again with that smile. "Then I guess you'd better kiss me quick."

Clay laughed, put his hands in her hair, and did what he was told.

EPILOGUE

Elena Reyes Indicted

Luke Eyenga, People's Voice Senior Writer

Manhattan Water and Power COO Elena Reyes is going to jail, and she won't be buying her way out.

As previously published in The People's Voice exclusive story yesterday, Reyes stands accused of many charges, principal among them being that she masterminded the creation and distribution of Elixir, the drug that's become an epidemic in Brooklyn and elsewhere around the country. Now she's been indicted, ordered behind bars with no bail by New York Justice Anna Takahashi.

Reyes's capture comes thanks to the work of the late Terry Foster, formerly of Shun Ten Industries; her husband, Officer Clay Foster of the Brooklyn PD; hero cop Inspector Dennis Haley of the NYPD; and the late Alex Szarka, formerly the CEO of Manhattan Water and Power. Through their efforts, a vast array of evidence has been raised that the NYPD claims proves not only that Reyes created the drug and sent it out into the world but also that she used her personal bodyguard as an assassin, killing many of those who opposed her. The list of casualties includes both Mr. Szarka and Mrs. Foster and very nearly included Officer Foster as well. He's recuperating at Our Lady of Mercy Hospital in Midtown, awaiting the hero's welcome that he'll no doubt receive both here and in Brooklyn.

Anuhya Imran, also implicated in the conspiracy, faces charges of aiding and abetting Reyes in developing some of the drug's components. She remains free after posting bail and has vowed to help in any way she can to repair the damage she unwittingly helped to cause. Her work on the prototype cure for Elixir addiction has already begun, and early tests are promising.

We'll have more coming throughout the day as this story evolves, including a statement from Alex Szarka's nephew and a full transcript of the highly anticipated press conference being jointly given by Police Chief Andre Bartolo and Mayor Cooke. Stay tuned, readers … this is only the beginning.

- Luke Eyenga

THE END

WANT MORE INFORMATION?

There's lots of ways to stay in touch!

- Visit Christopher Buecheler's Website
  http://cwbuecheler.com/

- Follow @cwbuecheler on Twitter
  http://www.twitter.com/cwbuecheler

- Like Christopher Buecheler on Facebook
  http://on.fb.me/iOAdA1

- Christopher Buecheler's Writing Newsletter
  http://cwbuecheler.com/newsletter

ACKNOWLEDGMENTS

In the break between The Broken God Machine (2013) and Elixir (2018), I've learned such an incredible amount about the art, the process, and the business of writing. It's my great pleasure to thank those who've helped me shape Elixir into the best book I could.

- My wife, Charlotte, once again takes first billing. These books have to get past her before they get to anyone else, because I trust her to be gentle and brutal in equal measure. She's never failed to deliver.

- Kirsten Carleton, then of Prospect Agency, represented me as my literary agent on this book. In addition to being a tireless champion for the novel, she's also a terrific editor whose suggestions further helped refine the manuscript.

- Peter Gelfan gave me two brilliant content edits on this book that took it from an extremely rough product, riddled with amateur mistakes, to a manuscript that garnered offers of representation from multiple agents. I am a better writer today because of his help.

- Doug Wagner provided the final proofread for this book. If any typos, grammar flaws, punctuation issues, or other oddities remain, know that it's my fault and not his!

- My advance readers, Charles, Lindsay, Tracy, Sheri, and Nora, whose early feedback was immensely useful in shaping the story.

- My fans, who've waited patiently for me to get something new into their hands! Thank you for your words of support in reply to my newsletter, on Twitter, and on Facebook.

ABOUT THE AUTHOR

Christopher Buecheler is a professional web developer, an author, an award-winning amateur mixologist, a brewer of beer, a player of the guitar and drums, and an NBA enthusiast.

He lives a semi-nomadic existence with his wonderful wife, Charlotte, and their two cats, Carbomb and Baron Salvatore H. Lynx II. Currently they reside in Providence, Rhode Island.

You can visit him at http://cwbuecheler.com/

OTHER BOOKS
BY CHRISTOPHER BUECHELER

The Blood That Bonds

Two is Trapped. She's hooked on heroin, held as property, forced to sell her body to feed the addiction. Time brings her ever closer to what seems an inevitable death and Two waits, uncaring, longing only for the next fix. That's when Theroen arrives. The only problem? Theroen is a vampire.

http://iiamtrilogy.com/tbtb/

Blood Hunt

It's been six months since the events of The Blood That Bonds. As Two Majors and Tori Perrault struggle to adapt to their new realities, they are drawn into a world that neither knew existed. Two must deal with the machinations of the vampire council, while Tori must make a decision that will change not only her life, but the lives of all of the vampires in America, and perhaps the world.

http://iiamtrilogy.com/bloodhunt/

The Children of the Sun

Two and a half years have passed since Blood Hunt, and in that time a fragile peace has been maintained by the American council of vampires and their allies. Two Majors has spent the years focusing on rebuilding the life that was torn away from her. When the Children of the Sun, the militaristic cult of vampire hunters, strike at a trio of vampires visiting Chicago, the peace is shattered.

http://iiamtrilogy.com/tcots/

The Broken God Machine

Pehr is sixteen, strong and fit, about to take the Hunter's Test and become a man when a horde of vile beast-men known as the Lagos descend upon his village. He finds himself thrust into an unlikely adventure, journeying through jungles, mountains and plains to find the land of the ancients and the advanced technology they left behind.

http://brokengodmachine.com/

Made in the USA
Middletown, DE
24 December 2018